UNINTENDED

CONSEQUENCES

SHERRYL D. HANCOCK

Published by Vulpine Press in the United Kingdom in 2020

ISBN 978-1-83919-310-1

Cover by Claire Wood

www.vulpine-press.com

Also in the *MidKnight Blue* series:

CHAPTER 1

Dave Dibbins walked into his house, glancing at his watch. It was 11:30 p.m. He grinned. Good, he still had time. In his bedroom, he saw Susan sleeping. He stood staring at her for a full minute. He was still constantly amazed that this beautiful, sophisticated woman was his wife. She was a full sixteen years younger than him and a whole league of worlds different. Her family was rich, she'd been brought up in a mansion, she was an English nanny, highly educated, very cultured. And she loved him—that was the amazing part.

Dave Dibbins grew up in a trailer park in one of the poorest areas in San Diego. His family was dysfunctional to the nth power. In fact, one of his first arrests as a narcotics officer had been his parents, for running a meth lab out of their trailer. He had barely finished high school; any higher education he'd achieved had been on the streets. He was an undercover narcotics officer with very little to his name, save a house and a muscle car he'd rebuilt himself.

They were an unlikely couple, but Dave had never been as happy in his life as he'd been for the last three years. Taking off his jacket, then his boots, his holstered weapon and his shirt, he got into bed next to his wife, touching her on the shoulder.

"David?" she said softly as she turned over to look at him.

"Hey, honey," he said, smiling down at her.

She moved to wrap her arms around him as he leaned down to kiss her softly.

"You've been gone forever," she said petulantly.

"I know, honey, I'm sorry," Dave said, kissing her again. "This case is giving me a lot of grief."

"It's alright, David," she said, reaching up to touch his cheek. "I know you come home as soon as you can."

Dave hugged her close, kissing her temple. She always understood. Susan was the haven he came home to every chance he got. He worked deep undercover, requiring him to be away from her for literally days on end. But when he was home with her, he was completely hers. He spent all his time with her, even if it meant staying with her while she did her job of taking care of the Sinclair children.

He leaned in to kiss her again, deepening the kiss as he pulled her closer. Her arms tightened around him as she pressed still closer to him. He always excited her senses.

"Susan, there was a—" came a voice from the doorway.

Dave's head snapped around as he tensed. Then he recognized his sister-in-law's voice and grinned.

"Hello, Liz," Dave said smoothly.

"Hi, Dave," Liz said, grinning.

"You were saying?"

Liz smiled self-consciously. "I was saying there was a noise, but I guess you would be the noise…"

"Not yet," Dave replied, giving Liz a wink.

"Oh lord," Susan said, rolling her eyes.

Liz only laughed. "Welcome home, Dave," she said. "I'll leave you two alone now."

Liz closed the door with a pointed look.

Dave looked back down at his wife. "Your sister is here… why?"

Susan bit her lip. "She's staying with us."

Dave narrowed his eyes at her. "Why does that have an indefinite ring to it?"

Susan grimaced. "Because I don't know how long she'll be with us."

"What happened this time?" Dave asked, sighing.

"Oh, the usual scandal," Susan said, grinning.

Elizabeth was always in some sort of trouble—Dave knew that. He liked his wild sister-in-law in spite of her thirst for trouble.

"So what else has been going on?" he asked, settling on the bed comfortably.

Susan proceeded to tell him all the latest on the kids she was responsible for, what had happened in the house, everything she could think of. Dave glanced over at the clock as she ran out of things to tell him, then leaned over, kissing her deeply. He reached for the box he'd set on the nightstand when he'd walked in and handed it to her as their lips parted.

"Happy anniversary," he said softly.

"David… you remembered," she said, her voice tremulous.

"Of course I remembered, honey. I told you I'd always be here for you, especially our anniversary and your birthday, and most holidays. I will have to make an exception for Groundhog Day, because I don't think that's an official holiday." He said the last grinning.

Susan laughed softly, shaking her head.

"Are you going to open it?" he asked gently, gesturing to the box.

"Yes, of course," she said, smiling.

She opened the box. Inside was nestled a sapphire pendant. It was a teardrop shape with tiny baguettes all around it, hanging on a gold chain.

"Oh, David…" she breathed, her eyes shining. "It's beautiful."

"You like it?" he asked, smiling.

"Oh my, yes," she said, leaning forward to kiss him. "As usual, you spoil me far too much."

"I don't spoil you, Susan," he said. "I love you."

She smiled warmly.

"Well, now I can give you your anniversary present too," she said, moving off the bed.

Dave turned over on his stomach and watched her walk toward the closet. She turned around, looking at him.

"What are you doing?" she asked, grinning.

"Admiring the view," he replied, grinning back at her.

"Well, stop that and close your eyes," she said, laughing softly.

"Yes, ma'am," he replied, and closed his eyes.

He heard some rustling, and the closet door opening and closing.

"Okay, open your eyes."

Dave opened his eyes, and his mouth dropped open. He got off the bed and stood staring at what his wife stood next to. It was a surfboard.

"Oh my God, you got me the Yater," he said, awed.

Susan smiled, thoroughly enjoying his reaction. He was one big kid when it came to surfboards and cars. They were his two major hobbies.

Dave walked over to the board, which stood nine and a half feet tall. He ran his hand down it, his look reverent. Taking it gently from Susan's grasp, he turned it around, looking down at the tail of the board.

"Tri fins," he said, all but a sigh.

He looked at Susan then. "Have I reminded you lately how so very much I love you?"

"Constantly, love," Susan said, winking at him.

"Well, I love you even more now," he said, smiling. "Thank you, honey, so much."

He kissed her deeply, one hand on the board, the other wrapping around her waist to pull her closer.

"Happy anniversary, David," she whispered.

Dave set the board against the closet and took her in his arms, kissing her properly, caressing her back. Finally she pulled away, looking up at him.

"I have one more thing to give you."

"Oh, honey…" he said, shaking his head. "This was plenty."

He knew the board was about $700, so she'd already gone way overboard. She led him back over to the bed and sat him down.

"Close your eyes again."

He grinned, doing as she said. Once again there was rustling, then she told him to hold out his hands. He did, and she placed something in them.

He opened his eyes and looked down. He stared for a long moment. It was black, and clothing. He touched it; it felt like wetsuit material. He naturally assumed she'd bought him a new wetsuit for surfing. But then he held it up, and it was tiny.

"Um, babe…" he said, his tone querying. "I think it's a little small…" His voice trailed off then as it hit him.

One glance at her face told him he was right.

"Oh my God," he said, staring up at her. "Are you telling me…" he began, unable to finish the sentence.

Susan took a deep breath and nodded. "David, I'm pregnant," she said softly.

He stared at her openmouthed for a full minute. "Oh my God…" he said again, shocked.

Susan wasn't sure what to make of his reaction. Was he happy?

Mad? Unhappy? Or just shocked?

"David?" she queried finally.

He shook his head as if to clear it, then stood up, taking her into his arms and hugging her close.

"I love you," he said, and his voice held so much sincerity, Susan had tears in her eyes instantly.

She put her arms around him, feeling his heart pounding in his chest. Reaching between them, she put her hand on his heart. It was indeed beating madly.

"David, are you alright?"

He pulled back, looking down at her hand, then up at her. He nodded, and then Susan saw it in his eyes.

"You're terrified, aren't you?" she asked, shocked.

"As hell," he replied, grinning.

"Oh, David," she said, laughing and crying at the same time. "Why?"

He took a deep breath, blowing it out slowly as he sat down on the bed, setting the miniature wetsuit aside. He pulled her down onto his lap, holding her there.

"I just want to be a good father."

"You will be, David," Susan assured him. "You're the best man I know."

"That doesn't make for a good father."

"It makes for an incredible start."

He looked considering, then nodded. They sat together for a long time. Finally, she could see that he was getting tired, so she moved off his lap and pulled him down on the bed with her. Dave fell asleep lying against her stomach, his arms wrapped around her waist. She sat watching him for a long while, stroking his hair. It was an incredible feeling, loving someone so much. She was excited at the prospect of raising a child with this man.

She had been totally honest when she said he was the best man she knew. He'd always been everything to her. He was open and honest with her, kind and loving, yet never weak by any means. When he believed something, he would discuss it with her to try and give her his viewpoint. He never raised his voice to her, yet when he disliked something, he was able to show her without anger. He gave himself to her totally. There was never a question she wasn't allowed to ask. Never a moment where she worried about his reaction to something. She never wanted to disappoint him, but she knew that if she ever did, he would accept it and stay with her regardless. Dave Dibbins was the very best man she knew, and she loved him beyond all reason.

***

"I really hate to do this, Blue, but you're under arrest."

It was the last thing Christian expected to hear from the beautiful blonde.

"I'm what?" he asked, too stunned to even think as she spun him around and shoved him against the wall.

His hands went out instantly to brace himself, and then he realized he was taking the stance of someone being arrested.

"Whoa! Wait! Hold up here!" he said, turning to face her again.

"Don't make this harder, Blue, just turn around," she said, gritting her teeth.

She grabbed his wrist, spinning him back around with surprising strength and shoving his arm up behind his back.

"Fuck!" he yelped as she pressed him against the wall. "Cat, will you just fucking listen for a second?"

"I don't want to hear it, Blue, I'm sorry," she said, shaking her head.

Christian turned his head, leaning down to her, wincing as his arm was lifted higher.

"I'm a cop, Cat," he said softly.

She looked at him for a full minute.

"And can you let go of my arm before you break it?" he asked calmly.

She let go of him instantly. He turned to her, reaching quickly into his pocket as he did. He saw her tense and held his hand up, forestalling whatever defensive gesture she was going to take.

"Easy…" he said as he took out his badge and showed it to her.

She looked at the badge, then at him, her face showing complete shock.

"You're a cop?" she asked, as if he hadn't just told her that.

Christian nodded, his lips curling sardonically. He reached into his inner jacket pocket and pulled out his credentials with his picture on it, showing her.

"Holy fucking shit!" she exclaimed, shaking her head.

"And then some," he agreed, grinning.

"How the hell…"

"Lack of communication, beautiful, happens all the time," he said, winking at her.

He was really shocked by the whole thing, but as usual he hid it well.

He'd met Catalina, "Cat," in the house of the dealer he'd been working for the last month. She'd been sent up to him by the dealer, after he'd sent the first girl back, claiming he preferred blondes. He hadn't seen a blonde in the dealer's company before that, so he'd figured he was in the clear. But twenty minutes later, Cat had appeared at the door to the room he was staying in at that moment.

Thinking back, he realized he'd noticed she was on edge, but he'd just assumed it was because the girl wasn't sure what he'd be like. He couldn't fathom being sent up to some strange person to have sex with them, never knowing what kind of nut that person could be. He'd chalked her nervousness up to that, and set about relieving that nervousness.

"Look," he'd said, moving to sit up on the bed. "Do me a favor—just take your clothes off and get into bed."

Her eyes had widened at that.

"No," he'd said, shaking his head. "I don't want to have sex with you. I have a lady back home that'll fuckin' castrate me if I screw around on her."

He'd been telling the truth; his wife, Stevie, would beat the living shit out of him, verbally and physically, if he screwed around on her, even in the name of the job.

The girl had visibly relaxed then. She'd gotten into bed next to him, and they'd talked for a little while about basically nothing. She'd told him her name was Cat, and that it wasn't that she didn't want to have sex with him but that she was involved with someone too. Christian had told her that it would be their secret that they hadn't had sex. She'd seemed grateful for that.

After that, she'd been a general fixture around him. Especially after she'd been chased down by another man in the household. She'd run straight to Christian, who'd told the guy that she was with him and to leave off. At one point, when someone had knocked on the door then opened it, she'd leapt at him, planting a major kiss on his lips. He'd responded to the kiss, knowing she was trying to convince these men she was with him.

After the man had turned and left, she'd pulled back to look at him.

"Damn, Papi," she'd said, her blue eyes twinkling at him. "Your lady's one lucky shorty."

Christian had looked back at her for a moment, then shook his head, grinning.

"Is she a hottie?" Cat asked.

"She's very hot, yes."

"Mmm," she'd murmured, reaching up to touch his jaw, running her nail along it. "I'll bet she's a hot one in bed too."

Christian's brows had furrowed then, detecting the odd tone to her voice.

Cat laughed, winking at him. "Relax, Papi. I swing both ways."

That comment had floored Christian.

She'd commented on it a few times over the next three weeks, saying a few times how she'd love to see the woman that could keep a man as hot as he was faithful. Christian had only laughed, shaking his head. He'd also decided he liked her; she was feisty without being obnoxious. She reminded him a bit of his wife, who he hadn't seen in three weeks.

He and Stevie were on separate cases, and when he was home, she wasn't. It had happened that way for too long—he was missing her to the extreme at that point.

Because he liked Cat, he'd tried to suggest a few times that she find a new place to "hang," but she hadn't listened to him. She had in fact suggested a few times that he might want to make a deal with someone else. Now he knew why.

In the end, he found out that Cat worked for the San Diego Sheriff's Office narcotics team. They had a good laugh about it, and were both very relieved not to have to arrest each other.

Christian walked into his and Stevie's house at noon. Kicking off his boots, he lay down on their bed, and was asleep a few minutes later. He woke at 6:30 p.m. He got up from the bed and went into the bathroom. Dropping his clothes, he got into the shower. Afterward he shaved, and then went to the kitchen to make himself something to eat. He ate Top Ramen for dinner, since there was nothing else in the house. He sat on their bed, watching TV and drinking a beer.

At nine o'clock, Stevie walked in. Christian was sitting bare-chested on their bed, wearing only black shorts. She was sure her heart stopped at the sight of him, with his jet black hair, complete with jet black eyebrows and eyelashes, and his dark complexion, combined with his light blue eyes that seemed to glow in his face. She could never get over how handsome her husband was. He was beyond handsome; he was someone that couldn't be described—you had to see him to believe how gorgeous he was. Women stopped dead in the street to look at him. On top of that, he had the dangerous, mysterious quality about him that drove women wild. He still drove her wild even after a year of marriage.

Christian glanced up from the TV, sensing her in the doorway.

"I remember you," he said, grinning.

"You better," she said, smiling as she dropped her bag and walked over to him.

Getting up on the bed and straddling his lap, she leaned down, kissing him deeply. His arms were around her instantly, pulling her closer and deepening the kiss.

"Mmm…" she moaned against his lips, even as he pulled her shirt from the waist of her jeans.

He made quick work of pulling her clothes off, pushing her back on the bed and kissing her deeply, making her writhe under him. At one point, he pulled back, looking into her eyes, which burned like emerald fire.

"Did you miss me?"

"Nope," she replied, with a quick grin.

"Uh-huh," he said, leaning down to kiss her lips again. "I missed you like crazy too," he murmured.

Within minutes they were making heated, passionate love, reminding each other how compatible they were. The sex between them never seemed to grow boring. They were always hot for each other, and always willing to try anything.

Afterward they lay together, going over their cases, how things were going.

"Well, my case took an interesting twist," he said, grinning.

"How?" she asked, moving to lie with her head in his lap as he sat up and reached for a cigarette.

Christian lit his cigarette, taking a long drag and blowing it out pointedly toward the ceiling.

"Remember I told you about Cat?"

He'd told Stevie all about her, what had happened, what Cat had said to him. He'd been honest with Stevie about kissing Cat when someone walked in, and he'd even told her that he had kissed the girl back, to make things believable. Stevie had agreed that it was the smartest thing to do in that instance. She knew who he loved. He'd been happy to note that she wasn't quite as jealous as she'd been before. She'd also proceeded to tell him that she'd run into the same situation with Kevin Elmasian, and had hesitated to "prove" anything to the dealer they were working, for fear Christian would get mad.

"I want you to be safe," Christian had told her. "And if the dealer you're working isn't convinced you're with Mace, then you're not safe. Do what you need to, babe."

It had said a lot to Stevie then too. It had told her that he trusted her. That was something that she valued. They'd had a very dark period in their relationship the year before, when Christian had pushed her away, fearing the commitment their relationship took. Stevie had walked away from him, and into the arms of his cousin Joe Sinclair. Christian had been devastated, so much so he'd attempted to take his own life. It had scared Stevie to death, and in the end, they'd gotten back together and ended up married, both of them throwing aside their fear of commitment to be together. Now they were both determined not to lose what they had ever again. To that end, they were always honest with each other.

"Yeah, I remember Cat," Stevie said, nodding and grinning at the same time.

"Well, she tried to arrest me today," Christian said, his tone so normal that Stevie wasn't sure she'd heard him right.

Then, when she realized she had, by the way he was looking at her, she sat up, staring at him with wide eyes.

"She's law enforcement too?"

"Yeah," Christian said, grinning. "She's with the SO."

"Lovely, blue on blue," Stevie said, using the term for when cops were working other cops and didn't know it.

"Nicely dangerous," Christian said, disgusted.

It was always a dangerous situation when a cop was undercover. Add to that another cop working undercover, without the knowledge of the first officer. A weapon could be pulled in the line of duty, and be mistaken as a hostile act by the other officer. It could get a cop killed. Hence "blue on blue" was usually avoided at all costs.

"Jesus..." Stevie said, shaking her head.

"Tell me about it," Christian said, rolling his eyes.

"You're going to make sure Midnight hears about that, right?"

"Of course. I want to hear it when she calls up the SO to chew their asses out."

"Good."

"So, what's up with your case?" Christian asked, wanting to divert his wife before she really got going on the ramifications of what could have happened earlier that day.

Stevie had lost two family members to law enforcement actions. Her father had been killed in the line of duty, and her brother-in-law too. Christian knew how worried Stevie could get about him, thinking he could get killed in the line of duty.

"Uh, we're going to get to go on a boat," Stevie said brightly, even as she made a disgusted face.

"A boat?" Christian asked, raising a jet black eyebrow.

"A yacht," she qualified.

"For how long?"

"God, who knows!" Stevie said, shaking her head.

"You ever even been on a boat?"

"Nope," she replied, looking even more disgusted.

"So you have no idea if you get seasick or not. You're bound to be a barrel of laughs," he said, grinning. "Better Mace than me."

She laughed. "Oh, very nice."

Christian laughed too. They talked late into the night, making love again before falling asleep with their bodies still intertwined. They slept late the next morning. When they woke, they got out of bed, took a shower together, making love again. Afterward they spent the day lounging around watching TV, relaxing, and just spending time with each other. They even took an evening nap, having talked about going out that night, since it was Friday. Stevie woke before Christian. Sliding carefully out of bed, she put on her silk robe. It was 7:00 p.m. She decided to order them Chinese food, knowing Christian would be hungry when he got up.

14

She'd just dialed the number when there was a knock at the door. Walking over to the window, she looked out and saw a blonde woman standing there. Just then the restaurant answered and put her on hold.

Stevie opened the door a crack.

"Yes?" she asked, stifling a yawn as she hung up the phone.

"Oh shit, did I wake you?" the woman asked.

"It's okay, I had to get up at some point today," Stevie said, her emerald green eyes sparkling with humor. "What can I do for you?"

"Does, um, Sergeant Collins, live here?" the woman asked, looking down at a piece of paper in her hand.

Great, Stevie thought. *I get to deal with a process server.*

"Yes, he lives here," she said, opening the door wider, knowing she was going to have to sign something.

Catalina looked back at the redhead, thinking, *This has got to be his lady.* The woman was gorgeous, with long, rich-looking red hair, a perfect sweetheart-shaped face, gorgeous emerald green eyes—and from what little the small silk robe didn't hide, Cat could tell the woman had a killer body as well.

"You must be his girlfriend," she said, smiling.

Stevie looked back at the woman for a long moment. Then it clicked. The blonde was "Cat," who had thought her husband was a great kisser, and who had told him she'd like to meet his lady who kept him so faithful. *No wonder she just checked me out thoroughly,* Stevie thought. Then she recalled that Christian had also told her that this woman was bisexual, and would most likely think Stevie was hot too.

"Actually," Stevie said, grinning as she held up her left hand, where she wore her wedding rings. "I'm his wife."

"Oh." Catalina's eyes widened slightly. Then she nodded. "He

15

only ever said his 'lady'—I just assumed wrong," she said, without a hint of jealousy.

Stevie nodded. "I'm Stevie," she said, extending her hand.

"I'm Cat," Catalina replied, taking Stevie's hand and shaking it, her blue eyes looking right back into Stevie's.

Stevie was surprised by how direct the woman was, but she also found she wasn't repulsed by the idea that the woman found her attractive. Stevie had never been one to have a closed mind. She'd try anything once, and again and again if she liked it. She'd never actually been with a woman sexually, although she had shared a fairly passionate kiss with one at one point in her life. It had been interesting—she hadn't been able to deny that—but nothing had happened after that.

"It's nice to meet you," Stevie said honestly. "Christian was telling me last night about what happened with your cases crossing."

"Christian?"

Stevie grinned. "That's his real name."

"I only knew Blue," Cat said, grimacing.

"Well, that's really his nickname too," Stevie said. "And most people call him that, so you weren't far off."

Cat laughed softly, nodding. "Easier if you use something you yourself recognize."

"Oh yeah. I know, I can't ever imagine using anything but my own first name."

At that, Cat canted her head to the side. "You're a cop too?"

"Yep," Stevie said, grinning. "I'm on the same team as Christian."

"Wow," Cat said, truly surprised. "My department would never allow that kind of thing."

"Well," Stevie said, "Midnight is pretty lenient on that kind of thing, as long as it doesn't cause problems."

"And it hasn't so far?"

"Nope. Not in the year we've been on the team together and married. There's another married couple on the team too," she said, shrugging.

Cat shook her head in amazement. "Where do I sign up?"

"Don't laugh," Stevie said. "We need a sixth on the team."

"Oh yeah?" Cat asked, looking like she might be interested.

Stevie nodded.

"Something to think about," Cat said, nodding too. "I don't know if I'd have enough experience to qualify."

"If you could play my husband, you have enough experience."

Cat laughed. "He's that good, huh?"

"His instincts about people are pretty sharp."

"Well, I had no idea he was a cop either. He just seemed like some out-of-work movie star."

Stevie laughed. "That's how he gets them every time. Speaking of which, let's go get his ass up," she said, and led the way back to the bedroom.

Cat hesitated, surprised that Stevie was apparently fine with her following her into their bedroom. She shrugged, and did just that. Stevie's nice shape walking in front of her was definitely a great view, Cat thought. She shook her head, telling herself to stop being such a tramp.

The first thing that hit her about their bedroom was the big, heavy-looking dark-wood bed, with stark white sheets against the wood. She didn't have time to think of much more as her eyes went to the center of the bed. Christian was asleep, on his stomach, his back totally bare. The white sheet that covered him barely did so— one long, dark, well-toned leg was exposed, as well as his entire back all the way down to the curve of his ass.

Damn! Cat thought, finding it hard to breathe for a moment or two.

The sight was just too fantastic not to stare at. The man was too goddamned sexy for his own good. There was no getting around that. All lean muscle, jet black hair curling just past his broad shoulders, muscular arms wrapped around the pillow under his head.

"Babe?" Stevie said, walking over to the bed and sitting down next to him.

She reached down, touching his back, and Cat was struck by the contrast of their skin. Stevie's hand was pale, a creamy tone like the rest of her, with just a hint of a tan. She wore a burgundy polish on well-manicured nails. It was just a very visceral picture to behold against his dark skin.

"Mmm?" Christian murmured as he stirred.

"You have company," Stevie said, grinning at him.

"I have what?" Christian asked, his English accent thicker when he was tired.

He turned over, exposing his incredibly well-muscled chest, his light blue eyes going to Cat.

"Hey," he said, grinning. "What are you doing here?"

"Paperwork," Cat said, laughing as she held up the piece of paper in her hand.

Christian shook his head. "Damned SO, always hassling us."

"Well, if you'd keep your nose out of my case…" Cat said, giving him a narrowed look.

"And if you'd keep your ass out of my case…" Christian echoed, chuckling.

Cat put her hands on her hips, giving him a challenging look. He looked back at her as he leaned back against the headboard of his bed. Stevie watched the two of them, grinning.

Finally Cat blew her breath out, shaking her head.

"Fine, you win. It was your case, and I stuck my ass in it," she said, sounding anything but conciliatory. "Now, can you sign my paperwork?" She asked the last with a sweet smile.

Christian narrowed his eyes, knowing she was teasing him. He glanced at Stevie, who looked back at him and shrugged, shaking her head. Then he looked back at Cat.

"I suppose," he said finally, giving a long, suffering sigh.

"Oh, stop," Cat and Stevie said at the same time.

They looked at each other with wide eyes, then started laughing.

"Sign her paperwork, Collins, or I'll box your ears," Stevie said.

"Oh, I see how it is now," Christian said, narrowing his eyes at his wife. "Side with her."

"Always side with the winning edge," Cat said, her look cocky, even as her eyes twinkled with humor.

"Or the cute blonde," Christian said, making a face at his wife, then glancing at Cat.

Cat's eyes widened slightly, but she said nothing.

Stevie laughed, shrugging. "Gotta side with the girl, babe. Sorry."

"Not as sorry as you will be," Christian replied, his grin evil.

Stevie looked at him for a long moment, then over at Cat. "And I'm moving in with you when?"

Cat laughed. "Anytime, honey, anytime."

"Oh, I see how this goes…" Christian said.

The three of them laughed then.

"Look," Christian said. "Let me get up and we'll figure out what you need from me."

"Sounds like a plan," Cat said.

"I'll be out in a sec," Stevie told her.

Cat nodded, and left the bedroom.

Stevie turned back to Christian.

"You didn't tell me she was really gorgeous," she said, her eyes narrowed.

"I told you she was pretty," Christian said, reaching up to touch her cheek. "You're really gorgeous to me."

Stevie gave him a measured look, then grinned, leaning over to kiss him on the lips.

"Got out of that one nicely, Collins," she said, laughing softly.

She got up, picking up the camisole top she'd been wearing earlier and the shorts. She dressed quickly, then sat down on the bed, watching him as he got up and stretched. She found it necessary to reach out and touch his stomach as he did. He looked down at her, his eyes shining brightly as he smiled.

Stepping forward, he put his arms around her. She wound her arms around his waist, putting her cheek against his flat stomach. Turning her head, she kissed his stomach, then moved to get up. She headed for the door.

"Steve?" Christian said.

"Yeah?" she asked as she turned around.

"I love you," he said, his voice sincere.

"Just remember that," she said, winking at him.

He chuckled as she left the room.

Out in the living room, Cat was looking over the pictures on the mantle when Stevie walked in. Cat glanced over her shoulder, her eyes doing a quick scan of Stevie's body again. *Definitely nice.*

"Who's this?" Cat asked, pointing to a picture of an officer in uniform.

"That was my dad," Stevie said, smiling softly.

"And this?" Cat asked, pointing to another officer, a young man.

"That was Jason," Stevie said, her voice softer now. "He was my brother-in-law."

Cat looked at her for a long moment, noting that she'd said "was" about both men. Stevie stared back at her. Cat grimaced, nodding slowly.

"I need a drink," Stevie said, her tone upbeat but her eyes reflecting sadness.

"Me too," Cat said, smiling.

Stevie laughed softly, walking over to the cabinet in the kitchen where the alcohol was kept.

"What's your poison?" she asked. "We have vodka, tequila, Jack, and Southern Comfort."

"Southern Comfort works."

"Works for me too," Stevie said as she brought down the bottle.

She also took out the bottle of tequila. Cat raised an eyebrow.

"Christian drinks tequila," Stevie explained. "And he never lets me drink alone."

"Probably a good practice."

"What is?" Christian asked as he walked out of the hallway.

"Not letting me drink alone," Stevie said.

"We're drinking?" Christian asked, even as Stevie poured him a shot then grabbed a lime out of the refrigerator and cut it.

"Yes," she said, handing him the shot and the lime. "We are."

"Good plan," Christian said, searching his wife's eyes.

Stevie nodded as she poured shots for herself and Cat.

"To good plans," Stevie said, holding up her glass.

Cat and Christian did the same, and the three of them drank. It was the beginning of an interesting evening. They ended up settling in the backyard with the bottles, Cat with her cigarettes and Christian with his. Christian and Stevie sat in chairs on the patio; Cat sat on the ground, facing the two of them. It was a nice evening outside, not cold but not too warm either. They talked about police work, about the house, about anything that came to mind.

Cat found that she liked the two of them very much. Stevie was a very friendly, witty woman, with a very direct attitude. They talked about what had happened between Cat and Christian at the house of the drug dealer. Stevie told Cat that she hadn't worried about her kissing Christian, that Christian knew what he had at home. Christian grinned at her words, nodding in agreement

"So how did you two meet?" Cat asked at one point.

"We were working a case together," Stevie said, leaning back in her chair, the breeze ruffling her hair slightly.

"What kind of case?" Cat asked, glancing at Christian, who'd begun to grin.

"Oh, it was a sexual predator case," Stevie said.

"So what got you two together?" Cat asked, her eyes going back and forth between them.

Christian dropped his head back, laughing; it was a deep, rich sound. He looked over at Stevie, and she shook her head at him, grinning widely. Finally Stevie looked at Cat.

"Sex," Stevie said simply.

"Sex?"

"Sexual tension," Christian qualified, looking over at his wife fondly. "This case took place in a chat room, where Stevie had to entice these preds to come after her. She was playing a sixteen-year-old girl. To get interest, we did a bit of cybering in the room…" He trailed off as a grin curled his lips. "Let's just say, Stevie had me wound tight by the end of most nights online."

"Oh ho…" Cat said, looking over at Stevie and laughing.

Stevie nodded. "Trust me, it was just as rough on me," she said, her look at her husband accusing. "Then he shows up over at my house one night after we'd gone offline. He said he'd come to fix my connection, since it kept dropping."

"And there she was in bed, wearing absolutely nothing," Christian put in.

"I was in bed for the night, Collins, unlike some people," Stevie said, her look narrowed.

"I wanted to be in bed." He laughed. "Just yours instead of mine."

Stevie laughed too.

"So what happened?" Cat asked, gesturing with her hands for them to continue.

"I fixed what was wrong with her laptop," Christian said. "And she asked if I wanted to show her what I'd done to fix it."

"He asked me if I was wearing anything under the sheet I had on," Stevie said, smiling. "I told him that no, I wasn't."

"I told her that she'd better stay where she was, or more than her computer was going to get taken care of."

"Ohhhh…" Cat said, making a face that reflected her enchantment.

"And you took care of me," Stevie said, biting her lip as she stared into his eyes.

"Oh yes," he said, nodding, taking her hand and pulling her onto his lap.

Stevie straddled his lap, leaning down to kiss him deeply. He buried his hands in her hair, caressing her neck. When their lips parted, Stevie turned around, leaning back against him.

"You know what?" she said, glancing up at the sky.

"What?" Cat asked.

"We need food."

"Food sounds good," Christian said, nodding.

"Yeah, I'm starved," Cat said.

Christian moved to stand, taking Stevie by the waist and setting her on her feet. He put his hand out to Cat, to help her up off the ground. She took his hand, and he pulled her up and right into him. She laughed as she stumbled slightly. They'd been drinking for two hours, so none of them had great balance at that point. Stevie was the one to grab her arm and stabilize her.

"Thanks," Cat said, smiling.

"No problem," Stevie said, her hand sliding down Cat's arm slowly.

Cat shivered. It hadn't been something she'd expected, but it had been a slight thrill all the same. When she glanced at Stevie, Stevie winked at her. Cat canted her head to the side, her look questioning. Stevie said nothing, only shrugging and walking inside. Cat glanced up at Christian, who stood next to her. His light blue eyes looked down at her, then to where his wife had just walked inside, considering. Cat narrowed her eyes at him. He only laughed, and walked inside too. Cat thought about it. They were all getting pretty close to being drunk. That tended to lower people's inhibitions.

They ordered the Chinese food Stevie had originally planned to order.

They had a few more drinks sitting in the living room waiting for the food to come. Christian sat on the couch, Stevie lying there with her head in his lap, and Cat sat on the floor next to Stevie.

"So you two have been together how long?" Cat asked.

Stevie and Christian looked at each other, grinning.

"Well, that depends on if you count breakups," Stevie said.

"Breakups?" Cat asked, pouring another shot.

"Oh, a couple," Christian said casually.

"Bad?" Cat asked, drinking her shot and handing Stevie the bottle.

Stevie nodded, sitting up and drinking straight from the bottle.

Christian reached over, taking the bottle gently from her hands and handing it back to Cat. Cat watched, knowing there was something deeper than breakups involved in that story.

"Suffice it to say," Christian said, pulling Stevie back against him and leaning down to kiss her lips softly, "we won't be breaking up again."

Stevie shook her head, burying her face against his shoulder and neck. Christian grinned, the look on his face soft. Cat looked on, seeing how deeply in love these two were. She thought it was great. She herself had never been in love, nor did she really care if she ever was. She was enjoying being single, free, and doing anything she wanted to do.

"I'm sorry," Cat said. "I didn't mean to bring up any bad memories. Breakups suck," she added, reaching out to touch Stevie's hand, which rested on Christian's leg.

Stevie turned around, lying back down and putting her cheek on Cat's hand.

"Trust me, the breakups with this guy never end well," she said, making a face as she glanced up at Christian.

Christian grinned. "They're fairly deadly, aren't they?"

Stevie narrowed her eyes at him. "That first time wasn't my fault."

"The hell you say. If you'd just let me kiss you..."

"They would have shot both of us," Stevie finished.

"Shot?" Cat asked, shocked. "You mean with a gun, shot?"

"I mean with an AK47 shot, babe," Christian said, winking.

"Are you kidding?" Cat asked, sure he had to be.

Christian reached down, lifting Stevie's shirt to just under her breasts and pointing to a small scar. "There," he said, then pulled the top of her tank top down to just above the curve of her right breast, pointing to another scar. "There, and"—he pointed to her right shoulder, resting against his leg—"there."

"Three times?" Cat asked, having noted the nice expanse of skin he'd exposed but not commenting on it.

Stevie nodded, then sat up, pulling Christian's shirt off and tossing it aside. "And there," she said, pointing to a longer scar on his right shoulder.

"You were hit too?" Cat asked, growing more and more aghast.

"He was hit trying to protect me," Stevie said, looking a bit stricken.

"Don't start," Christian said, leaning toward her and kissing her neck.

"Everyone says that he took the fourth shell that would have killed me," Stevie said, narrowing her eyes at him. "He saved my life."

Christian narrowed his eyes back at her. "You shouldn't have been shot at all."

"No, but it wasn't something you could have prevented, so shut up, Collins."

"Only if you will."

"Only if you think you can shut me up," she shot back, her look challenging.

"Easily done," he said, grabbing her by a handful of hair and pulling her to him.

He kissed her deeply while Cat looked on. Stevie's hand slid up his chest, her nails leaving light marks. Christian groaned deep in his throat. Stevie grinned in response, moving her lips to his neck, and then down his chest. Christian's hand stayed in her hair, guiding her head. He gasped out loud, his eyes on Cat, as Stevie's mouth closed over his nipple. A moment later, Stevie sat back up, kissing his lips, then lay back down on the couch as if nothing had happened.

Cat grinned, looking at Stevie, then up at Christian, who shook his head. His wife had just reminded him how easily she could get to him. The doorbell rang then, and Christian moved to get up. Stevie sat up to allow him to. Cat reached into her pocket, pulling out some money to help pay for the food. Christian walked to the door.

"Put that back," Stevie said. "We got this."

"No way," Cat said, shaking her head. "You two have been supplying the alcohol—I need to pay for the food."

"Nope," Stevie said with a grin.

Cat moved to stand up, with the intention of going to hand Christian money. Stevie grabbed her hand and pulled her down on the couch, taking the money and shoving it back into Cat's pocket. Cat laughed, reaching for Stevie's hand and pulling it out of her pocket, holding it away from her and reaching into her pocket with the other hand to get the money. Stevie laughed too, grabbing Cat's other hand to keep her from getting the money out again. It became a battle of wills—both women were strong, so it was a matched fight.

"And what's going on here?" Christian asked, holding the bag from the restaurant and raising a jet black eyebrow at the two of them.

Stevie glanced up at him, not releasing her hold on Cat's hands. "We're fighting," she said.

"That ain't how you fight, babe," Christian said, winking at her.

Stevie laughed, turning her head back to Cat. "He already paid for it—you lose."

"I'll just give him the money," Cat replied, still trying to reach for it, Stevie's hold on her hands keeping her from doing so.

"Nope," Stevie said, grinning.

"Come on," Cat said, laughing. "Just let me pay for it, okay?"

"Nope."

There was more struggling, while Christian looked on indulgently.

"I'm paying for the food," Cat said, narrowing her eyes at Stevie.

"No, you're not," Stevie said, narrowing her eyes back.

Cat made a move to reach for her pocket again, and Stevie stopped her again.

Cat growled. "Let go!" she said, laughing all the while.

"No!" Stevie replied, laughing too.

"I can make you."

"Cannot," Stevie replied, grinning confidently.

"Wanna bet?" Cat asked, her eyes sparkling with mischief.

"I'll bet you anything you want."

"Anything?"

"Yep."

"You got it," Cat replied, then leaned in, kissing Stevie on the lips.

Stevie was shocked at the action. Even Christian's mouth dropped open for a moment, but then he started to grin, because Stevie did indeed let go of Cat's hands. Cat leaned back, grinning triumphantly.

"That wasn't fair," Stevie said, the beginnings of a grin on her lips.

"It was fair," Cat replied, smiling.

"Brat," Stevie said, sounding petulant.

"Poor loser," Cat countered, laughing.

"She got ya, babe," Christian said as he moved to sit back down on the couch, setting the food on the coffee table next to Cat.

"Yeah, yeah," Stevie said, giving Cat a narrowed look. "And I'm gonna get her back."

"Ohhh… that sounds exciting," she said, her eyes sparkling.

"Shut up," Stevie said. "Or I'll make you shut up too."

"And you think that's a threat to me?" Cat replied, reaching for the bag and starting to unpack the white boxes.

Stevie sat down on the floor next to Cat, helping her.

"Nah, you'd enjoy it too much," she said, grinning.

"You think you're that good?" Cat said, giving her cynical look.

Stevie glanced back at Christian. "Ask him."

Cat shook her head. "It's different with women, babe."

"Are you an expert?"

Cat gave her a measured look. "Let's just say I've had a lot more experience than you probably have."

Stevie nodded, acquiescing the point. "But good is good, no matter what."

Cat grinned. Stevie didn't give up, did she.

They started eating then, each of them taking an entree box.

"Let me try that," Stevie said to Christian when he had the shrimp.

Christian grinned, putting a shrimp between his teeth and leaning down to her. Stevie laughed, taking the shrimp with her mouth then kissing him deeply.

"No fair," Cat said, grinning.

Christian put another shrimp between his teeth, glancing at Stevie as he did. Stevie grinned and gestured with her head toward Cat. Christian leaned toward Cat. She hesitated for a moment, then leaned forward, taking the shrimp then kissing Christian too.

"You're right, that tastes much better that way," Cat said, winking at Stevie.

"Uh-huh," Stevie said, smiling.

"So what have you got there, babe?" Christian asked, looking pointedly at Stevie.

"Pork," she replied, grinning at her husband.

"Gimme."

They repeated the routine, kissing deeply afterward. Then Stevie turned to Cat, canting her head to the side.

"You want to try some too?"

A smile played at Cat's lips as she glanced at Christian, who was watching her expectantly. Cat had no intention of turning down that offer. She nodded, her eyes on Stevie's. They repeated the exchange of food, and then kissed. Cat's hand came up, pulling Stevie closer, kissing her deeply. Stevie shuddered, and then gave herself over to the kiss, making Cat groan softly. Christian looked on, thinking this was likely to be an interesting evening indeed.

In the end, the three of them moved back to Christian and Stevie's bedroom. On the bed they kissed, touched, and did whatever else came to mind. Eventually clothing was shed and things really began in earnest.

"My God, you two are beautiful…" Cat said, looking at Stevie and Christian as they lay next to each other, kissing.

Stevie reached out, taking Cat's hand and pulling her closer to them, leaning over to kiss her again. There was no more talking then, only sounds of pleasure and cries when releases were reached.

Afterward the three lay together, Christian in the middle, with Stevie and Cat on either side of him. Stevie rested her head on Christian's shoulder, her hand on his chest. Cat lay with her head against his lower torso, her arm over his waist. Every so often, Stevie would reach down and stroke Cat's hair. Cat would move her head, kissing Christian's stomach, reaching over to stroke Stevie's skin.

Christian leaned over kissing Stevie softly. He was amazed she'd indulged in this act with him, but he was also thrilled that she'd been willing to. He knew that was what kept his relationship with Stevie alive, her willingness to try anything with him. It wasn't that he needed other women—he didn't—but he'd lived a life full of sexual adventure, and that was what had always scared him about commitment, losing that adventurous life. Stevie loved him enough and trusted him enough to explore things with him, and it kept their marriage exciting.

After a while, the three of them got up, got dressed, and went back to finish the now cold Chinese food. They also continued to drink, and they ended up making out in the living room again. They found quickly that they were very comfortable together. Cat constantly told them what incredibly beautiful people they were.

"You're one helluva hottie too, love," Christian said.

"Mmhmm," Stevie agreed, reaching out to touch Cat's cheek.

Cat rewarded each of them with a kiss. It was a very nice night.

In the wee hours of the morning, the three of them lay in bed once again.

"You should seriously think about joining Rogue Squadron," Stevie said, reaching out to touch Cat's hair, which rested against her leg.

"You're thinking about leaving the SO?" Christian asked, glancing down at Cat.

"They're not, uh, shall we say, 'family' oriented," Cat said, giving him a pointed look.

"Oh," Christian said, nodding. "Well, hell yeah, you should think about joining our team. We need a third female."

Cat shrugged. "I'd have to apply and all that. I don't know if they'd even take me."

Stevie glanced up at Christian. "We could get her a meeting with Spider."

"Spider?" Cat asked.

"He's our LT," Christian explained.

"Well, Dave should probably be in on that too," Stevie added.

"Dave?"

"Dave Dibbins, he's our lead," Christian said.

"You mean *the* Dave Dibbins?" Cat asked, looking awed.

"That's the one," Stevie said, grinning.

Dave Dibbins was renowned as the best narc in the country. Anyone who did narcotics work knew who he was.

"Okay, now you got me," Cat said, grinning. "I'd give anything just to meet that guy."

"Well, you got it," Stevie said, smiling.

"Well, we already knew that," Christian said, winking at Stevie.

Stevie laughed, as did Cat.

***

"Yes?" Midnight said, answering her intercom and glancing apologetically at Kyle.

"Chief, Sergeant Dibbins is here to see you," Cassandra said.

Midnight smiled. "Send him in."

Dave walked in a few moments later. Midnight smiled warmly at him. Dave returned it, extending his hand to Kyle.

"It's about time you blew back into town," Midnight said.

"Yeah," Dave said, looking tired. "My sentiments exactly."

"How's Rogue Squadron doing?"

"I don't know yet," Dave said, grinning. "I need to go check in with Spider next."

"I feel privileged then—I was your first stop."

"That's because I need a favor," Dave said, still grinning.

"You name it, you got it."

"Well," Dave said, grimacing, "I need to get approval to take the test for lieutenant."

Midnight's eyes widened. "Why do you need approval?" she asked. Dave had avoided taking the lieutenant's test for years.

"Because the final filing date was a week ago," Kyle put in with a grin.

"Oh," Midnight said, nodding, still looking at Dave quizzically. "Explain, Dibbs."

Dave grinned widely. "I need to be home with my wife more."

"Why...?" Midnight asked, her tone leading even as her face shone expectantly.

"Because she's pregnant," Dave said, smiling.

"Oh my God!" Midnight exclaimed, jumping up from her desk and running around it to hug Dave, who had stood also.

Susan was Midnight's niece, through her marriage to Rick. Also, she and Dave had been working together for many years. Dave was part of what Midnight considered her extended family. She was thrilled for them.

"Congratulations," Kyle said, extending his hand to Dave.

"Thanks," Dave said, grinning.

"So you're going to take the test, then?" Midnight asked.

"Yeah," Dave said. "I'll be damned if I'm going to be away from my wife *and* child that much. It's been hard enough being away from Susan."

Midnight smiled. She loved that her niece had found a man that loved her so much. She loved even more that in finding that man, Susan had made Dave a very happy man as well. Fate had been very kind to them, and it was great to see.

"Well," she said, glancing over at Kyle, "I'm sure that we can make an exception in your case, Dave, for the filing date, considering you were in the field at the time the date passed."

Kyle nodded his affirmation.

Dave grinned, knowing that Midnight was bending the rules for him and appreciating it. The fact of the matter was, Midnight had been begging him to take the test for years now. She wanted to put him and Spider in charge of narcotics, since the unit seemed to do nothing but grow.

Dave left Midnight's office feeling better about taking the test. He knew it was the right thing to do. He couldn't take as many chances with a child on the way, and he was serious about being home more with Susan. He headed downstairs to Spider's office. Knocking as he walked in, Dave was surprised to see a blonde woman sitting in the chair across from Spider.

"Oh, sorry," Dave said.

"Hey, Dibbs," Spider said, smiling. "Just in time, actually."

"In time?" Dave said, his eyes going to the woman, who'd snapped her head around to look at him at the mention of his name. "For?" Dave asked, glancing at Spider.

"Yeah," Spider said, grinning now. "Dave Dibbins, meet Catalina Roché, the newest member of Rogue Squadron."

Catalina stood up, turning to Dave, her hand extended, her eyes bright as they looked into his.

"It's an honor to meet you," she said sincerely.

"An honor?" Dave asked, taking her hand and shaking it firmly.

"Yes, sir," Cat said. "You're the best narc in the country, and that's what I want to be."

Dave looked back at her, his blue eyes giving nothing away. "How long have you been doing narcotics work?"

"Two and a half years," she answered crisply.

"How many cases have you made?"

"Twenty-seven. Twenty-three of which have gone to trial and were convictions."

"And the other four?"

"One pleaded out," Cat said. "And the other three…" She narrowed her blue eyes ever so slightly. "Got off on technicalities."

"Your mistake?"

"Yes, sir," Cat replied promptly.

Dave looked back at her for a long moment, then nodded. He liked that she took responsibility for her mistakes. There was nothing worse than an officer that refused to do so. He liked her direct manner, and she definitely didn't look like a narc.

Dave gestured for her to sit down. She did, and he took the seat next to her.

"Cat is coming to us from the Sheriff's Office," Spider said, his eyes glittering with suppressed amusement.

"Okay…" Dave said, giving Spider a narrowed look. "And?"

"And she played your boy," Spider said, grinning.

Dave gave Spider a deadpan look, then glanced over at Cat.

"He played me too, sir," she assured him.

"Which one?" Dave asked seriously.

"Blue, sir," Cat said, wondering if Dave was mad.

Dave's look changed to one of amazement. "You played Blue?"

"Well, sir, I didn't know he was a cop, and he didn't know I was."

"She tried to arrest him," Spider said, grinning still.

Dave started chuckling then.

35

"Did you manage to get him cuffed?" he asked.

"I almost did," she said, grinning now too.

"Almost doesn't count," Dave said, shooting Spider a dirty look. "But playing one of my best guys does," he continued, looking over at Cat. "Welcome to the team."

"Thank you, sir," Cat said, smiling now.

"And it's Dave, or Dibbs, not sir."

"Okay."

"Or it might be LT in the future," Dave added evenly.

"What?" Spider exclaimed.

Dave grinned, nodding.

"You're finally taking the test?" Spider said.

"Yup."

"Wait, why?" Spider asked, narrowing his eyes.

Dave just looked back at him, his blue eyes widening slightly.

"Holy shit, Susan's pregnant," Spider said, breaking into a wide smile.

Dave nodded, smiling now.

"You tell Debenshire yet?"

"One of them."

"Which?"

"Midnight. Had to get an exception to file after the close."

"Oh, I see, tell the chief before you tell your best friend," Spider said, looking disgruntled.

"Hey, gotta get my priorities straight here," Dave said, laughing.

"Yeah, yeah," Spider said, waving away Dave's comment. "Get out of my office and take your new girl with you. Mace, Jeanie, and Pony need to meet her yet."

"You've met Stevie?" Dave asked, surprised. Stevie had been on undercover status for a while.

"Yeah," Cat said with a mysterious grin. "I've met her."

Dave narrowed his eyes, knowing there was more behind that grin but not sure what. He nodded toward the door as he stood up.

"I'll talk to you later, Spider," he said. "Once I've gotten up to speed on everyone's cases."

Spider nodded. "Tell your wife I said congratulations," he said, his grin sly.

"Not congratulating me?" Dave asked, raising an eyebrow.

"Why?" Spider asked. "Susan's the one that not only managed to nail your ass down, but now she's managed to get you to take the lieutenant's test. That's worth congratulating. All you did was sleep with your young and extremely beautiful wife."

"Fuck you," Dave said simply, his grin in place.

Spider laughed.

Dave and Cat left Spider's office then, walking out toward the offices Rogue Squadron used. Since they were an official team now, they'd been allotted an area just for them. There was a sign over the door to the offices that said: *Enter at your own risk. High-strung, tired, or just plain mean narcs within.* Cat grinned when she read it.

"So how did the name Rogue Squadron come to be?" she asked.

"It's my understanding," Dave said with a grin, "that when Blue, Jay, Steve, and Pony worked a setup once, Midnight made the mistake of referring to them as the Fab Four. Being the kids that they are, they balked at that. The name Rogue Squadron was settled on, since Blue's a Star Wars fan, and they tend to be the rogues in the department. But I'll let them explain further," he said, smiling as they rounded the corner.

The unit was set up with open cubicles with low walls, since the team had a tendency to yell over the cubicles at each other anyway. There were two desks in the center, facing each other, two next to each other on one wall, and two next to each other on the other wall. Dave's office was situated so he could see everything going on. He always left his door open so they could come in and talk to him when he was in. It was his way of doing things.

Kevin was sitting at his desk in the center of the room, on the phone. Christian was working on the computer on the opposite wall. Jeanie and Donovan were at their desks on the other wall, currently engaged in a good-natured battle over why Glocks were not better than Sig Sauers.

"You try wrapping my tiny little hands around a Sig, babe, and you'll see why my Glock is better," Jeanie said, giving her husband a "so there" look.

"For you," Donovan said. "Some of us don't have a tiny-hand handicap."

"Are you calling me handicapped?" Jeanie asked, widening her eyes at her husband.

"Only because you're married to Curtis," Christian put in from his desk.

That had the whole group laughing. Cat grinned too, not even knowing most of these people but happy to note their casual banter.

"Oh look, the boss is back…" Christian said, winking at Cat.

"Yeah, don't start with me," Dave said. "I've had about an hour of sleep."

"Zan keepin' ya up late, huh?" Christian said.

"It's was our anniversary yesterday, thank you very much," Dave said. "So let me get up to speed and out of here so I can go home and get some more sleep."

"Well, happy anniversary for yesterday," Jeanie said, smiling at Dave.

"Thanks, Jay," Dave said, smiling back.

He looked at the group then. "Where's Steve?"

"She's headed into the office now," Christian said. "She had a doctor's appointment."

"Her shoulder again?" Dave asked, raising an eyebrow.

Christian nodded. "Same shit, different year. She jammed it on a raid yesterday though."

"That never helps," Dave said, shaking his head. "Okay, well, she can catch up later then."

"Catch up on what?" Stevie asked as she walked in.

"Never mind, you haven't missed anything yet," Dave said, grinning.

Stevie walked by him, giving him a smile, and then moved to sit on Christian's desk, her eyes going to Cat.

"Mace, you with us?" Dave asked, glancing at the younger man.

"Yeah," Kevin replied, hanging up his phone and turning his chair around.

"Okay, a couple of things here," Dave said, moving to lean a hip on an empty desk in front of him. "First of all, we have a new team member here." He gestured at Cat. "For those of you that don't know her," he said, glancing at Stevie and Christian, still puzzling over the fact that they both knew her, "her name's Catalina Roché, and she's from the SO's narcotics team."

"Ah, we stole another one," Jeanie said, grinning.

"Hey, Blue, is this the one that—" Donovan began.

"Shut the fuck up, Curtis," Christian growled, his eyes sparkling with humor.

Donovan laughed, then looked at Cat. "It's good to meet anyone that can play Blue."

Cat dropped her head, grimacing, then looked over at Christian with one eye closed comically.

"Nah, live it up, Cat," Christian said. "I haven't told them your side of it yet."

Cat's mouth dropped open as she started to laugh.

Then she shrugged. "He played me too. I had no idea he was a cop."

"He doesn't have the decency to look like one," Donovan said, his tone disgruntled, even as he grinned.

"Neither does she," Kevin put in from his desk, nodding at Cat.

"That's Mace," Dave told Cat as she turned to look at Kevin.

Kevin nodded to her.

"And that's Pony," Dave said, pointing to Donovan.

"Or Donovan," Donovan put in, extending his hand to Cat as he stood up.

"Or the boy scout," Christian muttered, getting smacked on the arm by his wife shortly thereafter.

Dave grinned, shaking his head. "And that's Jeanie, or Jay," he said, nodding to her.

"Or the poor sod married to Curtis," Christian put in, ducking and laughing as Stevie moved to smack him again.

"He always hassle you like that?" Cat asked Donovan.

"Always," Donovan said, grinning.

"Well, we'll just have to gang up on him," Cat said, smiling and raising an eyebrow at Christian.

"You wouldn't dare…" Christian said, narrowing his eyes at her.

"Wanna bet?" Cat asked, smiling evilly.

"See? I like her already," Jeanie said as she stood up to shake hands with Cat.

Cat looked over at Christian. "See? Three against one," she said, grinning.

"Four," Stevie put in, winking at her husband.

Christian stared openmouthed at Stevie. "I'm hurt."

"Uh-huh."

Christian looked over at Kevin. Kevin nodded. "I'm with ya, Blue."

"Ah, problem child agrees with me," Christian said.

"Just for that…" Kevin said, grinning, trailing off as he shook his head.

"Shit," Christian said, grimacing.

Everyone laughed then.

"Cat," Dave said. "You can sit here with Mace." He gestured to the desk he was leaning against.

Cat nodded, moving to sit in the chair in front of the desk, facing Dave.

"Okay, the other announcement I have is that I'll be taking the lieutenant's test next month."

There were a number of shocked noises and "*What?*"s.

"You leavin' us, Dave?" Stevie asked.

"Nah," Dave said, grinning at her. "I can't get out of this assignment that easy. No, I'm taking the lieutenant's test so I can get out of the field."

"Why the hell would you want to do that?" Christian asked.

Dave turned his head, looking straight at Christian. "Because my wife is pregnant."

Cat glanced at Christian and saw the look on his face.

Christian was shocked at first, then started to nod, even as the rest of the team jumped up to congratulate Dave. Christian was the last to stand, walking over to Dave. Cat watched as the rest of the group parted. Christian extended his hand, nodding.

"Congratulations, man," he said. "Tell Zan I'm very happy for her."

"Tell her yourself," Dave said, smiling.

"She home?"

"Yeah. You can stop by there when you take Cat out to the range to have Joe gear her up."

"I'll do that," Christian said.

The meeting proceeded then, with Dave getting everyone's status. Cat noticed the easy way he handled everything. When there was a problem, she saw that Dave gave all of them an opportunity to come up with answers. If no one came up with anything, Dave told them what he suggested, and then a discussion would ensue. She found that she liked Dave's style very much. She could easily see why he was a good narc. He never threw an idea out; he looked at every angle and decided which he thought would be best, but even then he gave each team member a chance on some input. It was a refreshing change from the attitude of her former lieutenant, who'd treated her like she was an idiot and always just ordered her to do things his way.

Later, in Christian's Viper, Cat looked over at him.

"Can I ask you a question?"

"Sure," Christian said, nodding.

"Why were things, ah, a bit weird when Dave announced that his wife is pregnant? I mean, for you, that is."

Christian grinned. She did have good instincts.

"Well, Dave's wife and I dated for over a year," he said. "And I could never commit to her."

"This was before Stevie?"

"Yeah," Christian said. "In fact, I was still officially dating Zan when I started sleeping with Stevie."

"Officially?"

"Well, we hadn't broken up, but I was sleeping with other

42

women, and she knew about it," Christian said, not looking the least bit ashamed.

"And she put up with that?"

"Well…" Christian winced. "I didn't give her much of a choice. If she wanted to still be with me, she had to put up with my way."

"You were an asshole," Cat said simply.

Christian looked over at her, surprise on his face. Then he started to laugh, nodding.

"Yeah, I guess I really was," he said. "But I loved her, and I just figured she'd wait."

"You loved her, but you slept with other women?" Cat asked cynically.

"God, you sound like Steve now," Christian said, rolling his eyes. "Susan was the first women I fell in love with, but I just needed more. She's very beautiful, very nice, very sweet…"

"Too sweet," Cat put in.

Christian looked over at her again, then nodded. "Yeah."

"So you slept with other women for the excitement."

"Pretty much."

"And Stevie captured your heart."

"And then some," Christian said, grinning.

Cat nodded, understanding better now.

"How old is Dave?" she asked, thinking that a woman that was dating Christian couldn't be too old, but Dave Dibbins had been around for years.

"He's forty-one."

"How old is she?"

"Twenty-five now, I think."

"Oh," Cat said, widening her eyes.

"Oh, trust me, they're perfect for each other," Christian said.

"Wait till you meet her."

"What's she like?" Cat asked, curious about the kind of woman a guy like Dave Dibbins would be married to.

"Cultured, smart, beautiful, sophisticated," Christian reeled off. "And she takes good care of him."

Cat looked surprised, then nodded, thinking she'd reserve judgment until she'd met Susan. She was indeed surprised that Dave would be married to someone that sounded like she was very classy. Dave was a narc, after all—wouldn't he want someone more down to earth?

Christian pulled up to Dave and Susan's house. He and Cat got out of the car and walked to the door. Christian knocked, disdaining the use of the intercom that Dave had installed. He was very surprised when Elizabeth, Susan's younger sister, answered.

"Oh my lord, Blue!" Liz said, smiling brilliantly up at him as she reached up to hug him.

"What are you doing here?" Christian asked, narrowing his eyes at her but grinning.

Liz grimaced. "Don't ask."

"Oh, Christ," Christian said, rolling his eyes. "Just tell me it wasn't a member of the royal family this time."

"Nope," Liz said, smiling brightly. "But the scandal was immense."

Christian shook his head. Elizabeth Endicott was constantly in trouble. She seemed to live for just that.

"Oh," he said, glancing at Cat, who was watching with interest. "Liz, this is Cat. Cat, this is Liz. She's Susan's younger sister."

Cat nodded, grinning as she looked right into Liz's eyes. "It's nice to meet you."

"You as well," Liz said, smiling. "Are you working for Blue?"

"With," Cat clarified. "I'm working with Blue."

Christian grinned at the exchange.

"Where's your sister?" he asked.

"Susan!" Liz yelled, her eyes still on Cat. "Your ex is here."

"My what?" Susan asked as she came around the corner. Then her face lit with a brilliant smile. "Christian," she said, her English accent elegant.

Christian hugged Susan, kissing her cheek.

"Come in," Susan said, giving her sister a dirty look for keeping Christian and the lady with him standing on the porch.

"Zan, this is Cat. She's working with Rogue Squadron now," Christian said as Susan led them to the living room.

Susan turned around, smiling at Cat and extending her hand.

"It's lovely to meet you," she said.

Cat nodded, smiling too. "Nice to meet you too."

Elizabeth had moved to perch on the counter in the kitchen, watching them talk. Cat noticed her, and wondered why the girl was so interested in the conversation.

"So, I heard some news this morning…" Christian said to Susan, his eyes on hers.

Susan smiled, nodding and biting her lip.

Christian hugged her again. "Congratulations, babe," he said softly. "I know how long you've wanted this."

"Thank you," Susan said, her voice equally soft.

"Any due date yet?"

"Not yet. I don't have my first appointment until next week." She looked at Cat. "So you're having to work with Christian?" she asked, her voice still nice even if her words indicated condolence.

"Yeah," Cat said, grinning. "It's a burden I'm bearing in silence."

"Oh, shut up," Christian said, laughing. "She begged to work

45

with me," he told Susan.

"I can't imagine why," Susan said, making a face.

"Oh, nice," Christian said. "I come all the way here to congratulate you personally, and this is how I'm treated?"

"Oh, stop," Susan said, putting her hand to his cheek. "You know I love you. I just enjoy teasing you a great deal."

"Uh-huh," Christian said, giving her a narrowed look.

Susan laughed softly, shaking her head.

"You can always dish it out, but you can never take it, Christian Joseph Collins," she said, sounding like a mother.

"Joseph?" Cat echoed.

"Don't you start," Christian warned her.

Cat smiled in response, her blue eyes glittering with mischief.

"Well, we better go," Christian said. "I just wanted to come by and see you." He reached out to hug Susan again. "And congratulate you."

"Thank you, Christian," Susan said as she kissed his cheek.

She walked them to the door. Cat noticed Liz following at a distance.

Once back in Christian's Viper, she looked over at him.

"Susan seems very nice," she said, shaking her head. "I still can't reconcile her with a guy like Dave though."

"Most of us couldn't," Christian said. "But they seem very happy. Midnight's view on it is that Susan has a need to take care of people—I'd never let her take care of me, but Dave actually needs someone like that. So they have a mutual need for each other."

"Which makes for love?"

"I guess so," Christian said, grinning. "In their wedding vows, Susan even cited the fact that he allows her to take care of him as one of the reasons she loves him."

Again Cat nodded, and shrugged. "Guess that's it then. What's the younger sister's story?" she asked mildly.

"In terms of?" Christian asked, a jet black eyebrow raised.

"She just seemed to… I don't know… lurk, is the best word I can think of."

Christian grinned. "Probably because she's not sure how much Susan knows."

"About what?"

"About how far things went between her and I, while I was dating Susan," Christian replied simply.

"Ohhhh…" Cat said, grimacing. "Her too?"

Christian laughed. "Yeah, her too. And Jay as well."

"You slept with Donovan's wife?"

"She wasn't his wife then," Christian said, giving her a sour look. "Actually his ex-girlfriend at that point."

"I see," Cat said, nodding. "You really were a high-level player, weren't you?"

"Oh yeah."

"But I'm betting Stevie was too, wasn't she?"

"Better than me, in most cases," Christian said, grinning.

"Oh, that explains a lot."

"About what?" he asked, sounding very English.

"She was the ungettable get," Cat said, grinning.

"The what?"

"She was the one that you couldn't catch, so you wanted her more."

"She was the one I couldn't keep to save my life," Christian said. "And the only one I ever wanted to."

Cat nodded. "You got yourself caught then, by a better player."

Christian grinned. "That I did." He looked over at her then. "So you've never been got?"

Cat shook her head. "I play them, not the other way around."

"Careful—that can bite you in the ass when you least expect it."

"Like it did you?"

"Indeed," Christian said, not looking too unhappy with that.

Cat nodded, grinning at him.

It was just plain sick, being that happy in love. Better him than her, was all Cat could think. Although she did respect his and Stevie's relationship totally, she had no desire to be in love ever. She liked being in control of how she felt and did things, thank you very much.

CHAPTER 2

Mikeyla Debenshire stared openmouthed at Nick.

"So what are you saying?" she asked, her tone very much like her mother's in its acerbity.

Nick sighed, knowing he was about to get called just about every name in the book, not the least of which was "pig."

"I'm saying, I think we need to break up," he said, crossing his arms over his chest in a subconsciously defensive gesture.

"Because I won't sleep with you," Mikeyla said, narrowing her blue eyes at him.

Nick sighed, shaking his head. "Because we can't stop fighting at all now."

"Because I won't sleep with you."

"Mikeyla," he said, putting his hands down on the table in front of him. "I've been honest with you. I do want to sleep with you. I've also respected the fact that you don't want to do that, at this point."

"But not so much that you want to stay with me," Mikeyla said, shaking her head in disgust.

"Damnit, Keyl," Nick said, his temper flaring. "Don't make me out to be a total jerk here—that's not fair."

"No," Mikeyla said, flipping her copper-blonde hair over her shoulder, her look cynical. "You just don't want to fight anymore."

"No, I don't," Nick replied, his eyes narrowing.

"Fine," Mikeyla said, standing up. "You want to break up, it's done. But don't try to bullshit me, Nick. It's a case of 'Don't put out, I'll put you out.'" With that, she turned and walked away.

Nick watched her go, pressing his lips together in irritation. She was right. He couldn't even think straight anymore around her. He was so obsessed with making love to her that his mind just couldn't function when she was near him. And she wasn't even considering sleeping with him. He knew that too. The idea that he wanted her so much and she wouldn't even consider it drove him crazy. That made him mad, and being mad had caused a lot of the fights, had made him frustrated and just plain tense with her constantly.

It wasn't like he hadn't had sex—he'd been having sex since he was thirteen and the girl down the hall from them in New York had initiated him into the world of sex. She'd told him he was the hottest-looking guy she'd ever seen, and she wanted to show him things. She'd shown him things alright, a whole world of things. It had been part of the reason he'd been so pissed at his father for moving them to San Diego less than a year later. In truth, he'd been mad at his father since his mother had died of breast cancer. He blamed his father; somehow it had to be his fault that she had died.

He'd scored a number of girls in San Diego too, however. But Mikeyla Debenshire wasn't like any of them. She was beautiful to the extreme, and sexy beyond belief, even though she didn't even seem to know it, with her long copper-blonde hair and her deep blue eyes. She had a perfect tan, since she lived on the beach, and a well-shaped body, petite but nicely rounded as well. At almost sixteen, Mikeyla had legs to die for and a body that kept him awake nights.

They'd been dating for just over a year, and they'd done little more than make out. She never let him touch her other than over her shirt and bra. Nick was smart enough not to push it, since her father was a very intense and frankly very dangerous cop, and her mother was the Chief of Police of the San Diego Police Department and his dad's boss.

Nick had just turned sixteen. He couldn't believe he was dating a girl that refused to sleep with him. It wasn't like he wasn't getting offers left and right. Girls found him incredibly sexy. He was Italian/Irish, with jet black hair and rich blue eyes. He was six foot one inch tall, with a well-toned body. The body he'd garnered by working out with his father, who was an ex-Navy Seal. Nick had an easy manner, with just enough charm to be a cut above the other guys in his class, and plenty of style. On top of which, he still had just enough of his New York accent to give him a different quality from the California guys.

Mikeyla Marie Debenshire was one of a kind, though, and he knew it. But the fact of the matter was, he knew if she wouldn't sleep with him, he'd end up cheating on her just to relieve the frustration she stirred up in him every time he saw her. Taking care of it by himself at night just wasn't cutting it anymore—he needed to have real sex with a real woman. He wished like hell it could be Mikeyla, but wishing never made things happen. He'd learned that when he wished that his mother wouldn't die.

Getting up from the table, Nick made his way out to the Monte Carlo his father had given him to celebrate getting his license. The car had been his father's; all the same, it was top of the line all the way. Black with black leather interior, automatic everything, six-CD player in the dash, Cyclone speakers, and a high-performance 200-horsepower V6 engine. It was a beautiful car, and Nick had been floored when his father handed him the keys.

Kyle Masterson and his son had seen some very difficult times, especially when Kyle met and fell in love with Rhiannon Templeton. Nick had rebelled totally against his father marrying another woman.

He'd refused to accept Rhiannon and had been outright rude to her a number of times, even when she did everything in her power to keep Kyle and Nick from fighting. Kyle had come very close to hitting his son more than once, something he'd never done before. It had taken an emergency for Nick to finally comprehend the possible repercussions of his behavior.

Rhiannon had gotten pregnant and had subsequently miscarried the baby. Kyle had been out of town that night. Nick had been the one to call the ambulance and stay with Rhiannon. The emergency had brought out the good man Nick was meant to be, the man his mother had wanted him to be—Kyle had said so himself. The doctors had indicated that stress could have caused the loss of the baby. Nick had felt responsible. In feeling such remorse, he'd finally begun to see in Rhiannon the kind, caring woman that she really was. It had, in fact, been Rhiannon's sound advice that had helped him to capture and hold Mikeyla's attention after a botched first date.

Nick had grown up a great deal during that time, and he was grateful now for his stepmother. She made his father extremely happy, and his younger brother, Brenden, had blossomed under Rhiannon's care. Brenden had only been two when their mother died, so he'd never truly known her. He'd been very open to Rhiannon's entry into their lives. And although Rhiannon had never had children of her own, she seemed a natural mother, seeing the good in both Kyle's sons and constantly pointing out different viewpoints to Kyle on raising them.

Nick had honestly begun to believe that Rhiannon had truly been sent to them to heal them all. Rhiannon had sustained very painful losses in her life too, having lost her father, a police officer, in the line of duty when she was fourteen. She also lost her husband of eleven years, Jason Templeton, in a car accident during a pursuit. The irony was that Jason had been killed the exact same day that Barbara Masterson had succumbed to breast cancer. Everyone believed that it had been fate that had brought Kyle and Rhiannon together to heal each other and bring each other back from the half-lives they'd been living. Nick believed that too.

Nick drove around for a couple of hours, finally going home. Walking in, he smelled dinner cooking. Rhiannon was a good cook; he had to fight the effects of it at the gym regularly. Walking into the kitchen, he saw her leaning over the counter, reading the paper.

"Hey, Rhi," he said, leaning down to kiss her cheek.

"Hi, Nick," Rhiannon said, glancing up at him.

"Anything new in the news?"

"Just the usual mayhem and bloodshed," Rhiannon said wryly.

Nick nodded, opening the refrigerator and looking inside with a heavy sigh.

Rhiannon glanced back at him. "What's the sigh for?"

"Keyl and I broke up."

Rhiannon winced, canting her head to the side. "I'm sorry, Nick," she said sincerely. "What happened?"

Nick shook his head. "We just don't want the same things any-more," he said, trying to put it as delicately as possible.

Rhiannon nodded. "That happens. Still, I'm sorry."

"Thanks," Nick said, looking unhappy. "I think I'll go hang out on the balcony."

"Just don't jump," Rhiannon said, grinning.

"It's about an eight-foot drop, Rhi. I think I'll be okay," he said, grinning too.

He walked over, hugging her, grateful for her way of being able to make him smile, even when he felt like shit. He knew it was that

53

quality that had brought his father back from the depths of an emotional coma.

"Thanks, Rhi," Nick said softly.

"Any time, Nick."

Nick made his way out onto the balcony, watching the waves on the beach as they rolled in. The house Kyle had been renting from Joe Sinclair and had now purchased from him was nothing short of a mansion. It was incredible.

Kyle Masterson drove home feeling a bit harried. It had been a long day—it was year end, and the department's budget was a constantly moving target for him to plot. Walking into the house, he inhaled the scent of stroganoff, one of his favorite meals. He grinned to himself. Rhiannon always seemed to know when he needed something special. He loved her for that, and a whole boatload of other incredible qualities.

"I love you," he said, walking into the kitchen.

"Boy, you're lucky I wasn't the maid," she said, grinning as she straightened from the counter.

"We don't have a maid, honey."

"Oh yeah…" Rhiannon said as he walked over, taking her in his arms and kissing her softly.

"Trying to tell me we need one?" he asked, grinning down at her.

"Nah," she said, shaking her head. "We've got Bren—he loves to do housework!"

Kyle rolled his eyes, chuckling. Just the day before, Brenden had used an entire canister of Clorox wipes to "clean" his walls. Once Rhiannon had stopped laughing, she'd instructed Brenden to "help" her by picking up the wipes strewn about the room. When Kyle had gotten home that night, Rhiannon had handed him a basketball-sized wad of them and reported that his son had been cleaning again. Kyle had gotten a good laugh out of the incident as well.

Kyle glanced out at the deck, noting his son looking unhappy. He nodded toward the deck.

"What's wrong with Nick?"

"He and Keyl broke up," Rhiannon said, looking unhappy.

Kyle nodded. He knew that the couple had been fighting a lot lately. Many dates had ended early, with Nick coming home irritated and locking himself in his room.

"I think maybe you should talk to him," Rhiannon said. "I tried to, but I think this might be a guy kind of thing."

Kyle nodded, leaning down to kiss her lips. He went out onto the back deck, reaching up to loosen and pull off his tie and undo the top two buttons of his shirt.

"Hey," he said, moving to lean on the rail next to where Nick stood.

"Hey, Dad."

"So what happened with Keyl?"

Nick took a deep breath and sighed, shaking his head. Then he looked over at his father.

"Have you ever met a girl or a woman that just got inside your head so much that you couldn't think past getting to her?"

Kyle grinned, nodding. "Your mother."

"Yeah?" Nick smiled. "That bad, huh?"

"Oh yeah," Kyle said. "But I was really cautious with getting involved with her, because of her family ties. She was pretty on her guard with me too."

Nick nodded. "Keyl won't even discuss it."

Kyle pursed his lips. "She's only fifteen, Nick."

"She'll be sixteen in two months," Nick replied.

"Okay," Kyle said. "But if she's not ready, she's not."

"I know, Dad. You've drilled it into my head that when a girl says no, it means no. But that doesn't keep me from thinking about it constantly."

Kyle grimaced, nodding. "I know what you mean."

"I don't want to cheat on her, but Jesus, I'm goin' nuts here," Nick said. "I just touch her arm and I want her more than anything."

Kyle blew his breath out, shaking his head. "I can see the problem there. So you figured breaking up with her was the best thing to do? Or did she break it off with you?"

"No, I broke up with her," Nick said, looking extremely unhappy about it. "She doesn't understand at all—she just thinks it should be easy for me to wait."

"Girls don't feel it like we do, Nick," Kyle said. "It's not all external and intense for them."

Nick nodded. "I just don't know what else to do here."

"Well, it sounds like you did the best thing you could at this point. Maybe getting away from her for a while and hooking up with someone else will help."

"God, I hope so," Nick said. "But I'll tell ya, if someone else gets to her, I'll probably kill the guy."

Kyle rolled his eyes. "You didn't just tell an Assistant Chief of Police that," he said, grinning.

"Nope," Nick said, grinning too.

***

Joe Sinclair sat up fully awake, his senses working overtime. He knew someone was in his house. He was reaching for his gun when the door to his bedroom opened. Tensing, he glanced over his shoulder.

"You're gonna get yourself shot one of these days, beautiful," he

56

said as he grinned.

"You're too good for that, Joe," Jordan said as she climbed onto the bed on all fours, crawling over to him seductively and kissing him.

"Always counting on that, aren't you?"

"Yep," she said, staring back into his eyes.

Reaching up, he touched her under the chin, guiding her lips back to his. His hands slid over her shoulders and down her arms to pull her closer. She moved to straddle his lap, their lips never parting. Suddenly Joe pulled away, his eyes unfocused. Jordan started to say something, just as Joe leaned around her to locate the second person in the room.

"Hey, Jim," Joe said, addressing Jordan's new bodyguard, who was standing in the doorway.

Jim looked back at Joe for a long moment, his face showing surprise that Joe had sensed him. Then he nodded to the other man.

"I think I can protect her from here," Joe said, his look pointed.

Jim looked rebellious for a moment, and Joe felt Jordan tense as her head whipped around and she gave Jim a narrowed look.

What's goin' on there? Joe wondered.

"Jim?" Jordan queried, irritated. "Think you could leave me and my man alone for a bit?"

There was a very definite look of disdain exchanged, then Jim nodded and turned around.

"You could close the door!" Jordan called after him.

When Jim didn't return to do just that, Jordan made a noise of disgust in the back of her throat and got up to go and close the bedroom door. She turned around to find Joe watching her with a curious look on his face.

"Don't ask," she said, sighing as she kicked off her boots, once again climbing onto the bed.

"He's trying to do his job, babe."

"He's being a pain in the ass, Joe," she said, kissing him to forestall further comments.

She wrapped her arms around his neck, pressing closer to him as they kissed. Joe forgot about the issue with Jim and allowed himself to be absorbed in her presence. It was a rare treat having his rock star girlfriend show up to surprise him—he wasn't about to waste it.

They made love for hours that night, enjoying each other thoroughly. It amazed Joe when he thought about it—Jordan Tate was a world famous pop/rock star. People knew her face wherever she went. And she loved him. To his way of thinking, he was just some cop from San Diego, a nobody. To Jordan he was the man that she could never get enough of and wanted to spend every free moment she had with. She'd spent a small fortune on a plane to be able to see him more often; she also spent hundreds of thousands on flights when the Gulf Stream she'd bought wouldn't get her to him fast enough.

It was a very difficult relationship to manage, since he worked in San Diego and was rarely able to get free long enough to go and see her. She was on a tour to promote her third album. She had finished her European tour four months before. She started her tour of America after spending as much time as she could with Joe during her two month "break." She owned a house in Los Angeles, but basically spent all of her time with him at his townhouse in San Diego, whenever she was free. All the same, they spent a lot of time apart.

It was a difficult adjustment for Joe, who'd been married to one woman for fifteen years and was used to having the woman he loved with him all the time. To his credit, he managed it. It was an adjustment for Jordan as well; she wasn't used to needing a man as much

58

as she needed Joe. She did her best not to dwell on the fact that he didn't really have to work—he was worth literally millions of dollars all on his own. He'd inherited the money from his parents when they'd died years before. His guilt over indirectly being the cause of the accident that had killed them was what made him work. Jordan would be completely happy if Joe would give up his job and travel with her full time, but she knew that wasn't his style. He'd avoided being a rich playboy for years, and just because he'd fallen in love with a singer, it didn't mean he should change his standards and work ethic now.

They fell asleep with their bodies intertwined. Joe lay half over her, his lips against the hollow of her throat, his arm and leg thrown over her possessively. Jordan lay with her hands holding on to his arm and her legs wrapped around the leg he had over her. It was obvious they'd missed each other.

Jim opened the door to the bedroom quietly, hoping that he was right and they were both asleep. He looked at Sinclair first, knowing the man had uncanny senses and would be aware when someone was in the room. *She must have worn him out*, Jim thought, noting that Sinclair didn't even move. Jim knew he had to think of a way to keep Sinclair out of the picture if he was ever going to get to Jordan. The woman was just too hot, and he was going to nail her if it was the last thing he did. It was the reason he'd become a bodyguard in the first place, to have a better shot at the women no one else could touch. It wasn't like he didn't have the looks; he was tall, dark, and he thought pretty handsome, with the whole Italian stallion thing going on. Jordan wanted him, she was just playing it to get to him.

Joe Sinclair was a problem though. Jim had met him right after they got back from the European tour. Jordan had introduced them, giving Jim a pointed look as she did. Jim read the look as "Don't say anything about Europe." In Europe they'd gotten pretty close, he and Jordan. He knew she didn't want her boyfriend to know about that, so Jim had played it cool. But he wasn't going to be able to stand Sinclair around Jordan for too long. He was her protection, not Sinclair, the cocky bastard.

Jordan woke the next morning with the eerie feeling of being watched. Sure enough, she caught a glimpse of Jim just moving away from the door. *Damnit!* she thought as she gritted her teeth. Brenden, known to the world as BJ Sparks, the man that owned the record label she recorded under, had hired Jim to protect her. After a very nasty break with her former manager and stepbrother, Mark, Jordan had started receiving threatening phone calls from him. Mark told her he was going to kill her for throwing him aside now that he'd made her a star. Jordan had laughed at him, telling him that BJ Sparks had made her a star, not Mark.

Mark was her stepbrother by her father's marriage to Mark's mother. Mark had also been after Jordan since she was fifteen years old. He'd finally managed to finagle some semblance of a relationship from her when they'd both lived in Los Angeles, while she was attending Musicians Institute. She'd been twenty at the time. When Jordan had been unable to feel anything for him other than the sense that them being together sexually was wrong, she'd broken it off. He'd gone ballistic and beaten her. She ran home to London to her father. Mark had followed shortly after that, magnanimously offering to manage her fledgling singing career. Since their father knew nothing of their relationship, Jordan had found it impossible to refuse Mark's "help."

What had ensued was years' worth of threats, bruises, and even sexual assaults whenever Mark felt his place in her life was threatened. The last sexual assault had been right after Jordan had met Joe in London. Joe had sensed something wrong, and in the end confronted her with what he believed was going on with her "manager." Jordan had admitted that Mark was abusive, but that she was bound by a contract to him. In truth, she had been terrified that Joe would find out the "sick truth," as she saw it, that she'd actually had consensual sexual relations with her brother. Eventually it had come out that Joe knew that Mark was her stepbrother, and that he didn't see anything wrong with that aspect. What he found unacceptable was that she was tied to Mark through a contract. It had been Joe who had paid her way out of that contract. He'd had his lawyer, Robert Debenshire, read over it and find the out clause. Joe had paid $750,000 to get her out of the contract.

Mark had left quietly at that point. It had taken him six months to muster the courage to start threatening Jordan. Jordan suspected that he was using drugs heavily, as he had many times before, and had probably run through the money Joe had paid him. When Jordan had told Joe about the phone calls Mark had been making, Joe had told her in no uncertain terms she needed a bodyguard. She'd shrugged it off. Finally, Joe had contacted BJ, Jordan's best friend, and made sure he was aware of what was going on. As Joe had suspected, BJ knew nothing about the threats. Brenden had assured Joe that Jordan would have a bodyguard the next day. Jim had been hired and sent to Europe with her.

Neither BJ nor Joe knew what a slimy piece of crap Jordan really thought Jim was. The guy tried to come across as protective, but in reality he was a jerk. He tried to say things to be "supportive," or what he thought supportive would be, but it always came across as some kind of come on. Jordan had spent the entire European tour avoiding being alone with him. When they were alone, Jim constantly told her what a beautiful woman she was, how she was probably really lonely on tour a lot. He was always suggesting that if she needed to talk or just hang out, they could do that. It made Jordan's skin crawl.

She had purposely taken Jim down to San Diego after the European tour to introduce him to Joe, so he could see that she had a man. Not only did she have a man, but she had one that took care of her every possible need, desire, and want. She'd hoped Jim would get the message. He hadn't. She figured he was basically harmless, just annoying as all get out.

Carefully, Jordan got out from under Joe, knowing he'd wake up the minute she moved. True to form, Joe stirred, opening his eyes and looking at her.

"And you're going where?" he asked, grinning.

"I need to take care of something," she said, leaning over to kiss him. "I'll be right back. You stay right where you are, sexy man."

Joe nodded, turning over onto his back and going back to sleep.

Jordan pulled on her jeans and Joe's shirt and walked out into the living room. Jim was sitting on the sofa watching cartoons. *Brilliant*, Jordan thought.

"We need to get something straight," she said without preamble.

"What's that?" Jim asked, glancing up at her.

"When I'm here with Joe and you insist on accompanying me here, you need to leave after I'm safely in the townhouse."

"I can't do that," Jim said, his look defiant.

"Why not?" Jordan asked, putting her hands on her hips.

"Because BJ Sparks told me you were to be protected at all times," he replied, thinking how smart he was for outwitting her hard-to-get ploy.

"Jim," Jordan said, exasperated, "Joe's a cop. He can protect me better than any man in this country, and probably a few other countries. If I'm with him, I don't need you."

"That's not what BJ Sparks said."

"I don't fucking care, Jim!" Jordan whispered fiercely. "I'm telling you that if you don't leave me the hell alone to be with my boyfriend, I'm going to let him kick your ass for peeping on us when we're sleeping. You got it?"

Jim looked back at her for a long moment, his lips drawn, twitching at the mention of her boyfriend kicking his ass. He wasn't afraid of some old cop—he didn't care how much money the guy supposedly had.

Jordan didn't wait for him to formulate a response. She simply turned and walked out of the living room and back to Joe's room, shutting the door and locking it. Dropping the clothes she'd put on, she climbed back into bed with Joe, snuggling against his chest and kissing his neck. His arm slid around her, pulling her closer to him as he stirred. She leaned up over him, kissing his chest, moving her mouth to one nipple and sucking at it.

"Mmm…" Joe groaned softly, his hand tightening at her waist. "You can't still be unsated," he said, his voice tired.

"I never get enough of you, Joe," she said, grinning at him.

Joe smiled, his eyes still half closed. He reached for the phone, dialing as she lowered her head to kiss his chest again. His hand moved to her hair, gripping a handful and guiding her head to his nipple again, even as he started to talk on the phone.

"Hey, Night, it's me," he said, closing his eyes as Jordan's tongue slid over his nipple, forcing his voice to sound normal as he continued. "Jordan got here last night, so I'm gonna take a day off, okay?"

Midnight chuckled. "Can't handle that all-night stuff anymore, huh?" she asked knowingly.

"Nope," Joe said, grinning. "So I'm gonna take the day off to recover."

"Uh-huh," Midnight said, unconvinced.

"I don't have anything pending on my desk."

He had to hold back a groan, and his hand tightened on Jordan's hair as she tried to move lower on his body. He knew he couldn't handle that and be on the phone talking normally.

"I'm not worried about it, Joe," Midnight was saying. "Just have fun."

"Oh yeah," Joe said, giving Jordan a pointed look as she grinned at him mischievously.

He and Midnight hung up a moment later, and he loosened his hold on Jordan's hair. She moved down his body, and he groaned loudly as her mouth slid down over him. There was never a dull moment with this woman, that was for sure.

Jordan and Joe spent that day together, leaving Jim at a nearby hotel and going for a walk around the beach, having lunch, going back to the townhouse and making love. Whatever struck their fancy. Jordan loved that about Joe—he was able to just take things in stride. He didn't have to have a plan for everything. He was easygoing, laidback, but also very intense when the occasion called for it. There was nothing boring about the man. Jordan enjoyed every day with him.

That night, they were watching a movie on his couch when his pager went off. He checked it and shook his head, grinning.

"What?" Jordan asked, looking up at him from where her head rested in his lap.

"Midnight," he said, rolling his eyes as he reached for the phone. "She can't live without me for even a day."

Jordan laughed.

Joe dialed Midnight's number and was surprised when Mikeyla picked up. He wondered for a moment if he'd only assumed that

Midnight had paged with her home number.

"Keyl, it's Joe. Is your mom there?"

"She's here," Mikeyla said. "But I paged you."

"You did?"

"Yeah, I wanted to ask you a favor," Mikeyla said, biting her lip.

"You got it, little one, whatever it is," Joe replied, grinning.

Mikeyla smiled. "I was hoping you were having a range day here soon, and that I could come to it."

"Ahhhh," Joe stammered. "Well, I've got one scheduled for tomorrow. Does Night know about this?"

"I talked to her about it, Uncle Joe—she said it would be okay."

"Oh, well," Joe said, taken aback. "Then yeah, if you want to come along, that would be fine. Do you want me to swing by and pick you up in the morning?"

"That would be great," Mikeyla said. "What time?"

"I usually leave the house at six thirty," he said, grinning.

"Yikes," Mikeyla said, widening her eyes. "That early?"

Joe chuckled. "Yeah, babe. I have to do a lot before the trainees get there at eight. Still want to come?"

"Yeah, I want to. I'll be ready."

"Okay. So, why the sudden interest in the range?" Joe couldn't help but ask.

"I just thought it would be something new to experience," Mikeyla said, shrugging. "And since I'm on summer vacation, I don't want to waste it."

Joe nodded, knowing there was more to it than that but not wanting to put her on the spot.

"We'll see you at around six forty-five then."

"We?"

"Jordan's here."

65

"Oh, cool," Mikeyla said, thrilled that she'd maybe get to hang out with Jordan.

Joe grinned. "Sure you didn't know that ahead of time?"

"I'm sure, Uncle Joe," Mikeyla assured him.

"See you in the morning, Keyl."

They hung up then.

"What was that about?" Jordan asked.

"That was Midnight's daughter. She wants to go to the range with me tomorrow. You are coming too, aren't you?"

"If you're there, I'm there," she said, smiling.

He grinned. "Alright then."

"So why does she want to go to the range?" Jordan asked. "You'd think she'd be all copped out, living with two of them all the time."

"All copped out?" Joe asked, raising an eyebrow at her. "Are you saying that she should be bored with law enforcement personnel?"

Jordan laughed, shaking her head. "I never get bored with mine," she said, winking. "But I would think hanging out at a gun range would be kind of boring for a teenager."

"You aren't saying that shooting is boring, are you?"

She narrowed her eyes at him, sighing as she shook her head. "I'm only digging myself in deeper, aren't I?"

"Basically," he said, grinning.

She sat up, turning to face him, and kissed him. That was enough to distract him.

The next morning, Joe drove his black Escalade up to Rick and Midnight's house. Rick was just walking out to his Mustang, gear bag in hand.

"Hey, old man," Rick said, grinning at Joe.

"Fuck you," Joe replied mildly.

"Not even if you begged," Rick shot back smoothly.

Joe laughed. "Your kid ready?"

"Yeah," Rick said, leaning against his car. "Had to drag her ass outta bed about a half hour ago."

Joe shrugged. "She called me, man."

"I know," Rick said he leaned forward, nodding at Jordan. "Hey, Jordan."

"Hi, Rick," she said, smiling at him.

"Still hangin' around this loser, huh?" Rick asked, gesturing to Joe.

"Uh-huh."

Mikeyla came hurrying out of the house. She ran up to her father, giving him a hug and saying a hurried "Bye, Daddy!" Then she ran around to get into the Escalade.

"Take care of my little girl, Joe," Rick said, his tone light but his eyes indicating that he meant it.

"I'll do that," Joe assured him.

Rick looked at his best friend of thirty-five years, nodding, knowing that Joe would make sure Mikeyla was safe above all else. It just made him edgy, knowing she was going to be around guns.

"Rick," Joe said, his tone softer now. "When's the last time I had an accident on my line?"

"You never have."

"Right," Joe said. "I don't intend to start with a member of my family, okay?"

Rick blew his breath out, nodding. "You're right. I'm sorry."

Joe shook his head. "No need to be."

He drove off a few minutes later, pushing a CD into the player and reaching for a cigarette.

"You're smoking again?" Mikeyla asked, surprised.

Joe glanced back at her, grimacing. "Uh, yeah," he said, a little bit abashed.

Joe caught Jordan's grin and narrowed his eyes at her. They'd had this same discussion the day before when he'd lit up.

"I'll open a window—you won't get any smoke," Joe said.

"No, but you will," Mikeyla countered.

"Jesus Christ," Joe said, rolling his eyes even as he laughed. "Do you realize how much you sound like your mother these days?"

Mikeyla grinned, knowing that coming from Joe that was actually a compliment. It had taken a long time to understand her mother's relationship with Joe Sinclair. She'd known for years that Joe and Midnight had been a couple for years before Midnight had met Rick. She also now knew about a minor affair Midnight had had with Joe when her and Rick's marriage was on the skids. Growing up, Joe had always been part of her life. He was the steadfast man in her life that never really changed.

She'd been surprised when, a year and a half before, Joe and Randy, his wife of fifteen years, had gotten divorced. It had made her very nervous. Rick and Midnight had always had fiery arguments, and Mikeyla was afraid that if Joe could divorce his wife after such a long time, then maybe her mother and father could do that too. When she'd talked to her parents about it, finally voicing her concerns, they'd been frank with her.

Midnight had told her that Joe not only leaving Randy but also starting to date a much younger woman had bothered her a great deal. She said that it had been at the same time that a young woman that worked with Rick had been coming on to him. It had only polarized the whole situation for Midnight. She'd admitted that she had judged Joe based on her own feelings and prejudice, and had been unsupportive of him for that reason. Midnight also told her she'd regretted it, because she knew Joe better than that. It was an interesting insight into her mother.

Seeing her mother fight and beat the girl that had been after Rick had been a much more eye-opening experience, however. She'd never seen her mother fight, although she'd heard from members of her extended family that Midnight was a very good street fighter. She'd been scared to death when the much younger woman, Angelina, had pulled a knife on Midnight in the parking lot of the police department. Midnight had been unfazed by the knife itself, but she'd been infuriated that the action had put her officers in danger when they'd all drawn their weapons to protect her. Then Midnight had been mad, and that had caused Angelina's eventual loss. Mikeyla had learned a lot about her mother that day, and discovered that she wanted to be a lot like her when she finished growing up.

Mikeyla listened to the song that was playing on the stereo. She knew it was Joe and her father's favorite band, Def Leppard, but she didn't recognize the song. The drift of the song had her fuming, though—it was basically about sex, wanting it, having it, and not wanting anything else.

When it ended, Mikeyla spoke up.

"That's really all guys think about, isn't it?" she said derisively.

Joe glanced back at her, perplexed. Then he looked over at Jordan. Jordan shook her head, not sure where Mikeyla's comment had come from.

"Excuse me?" he said, glancing at Mikeyla again.

"Sex," Mikeyla said. "That's what that song was about, right? Sex?"

"Uhhh," Joe stammered, having to think about what track had just played. He'd been thinking about the day ahead of him, not the song on the CD player. "Oh, 'Slang'?"

"Yeah."

"Uh, yeah, that would pretty much be it," he said, nodding. "The song, that is, not what guys think about," he quickly clarified, catching Jordan's grin.

"But that is all guys think about," Mikeyla said, looking disgusted.

Joe opened his mouth, his look considering. "Actually, I'm a guy and I manage to think about lots of other things besides sex," he said, his light blue eyes narrowing slightly. "Are we talking about a specific guy?"

Mikeyla looked hesitant then, not sure what she should say to her father's best friend. She'd just realized she'd opened a can of worms in front of what her mother called one of the best investigators she knew.

"I, uh…" she stammered, looking nervous.

"Nick, perhaps?" Joe said, his tone indicating that he knew he was right.

Mikeyla blew her breath out in a sigh, then nodded.

Joe nodded. "Okay, then let me rephrase—teenage guys, yeah, that's pretty much all they think about."

"I knew it," Mikeyla said, looking more unhappy at being right.

"So what's goin' on?" Joe asked, knowing there was more to this.

Again Mikeyla hesitated. Finally she shrugged. "Nick and I broke up."

Joe nodded, his light blue eyes on her, as he was stopped at a light. He was waiting for the rest of the story.

Mikeyla sighed again. There wasn't any way out of this other than lying. She knew better than to lie to her mother's friends; it had come back to bite her in the ass consistently over her lifetime. They

70

all talked to each other, she knew that.

"He said it's because we fight too much now."

Joe nodded. "But you don't believe that."

"No," Mikeyla said. "I think it's because I won't sleep with him."

Joe glanced at Jordan, who pointedly looked out the window.

"Tell me you didn't tell your father that little bit of information."

"No," Mikeyla said, looking at Joe like he was nuts. "I don't want Nick dead," she added, sighing. "I just want him to be honest with me."

Joe nodded, grinning. Rick would indeed more than likely kill Nick Masterson for trying to get his daughter to have sex with him.

"Have you and Nick been fighting a lot?"

Mikeyla nodded unhappily.

"But you think it's related to the sex thing?"

"Well, we didn't start fighting a lot until he asked me to have sex and I said I didn't want to. I think that says it all."

"Well, it does probably indicate that a certain frustration level is attributed to the fights."

"Frustration level?"

"Uh," Joe stammered, trying to think of a way to put things that wouldn't come out sounding too crude. "Let's just say, when you want something and you're not getting it sexually, things get rather… uncomfortable."

Mikeyla canted her head to the side. "What does that mean?"

Jordan glanced over at Joe, grinning. She knew he was talking himself into more complications, not less. She turned around, looking at Mikeyla.

"When you and Nick would fight," Jordan said, "was it usually after you two made out a lot?"

Mikeyla looked nervous, afraid to answer that.

71

"Don't worry," Jordan said. "This stays between the three of us."

Mikeyla looked relieved, and nodded.

"Okay," Jordan said. "Then basically what happened is he got going and then you put the brakes on."

"But he knew I'm a virgin," Mikeyla said, confounded.

"Right, but that doesn't stop his physical reaction to that kind of intimacy," Joe put in.

Mikeyla bit her lip. "So you're saying I shouldn't have made out with him at all if I wasn't willing to go all the way?"

"No," Jordan said, shaking her head. "That's not what we're saying at all, Mikeyla. It's just that men are very reactive when it comes to sex. If they get going, and they get told no, they react. That reaction is almost always anger."

Joe glanced over at Jordan, his look pained. He knew she'd been attacked a few times by Mark because she'd told him no, and he was fairly sure that was what she was thinking of.

"Well, he definitely got snotty," Mikeyla said. "But I wouldn't say he was mad."

"You just didn't see that part," Jordan said. "That actually says a lot about Nick's character—he's able to control it to some point."

"How do other guys react?" Mikeyla asked, knowing that Jordan would know.

"Sometimes violently, other times just by getting quiet and walking away for a while," Jordan answered, glancing over at Joe.

Mikeyla nodded. "Nick did that too. Walking away, I mean," she clarified quickly when she saw Joe tense, his head snapping around to look at her. "He'd say he had to go, and would leave really quick."

Joe nodded, his lips twisting in a grin.

"I just don't know what to think," Mikeyla said, shaking her head.

"Well," Joe said, reaching for another cigarette and rolling his window down, "I can tell you, Keyl, that it looks like he's trying to do the best thing for both of you at this point."

"What do you mean?"

"Well," Joe said, glancing over at Jordan as he lit his cigarette, "I think he's trying to respect your wishes."

"By breaking up with me?" Mikeyla asked, sounding exactly like Midnight when she thought Joe was losing his mind.

"Keyl," Joe said, looking at his hands and wondering how the hell he'd ended up on the advice-giving end of this whole thing. "As a guy, I can tell you that when you want someone, sexually, that's not an easy thing to ignore. It's worse still when that woman is your girl-friend and you spend a lot of time in close proximity to her. And if you two are making out a lot, that just makes it worse…" His voice trailed off as he glanced at Jordan again to see if she agreed with him; she was nodding. "He wants something you're not willing to give, and he's respecting that."

"The thing is, Mikeyla," Jordan said when Joe paused, "respect-ing your wishes doesn't really solve the problem for him."

Mikeyla bit her lip. "So he's breaking up with me so he can sleep with someone else," she said, not sounding happy with that prospect.

Joe grimaced. "I don't think that's his sole purpose, but basically, he needs what he needs at this point. If he cares enough about you to not want to cheat on you, then he probably feels like this is his only option."

"Why can't he just, you know…" Mikeyla said, trailing off as she grimaced, turning a number of shades of red.

Jordan laughed softly, looking over at Joe. Her look told him he was going to have to handle this one. He narrowed his eyes at her as she started to grin.

"Well, Mikeyla," Joe said, thinking he was going to send Midnight a bill for the therapy he was currently conducting, "that only does so much. There's a point at which you need the real thing."

"Oh," Mikeyla said, still embarrassed at having alluded to such a personal subject.

"I take it Nick's already had the real thing?" Joe asked.

"Oh yeah," Mikeyla said, nodding. "Since he was like fourteen," she added, her tone indicating her incredulity over that fact.

Joe laughed out loud at that. "You sound like you think that's young."

"Isn't it?"

"Uh," Joe said, rubbing the bridge of his nose with his forefinger. "Your father was fourteen the first time he had sex."

"Seriously?"

"Yup."

"How old were you?" Jordan asked, giving him a pointed look.

"I was old," Joe said, grinning. "Sixteen."

"Uh-huh," Jordan said, narrowing her eyes at him. "Real old, Joe."

He laughed.

"So then that's not really weird..." Mikeyla said, more to herself than to anyone else.

She'd thought it was strange that Nick had started having sex so early, but if her own father had done the same, then maybe it wasn't. She didn't see her father as being a pervert or anything. In fact, she'd always thought her father must be a great lover, considering the passionate relationship he and her mother seemed to share.

Joe glanced back at Mikeyla, seeing her mind working. He was sure he'd catch hell from Rick for telling Mikeyla how young he'd been when he'd first had sex, but too bad. Rick wasn't the one on the hot seat right now, and it was, after all, the truth. Never mind the fact that the woman that had inducted both him and Rick into the world of sex was Rick's younger sister's nanny. That was a whole other story.

Fortunately for Joe, they arrived at the range shortly after that. Jordan noted that he beat a hasty retreat from the vehicle, saying that he had to take care of some stuff before the students got there. She found it amusing.

"So," Mikeyla said, looking at Jordan. "How old were you the first time?"

"I was seventeen."

"Did you love the guy?"

Jordan shook her head. "I just wanted to get it over with."

"Over with?" Mikeyla asked, widening her eyes.

"The whole losing my virginity thing," Jordan said, making a face. "Everyone always made such a big deal about it, and I couldn't stand the worry about it anymore. So," she said, shrugging, "the first guy that seemed like he knew what he was doing got to be my first."

Mikeyla looked dismayed. "But isn't it supposed to be special?"

Jordan looked back at the girl, thinking she'd been reading way too many romance novels.

"Fact of the matter is, Keyl, chances are real good it'll hurt, so that pretty much negates special." She could see that Mikeyla was waiting for more. "Look, you should do it with someone you really feel good about, but don't be expecting violins, flowers, and fireworks, because it just doesn't happen that way most of the time."

Mikeyla nodded. "My mom said that I should make sure it's with someone I'm comfortable with."

Jordan nodded. "That's true. Sex gets very intimate. Obviously," she said, rolling her eyes. "But if you're not comfortable with the guy, then you end up worrying more about 'What does he think of my body?' 'Am I kissing right?' 'Am I making the right sounds?' than you are about the fact that you're actually having sex for the first time."

Mikeyla laughed, nodding. "I've already thought that a billion times with Nick, and we haven't had sex yet!"

Jordan laughed. "I know. We all do it, trust me."

"Really? Not you, no way," she said, shaking her head.

"Oh yeah, me, Mikeyla," Jordan assured her. "The more I want someone, the more self-conscious I get. I feel like I'm being a total dork, or saying all the wrong things, or whatever."

"Were you like that with Joe?"

"Oh God, yes," Jordan said. "I spent the entire day talking to him, getting distracted by his lips and his chest. By that night I was totally unable to concentrate on what was being said, because I was so busy wondering what he kissed like. And did he even want to kiss me?"

Mikeyla shook her head in astonishment. Even a star like Jordan had doubts? Was there no such thing as automatic confidence?

"So…" she began, biting her lip. "Does he kiss good?"

"Joe?"

"Yeah," Mikeyla asked, her look anticipatory.

"Joe does *everything* good."

Mikeyla made an "Oh" face, widening her eyes.

Jordan laughed. "And he'll kill me if he knows I told you that."

"I won't tell," Mikeyla said, crossing her heart with two fingers.

"Good," Jordan said. "I don't need to be in big trouble with my man," she added, winking at Mikeyla as Joe walked by.

"For what?" Joe asked, narrowing his blue eyes.

"Nothing," Jordan replied sweetly.

"Uh-huh," Joe said, sounding unconvinced, but continued on

toward the range.

It ended up being a nice day. Mikeyla was thrilled when Joe offered to teach her to shoot. Joe knew he was risking getting his head knocked off by either Rick or Midnight. He honestly felt, however, that since Mikeyla lived in a house with guns, she should know how to shoot one. He taught her safety first, how to handle a weapon, how to check to see if it was loaded. He taught her to load the ammunition clip and how to chamber a round. Then he showed her how to shoot it. Mikeyla was shocked at how hard the gun kicked. Joe taught her to tighten her grip and concentrate on keeping the muzzle down when she fired.

By the end of the day, Mikeyla was shooting as well as the cadets Joe was teaching.

"You're like your mother," Joe said. "You learn quickly and well."

Mikeyla was happy to be compared to her mother, especially by Joe. She went home that day feeling better about a lot of things. She thought about what Joe and Jordan had said, and did her best not to judge Nick solely on the idea that he broke up with her because she wouldn't sleep with him. It still hurt that he hadn't been willing to wait for her, but she also knew it would have hurt a lot more to have him cheat on her with some other girl.

That night, Jordan complimented Joe on his handling of the situation.

"You did really well, considering…" she said, grinning.

"Considering what?" he asked, narrowing his eyes at her.

They were lying in his bed, having just made love after taking a shower together.

"That you're male, and men tend to protect their own," Jordan said, her look blithe.

"Hey, the kid could have either pushed her to the point of giving in," Joe said, his tone conversational, "or he could have screwed around on her and brought God knows what back to her. I think he did the smartest thing possible at this point."

"I think you're right. But I also think it's not so easy for women to understand men and the absolute insatiable need for sex."

Joe looked back at her for a moment, then leaned down to kiss her. "I do believe, Ms. Tate, that you attacked me tonight, not the other way around."

"Yeah, 'cause you have me addicted to your body," she replied, giving him a narrow look, as if he'd done it on purpose.

Joe laughed. "Yeah, yeah, always my fault."

"That's right," she said, smiling.

"I love you," he said, his look serious.

"I love you too, Joe," she said, putting her hand to his cheek. "And I think you're going to be a great father when your daughter is a teenager."

Joe grinned. "When it's Kat. She's not getting anywhere near a guy that looks like Nick Masterson."

"Joe!" Jordan said, astonished.

"Hey," Joe said, shrugging. "Rick was stupid to let the girl go out with the kid—he's a comer if I ever saw one. Rick should have been smarter than that."

"And?" Jordan asked, raising an eyebrow.

"And shot the little bastard before he could get near his daughter," Joe said, laughing.

Jordan laughed, shaking her head. "You're hopeless."

"Nope, just a father."

"Joe taught our daughter to shoot today," Rick informed Midnight when she walked into their bedroom that night.

"He what?"

"Taught Keyl to shoot," Rick repeated, grinning.

"I'll fuckin' kill him."

"Oh, stop it. Night, the fact is it's smarter that she knows how to shoot the guns that are in this house than to be totally ignorant of them. I agree with that."

"Yeah, I'm betting you didn't originally though," Midnight pointed out.

"True," Rick said, chuckling as he pulled his gun out of his holster and placed it on his dresser. "And then I realized that Joe would teach her how to be safe first, then teach her to shoot."

"Doesn't necessarily make it easier though."

Rick sighed, shaking his head. "She's growing up too damned fast, Night."

Midnight smiled. From where she sat on the bed, she could sense his tension. "It seems like yesterday when she was born, doesn't it?"

"Yeah," he said, moving to lie down on his stomach on the bed, putting his head on her lap and wrapping his arms around her waist. "Can't we go back to when she was like ten?"

"I don't think so, babe," Midnight said, reaching down to stroke his hair.

"So how was your day?" he asked after a few minutes, turning over to look up at her.

"It was alright. Same shit, different day," she said, shrugging.

"The rigors of being the chief, I tell ya."

"Shut up," she said, giving him a narrow look. "Or I'll quit and make you support me for the rest of my life."

"I could get so lucky," Rick said, reaching up to touch her cheek.

"You'd get bored with me, really fast," she said, grinning at him.

"I'd thoroughly enjoy having you all to myself."

"You have me all to yourself right now," she said, her look pointed.

Rick sat up, facing her. His hand slid under her hair as he leaned toward her, kissing her lips deeply. She responded instantly, her hands sliding up his chest and unbuttoning the shirt he wore. He groaned as she touched his bare skin.

"God, what you do to me…" he murmured against her lips.

"No less than you do to me, babe," she replied, moving her lips down his neck.

His hands were buried in her hair, caressing her, holding her to him. She pushed him back on the bed, leaning over him, kissing him over and over again as his hands pulled at her. She grinned, knowing she was making him crazy but enjoying the feel of him wanting her so much. It was constant with them, a need to be close, to touch, to feel each other. She was always amazed by her reactions to him, as he was with his reactions to her. They had chemistry that was absolutely unmatched by anything else they'd ever had. They knew it, and they guarded it zealously.

There was a light knock on their door. Rick growled quietly, even as Midnight chuckled.

"So much for all to myself, huh?" he said, grinning as he sat up and she moved back, allowing him to do so.

"Come," Midnight said, tossing her hair back over her shoulder.

Mikeyla opened the door, looking pensive.

"Am I interrupting?" she asked, noting that her father's shirt was unbuttoned.

"Yes," Rick said, grinning.

"Richard!" Midnight said, swatting him on the arm as he

laughed.

"No, Keyl, I can attack your father anytime," she continued, giving Rick a mock angry look. "Or never again."

"Like you could," Rick said, rolling his eyes.

"So what's up, hon?" Midnight asked Mikeyla.

"I just wanted to let you guys know that I had a really good time today," Mikeyla said, biting her lip. "And I kinda learned how to shoot a gun."

"Kinda?" Rick said, raising an eyebrow. "I know Joe better than that—he either taught you well or he didn't teach you at all."

Mikeyla laughed, relieved that they apparently weren't angry. "Well, I did manage to hit center mass with my last two shots," she said proudly.

Rick glanced at Midnight in surprise. "Damn, girl," he said. "Maybe we should be sending you to the academy next."

"Oh, I don't think so," Midnight said, shaking her head.

"Why not?" Mikeyla and Rick asked at the same time.

Midnight looked back at both of them like they were nuts.

"I'm doing this," she said, gesturing at her badge on her dresser, "so you can do better with your life, Mikeyla."

"Mom, you're the Chief of Police," Mikeyla said. "I don't think that would be considered a bad thing."

"No," Midnight said. "But it's not the kind of life I want for you. I didn't start out as the chief, Keyl. I've been shot, stabbed, beaten, you name it… I don't want you going through that."

"But what if that's what I want?" Mikeyla asked, surprised by her mother's attitude. "I don't mean the violence part, but what if I want to be a cop like you and Daddy, and Uncle Joe, and basically my entire family. You're saying I can't?"

Midnight looked at Rick, seeing the questioning in his eyes too.

She sighed, shaking her head.

"I'm never going to tell you what you can and can't do with your life, Mikeyla," Midnight said. "I just want you to be safe, and police work isn't safe."

"Neither is breathing nowadays," Rick said.

"Rick…" Midnight said, her tone begging him not to make light of this.

"I'm serious, Night. It's dangerous walking down the street, it's dangerous getting on a bus, it's dangerous driving too nice of a car." He shook his head. "She's seen us make a difference her whole life, Night—maybe she wants to make one too."

"And she can," Midnight said. "Anywhere. I thought you of all people would be in agreement with me on this."

Rick shook his head, sighing. "I want her safe too. I just can't blame her for wanting to go into what is basically the family business around here."

Midnight looked at both of them, not happy with the direction of the conversation, so she changed it.

"I need to get ahold of everyone and make sure they're coming to Joe's party."

"They'll come," Rick said, grinning, knowing she was avoiding the other topic.

"They better."

Midnight was planning a surprise party for Joe for his birthday. She knew he'd never agree to a party otherwise, so she decided he was going to be "surprised" if it killed her. She'd planned it at Kyle's house, knowing it would be too obvious if it was at hers or Randy's. It was to take place in two days, and actually a full week before Joe's birthday, so he wouldn't suspect anything.

CHAPTER 3

Kana met Cat three days after she'd started with the department. There'd been a raid and Kana had run into the girl afterward. She'd been stunned to discover the beautiful blonde was gay. Later that day, Kana walked into Christian's cubicle, coincidentally located right across from Cat's. Christian looked up from his computer, smiling at Kana.

"Hey, K."

"Heya, Blue," Kana said, moving to lean against the vertical cabinets along the wall of the cubicle, glancing quickly across at Cat.

The girl was sitting typing away at her computer, her headphones on and oblivious to the fact that she was being observed.

Kana handed Christian the report she'd written for the runaway suspect, then glanced over at Cat again. Christian caught the glance and grinned, not saying anything. Kana saw it and narrowed her eyes at him.

"You knew I'd want do meet her," she said quietly.

"You want to meet Cat?" Christian asked, doing his best imitation of surprise.

"You know, Collins…" Kana began darkly.

"I know," he said, a grin still playing at his lips. "I gotta ask, though," he went on, moving to lean back in his chair. "How did you pick up on her so quickly?"

Christian knew that Kana had only met Cat that day at the raid.

Kana gave him a blasé look. "I have excellent gaydar."

Christian laughed at that. He liked Kana a great deal; she pulled absolutely no punches.

"What I want to know is how *you* know her," Kana said.

It was Christian's turn to look nonchalant. "Suffice it to say, Stevie and I *both* know her."

Kana's mouth dropped open. Then she shook her head. "I'm hurt, Collins," she said, grinning then.

"Hurt?" Christian repeated, his light blue eyes twinkling mischievously.

"Yeah, you know I've wanted to nail your wife, and she finally goes there and you don't call me?" She shook her head, scowling at him. "I thought we were friends."

Again Christian laughed. "I'm sorry, K. What can I say? You'd have to take that up with my wife."

"Don't think I won't," Kana said, still scowling at him, even as her eyes sparkled with humor.

"Uh-huh," Christian said, nodding as he grinned.

"Hey, Cat!" he said then, his voice loud so she could hear him over the music she was listening to.

Catalina glanced over at him, her eyes skipping to Kana then back to him as she took her headphones off and turned her chair to face him.

"Yeah?" she asked, her eyes going to Kana again for a moment, then back to Christian.

"Have you officially met Lieutenant Sorbinno?" Christian asked, referring to Kana by her recent rank change.

Cat's eyes went to Kana and stayed on her. "Not officially, no," she said with a grin. "But she did lend me some critical assistance this morning."

Kana grinned too, stepping forward to extend her hand to Cat, her eyes meeting the other woman's.

"I think that would be considered follicle assistance," Kana put in.

Cat laughed, nodding. She took Kana's proffered hand, holding it a moment longer than necessary.

"Either way, it was greatly appreciated, Lieutenant," Cat said, her look once again direct.

"Call me Kana," Kana replied, her eyes narrowing ever so slightly as their hands parted.

"Then call me Cat."

"Oh yeah," Christian said. "Kana, that's Sergeant Catalina Roché. She just transferred from the SO."

Kana canted her head to the side, glanced back at Christian, then back to Cat.

"Is this the woman that got the drop on you, Blue?" she asked, her tone slightly awed.

Christian laughed, nodding, even as Cat rolled her eyes.

"Well, anyone that can get the drop on Blue is a friend of mine," Kana said to Cat, winking at her.

"Oh, good information to have," Cat said, grinning as she glanced at Christian and gave him a wink.

Cat's phone rang then, and she glanced back at it, then looked at Kana. Her long hair dropped over her shoulder, and Kana knew the girl had no idea how sexy she looked at that moment, but she found herself a bit flustered by it.

"Excuse me a sec," Cat said, smiling at Kana again and moving to answer the phone.

Kana stepped back toward Christian's cubicle. His look was speculative.

"Don't even start," she said.

Christian held his hands up in surrender. "All I was gonna say is, welcome back."

Kana narrowed her eyes at him again, but only shook her head. She got a page a few minutes later.

"I gotta go. Midnight's callin'."

"I'll give Cat your goodbyes," Christian said, winking at her.

"Go to hell, Collins," Kana said, even as she smiled.

"All in good time, love," Christian replied, smiling unrepentantly.

Kana glanced at Cat again, her look regretful, then left the office.

Later that afternoon, Kana was sitting in her office when the phone rang.

"Sorbinno," she answered.

"She's heading to The Pit for lunch," said a very familiar English-accented voice.

"Oh yeah?" Kana asked, grinning.

"Better hurry."

"I owe you," Kana replied, hanging up a moment later.

Cat had just given her order to Tom when she heard "Taking that to go?" from behind her.

She turned to look up at Kana, and smiled broadly as she nodded.

"Eating alone is bad for the digestion, you know," Kana said, grinning.

Cat shrugged. "Didn't have another option," she said, staring directly into Kana's eyes. "Now, if you're offering to stay and eat with me, then I won't have to eat alone at my desk." Her blue eyes scanned the restaurant. "Although there don't seem to be any tables open."

"There's one open," Kana said confidently. She looked over at Tom. "Hey, Tom, make that last order for here, and give me my usual."

"You got it, K," Tom said, his eyes twinkling.

Tom, like many members of the Gang, hadn't been totally shocked by Kana's not so subtle announcement about her sexuality. And like the rest of the Gang, he wanted her to be happy. He knew that the breakup with Palani had hurt Kana a great deal. It warmed his heart to see her obviously flirting with a new woman.

"Come on," Kana said, gesturing for Cat to follow her.

Kana led Cat back to the table permanently reserved for FORS members. It was at the back corner of the restaurant. It was a place where many members liked to be if they didn't feel like being bothered.

"Wow…" Cat said, seeing an empty table in a restaurant full of people.

She saw the little metal plaque on the side of the table, an engraved sign that read *FORS members only. Don't even dare!*

Cat laughed, and Kana grinned as they sat down.

"So you're a FORS member?" Cat asked.

"Former," Kana said, inclining her head.

"Ah, and once a member, always a member?" Cat said, canting her head to the side.

"Pretty much," Kana said, laughing. "Everyone in the Gang is allowed at this table, as well as FORS members."

Cat nodded, narrowing her eyes. "Now this is the 'Gang' I keep hearing about, right? The best of the best?"

"Yeah, that would be us," Kana said, her tone confident without being cocky.

"So what's the story behind all that?" Cat asked, having been curious about this "Gang" since she'd first heard about them.

Kana leaned back, putting one arm on the table, the other up on the back of the booth.

"Well, most of us were members in FORS when it first started up, way back when. Since we all used to be gang members or leaders, people still saw us that way. So that's apparently what they started calling us. As the years went by, people became part of the Gang by association. Like Pony—he's the brother of the woman that Joe Sinclair was married to for years. Jeanie's with Pony, so she's part of it. Blue is Joe's cousin, and Stevie became part of the Gang when Dave brought her back to the department. Kyle Masterson dated the chief years ago before she was with Debenshire, and as the AC now, Kyle gets into the Gang by default." Kana said the last grinning.

"Okay, name them all off," Cat said. "With their ranks now."

"Well, there's Midnight, the chief. Rick Debenshire, he's the LT in charge of FORS."

"Which Midnight Chevalier originally started, right?"

"Yeah," Kana said as Tom brought their food to the table.

"And Tom's the reason Midnight is still with us today," Kana said, winking at the older man.

"Really?" Cat asked, looking at Tom.

"Ain't all that," Tom said, shaking his head.

"Tom's the one that was there for Midnight when her world caved in," Kana said seriously.

Cat looked at Tom again, surprised.

"She needed someone," Tom said, shrugging.

"And you were there," Kana said.

Tom nodded.

"How much do I owe you?" Cat asked Tom, gesturing to her

lunch.

"It's on the house," Tom said, even as Kana said, "I'll take care of it."

Tom and Kana looked at each other with a challenge in their eyes.

"You runnin' a charity now, Ryan?" Kana asked, raising an eyebrow.

"No, I'm celebrating," Tom replied, smiling.

Kana looked perplexed. "What are you celebrating?"

"A friend of mine just came out of a six-month coma," he replied, winking at her as he walked away.

Kana gave a short laugh, dropping her head and shaking it.

Cat looked at her, totally lost. Kana glanced over at her and grinned.

"Don't ask," she said.

"Okay," Cat said, nodding. "So go on. You said Chevalier and Debenshire—now they're married, right?"

"Right," Kana said. "Then there's Joe Sinclair. He's a captain over vice right now."

"And he was married to Donovan Curtis' sister," Cat said, correlating what had been said before.

"Right," Kana said. "He's dating a rock star right now."

"Seriously?"

"Yeah, Jordan Tate."

Cat nodded, her look contemplative. "I think I heard that somewhere along the way, but I didn't know who he was at that point."

"And there's Kyle, the Assistant Chief, who's married to Rhiannon. Who's Stevie's sister."

"Wait," Cat said, holding up a hand. "Stevie O'Neil? Her sister is married to the Assistant Chief?"

"Right," Kana said, grinning as she reached for her fork and started eating her salad.

Cat shook her head. "It's pretty complicated with you people, isn't it?"

"Oh, that's just the half of it," Kana said, laughing. "There's Spider, the LT in charge of narcotics, who's married to Tammy, former FORS member. There's Dave, who's married to Susan, who's Joe's kids' nanny and Rick Debenshire's niece. There's my former partner, Tiny Ako, who you met this morning too. He's a sergeant in homicide who's married to Jess, who came down here from Sacramento because she had a crush on Joe. Oh, and now there's Mace, from your team, who's dating Erin, who was dating Donovan when he and Jeanie broke up."

"Holy shit," Cat said, looking shocked as she shook her head. "How do you keep it all straight?"

Kana shrugged. "It's our family history."

"So the Gang is like a family?" Cat asked, reaching for one of her french fries and eating it.

"For most of us, it's the only family we've had for years."

Cat nodded. "So were you a gang member once?"

Kana nodded. "I was the leader of a gang in Honolulu."

"What was the gang called?"

"Sisters of Samoa," Kana said. "Basically your female equivalent to the Bloods or the Crips."

"That fierce?" Cat asked, surprised.

"Pretty much," Kana said, grinning as she took another bite of salad.

"Why were you in a gang?" Cat asked, wanting to understand this woman all of a sudden.

"When I was a kid, I never looked like all the other girls. They were all these tiny little perfect dolls. I was always big, fat, and tall. So I was excluded a lot from their groups. I found out when I was about twelve that I could throw a mean punch. And that made people like those little dolls respect me."

"You mean fear you," Cat put in.

"That too," Kana replied, grinning. "One of the leaders of the Sisters recruited me when she saw me knock down a boy that was two years older and a foot taller than me. After that, I felt like I belonged to something," she said, shrugging.

"So how did you get into law enforcement?" Cat asked as she pulled her hamburger over and took a bite.

"I met Midnight at a gang fight."

"Was she in a gang?" Cat asked, shocked.

"At that point, no. She led a gang when she was eight, but that's a whole other story," Kana said, waving her hand. "When she ran FORS, she'd take out gangs by any means necessary. Sometimes that meant fighting and defeating the leader of the gang. This was one such incident."

"Were you in the gang?"

"I was considering getting into the gang—I hadn't decided yet," Kana said. "But when I saw little five foot, five inch Midnight Chevalier beat a woman that was almost as big as me, and do it without even breaking a sweat… I knew I wanted to be in her gang."

"And her gang was FORS?"

"Yup," Kana said, nodding.

"So you became a cop then?"

"No, I was a CI for a while—I was only eighteen at that point."

"Oh, but you became a cop later, obviously," Cat said, nodding to herself.

"Right," Kana said. She canted her head. "And how long have

you been a cop?"

"Seven years."

"So that makes you…"

Cat smiled. "That makes me twenty-eight. And you're…"

Kana grinned. "I'm thirty-two."

Cat looked surprised for a moment, then shook her head. "I'm sorry, that surprised me."

"Why?" Kana asked.

"You just look a lot younger than that."

"A lot?" Kana asked, grinning wryly.

"Well, you look like you're maybe, like, early twenties."

"Well, thankfully, I'm not."

"Thankfully?"

"That's in the category of been there, done that," Kana said, making a face.

"Oh," Cat said, grinning.

They ended up talking for the next hour, neither of them eating much of their food. Kana found that Cat was definitely an interesting woman, very up and outgoing. It was a very interesting lunch.

***

Elizabeth wandered around Kyle's house, making a point of disappearing before her sister dragged her into more work. She'd come with Dave and Susan, but she had no intention of sticking with her sister the whole night. Taking a long drink of the cocktail in her hand, Liz walked into the family room of the large mansion. She saw a dark-haired young man, his eyes closed, his head back on the overstuffed chair he sat in.

"Excuse me?" Liz queried, her English accent clear in the quiet room.

He lifted his head, looking at her. Elizabeth felt her body react simply at the look of him. He had jet black hair and blue eyes, not light like Christian's but a rich color, more like her own. She found him very attractive, even as she tried to figure out who he was.

"Can I help you?" the young man asked.

"Perhaps," she said, grinning. "But first you'd have to tell me who you are." She walked over to him and sat on the ottoman in front of his chair.

Nick looked back at the woman. He was surprised by her brashness. He was also taken aback by how pretty she was. She looked vaguely familiar, but he was sure he'd never met her. She had straight honey-blond hair, cut to frame her face and fall a few inches past her shoulders. She had a very nice face, and from the little that her bikini top and short denim skirt hid, an incredible body. *Nice*, was all he could think.

"Oh," he said, realizing she'd asked who he was. "My name's Nick. My dad owns this place."

"So you're Kyle Masterson's son?"

"Yeah. You know my dad?"

"Only through my aunt."

"Your aunt?"

"Midnight."

"Oh," Nick said, taken aback again. She was the chief's niece?

"I'm Elizabeth Endicott," Liz said, extending her hand, her look direct.

He took her hand, holding it for a long moment, canting his head to the side. "Where have I heard that name before?"

"Lord only knows," Elizabeth said, grinning rakishly. "I'm notorious in this family."

Nick laughed, shaking his head. "No, I didn't mean like that. Is your sister Susan?"

"Yes," Elizabeth said. "You caught me. My sister is dull."

"But beautiful as hell," Nick said, grinning.

"You think so?" Elizabeth asked, narrowing her eyes at him.

"Must run in the family," he replied, grinning still.

"Very smooth, Nick Masterson, very smooth," Elizabeth said, smiling in spite of herself.

"Liz, there you are," Midnight said from the doorway. "I need your help," she added, glancing at Nick.

"What do you need?" Elizabeth asked, moving to stand up. Nick did the same.

"I need more alcohol and I can't spare anyone to go and get it. Do you have your ID with you?"

"Yes," Elizabeth said.

Midnight nodded, then glanced at Nick. "Maybe Nick can drive you," she said, glancing at the drink in Liz's hand.

"I'm not drunk, Midnight," Liz said mildly.

"I didn't say you were, Liz," Midnight countered gently. "But it doesn't take much to blow a point-oh-one nowadays, okay?"

Liz nodded, sorry that she'd sounded so defensive with her aunt.

"I can drive her, no problem," Nick said, stepping into the silence.

"Thanks, Nick," Midnight said, walking over to them and handing Liz some money. "Get as much tequila as you can get with that, okay?"

"No problem," Liz said, smiling.

"Thanks," Midnight said, hugging Liz quickly before leaving the room.

Nick looked at Liz. "My car is out front."

94

Liz nodded, setting her drink aside and gesturing for him to lead the way.

Once in the car, Nick turned on the radio, sensing that Liz didn't want to talk. As he drove he did his best to keep his eyes off her legs, but they were a definite draw to his attention.

Liz noticed his sly glances, and grinned.

"So why were you hiding out?" she asked after a few minutes.

"Who said I was?"

"You were. Why?"

Nick chuckled, shaking his head. "I was avoiding someone."

"Who?" Liz asked, direct as always.

"My ex-girlfriend."

"And who would that be?" Liz asked doggedly.

"Mikeyla."

"My cousin is your ex-girlfriend?" Liz asked, surprised.

She couldn't believe her uncle would allow Mikeyla to date a man that much older than her. She narrowed her eyes at him, something having just clicked in her head.

"How old are you?"

"Sixteen."

"That's all?" Liz asked, further surprised. She'd taken him for at least twenty.

"That's all," he replied, grinning.

"Bloody hell," Liz muttered.

"What?" he asked, glancing over at her.

She smiled at him. "Nothing. So why is she your ex, and why are you avoiding her?"

"One and the same. I did the breaking up, and she's not happy with me about it."

"And why did you break up with her?"

Nick looked back at her for a long moment, surprised by her direct questioning.

Finally he shrugged. "We wanted different things out of the relationship," he said, thinking that sounded safe.

"What did you want?"

"Uh," Nick stammered, not sure what he should say.

"Well?" Liz asked, her blue eyes looking straight into his.

"I wanted the relationship to move forward. She didn't," he said, hoping he'd managed to satisfy her curiosity.

No such luck.

"You wanted sex and she didn't, right?"

Nick's mouth dropped open, unable to believe she'd actually stated it so blatantly.

Liz laughed at the look on his face. "Oh, believe me, I've heard that story a number of times over the years."

"You have?" he asked, curious now. "Why have you heard that?"

"Certainly not because I've withheld sex," she replied simply. "More because I was the one that would give it to them."

Again Nick was stunned into silence.

"I have no idea what to say to that," he said, shaking his head.

Liz laughed. "You don't have to say anything, Nick. I was merely stating a fact. So you want to sleep with my cousin and she said no, right?"

"Right," Nick said, still surprised to be having this conversation with a total stranger.

Liz nodded. "You do realize her father would have killed you if you'd slept with her, right?"

Nick grinned, nodding. "If he found out about it, yeah."

"My uncle knows everything," Liz assured him.

"So I'm probably lucky, is what you're telling me?"

"Perhaps," she replied, sounding very English. "But also very brave, to even attempt it."

"So how old are you?" Nick asked, once again at a loss for what to say to her.

He pulled into the parking lot of BevMo!, putting the car into park.

"Twenty-two," she said, giving him a sidelong glance and grinning rakishly. "I don't suppose you're into older women?"

"Older is thirty-five," Nick said, his look direct.

"Oh," Liz said, looking right back into his eyes. "Well, sadly my aunt would probably kill me for befouling such a fine young man as yourself."

"Yeah, too bad," he said, shaking his head, thinking he couldn't get that lucky.

"Relax, Nick," she said, her accent so elegant. "You're in no real danger with me," she added, laughing softly as she got out of the car and walked toward the front doors of the store.

Nick stared after her, shaking his head, then followed her.

They got through the store, but not before Nick realized that Elizabeth Endicott was so far out of his league it wasn't even funny. He felt as if he'd gone from the frying pan into the fire.

***

To Midnight's surprise, Joe didn't shoot her for throwing him a surprise birthday party. Midnight was fairly sure it had everything to do with Jordan being in town. When the two of them walked in and everyone yelled "Surprise!", Joe stood looking around openmouthed as they all laughed at the look on his face.

He turned to Jordan, his eyes narrowed. "You knew about this, didn't you?"

"Duh," Jordan said, grinning. "Why do you think I've been here?"

"'Cause you love me?"

"Nah," she said, laughing. "Party!"

Everyone laughed. Jordan opened the hall closet and pulled out a wrapped present, handing it to him.

"My birthday is a week away."

"And I care because?" she asked, smiling. She rolled her eyes. "Just open it."

Joe grinned, setting the box on the entryway table and opening it. There was another box inside, then another and another. He finally got down to a box that was three inches square. He looked questioningly at her.

"You were just trying to see how dexterous I am still?"

"Oh, I already know that," she said, winking. "That's the last one, I promise."

"Mmhmm," he said, glancing around as the whole group watched him. "Someone get me a shot?"

A shot of tequila was quickly forthcoming. He knocked it back and handed the glass to Jordan with a kiss. Then he opened the box. There was a set of keys inside as well as a piece of paper folded up. He looked at Jordan, his smile confused.

Jordan pointed to the paper. "Open it."

He picked up the folded paper. Opening it, he saw that it was an invoice stamped *Paid in Full*. He read over the description of the item purchased, and his eyes widened as his mouth dropped open.

"You bought me a plane?"

"Yep," she said. "So you can come see me when you can get away."

"His and hers planes, how cute," Rick muttered, making everyone laugh.

"Jealous?" Joe asked.

"No," Rick countered. "My wife lives with me."

"Low blow, Debenshire," Joe said, grinning all the same.

"One I'm sure you'll drink me under the table for," Rick replied, laughing.

"Indeed," Joe agreed.

He looked at Jordan then, leaning in to kiss her deeply. He pulled back, looking down into her eyes.

"You didn't have to, babe," he said, knowing how expensive planes were, even though she'd purposely blacked out the purchase price and final cost on the invoice.

"I wanted to, Joe."

"I love you," he said. "Thank you."

"Hey, it's for me too," she said, grinning. "Hopefully I'll get to see you more this way."

"You will."

"Then I win too."

The party proceeded. Everyone drank and had a good time. At one point, Nick walked out onto the private beach behind the house. He saw Mikeyla standing talking to JT, Joe's eight-year-old son. Nick walked over, catching Mikeyla's wary look. JT turned to him, smiling widely.

"Hi, Nick!" JT said excitedly.

"Hiya, JT," Nick said, grinning down at the boy.

"Bye, Nick!" JT said as Randy walked out onto the beach calling to him.

Nick watched as the blond-haired boy ran off to see his mother, then looked back at Mikeyla.

"I was hoping we could talk."

"About what?" Mikeyla asked evenly.

Nick took a deep breath and blew it out in a sigh. "Keyl, I don't want you to hate me," he said seriously.

"I don't hate you, Nick," she said, her look unaffected. "I just don't like you much right now."

Nick nodded, dropping his eyes from her. Mikeyla walked away, leaving Nick standing staring up at the sky. He stayed out on the beach, not willing to go back into the house at that point.

"You look like you could use a friend," Elizabeth said from behind him.

Nick grinned. "It's that obvious?"

"Quite."

They ended up walking down the beach together, talking about whatever came to mind, nothing at all serious. He found that Liz was actually a very witty woman. She could take something he'd say and go on about it, seeing the humorous side of it. When they got to the pier about a half mile down, Nick found that he was feeling better.

"Feeling better?" Liz asked.

"Yeah."

"Good."

Nick leaned against one of the pilings of the pier, looking out at the ocean. Liz turned, putting her back to him, then leaned against him. Nick put his arms around her shoulders, leaning his chin on the top of her head. It was doing his ego a lot of good to have this beautiful, wild woman paying so much attention to him. He wasn't naive enough to believe there was some great love affair starting here. What he did know was that he had been feeling really shitty when Mikeyla had been so cold to him, and having Elizabeth Endicott show up when she had was just what he needed.

They stood watching the ocean for a while. The sun was going down. It was a nice moment, and for the most part innocent. Liz thought about starting something that she knew would be well received, but she also knew that he was too young, and the last thing she wanted was to tangle with her family about him.

Mikeyla had seen Elizabeth walk up to Nick after she walked away. She took a deep breath, blowing it out slowly. She knew her cousin was a wild child, and that if anyone would give Nick what he wanted, it was Liz. Mikeyla gritted her teeth as she saw them walk off down the beach. In truth, she'd begun to wonder whether or not she'd made a mistake in not having sex with Nick. It didn't seem to be a problem for anyone else.

Turning away from the beach, Mikeyla ran into Susan, who had been standing behind her watching the same thing. Susan did not like what her sister was doing. Mikeyla was their cousin, after all, and there should be some loyalty there, for their family.

"Susan." Mikeyla smiled, doing her best to hide how she was feeling. "I heard the good news," she said, moving to hug her cousin. "Congratulations."

"Thank you," Susan said, hugging her back. "I'm very happy about it."

Mikeyla pulled back. "Do you know when the baby is due?"

"No, not yet," Susan said, shaking her head. "Mikeyla, do you want to talk?"

Mikeyla looked considering, then nodded.

"Come along," Susan said, taking the younger girl's hand and walking her out to the beach.

"I don't know if we should be out here," Mikeyla said, glancing around uncertainly.

"Why not?" Susan asked conversationally.

"Well, Nick's out here," Mikeyla said, purposely not mentioning who he was with. "And I don't want him to think I'm out here trying to spy on him."

"We'll walk this way," Susan said, pointing in the opposite direction from the one Elizabeth and Nick had taken.

Mikeyla nodded as they began to walk.

"Mikeyla," Susan began, "I know Nick's with my sister right now, and I'm very displeased with her for that."

Mikeyla shrugged. "She's single and beautiful, and Nick's a good-looking guy. Why shouldn't she go for it?"

"Because he's your boyfriend, and he's far too young for her," Susan said, sounding appalled.

"Ex-boyfriend, Susan, remember?" Mikeyla said, knowing that the entire Gang had likely heard by now. She wasn't wrong.

"All the same," Susan said, shaking her head. "Elizabeth is far too reckless with other people's feelings, and she needs to stop that."

Mikeyla said nothing. She wasn't going to say it didn't hurt that her cousin was going for Nick. She also wasn't willing to crucify Elizabeth. Nick was handsome to the extreme. Mikeyla was used to every girl in the whole school wanting him, so someone else being interested in him wasn't new.

"Susan?" Mikeyla said after a few minutes. "When you had sex for the first time, did it hurt?"

Susan looked considering, then nodded. "Yes, but I don't know if the man I had it with exactly knew what he was doing either."

"It wasn't with Blue?" Mikeyla asked, surprised.

"Lord no," Susan said, rolling her eyes. "I could only imagine how Christian would be with a woman who was a virgin. No, it was with Warren—remember, my fiancé?"

"Oh yeah…" Mikeyla said. "Funny that you ended up marrying

someone totally different from him, isn't it?"

Susan smiled fondly, touching her wedding ring. "No, I married for love, whereas before I was doing what I thought I was supposed to do."

Mikeyla nodded. "See, that's what I'm worried about."

"What do you mean?" Susan asked, sensing they were getting to the heart of the problem now.

"Well, I won't have sex with Nick because I feel like my parents will be disappointed in me. I mean, my mom didn't have sex until she was like nineteen!" she said, frustrated.

"Mikeyla, I doubt your mother expects you to wait until you're nineteen simply because that was when she lost her virginity," Susan said gently. "But I'm sure she wants you to make good, responsible choices about sex."

Mikeyla nodded, then sighed. "I've been doing that, but now I think I've lost Nick because of it."

"Mikeyla, if you lost him because he can't respect your wishes, then he wasn't worth keeping," Susan said, sounding very much like Midnight.

"But Joe said that he thought Nick was trying to respect my wishes by breaking up with me when he did."

Susan canted her head to the side. "Did he explain why?"

Susan had the utmost respect for Joe, a man she considered another uncle. If Joe had said that, Susan wanted to hear the logic for it.

"He said that he thought Nick was respecting what I wanted, about not having sex, but that Nick needed what he needed too. He said that it was probably pretty difficult for Nick to be around me, wanting me but not being able to have sex with me."

Susan nodded, not sure how to respond to that. Dave saved her from needing to.

"What are you two doing out here?" he asked, walking up.

"Talking," Susan said, smiling up at him.

"Well, it's getting dark, honey," Dave said gently, even as he glanced around them, his blue eyes scanning the beach. "You two mind an armed escort?"

Susan glanced at Mikeyla, who shook her head.

"Actually, David, perhaps you could give us your take on this," Susan said.

"On what?" Dave asked, falling into step beside them as they started to walk again.

"We're talking about Nick, and whether or not he was right in breaking up with Mikeyla when she, well, when she wouldn't…" Susan said, trailing off when it came to saying it in front of her husband.

Dave nodded, understanding what she meant, and knowing her ways well enough to know she was embarrassed to say "sex" in front of him.

"And I told her that I thought Nick wasn't worth keeping if he couldn't respect her wishes," Susan said.

"But Uncle Joe said that he thought Nick was respecting my wishes," Mikeyla said. "Because things were difficult for Nick, being with me and wanting that."

Dave nodded. "Did Nick say that's why he was breaking up with you?"

"No," Mikeyla said. "He said it's because we fight too much, but that all started when I refused to have sex with him."

"So the fights are in direct relation to the refusals?"

Mikeyla nodded.

Dave shrugged. "It seems like it was better for both of you to break up at this point."

"Why?" Susan asked, surprised.

"Well, Nick's on a different level, sexually, than Mikeyla is at this point. Staying together in spite of that will only cause more frustration for both of them. And I think Joe's right—Nick is respecting what Mikeyla wants. Sometimes it's better not to try and stick things out. What may end up happening would be worse than breaking up."

Mikeyla nodded, remembering what Jordan had said about how men got frustrated sexually and that sometimes their reactions to that were violent.

"So, you're saying that things will go the way they're meant to go," Susan said, grinning at her husband. It was the philosophy of his entire life.

"Exactly," Dave said. "Mikeyla, there's probably something you're meant to learn from this, or it's teaching you to stick to your guns when it's something you believe in."

"But how do I know for sure?" Mikeyla asked. "How do I know what the right thing is to do?"

"You'll know, Keyl," Dave said, touching her under the chin. "You'll feel when it's right. Just let things go the way they're meant to."

She nodded, sighing deeply.

They walked back to the house then, and Mikeyla went to get a soda. Susan glanced up at Dave.

"I'm very unhappy with my sister," she said, looking outside.

Dave looked down at Susan, then followed her line of sight to where she was watching Nick and Elizabeth as they headed up the sand toward the house. He wondered what was going on between the two.

"I'll be right back," he said, leaning down to kiss his wife on the cheek.

He walked outside, intercepting Nick and Elizabeth.

"I think you two should arrive separately at this point…" Dave said, his eyes on Liz.

"It's completely innocent, Dave," Liz said, irritated.

"Sure it is, Liz," Dave replied. He knew his sister-in-law, and she was rarely discreet, or wise about how she conducted herself. Liz looked defiant. "No matter what did or didn't happen, you know what everyone is going to assume, so just don't push it."

That got her. Elizabeth knew Dave was right. If she went in there now, it would cause a huge stir, and she didn't know for sure that anyone would hesitate to say something. The last thing she wanted was to call down the thunder of her uncle's disapproval on her head. Rick was extremely vehement in his reproach when he thought she was out of line. He always had been. She really wasn't in the mood to have his razor-sharp tongue turned on her at this point in time.

She nodded, still looking displeased at being chastised by her brother-in-law. Dave narrowed his eyes at her for a moment, then glanced at Nick. Then he turned and walked back into the house. Elizabeth growled low in her throat, walking over to sit on the stairs leading from the deck to the beach. Nick came over, leaning against the deck.

"Guess I'm not the only one that's the assumed asshole here, huh?" he said.

"Not hardly," Elizabeth said. "You're just the victim."

Nick looked at her, his face showing surprise at her words.

"The victim?"

"Of my wild ways," she said pertly.

Nick nodded. "I see. So do you always cause problems in your family? Stealing your cousin's boyfriends and all that?" he asked wryly.

106

"No. I take what I want, when I want it," Elizabeth said, narrowing her eyes. "And to hell with what anyone thinks."

"That's why you're out here now, because you do what you want?" Nick asked, grinning.

"Have you ever seen my uncle angry?"

Nick looked down at the ground, grinning still. "No, but I've heard that when he is, fire-breathing dragons are less dangerous."

Elizabeth laughed at that. It was fairly accurate.

"Is that why you broke up with Mikeyla?" she asked, canting her head to the side.

Nick didn't say anything for a moment, then looked up at the darkening sky.

"I want her more than I've ever wanted anything in my life," he said, sighing. "And I knew there was going to come a time when I made her change her mind, one way or the other."

"And if it had been the other, my uncle would have killed you."

"And then some."

"Precisely," Elizabeth said, grinning.

Back inside the house, Liz went to the bar. Joe was there, drinking a shot.

"Happy birthday, Joe," Elizabeth said, reaching up to hug him.

"Well, thank you, Liz," he said, grinning.

Liz picked up the bottle of tequila Joe had just set down and poured two shots, handing one to him.

She held her glass up. "Cheers," she said, then threw back the shot.

"Cheers," Joe echoed, shaking his head even as he took the shot. He walked away to go and find Jordan. Elizabeth poured herself another double shot, drinking it and then pouring herself a JD and

Coke. Nick looked on, thinking that the woman was just a bit crazy.

Midnight was leaning against a wall, talking to Kana. They were deeply involved in a conversation on the merits of SUVs versus sports cars. Kana's eyes caught Nick and Elizabeth walking in together. She glanced at Midnight, then nodded in the direction of the bar.

"Yeah," Midnight said. "I saw that one coming from a mile away."

"She's a lot older than him, isn't she?"

"Yeah. But I don't think that matters to him at this point, and possible impropriety never matters to Liz."

Kana glanced back at Midnight, canting her head to the side. She was wondering why Midnight wasn't irritated that her daughter's ex-boyfriend was apparently already carrying on with someone else.

"So what's up with that?" she asked, raising an eyebrow.

Midnight shrugged. "He wanted something Keyl didn't want to give him yet. He's apparently found it elsewhere."

"And that doesn't piss you off?"

"No. Better Liz, who's been with a lot of men, than my fifteen-year-old daughter who's a virgin."

"Yeah, but…" Kana said, still thinking it should irritate Midnight.

"K, if Nick's anything like Kyle was, he's going to have an insatiable sexual appetite." Midnight spread her hands plaintively. "That's not something I want Keyl to have to deal with until she's ready."

Kana looked back at Midnight for a long time, finally shaking her head. "You amaze me sometimes, Chief."

"Why?" Midnight asked, grinning.

"You see things way clearer than normal people."

"No, I just happen to know that particular type of man," Midnight said, nodding toward Nick as Kyle walked over to talk to his son.

"Uh-huh."

Everyone in the Gang remembered well the relationship between Midnight and Kyle Masterson, known as Masters to them then. It was in the early days of FORS, and they would literally spend weekends together in bed. Joe had started calling Kyle "The Train," because whenever he'd come through town, Midnight would be wrecked for the next few days.

"Everything okay over here?" Kyle asked, having seen Nick and Liz come into the house together and assuming what everyone else was assuming.

"No problem, Dad," Nick said.

Kyle nodded, his eyes staying on Liz for a moment, his look measuring. Then he walked away. Liz watched him go, then turned to Nick.

"Your father is disgustingly handsome," she said, grinning.

Nick nodded. "I've heard that a lot."

Elizabeth turned and scanned the room. "In fact, there are any number of men in this very room I'd happily do," she said, her eyes sparkling mischievously. "Even a few women," she added with a wink.

Nick's mouth dropped open. Then he grinned, shaking his head. The girl did love to shock, didn't she?

Kyle walked back over to Rhiannon, leaning over to kiss her lips.

"All is well."

"Okay," Rhiannon said. "So what's he doing with Elizabeth Endicott?"

Kyle gave her a searching look. "You're not seriously asking me that question, are you?"

Rhiannon looked back at him for a moment, then shook her head, sighing.

"He's going to be like you've told me you were, isn't he?"

Kyle nodded. "More than likely. As long as he picks the right kind of women to be like that with."

"You mean, not Mikeyla Debenshire."

"Right. A girl like her deserves someone that's going to be patient with her. I don't think Nick can achieve that right now."

Rhiannon grimaced. "And if he pushes her too hard…"

"Her parents will kill him."

Rhiannon sighed, shaking her head. "It's never simple, is it?"

"What?" he asked, glancing down at her.

"Raising kids."

"It's not easy. But I think you're right when you tell me not to judge them by my standards."

"It's not fair to," Rhiannon said. "You've developed your standards over the years—you weren't born with them. The boys have to learn their own way."

Kyle nodded, smiling at her. He could never get over how wise she was when it came to his sons. She'd always been that way, able to point out things that he didn't see. He loved her all the more for being so good to Nick and Brenden. Losing their mother had been very difficult, especially for Nick. Rhiannon had brought back a sense of family to their home. She had been a godsend to him since the first day they'd gotten together.

Rick found Mikeyla in the kitchen. She was sitting on the counter, staring off into space.

"What're you doing in here?" he asked.

She shrugged. "Just hanging out."

"And hiding from Nick?" Rick asked, canting his head to the side.

Mikeyla made a face. "Pretty much."

Rick nodded. He'd heard a few things about the breakup, not all of which he was pleased with. What he was pleased about was his daughter sticking to what she believed in—at least, he thought that was what she was doing.

"You can't avoid him forever," he pointed out.

"What else can I do?"

"Well," Rick said, moving to lean on the counter next to where she sat, "you can learn a thing or two about moving on. Or revenge," he added, grinning.

"Revenge?"

"Yes, love, you have men out there that adore you," Rick said, winking. "All you need to do is let them know you need moral support."

Mikeyla gave her father a lopsided grin. "You think they'd care?"

"Try it," Rick said confidently.

Mikeyla looked back at him for a long moment, then shook her head and hopped off the counter.

Walking back into the room where most of the group were standing or sitting around, she saw Nick and Elizabeth over near the bar. Glancing around, she noted Christian and Donovan standing talking. She walked toward them. She didn't see her father standing in the doorway to the kitchen, nor did she know that Christian caught

Rick's eye. She didn't see Rick narrow his eyes at Christian, then gesture with his head toward Elizabeth and Nick. Christian caught his meaning almost telepathically as he glanced toward the bar.

"You've been ignoring me all night, young lady," Christian said, putting his arm out to Mikeyla as she walked up.

"Have I?" she asked, grinning up at him.

"Yes," he said, leaning down to kiss her on the cheek then moving back to her ear. "And I'm very upset about it."

Mikeyla pulled back, smiling at him. Christian leaned in, kissing her softly on the lips.

"Nick's crazy, love," he said gently. "Stick with me, I'll show you a good time."

Mikeyla laughed.

"Hey, no hogging the girl," Donovan said, grinning as he reached out, taking her arm and pulling her into his embrace. "How are you, Keyl?" he asked, his teal-blue eyes searching hers.

"I'm okay," she said, nodding as she looked up at him.

It amazed her no end how handsome the men in her "family" were, or how incredibly gallant they could be. Christian and Donovan danced attendance on her most of the evening, joined by Dave at one point. Joe made a point of paying a lot of attention to her, as did Tiny and Spider. Even Kevin wandered over at one point, giving her a hug and telling her that Nick was an idiot. Mikeyla felt very loved. Nick, of course, noticed the attention she was getting. Instead of being jealous, he was actually grateful. He knew that the Gang was closing ranks around one of their own, and he felt oddly comforted by that.

He saw Mikeyla laughing and talking with men all night. She only glanced at him once, that he saw, and even then seemed to look right through him. It dragged at him, but he knew that he'd done the right thing with her, even if she didn't understand it and thought he was just a pig for doing it. Knowing it was right and living with it might be two different things. But he knew that he wanted to maintain his friendship with her, and the way things had been getting between them was going to ruin that. He didn't want that, so he'd broken it off. It made him asshole of the hour, but Nick also hoped that the people that knew him could understand it.

He was relieved when, at one point, Midnight walked over to the bar. Elizabeth was still standing near him, but was talking to Kana.

"Hey, Nick," Midnight said as she poured herself a drink.

"Hi, Chief," he said, smiling cautiously.

Midnight turned to him, drink in hand.

"You know, Nick, you can call me Midnight."

"I know," Nick said, nodding. "Just seems wrong somehow, ya know?"

Midnight grinned. "It's not wrong, Nick. You're almost an adult now. No more sitting at the kids' table, and no more calling me by my title. You got it?"

"Yes, ma'am," he said, grinning.

Midnight grimaced. "Worse!" she said, and laughed.

Nick laughed too, feeling relief flood his veins. If Midnight didn't hate him, then yes, people did know why he'd done what he'd done. Kyle walked over, and Nick was fairly sure his father intended to rescue him from Midnight's razor-sharp tongue. Kyle, too, looked relieved as he joined them and saw Midnight laugh.

"And what's going on here?" he asked, raising an eyebrow.

"Your son just called me ma'am," Midnight said, making a face.

"Never call a woman ma'am, Nick," Kyle said, curling his lips in a grin. "Unless you want to get shot."

"I thought that was a term of respect," Nick said, grinning.

"It's archaic," Midnight said sourly.

"Actually," Kyle said, his voice taking on an informational tone, "'ma'am' is an abbreviated version of 'madame.' Which would actually lend itself to hookers, wouldn't it, Midnight?"

Midnight stared openmouthed at Kyle for a full half minute, and he started to grin.

"You sonofa—" she said, swatting him on the arm.

Kyle laughed, as did Nick.

"What's goin' on here?" Rick asked, his tone all cop, even as he grinned.

"Kyle just called me a hooker."

"You did that?" Rick asked, looking at Kyle.

"Actually, my son did," Kyle said, laughing at the way Nick's mouth dropped open. "I was only providing a definition of the term."

"Oh, well, in that case," Rick said, shrugging and moving to the bar.

"Oh, nice…" Midnight said as she swatted her husband on the butt.

"Sinclair!" she yelled. Joe's head snapped up instantly.

"What?" he yelled back.

"I need backup!"

Joe headed straight over. "What's the problem?" he asked, glancing at Kyle and Nick, and seeing Rick grinning as he leaned against the bar.

"I'm being denigrated," she said, looking hurt.

"You told me not to call you chief," Nick said. "I called you ma'am."

Joe grimaced. "And he's still breathing?" he asked Midnight.

"So far," Midnight said, narrowing her eyes at Nick.

"Hey, hey now," Kyle said. "I can't have you shooting the kid."

"Why not?" Joe and Midnight asked together.

"The blood on the carpet," Kyle said, rolling his eyes. "Take him out back and shoot him," he added, gesturing toward the deck.

Joe, Midnight, and Rick got a good laugh at the look Nick gave his father.

It turned out to be a fun night.

Later, Rick and Midnight were lying in bed, and had just started kissing when there was a knock on their door.

Rick growled deep in his throat. Midnight grinned.

"Come," Rick yelled.

Mikeyla poked her head in their door.

"Am I interrupting?" she asked with a grin.

"If you had been, I would have told you to stay the hell out," Rick said, grinning as he moved to sit up.

"Richard!" Midnight exclaimed, laughing all the while.

"What's up, Keyl?" Rick asked, moving to lean against their headboard. Midnight leaned against him, her back to his chest.

Mikeyla sat on the bed.

"I just wanted to let you two know about what's going on with Nick," she said. "I mean, I know you probably saw stuff tonight, but I wanted to tell you myself."

Midnight nodded, glancing back at Rick, telling him with her look not to say anything yet. Rick's eyes caught hers, and he nodded imperceptibly then looked back at Mikeyla.

"Okay…" he said, his tone leading.

"Nick and I broke up, as you probably know. But what you may or may not know is why."

Rick and Midnight said nothing, waiting for her to go on.

"Anyway," Mikeyla said, sighing, "he said it was because we

115

were fighting a lot, and we were, but…" She hesitated, glancing at her father and hoping she wasn't making a mistake in telling them.

She took a deep breath and plunged in. "I think a lot of it is because I wouldn't sleep with him and he really wanted to."

She looked at her parents, waiting for their reaction. She didn't see Rick's hand tighten on Midnight's waist. Midnight sat up, glancing back at Rick and shaking her head, her look pointed.

"Keyl," Midnight began. "Were the fights because you wouldn't have sex?"

"Yeah, I think so," Mikeyla said, nodding, glancing at her father and seeing the dangerous look in his eyes. "But Daddy, he never got really mad at me. I mean, he never directed it at me—he always just got irritable, then something I'd say would start a fight." She could see that wasn't enough to calm her volatile father. "And he never got physical with me."

Rick took a deep breath, expelling it slowly, his lips twitching in his effort to calm down.

"Okay," Midnight said. "So it's probably better right now if you two aren't together."

Mikeyla nodded, looking miserable.

"Babe," Midnight said, touching her daughter gently under the chin. "You've got a right to set your own pace on this, okay?"

"I know," Mikeyla said. "But Joe told me that it's probably really hard for Nick, wanting me and being so close all the time."

"Joe told you what?" Rick asked, his tone edgy.

Mikeyla winced. "I kinda talked to him and Jordan about this the other day when we went to the range."

"Lovely," Rick said, dropping his head against the wall behind him and shaking it.

"Richard," Midnight said, giving him a stern look. "It doesn't matter who she talked to. I trust our family to give her the right advice."

Rick narrowed his eyes, but said nothing. Midnight looked back at him expectantly.

"What?" he said, sounding petulant now.

Midnight grinned. For a forty-year-old man, he certainly could be a temperamental boy at times.

"Is what Joe told her accurate?"

Rick curled his lips in distaste. "Yes, he's right. It's near impossible to be around a woman you want but can't have."

Midnight winked at him. "At least you don't have that problem, babe," she said, her tone conciliatory.

"For now," Rick said, his grin wry.

Midnight nodded, grinning too, then turned back to their daughter.

"It says a lot about how much he wants you, Keyl. But if you're not ready, then he's really just giving the two of you some space."

"And taking up with Elizabeth," Mikeyla put in.

Rick grimaced immediately. "Keyl…" he began, trying to think of a way to soften what she was thinking.

"It's okay, Dad," Mikeyla said, forestalling him. "I know why he's doing that."

"You do?" Midnight asked, hoping her daughter wasn't thinking it was just to make her jealous—although it was possible, it wasn't likely.

"No offense, Dad, but Liz is pretty loose with where she puts it out," Mikeyla said, her tone unaffected. "I know Nick is getting it somewhere else."

Midnight winced, giving her daughter a searching look.

Mikeyla started to grin, looking very much like Midnight had at her age. "But no matter what, she'll never be me, and I'm the one he wants and didn't get."

Both Midnight's and Rick's jaws dropped open. Then they started to grin.

"Now that's the young woman I raised," Rick said.

"And the girl that's got her own that I raised," Midnight said, winking at her daughter.

Mikeyla laughed.

CHAPTER 4

Kevin Elmasian sat tapping his fingers on the steering wheel of his Dodge Durango. He watched as Stevie crossed the parking lot. She walked up and got into his vehicle just as he lit another cigar. It had been a long night, and it was likely to be a long day too.

Stevie glanced at him, her grin wry.

"Bad yet?"

"Bad enough," he said, holding his hand up. It shook a bit.

"Well, we can stop by your house if you need some."

"Nah, I got some in my desk," he said, grinning.

"Ah, you are learning, aren't you?"

"Uh-huh," he said as he put the Durango in gear and drove toward the office.

They were talking about his Adderall, which he had to take for his Attention Deficit Disorder. If he didn't have his meds first thing in the morning, he had a really hard time concentrating and he got very irritable and shaky. It was something the entire team knew about, as well as the fact that he was a recovering alcoholic. They guarded him and his conditions zealously, just as they guarded each other's lives.

Over the last year and a half, Kevin had gotten more and more used to being part of a team. He'd come to trust the people he worked with, not something he was given to doing normally. He'd come from a dog-eat-dog department in Seattle, where the slightest weakness was exploited and used against you to keep you from getting promotions, assignments, or just decent treatment sometimes. His alcoholism had been a department-wide gossip tidbit; everyone knew, and everyone had whispered about it. Kevin had finally gotten fed up and left to move to San Diego. He'd joined the San Diego PD and had gotten lucky enough to get on with what he considered the best narcotics team in the department, city, or country.

Rogue Squadron was made up of people that Kevin couldn't help but respect for their various experiences. There was Jeanie, who'd been a street cop, an ABC investigator, and with the department since she was seventeen. She'd also gotten number one on the sergeant's test the first time she'd taken it and had her choice of assignments.

Then there was Curtis, who outwardly did seem like a boy scout, as Christian Collins often referred to him. However, Donovan had been part of a major investigation against dirty cops, an investigation that had almost gotten him killed not once but twice. He'd been shot in an attempted gangland-style execution. Surviving that, he'd gone down to Mexico with Chief Chevalier in an attempt to track down the bad guys. There he'd been caught by the explosion that had nearly killed Chief Chevalier and had thrown Donovan through a plate-glass window. Since that time, he'd made a number of narcotics cases. He was a pro, even if he was fairly clean cut.

Christian Collins, a man who'd left England after attempting to kill his own father, had come to San Diego to stay with his cousin, Joe Sinclair. Christian had shown a definite talent for computers, and Midnight had recruited him to help her fix an archaic inventory system. Christian's database had become a hot commodity, and his expertise had been requested by any number of departments to install and customize his system on their computers. This was not before, however, he ended up infiltrating the ring of dirty cops that were out to have Chief Chevalier murdered for her investigation of their illegal activities. It had been Christian who'd led Joe, Rick, and the rest of the Gang to the men responsible for what at that point they thought was Midnight's death. Midnight had thankfully been found alive, but not before her husband had gone through the horrible task of burying the woman he loved more than life. Since that time, Christian Collins had actually become a narc, after making a brilliant case against an Ecstasy and Rohypnol dealer at a local college. Christian Collins' instincts were ingrained, not something that could ever be taught.

Stevie O'Neil was yet another phenomenon. She'd left the department as a street cop, under questionable circumstances. What she'd done over the year and a half that had followed was nothing short of miraculous. She'd infiltrated the inner sanctum of one of the most notorious and slippery drug dealers in the western hemisphere. She'd done so for one reason, to get revenge for the brother-in-law that she'd lost when the dealer had run from a bust. Jason Templeton, Stevie's sister Rhiannon's husband, had been killed in a car accident during the pursuit of the dealer. The department couldn't make a case, but Stevie had. With the help of Dave Dibbins, who'd been sent in by Chief Chevalier to bring Stevie back to her law enforcement family, they put the dealer behind bars. Stevie had been making amazing cases since then. She was an extraordinary woman, even having been shot in a drive-by, getting hit three times with AK47 rounds and surviving it to go back to law enforcement.

Kevin felt fairly inferior to his teammates, but they welcomed him as part of their group, and it did feel good to be accepted. The case that he and Stevie were currently working was becoming bigger by the minute. The man they'd thought was a lower-level dealer had proven to be much higher on the food chain than they'd thought.

Apparently Sergei Paskal wasn't stupid. He played it off as being a very low-level operation that he had. The more Stevie and Kevin learned about the guy, the more they realized he was very connected. To the Russian mob, no less.

Sergei's latest shipment had totaled over 175 kilos, and he was expecting another one within the month. Stevie and Kevin intended to be around for that. They'd connected up with Sergei through the appropriate channels. Fortunately, he had found Stevie quite intriguing, and had started negotiations with her and Kevin for a serious shipment of cocaine. Stevie stuck close to Kevin, allowing, even pushing, the belief that she was with him. Christian's attitude about her staying safe would help that immensely. Although they hadn't had to resort to actual physical contact since the time Stevie had discussed it with Christian.

Stevie and Kevin made it back to the office, where she pointedly reminded him about the Adderall and told him he needed coffee too. Kevin laughed, used to her direct manner and way of dealing with him. It had taken a lot of getting used to. If she wanted to know something, she asked. If she thought something about you or your actions, she told you. There was no guessing with Stevie O'Neil-Collins; you always knew where you stood. Even if you stood in quicksand.

Kevin was at his desk no more than half an hour before Erin wandered into the office, coming straight over to him. She perched on his desk, her eyes searching his face.

"Yes, I took my Adderall," he said, grinning up at her, even as he threw Stevie a narrowed look.

Stevie looked back at him, her smile benign.

"I heard you two were back in the office," Erin said, winking at Stevie. "I wanted to come see you. Is that a crime?"

"Nope," he said, grinning as he leaned his head against her.

Erin put her hands to his head, leaning down to kiss the top of his hair. She knew he was only showing affection in front of the team; he'd never do it if they were anywhere else in the department. He was very careful to keep up his facade for the rest of the department. He'd just recently started letting his guard down around his teammates.

"Will you be home tonight, do you think?" she asked when he pulled back to look up at her.

"I think so," he said, rolling his eyes and shaking his head. "This guy's all over the map, but we think he's gone down to Mexico to buy a boat."

"Does that mean I have you at home for a few days?" Erin asked hopefully.

"It means I think I'm home for a few days," he clarified.

"Good," she said, hopping off his desk and leaning down to kiss his lips. "I'll see you after work then, hopefully."

"Yeah. If I can remember where we live…"

"Should I draw you a map?"

"You are such a funny girl…" he said, narrowing his eyes at her.

"I know," she said, winking at him as she left the office.

Later that evening, Kevin drove up to his house. He sat in his Durango for an extra moment, thinking about the changes in his life. Now when he came home, he had his girlfriend and her son to welcome him. Before, he'd lived by himself and would come home to one more long, empty, and usually sleepless night. Erin had a way of making him feel so good. He didn't know what it was about her, but she gave him everything he could possibly need. She gave him love; it was something he'd never really realized he'd never had. Sure, his mother said she loved him. Stacy, the mother of his daughter, claimed to love him. But he'd never *felt* it like he did with Erin.

Neither of them had actually said the words, not in the year and a half that they'd been together, but Kevin felt it. And to him, that was much more important. He was fairly sure that Erin hadn't said it to him because she was afraid to think like that again. She'd been in a relationship where she'd been in love but the man hadn't been in love with her. Kevin hadn't really said it for fear that doing so would make it go away somehow. He knew it was stupid, but he also knew that love wasn't really something he'd ever been meant to have. What they had was comfortable and good, and he didn't want to screw that up.

Walking into the house, he was greeted with the smell of dinner being cooked and the sound of the PlayStation on his TV.

He walked into the kitchen and saw Erin reading a book, leaning against the island. She hadn't heard him come in, so he leaned down, kissing her softly on the neck. She jumped, then smiled.

"Hi," she said as she turned to face him, putting her arms around his neck.

"Hi," he said, grinning as he leaned down to kiss her lips.

When their lips parted, Erin turned her head toward the living room, where Steven was playing a game.

"Steven, you need to turn that down," she said, which had her son turning to look at her to ask why.

That's when Steven saw Kevin. His face lit up.

"Kev!" Steven exclaimed, jumping up from the coffee table where he'd been sitting and running over to Kevin, throwing himself into his arms.

"Hey, little man!" Kevin said, laughing as he hugged Steven. "I see you're on the next level again. You're going to have me beat here soon."

"Yeah, I found a really cool trick!" Steven said. "Come here, I'll show ya." He grabbed Kevin's hand and pulled him toward the living room.

"Steven," Erin said, "Kevin's been working hard all week. Let him relax for a bit first, okay?"

Steven looked disappointed, nodding miserably as he let Kevin's hand go.

"It's okay, babe," Kevin said. "He's just excited. Let me go change first, Steven, then I'll come right back and you can show me, okay?"

"Cool!" Steven said, smiling brightly.

Kevin glanced at Erin, who was shaking her head at him but smiling all the same. Kevin always went out of his way to make both of them happy. She knew it cost him a lot emotionally, physically, and even financially sometimes. For that reason, she tried to make it up to him by doing as much for him as she could.

The evening passed with Steven showing Kevin all the latest tricks to get farther in their latest PlayStation game. At one point they got into a good-natured argument about which car was the best.

"Boys," Erin said, grinning, as she glanced up from her book, "if you can't play nice, I'll have to send you to your rooms."

Kevin turned his head to look at her. She was curled up on the couch, her legs tucked under her, her hair in a ponytail, with no makeup on. All the same, she looked so beautiful.

"Only if you'll come to my room with me," Kevin said, a mischievous twinkle in his eye.

"When it's bedtime," she said, winking at him. "Believe me, I will."

Kevin's smile widened as he winked back at her.

That evening, as they were putting Steven to bed the phone rang.

Erin went to answer it while Kevin finished tucking Steven in, leaning down to kiss him on the forehead.

"Are you going to be home for a while, Kev?" Steven asked hopefully.

"Couple days, little man," Kevin said, grinning down at the boy.

"Cool," Steven said, grinning too.

"Kevin," Erin said from the doorway, holding out the phone to him.

"Thanks, babe," he said, kissing her lips as he took the phone.

He walked into their bedroom as he talked. It was Stevie, wanting to go over a few ideas for their next move with Sergei. He was lying on the bed, still on the phone, a few minutes later when Erin walked into the bedroom. She mouthed to him that she was going to take a shower; he nodded as he listened to Stevie.

Erin was washing her hair when she heard the shower door open. Her breath caught in her throat as she felt his hands on her skin. Kevin held her waist as she smiled, her eyes closed to keep soap from getting in them. His hands touched her waist, pulling her to him, his lips touching her neck, sucking, nibbling at her skin. She gasped, feeling her body come alive, as it always did with his touch. They made love in the shower, taking their time and enjoying each other thoroughly.

Afterward he dried off haphazardly and then wrapped her in a large bath sheet, picking her up and carrying her to their bed, kissing her again. She wrapped her arms around him, kissing him back. He laid her on their bed, opening the towel and moving his lips over her skin, eliciting gasps of pleasure from her as he touched her, bringing her to the heights of passion again, only then sliding his body inside hers.

She grinned as he moved over her. It thrilled her to no end that he still had to make her orgasm before he could actually be inside her. He told her she played hell on his self-control, because her orgasms never ceased to cause him to lose it. So he spent a lot of time making her come before he'd allow himself to make love to her. Even after a year and a half, she still seemed to have that effect on him. She loved that.

After they'd made love again, he moved to her side, sitting up and reaching for a cigar. Erin got up, opening the bedroom window and pointing the fan outside to draw the smoke out of the room. It was habit for them now. Kevin smoked cigars because he couldn't smoke cigarettes anymore. As a recovering alcoholic, he'd found that he associated the taste of cigarettes with the taste of alcohol. He'd begun smoking cigars to assuage his craving for nicotine without tempting fate in terms of his other addiction.

Erin knew all of that. She knew just about everything there was to know about this man. He was amazing to her, that he had so many problems and yet he handled them every day and still managed to be a peace officer. He was actually a highly effective narcotics officer. Many people compared him to the likes of Dave Dibbins, because he had a tendency to be as cold as ice, with the clear impression that he was anything but even tempered.

People had referred to Kevin as "metal under tension," saying that they felt he could snap at any moment and take a lot of people out. It was the angle he played, and he was good at it. Only Erin saw him as the totally relaxed, sweet, caring man that he really was. His teammates and members of the Gang saw the more casual and fun side of him, but never the whole picture that Erin saw. It pleased her to no end that he was willing to show her this side of him. There had been a time at the beginning of their relationship when he'd tried to convince her that this was just another facade he played. She'd seen through that, and told him she thought it was the real him, but not something he wanted anyone to see. She was shocked when he'd told her that no one ever saw this side of him, not even his family.

Erin knew that a lot of people in Kevin's life had let him down, never loving him the way he should be loved. She knew that part of it was Kevin's own doing, pushing people away before they could get close enough to love him. It had been a vicious cycle for years. He'd dated women that were harder edged with a plethora of their own issues about love and relationships. It had fed his already jaded sense of love, and had made him run farther from the desire to ever feel love. Erin had managed to get in under the radar that he kept up constantly to stave off affection. In doing so, she'd won his heart with her sincere desire to make him happy. It was something he valued more than anything in life.

He fell asleep that night with his arm wrapped around her waist, his lips pressed against her temple. Erin slept on her back, her arm wrapped up around his shoulder, her other hand on his arm around her waist.

CHAPTER 5

They were once again gathered in Midnight's office. The entire gang, even Stevie and Kevin, had made it in from the field for whatever Midnight had called them together for this time. There was the usual tension, the worry that it was bad news. Midnight's tension didn't help; it was obvious she was nervous about something. Her fingers drummed on the arm of her chair as they waited for Kyle to get into the meeting.

He walked in a minute later, apologizing as he closed the door.

"Okay, so what the hell is up?" Joe was the first to ask.

Midnight looked at her oldest friend and made a face.

"Well, I need my family's advice on something," she said, standing up and glancing at Rick, who sat on the credenza behind her desk.

Of course, Rick knew exactly what she was talking about; they'd discussed it for half the night. Midnight had wanted to put it to the Gang, since it would affect their lives too.

"Don't do it," Dave said.

"It's a bad idea," Spider chimed in, grinning.

"It's worse than a bad idea," Tiny said.

"It's probably the worst thing you could have done," Kana added, grinning.

"I'll second that," Christian said.

"Didn't someone already do that?" Donovan asked.

"I think so," Stevie said.

"About four people ago," Joe put in.

"Okay, people, shut the fuck up, will ya?" Midnight said, laughing. "I haven't even told you the situation yet."

"Oh," Joe said, grinning evilly. "Well, get on with it, will ya. Jesus."

"If I have to shoot you, Sinclair…" Rick growled, giving Joe a narrowed look.

"Come try," Joe said, making a face at Rick.

"I swear to God, you people get more immature every year!" Midnight said.

"He started it," Joe said.

"Did not," Rick countered, both of them grinning now.

"I'll gag you both, I swear," Midnight said.

Cat was getting a first-hand look at the Gang at their finest, and was doing her best to not laugh out loud. It was easy to see how well these people got along; they really were like a big family. And Midnight was their mother.

"Only if you'll promise to tie me up while you're at it," Rick told Midnight with a wink.

"I've got cuffs—I hear those work better," Christian said, pulling out his cuffs.

"Hear?" Stevie asked, grinning as she raised an eyebrow.

"Ohhhhh…" Dave said, grimacing. "That had to hurt."

"Only for a minute or two," Christian replied, laughing.

Everyone else laughed then, and finally calmed down long enough for Midnight to go on.

"Thanks," she said when everyone was quiet again. "Okay, look, here's the thing," she went on, putting her hands down on her desk and leaning forward. "John Davies has asked me for a favor."

"John Davies, the governor John Davies?" Stevie asked.

"Yeah, him," Midnight said, nodding.

"Midnight's known him since he was the chief over at BNE," Joe told Stevie.

"Oh," Stevie said, her eyes wide.

"So what does he need?" Kana asked.

"Well," Midnight said, looking around the group, "he needs a candidate."

"For what?" Joe asked, thinking along the lines of the time he'd spent at the police academy in Sacramento, helping them at their range.

"For Attorney General."

There was absolute silence in the room for a long minute.

"For the state?" Tiny asked.

Midnight nodded.

"And he wants you," Joe surmised.

Midnight nodded again.

"You'd have to run?" Spider asked.

"Yeah."

"And if you won…" Dave began, his tone grave.

"She wouldn't be our chief anymore," Kana said, sounding upset by the idea.

Midnight looked at Kana, then nodded, her look somber.

There was another moment of silence as everyone in the room mulled that thought over. Midnight was their leader, and if she became the Attorney General, she wouldn't be their leader anymore. She'd be leaving their gang behind. It was a very difficult concept for them to grasp.

"At the state level, she'd be over the Division of Law Enforcement," Joe said.

"Which is over Narcotic Enforcement, Investigations, Forensic

Services, everything," Rick put in.

"She'd be the top cop," Dave said.

"She'd be running the California Law Enforcement Telecommunication System," Christian put in.

"Figures the computer geek would point out the computer system," Donovan muttered.

"Narc now, Pony, narc," Spider said.

"And it was hacker, Curtis, not geek," Christian said, making a face at Donovan, who did the same.

"She'd also be in charge of the Clearinghouse," Stevie pointed out. "Which keeps blue on blue from happening." She said the last winking at her husband and glancing back at Cat, who grinned. The Clearinghouse was an area that tracked multiple agencies' cases to ensure that one agency didn't accidentally interfere with another's case or blow an undercover officer's cover by mistake. It was a very important resource to officers in the field.

"She'd also be in charge of defending the people of the State of California in death penalty appeals," Kana said.

"And I'd rather have Midnight backing me up on my homicide cases than anyone in the world," Tiny put in.

"I'll remember that come eval time, Nathanial," Kana said, using Tiny's given name.

"Shit," Tiny said, grinning.

"She nailed you," Jess said, chuckling at her husband. Then she looked at the group. "I think we can all see how Midnight would be effective at the state level. So I think she deserves our support on this."

"Even if she sucks at politics," Joe said, grinning.

"Even if," Kyle said, grinning too.

"Don't laugh, Masters," Midnight said. "I'll need Special Assistant AGs."

"No law degree here, sorry," Kyle said, holding up his hands.

"Don't need one—it's a special appointment," Midnight said, smiling evilly. "So don't piss me off."

"She told you," Rhiannon said, grinning.

"She always does," Kyle said, shaking his head.

"Poor you," Rick said.

"Bite me, Debenshire."

"Let's not go there," Midnight said, holding up her hands to silence her husband as she saw him start with a comeback. "So, you guys think I should go for it?"

"I think that's what we've decided, yes," Joe said, nodding as he grinned.

"And if I don't get elected?"

"We'll still love you," Dave said, smiling.

"And then we'll know for sure that you suck at politics," Christian said.

"That's been established for years, handsome," Midnight said.

"So the state'll get a new attitude," Spider said.

"And then some," Rick put in.

Everyone laughed.

"Are they always like that?" Cat asked Christian later that day when they were headed out on a surveillance.

"Like what?" Christian asked as they got into her Blazer; his Viper was too obvious for use as a surveillance vehicle.

"So casual," Cat said, gesturing with her cigarette as she started the vehicle and drove out of the parking lot.

"Pretty much," Christian said. "These people have been friends for over twenty years, Cat. They've been through every kind of hell together. It makes for lasting friendships."

Cat nodded, having enjoyed the rapid-fire banter in the meeting. She'd been surprised to be invited to the chief's office for the obviously confidential meeting of only the people closest to her. She still wasn't sure if she'd been included because she was part of Rogue Squadron or because she was dating Kana. All the same, the experience had been quite interesting. The chief definitely had a lot of people's respect—that much had been easy to see, despite the negative comments.

Cat had read plenty about Midnight Chevalier over the years. It was hard to live in San Diego and not know about the spitfire that was the Chief of Police for one of the largest departments in the country. It had been Midnight Chevalier who had inspired her to become a cop in the first place. Who wouldn't want to be a cop when they saw the copper-blonde, petite powerhouse of a woman testify in a court case in support of a woman accused of trying to have her killed? In all black, her long hair flowing down her back, her gold shield at her belt shining in the courtroom light as she raised her right hand and swore to tell the whole truth, Midnight had exemplified a strong woman making it in a man's world.

When Cat had moved to San Diego to go to school, she'd started hearing about Midnight Chevalier. It had been before she'd become Chief of Police—she'd been a captain then. But even as a captain of vice, Midnight Chevalier had been a recognized figure in law enforcement. Many of Cat's professors in school had referred to her in terms of her law enforcement style of getting on people's level to work with them or against them.

When Midnight had become Chief of Police, Cat had just gotten her degree. She'd applied with San Diego Police Department and at the same time the Sheriff's Department. The Sheriff's Department had offered her a job first; San Diego PD did a more extensive background. So she'd become a deputy sheriff instead. Years before, when the country had thought Midnight Chevalier was dead, Cat had found herself grieving with everyone else. It was beyond belief. She'd also exalted with the world when Midnight had been found alive. Midnight was the one person that just seemed to come back from anything and everything in her life. When Cat had heard about the feisty chief getting into a fight and beating a younger woman a year before, she knew Midnight was still every bit the gang member she'd been in her youth.

Cat had always hoped to transfer to San Diego PD, but hadn't ever had the right opportunity. It had been for that reason that she'd jumped at the chance when Christian and Stevie brought up the idea. Now she'd seen Midnight in person, and it had been quite an experience.

"Think she'll get elected as AG?" she asked Christian.

"I think Midnight does whatever she sets her mind to," Christian said, reaching for a cigarette, looking a little agitated.

"And you guys are really freaked out that she might leave, aren't you?" Cat asked, her eyes narrowing slightly.

Christian didn't say anything for a moment, glancing out the window then looking back at her.

"We trust her. We have no idea what will happen to the department if she leaves. I don't want to work for anyone else."

Cat was surprised by his admission, but it was obvious how loyal these people were to Midnight. It took a very compelling individual to inspire the kind of loyalty Midnight received in abundance.

"She really is larger than life, isn't she?"

Christian considered the question, then shrugged. "Not in her

135

mind, no."

"But to everyone around her?"

"She's the reason we're all here."

Cat nodded. They were both quiet for a while.

"So, how's it going with Kana?" Christian asked.

"It's going," Cat said, grinning.

"Uh-huh. And you've looked awfully tired these days."

"Two weeks, Collins, that's all," Cat said, making a face at him.

"Right."

"Hey, good sex is hard to find," Cat said, laughing.

"I understand completely."

Cat was quiet for a few moments, then looked over at him.

"Can I ask you a question?"

"Shoot."

"Do you know who Kana was in love with?"

Christian winced as he nodded.

"What happened between them?" Cat asked, curious in spite of herself.

"You ask Kana?"

"No," Cat said, shaking her head. "That seems like a pretty sore subject to her."

"It is, I'm sure."

"This girl's the reason for the 'six-month coma' Kana was in, isn't it?" Cat asked, remembering what Tom had said the first day she and Kana had had lunch at The Pit.

"Oh yeah," Christian assured her. "Palani nailed her good."

"Palani?"

"That was her name."

Cat nodded, wondering what kind of name that was—it certainly wasn't common.

***

Dave was relaxing on his couch with his wife. His head was in her lap; she was reading a book, stroking his hair with her other hand. He was reading the paper. They were spending a lazy afternoon together, before Susan had to go pick Joe's children up from the summer camp Randy had enrolled them in. Most mornings, Susan had to fight waves of nausea to get the kids to school. When she got home, she spent another hour in the bathroom being sick.

Dave had been fortunate enough to miss that up until that morning. He'd been lying in bed, catching up on his sleep, having just returned from a case the night before. When he heard her in the bathroom, he was up and out of bed instantly and at her side. He smoothed his hand over her back as she retched, and winced at the sound of it. Knowing it was perfectly normal didn't in any way help him to feel better about his wife being so sick.

He'd spent the next hour trying to make her feel better. Susan had assured him that it always passed by noon. She was right, and it did. It didn't keep Dave from treating her like she was made out of glass all of a sudden. She found it quiet endearing that this hardened narcotics officer would spend a day off getting his wife tea, toast with the crusts cut off—his idea, not hers—and making sure she was comfortable. She'd finally gotten him to relax too, assuring him repeatedly that she was indeed feeling fine now.

"This is over soon, right?" Dave had asked, his tone pleading.

Susan had smiled at him, her deep blue eyes shining with restrained humor. "Yes, love, usually after the first three months."

"Three months?" Dave exclaimed, shaking his head. "I'll be a nervous wreck by then."

Susan laughed softly, touching his cheek. She'd subsequently pulled him over to the couch, where she sat down, pulling him down so he could rest his head in her lap. Eventually she'd started reading a book she'd been given by Randy called *What to Expect When You're Expecting*. Dave had finally grabbed the paper.

It was the scene Elizabeth walked into when she came into the house. There were still days when she couldn't reconcile her oh-so-proper sister with a man as rough-edged and incongruous as Dave Dibbins. She liked Dave a great deal, but Elizabeth had no idea how he handled being around her boring sister all the time.

Walking into the living room, she saw Dave glance back at her, his bright blue eyes wary as always. Susan looked up at her sister, noting the high heels with too-tight black jeans and the low-cut silk tank top. Elizabeth never toned herself down for anyone. Susan never understood having to be so outrageous constantly. She rarely understood her younger sister at all, hadn't for years.

"You'll be happy to know," Elizabeth said, leaning against the island that led into the kitchen, "that I've rented an apartment."

"You're staying in California then?" Susan asked, surprised.

"For the moment," Elizabeth said, shrugging.

"Where did you rent?" Dave asked, moving to sit up and look at her.

"Del Mar," Elizabeth replied, naming a more upscale area of San Diego.

Dave nodded. It wasn't like Elizabeth had to commute to work or anything. Del Mar was a rich beach community—she'd fit right in.

"And you're moving there when?" Susan asked, her tone polite but her look indicating that the sooner Liz moved, the better.

"As soon as I can."

"Do you need help with anything?" Dave asked.

"No. I think I've got it all handled."

"But thank you for offering," Susan put in, giving her sister a reproachful look.

Elizabeth gave her sister snide look, then turned to Dave.

"Thank you for offering, Dave," she said. "And my condolences for marrying our bitch of a mother," she added, then turned on her heel and left the room.

Susan stared openmouthed after her sister. She could not believe what the girl had just said. As far as she was concerned, now wasn't soon enough for Elizabeth to move out.

"Well, that was charming," Susan said indignantly.

Dave said nothing. In truth, he'd been a bit shocked by Liz's comment as well. He'd suspected for a while now that Susan had always been the favorite of the two girls. Elizabeth was just too much for Deborah, a very nice if a little incapable mother. Deborah had no idea how to handle her wild daughter, and her answer had always been to get her away from the trouble she was into. It wasn't the best way to handle the situation, but Dave didn't feel it was his place to cast aspersions about someone's parenting skills. He'd never been a parent, so he knew it was easier to say what he thought would be the best way to handle things.

In Dave's guest bedroom, Elizabeth lay face down on the bed, gritting her teeth and forcing away the anger she was feeling. She absolutely hated it when Susan treated her like a child. Susan had sounded exactly like their mother when she'd corrected her minutes before, and that had ignited Liz's temper. Turning over on her back, Liz stared up at the ceiling, thinking about what she'd been doing. She had gone out to find an apartment, knowing she couldn't continue to risk staying in Dave's house. Dave was suddenly home way too much.

It was just as well—she couldn't have any fun in this house anyway. Susan was nothing but a bloody stick in the mud. Having a narc for a brother-in-law was a bit of a cramp in her style too. She'd had to cut back seriously on her use. Once she was in her own place she could do as she pleased; she wouldn't have to answer to anyone.

As far as she was concerned, she'd spent too many years of her life being told what to do by people that had never had a day's fun in their life. She had no intention of being controlled like that anymore. At twenty-two, she was a full fledged adult and was going to start living her life her way. Not that she hadn't been over the last four years. Ever since she'd turned eighteen, she'd gotten herself into any number of scandals. It amused her to no end to watch her mother attempt to cloak her sins for her. Elizabeth never asked for anyone to get her out of trouble; Deborah always just found it necessary to step in and "take care of" things.

It was part of the reason Elizabeth had decided to stay in California for a while, rather than go back to London and deal with her mother. Of course, the drugs were much easier to get in London, without an entire family of cops watching her. But Liz had her ways of getting what she wanted, and she'd utilize them as soon as she was out of this house.

With that in mind, she got up off the bed. Opening the closet, she pulled out her suitcase and tossed it on the bed. Within an hour she had all of her clothing packed. The manager at the apartments had told her she could move in any time. Not like she hadn't noticed the lecherous little man's eyes all over her. Like she'd ever condescend to sleep with someone that ugly and downright disgusting. Not in this lifetime!

In the four years since she'd turned eighteen, Elizabeth had gone everywhere and done just about everything there was to do. She knew she came across to everyone as the spoiled little rich girl, and she couldn't care less. Spending a great deal of time escaping from her mother and father was her goal at this point. Unfortunately, in escaping from them, this time she'd ended up stuck with her sister, who'd apparently become more like their mother instead of less.

It was no surprise to Elizabeth, however, that Susan saw nothing wrong with being like their mother. The sun had always risen and set on Susan in the Endicott household; Susan naturally wanted to be like Deborah. Elizabeth wanting nothing like that. She had no intention of ever getting married, let alone to some stuffy bastard like her father.

She intended to live her life fast and free, and hopefully die before she was thirty so she wouldn't have to deal with getting old and boring. She refused to care about what anyone thought of her, and she refused to consider the consequences of her actions. If she wanted to do it, she'd do it, and the consequences be damned. Her father had berated her constantly about thinking about the consequences of her actions, how she needed to be responsible and aware of her standing in society, *like Susan was!*

Well, Daddy, that might have gotten you somewhere until you mentioned my perfect sister. Now you're out of luck.

Elizabeth had become an expert at hiding. She hid her feelings, her hurts, her insecurities, and her drug use. She hid everything that didn't present the picture of the perfect rebel. To hell with all of them—fuck them if they couldn't take a joke. That was her favorite way of thinking. It got her through.

Walking out of the bedroom, she carried the large suitcase she'd brought with her and her valise with her toiletries in it. Susan and Dave were still on the couch. It had only been an hour since she'd been in the room with them.

Turning to them, Elizabeth looked directly at Dave, refusing to even glance at her sister.

"Dave, as always, it's been a great pleasure," she said, her voice overly sweet. "I do hope to see you again in the near future. Call me, we'll do lunch," she added, her voice a parody of rich snob extraordinaire. "And thank you so, so much for allowing me asylum in your home. I do sincerely hope I wasn't any trouble. Adieu." She said the last with a sarcastic smile, and then turned and walked out of the house.

Dave stared after her, even as Susan made a shocked sound in her throat. Narrowing his eyes, Dave felt his sixth sense tingling. There was something not quite right about that departure. He had no idea how right he was. While packing her valise, Elizabeth had come across a vial of cocaine she'd completely forgotten about. She'd snorted a bit, to steady her nerves enough to make the calm, pointed exit she'd just pulled off.

"How dare she act like that," Susan said, affronted. "I swear, my mother should have boxed her ears much more often when she was a child."

Dave grinned at his wife. She was every bit the perfect lady; she'd never dream of being rude to anyone, least of all someone lending her shelter.

"Am I guessing that our child will get his or her ears boxed regularly?" he asked.

"No," Susan said, her smile softening her voice. "Our child will be a perfect angel, so there'll be no need."

Dave laughed outright at that. "With my genes, honey? I seriously doubt the words 'perfect' or 'angel' will be anywhere near applicable."

"I beg to differ, David," Susan said, lifting her chin regally.

He leaned down, kissing her lips softly. "Beg all you want, honey, the child is still going to be half me, no matter how hard you try."

"I happen to love you, David Ezekiel Dibbins, so I would hardly want our child to be anything but at least half you."

Dave narrowed his eyes at her.

"You're going to make me extremely sorry I told you my middle name, aren't you?"

Susan giggled, nodding. "It's highly likely, yes."

Dave shook his head

Susan had wheedled his middle name out of him one night when they'd lain in bed talking for hours. She'd been surprised. She'd gone on to surprise him by telling him how ironic his middle name really was. He hadn't known what she meant.

"You never read the Bible?" Susan asked.

"Honey…" Dave said, giving her a look that told her she should know better.

"Oh, right," she said, grimacing. "Well, the prophet Ezekiel is said to have been first the prophet of doom, but in later years, after the fall of Jerusalem, he was said to have become the comforter and an inspirer of his fellow men. When Israel was restored, Ezekiel became a lawmaker and codifier of Hebrew wisdom. Much like you are now the inspiration of the people under you in your work, whereas before you were a prophet of doom."

Dave had stared at her for a long moment, then shook his head slowly.

"I don't know how you always see me in a good light, honey, but I'm here to tell you it's a gift you have," he said, grinning.

"It's easy to see a good man in a good light, David."

143

He'd nodded, rolling his eyes, looking wholly unconvinced. Susan hadn't pushed the subject, but she'd felt that his name had really meant more than he'd ever realized. She found it quite ironic.

***

Liz drove the new Porsche Carrera GT she'd bought herself for the bargain price of four hundred and fifty thousand. It was extremely fast, very flashy, and very Liz. She made the twenty-minute drive to Del Mar and her new apartment in ten minutes, driving at speeds exceeding a hundred. At the apartment gate, she punched in the code and drove to her garage. Getting out, she went up to the second floor. It was a lovely place—hardly an apartment, more like a luxury townhouse. It was two stories, at least 1,300 square feet. It had hardwood floors and Berber carpeting. It was, to say the least, incredible. It cost her almost $3,000 a month, but it was a lovely place, and she just needed to get to work furnishing it.

Walking up the stairs to the master suite, she opened the French doors out onto a veranda and stood staring out into the night. She was very high, and she knew it, but she needed more… She also knew where to get that.

***

Donovan and Jeanie lay in bed, both exhausted. It had been a long day. They'd had a search warrant first thing in the morning, which had culminated in hours' worth of rummaging through the house they'd hit. It had been hot, since the house had no air conditioning and they were in their raid gear; the bulletproof vests alone added ten extra degrees to their body temperature. There had been some levity.

Cat was proving to have a great sense of humor, with an ability to make everyone laugh. She always found something to remark on that had the whole team laughing uproariously. Today had been no different.

After the raid there had been the usual mountain of paperwork. They'd been up since three o'clock that morning, and it was already past midnight when they got home. Eating had been dismissed in favor of a shower. They'd taken it together to save time. It was a testament to how tired they were—it was a strictly platonic shower. Once in bed, they kissed a few times, but mostly just held each other and mentally deprogrammed.

"I think I'm sleeping for the next three days," Donovan said, his voice gravelly.

"Works for me," Jeanie said, grinning. "Wake me up an hour after you get up."

"Oh sure, you always get the extra sleep," he said, laughing.

"I need my beauty sleep, buddy."

"Not hardly, babe," he said, smiling down at her. "You can't get any more beautiful."

"Ahhhh…" she said, her eyes shining up at him. "Just for that you can wake me up a half hour after you get up," she said with a wink.

Donovan laughed. He kissed her, then snuggled against her back, and she wrapped her arm around his. They fell asleep that way.

They were awoken at 6 a.m. by the phone. They both groaned.

"Shoot it," Donovan growled as Jeanie reached for the phone.

She chuckled as she picked it up.

"Curtis," she said, assuming it would be work at this hour.

There was silence on the other end of the line for a moment.

"Hello?" Jeanie queried again, thinking if this was a crank call…

145

"I was told Donovan Curtis was at this number," said a woman's voice.

"He is."

"Who are you?" the woman asked sharply.

"His wife," Jeanie replied, wondering who this woman was.

"Oh," the woman said, sounding shocked. "May I speak to Donovan, please?"

"Sure, why not?" Jeanie said sarcastically, then handed Donovan the phone with a pointed look.

Donovan's eyebrows furrowed as he took it.

"Hello?" he queried.

"Donovan, it's me."

Donovan closed his eyes, going pale.

Jeanie sat up, worried. She put her hand on his cheek. He opened his eyes, looking up at her. Her worry intensified—he looked scared.

"Donovan?" the woman on the phone said.

"Don't call here again," he said into the phone, pushing the disconnect button and tossing it away from him like a snake that might bite him.

He was taking deep, gasping breaths, and his hands were shaking.

"Donovan," Jeanie said, reaching down to take his hands, her eyes searching his. "Who was that?"

Donovan swallowed a few times, shaking his head as if trying to deny what he'd heard. His teal-blue eyes looked into hers.

"My mother," he said, his voice a grave whisper.

Jeanie was stunned. They both jumped when the phone rang again.

"I'll get it," Jeanie said, her tone strong.

"Jay," Donovan began, but Jeanie got out of bed, snatching up the phone and hitting the answer button.

"Yes?" Again, there was silence. Jeanie's eyes narrowed. "Look, lady, I don't know what you did to Donovan to make him react like this to hearing your voice now, but as far as I'm concerned, you call here again and I'll run a tap on your ass, then come hunt you down for whatever you did. Got me?"

When there was no answer to that, Jeanie hung up. Donovan was sitting up by this time. She put her arms around him, hugging him to her.

"Talk to me, babe," she said softly. "I know there's always been more to the story with your parents than you've told me." She put her hands to his face, turning it to look up at her. "Will you please tell me what we're up against now?"

Donovan swallowed. His eyes looked haunted now, even as he nodded. Jeanie moved to lean against the headboard, pulling Donovan with her. It took him a while to reconcile a way to tell her, but after a long silence he started talking.

"When I was four years old, my parents replaced the carpet in our house," he said, his tone solemn, and she could see that he was reliving it. "That's when the rule started about no food in the living room. The thing was, we'd always been allowed to eat in there, so it was habit…" He shook his head as his voice trailed off. Closing his eyes, he continued, "I think I was almost five when I decided that Kool-Aid wasn't food. I thought it was a brilliant deduction. I took it in there to watch cartoons. Of course, it got spilled—it was cherry Kool-Aid too. Nice, bright red stain," he said, his voice haunted. "I can still see it," he added, swallowing and opening his eyes, still not seeing the present.

Jeanie started feeling the sense of dread he was describing. Somehow she knew she wasn't going to like anything about what she was about to hear.

"I tried everything I could think of to clean it up," Donovan said. "My mother was at the store with Randy, and Darrell was there to watch me. He tried to help me clean it up too, but what does a twelve-year-old know about cleaning carpet? In the end, I sat on the spot on the carpet, thinking that if I sat there long enough, it would just magically disappear. When my mother got home from the store, I didn't move. When my father came home three hours later, I didn't move. Of course, by then my legs were totally asleep, but I just knew I'd be in big trouble if my dad saw the carpet. Eventually, of course, dinner was ready, and I had to get up to go eat. My father came in to yell at me to 'get up off my lazy ass.' I could barely move, and the minute I got up I fell down, because my legs were asleep. That's when he saw the spot." As Donovan said it, his face took on a grim, pained look. "And that's the first time he hurt me. He kicked me so hard I couldn't breathe. My father was a construction worker, so he wore steel-toed boots."

"Oh my God, Donovan…" Jeanie breathed.

"I tried to get away from him," Donovan said, taking slow, deep breaths. "But I couldn't feel my legs, and then of course on top of him kicking me, the pins and needles started. All I could do was lay there and cry," he said, disgusted with himself for not doing more.

"Donovan, you were a child—a small child."

He nodded. "Darrell finally stopped him, lying and telling him that he spilled the Kool-Aid. My dad beat him too. He said he didn't believe him that he'd spilled it, that he was beating him for lying about it."

"My God, Donovan," Jeanie said, shaking her head, unable to think of anything to say at this point and sensing there was more.

"It was like suddenly my father had discovered a new way to ease his tension, and we were it. I was the one that got it most often—I was a clumsy kid, so I was always doing something wrong. Darrell got too big after a couple of years for my dad to go after, so it all came down on me." His lips tightened in a grimace. "When I was eight he literally put me through a wall, because I'd broken a glass—not before shoving my face down into the broken glass," he said, his fingertip brushing the tiny scar at his jawline.

It was a scar she'd noticed dozens of times, the only imperfection on his perfect face—it was noticeable. She'd never asked him about it, never really thinking much of the tiny mark. Now she stared at it, imagining him as a small boy, with his own father shoving his face in broken glass. It made her feel sick.

"Jesus, Donovan," she said, her voice reflecting her revulsion. "It was basically a godsend when they left, wasn't it?"

Donovan nodded, his expression still tormented.

"Oh, babe…" she said, reaching down to touch his cheek. "What did your mother do?"

"Nothing," Donovan said. "She stood by and watched, and eventually started going to their room until it was over."

"Did she at least comfort you after it was over? She had to have…" Jeanie said, trailing off as he shook his head. "My God, what kind of mother is that?"

"Mine," he said cynically.

"God, I'm sorry, Donovan," Jeanie said, hugging him close to her and stroking his back, doing anything she could to comfort him.

She wanted to do anything she could to take that look out of his eyes.

Donovan let her comfort him, feeling so raw at that point. It had been years since he'd even thought about what had happened to him growing up. He'd managed to forget it and move on with his life. He basically told people he'd had a shitty childhood—that was it. No one had any idea how shitty but Randy and Darrell.

The phone rang again, and Jeanie grabbed it. She was almost praying it was Donovan's mother again, so she could tell her what she thought of her.

"Yeah?" she answered.

"Jeanie, it's Randy."

"Hi," Jeanie said, glancing down at Donovan.

"Is he there?" Randy asked, knowing he was.

"Yes. Hold on," Jeanie said, handing Donovan the phone. "It's Randy."

Donovan sat up, taking the phone and running a hand through his hair.

"Hey, Rand," he said, his tone still affected.

"They called you too, didn't they?"

"Yeah."

"Are you okay?"

"What do they want?"

"To see us," Randy said quietly.

"I don't want to," Donovan said, shaking his head.

"I know, Donny, I know."

"Are you going to see them?"

"I don't know yet," Randy said, still trying to reconcile the idea of their parents contacting them after all these years.

"If you do, make sure Joe is there."

"Why?"

"Because I don't want you alone with those people."

Randy nodded.

"Did you ever tell Joe?" Donovan asked.

"No," Randy said. "It was something I chose to forget about

once they were gone. By the time I met Joe, I'd convinced myself that it was part of our past, not something he needed to know about."

Donovan nodded, having thought along the same lines with everyone as well. Of course, his friends from the neighborhood, some of whom worked for the department, knew about it. He knew that was why over the years he'd put more and more distance between himself and them. He'd needed to put distance between his past and his present.

They talked for a little while longer, then hung up. Donovan got up, putting on a pair of jeans. Jeanie followed him, putting on her sweats and a tank top. He walked out to their kitchen, and predictably reached for the bottle of tequila over the stove. Jeanie leaned against the doorway. She knew he needed to calm his nerves at this point. She would let him do that, but she wasn't going to allow him to tear himself apart.

They spent the rest of the day together, not talking much, but Jeanie moderated his drinking. She also made sure he ate. Darrell eventually called, stating that if their parents showed up at the house "again" he'd shoot them both and that Donovan would have to bail him out.

"I'll let Randy do it," Donovan said, grinning in spite of himself. "She has more of a house to mortgage for the bail money."

Darrell laughed too.

"Did they say what they were looking for?" Donovan asked.

"I didn't let them get that far, Pony. But my guess would be absolution."

"Not gonna happen," Donovan replied sharply.

"I know. Not from this camp either—trust me on that," Darrell assured him.

"If any of us does, it'll be Randy."

"You're right, she's got that forgiving streak," Darrell said, making a face. "Probably a chick thing."

Donovan laughed. "You're probably right."

They hung up a few minutes later. Donovan felt surprisingly better having talked to Darrell. That was a notable instance, since Darrell usually irritated the crap out of him.

Setting the phone aside, he wrapped his arms around Jeanie, who lay in front of him on the couch.

"I love you," he said softly.

She turned her head, kissing his chin. "I love you too, Donovan."

He snuggled against her, turning the movie they'd been watching back on and doing his best to forget about his parents for a while.

CHAPTER 6

"You look like shit," Christian said to Donovan the next morning.

"Man..." Donovan said, shaking his head at the Englishman. "Not now, okay?"

Christian stared back at him for a long moment, his light blue eyes searching Donovan's face.

"What's up, Donovan?" Christian asked, his tone serious now.

"Bad day yesterday," Donovan said, moving to sit at his desk.

Christian nodded. "Well, if you need anything, or just need to go have a few good belts, let me know."

Donovan nodded, appreciating that Christian was able to change gears so quickly. Their relationship had never been close—they were far too different to be good friends—but Donovan knew that if he needed backup, Christian would always be there.

Cat walked in later that morning, taking one look at Donovan and knowing something was wrong. She walked over to his desk, perching there for a moment, looking down at him.

"I know it's totally none of my business," she said softly, "but are you okay?"

Donovan looked up at the newest member of the team. Cat was definitely direct, but she had a way of speaking that showed that she was sincere.

"Okay isn't exactly how I am," he said. "But I'll get there."

"Well, if you need a ride..." she said, smiling.

Donovan laughed softly, nodding. "Thanks."

Cat hopped off his desk and went to her own. Jeanie was out doing some legwork for a case she was working with Cat and Christian. They were working at getting to a local heavy hitter. Stevie and Kevin were off on their case, so Christian and Cat made a silent pact to keep an eye on Donovan. They dragged him off to coffee at one point, making him laugh with comments about the scary-looking guy that made their lattes.

By the time Jeanie got into the office after noon, bringing lunch in for the four of them, Donovan looked better again. The night had been rough on him. He'd had a number of nightmares centering around his childhood trauma. He'd awoken with a yell at one point; it had taken Jeanie two hours to calm him down enough to sleep again. She noted his lightened mood, and knew their coworkers had everything to do with that. Donovan had told her about the coffee trip. She appreciated their support, knowing it was things like that that would get Donovan through this. By three, she, Christian, and Cat headed out to the field. Jeanie gently suggested to Donovan that he call it a day and go home and try to get some more sleep. He nodded tiredly, and left as they did. Jeanie walked him to his car and stood talking to him for a few minutes.

Christian and Cat waited for them across the lot, leaning against her SUV, smoking and watching the exchange between Donovan and Jeanie.

"You know anything about what's going on?" Cat asked, nodding toward the couple.

"Nope," Christian said, shaking his head.

"He looks more than tired."

"Yeah," Christian said. "He looks like he's reeling from something."

Cat nodded.

Jeanie walked over to the two of them, glancing over her shoulder as Donovan drove out of the lot, accelerating out of the gate, his tires squealing. Christian raised an eyebrow. The boy scout didn't usually peel out.

"He okay?" he asked.

"His mother called yesterday," Jeanie said.

Christian's mouth dropped open, even as Cat glanced between the two of them. Why was that a big deal? Her mother called at least once a week. Christian glanced at Cat, realizing she had no idea what was going on.

"Donovan's parents have been out of the picture since he was eleven," Christian said, having heard the story from Randy years before.

"Ouch," Cat said, wincing.

"Oh, it's much worse than that," Jeanie said, shaking her head.

"What?" Christian asked, sensing instantly that there was a lot more to this.

Jeanie looked at him for a long moment. "Blue, you have to swear to me that you won't hassle him about this…"

"Jay, I don't hassle him about anything serious, you know that," Christian said. "What's the story?"

"His father apparently beat him regularly from the time he was about five," Jeanie said, rushing through the statement so she wouldn't feel it again.

"Beat him?"

"As in, put him through a wall when he was about eight."

"Holy shit," Cat said, her eyes widening.

"No kidding," Jeanie said, upset again.

"So what the hell does his mother want now?" Christian asked, already identifying with Donovan hating his father.

"Apparently they want some kind of forgiveness."

"After all this time?" Christian said bitterly. "Fuck that."

"I have to agree," Cat said, nodding.

"Well," Jeanie said, "Donovan doesn't want anything to do with them, and I have to respect that."

"But?" Christian said.

"I've just learned that in order to forget something, you have to forgive first."

"Or kill the bastard," Christian said, his light blue eyes sparkling maliciously.

Jeanie stared back at him for a moment, then shook her head, laughing.

"I don't see Donovan shooting his own father, Blue."

"And why not?" Christian said, grinning. "It's rather cathartic, ya know."

"And rather illegal," Jeanie said, shaking her head. "Even in this country."

"I missed something, didn't I?" Cat said.

"Oh, so much to tell, so little time," Christian said, looking at his watch.

"Ohhhh, that's low," Cat said, tossing her cigarette down and stubbing it out with her sandal.

"That's me," Christian said, grinning.

"Uh-huh," Cat agreed, getting into the Blazer. Jeanie did the same, and Christian climbed into the back.

"So we know where these guys hang out, right?" Cat said.

"Yeah, head down to Chicano Park, south side," Jeanie said. "You sure you can get us in?"

"Oh yeah," Cat said, grinning.

Twenty minutes later they were parked. Cat and Jeanie stood outside the vehicle next to the driver's door. Cat was smoking. Christian leaned against the rear of the vehicle, smoking as well, his light blue eyes scanning the crowd with an air of ease. Cat had her stereo cranked and the car window open, much like the people around them did.

This was definitely a meat market, and Cat knew how to play "the meat" when she had to. She wore a short black skirt and a sapphire blue silky camisole with spaghetti straps. On her feet she wore a pair of high-heeled strappy sandals. She'd let her long blond hair loose, and it fell around her face in a wild, sexy mane.

The music she had on wasn't the same rap stuff everyone else was playing. She wanted to be different. She was playing the Tomb Raider 2 soundtrack, the song "Jam For The Ladies." It was a fast-paced, beat-driven song. Cat's natural rhythm showed in the way her head moved to the beat, her upper body moving at some points. She gestured with her hand, like many rappers did, during parts of the song as she sang the words. She looked like she fit right into the crowd.

Jeanie watched the other girl, thinking, *Damn, she's good.* Cat *was* good—they'd all figured that out quickly. She had her own way of playing things, and she did it quite well. Leaning back against the Blazer, Jeanie also scanned the crowd. She noticed a great deal of attention directed their way. Jeanie was wearing black chino-style pants that fit perfectly to her tiny shape and a burgundy tank top that hugged her upper body, showing that she had absolutely no flaws.

Cat and Jeanie made an irresistible pair, with Cat's gold-blond hair and Jeanie's long chestnut hair. They were highly noticeable amongst the black and Latina girls at the park. Christian grinned as he saw guys' heads turning left and right to look at the girls. He leaned indolently against the Blazer, his arms crossed in front of his chest casually. The women were noticing him, of course—they always did. With his jet black hair and darker-toned skin combined with the light blue eyes, he had them every time.

"Got action," Cat murmured to Jeanie, turning her head in the direction she was talking about.

Jeanie turned like she was going to talk to Cat and glanced at the guys headed their way.

"Stay ready, just in case," Cat said, smiling sexily at Jeanie in case the guys were paying attention.

A moment later the two guys walked up to them. Both men looked like thugs, with their baggy jeans, bandanas on their heads, and the gold on their fingers, wrists, necks, and teeth.

"You shorties looking for a party?" the taller of the guys asked, glancing at Christian then back to the girls.

"We could be," Cat said, flicking her cigarette away as she blew her smoke out in a long stream. "What you got runnin', dog?"

"A banger tonight," the first guy said. His friend was busy looking Jeanie over.

"Cool," Cat said, nodding. "Can I bring my girlfriend and our friend?" she said, gesturing to Jeanie and nodding back toward Christian.

The taller guy—his pendant said *JDogg*—looked measuringly at Christian. Christian stared back at him. His look basically told the guy that if he wasn't invited, the girls wouldn't be there. JDogg hesitated. He didn't know if he wanted such a good-looking white guy there—he'd take all the shorties for himself. Then he looked at Cat again. This shorty really had it going on, and he wanted to tap that ass—so what if her man got other broads?

"Girlfriend?" JDogg asked hopefully.

"Oh yeah," Cat said. "Ya know how it is…" she added with a sexy wink.

"Ya, I know, it's cool," he said, grinning widely. "Let me go check, cool?"

"Cool," Cat said, grinning.

The two guys walked away, continually glancing at Cat and Jeanie. Cat watched as they got over to the guy that was obviously the big man.

"Think we're in?" Jeanie asked.

"I think I can clinch it for sure, if you're brave enough," Cat said, watching the men glancing back at them, the big man watching with interest.

"Whatever it takes," Jeanie said.

"Just remember you said that," Cat said, grinning as she leaned over, sliding her hand through Jeanie's hair and pulling her to her, kissing her lips.

Jeanie jumped slightly. To her credit, she adjusted instantly. She even put her hand to Cat's cheek as they kissed for the big man. When they parted, Jeanie widened her eyes at Cat. Cat just chuckled, as did Christian.

Cat smiled. "Sorry about that, but I know that's what they're hot for."

Jeanie shook her head, grinning. "The lengths I'll go to."

Cat laughed.

"You nailed 'em, Cat," Christian said, having watched the men's faces as they witnessed the girl-on-girl kiss. The big man had nodded at his cohort vehemently.

JDogg walked back over, his eyes on Cat with heightened interest now.

"You're in, girlie girl," he said, all smiles. "And bring your friends."

"Slammin'," Cat said, smiling and winking over at Jeanie.

Jeanie nodded, smiling widely as well. JDogg wondered remotely if he could nail both of them. As it was, he had a major hardon from watching them kiss. He handed over the big man's card with the address of the party on it, making sure to slide his hand over Cat's as he did. Cat smiled widely at him, not giving anything away.

After JDogg walked away, Cat glanced at the other two, nodding. They hung out at the park for a little while after that, so they didn't look as if they'd come and gotten what they wanted and then left.

On the way back, Cat glanced over at Jeanie.

"You recovered now?" she asked with a sly grin.

Jeanie laughed. "Jeez, do I seem like that big of a prude to you people?"

Cat looked at her thoughtfully, then glanced back at Christian.

"Pretty much," they said at the same time.

"Hey, I can be wild with the best of them," Jeanie said haughtily.

"Uh-huh…" Christian said from the back seat.

"Shut up, Blue!"

"Seriously, though," Cat said. "If that was over the line, let me know, okay?"

Jeanie looked over at her for a moment. "It's not a problem, Cat. I know you know what you're doing—you just have a different angle on things than I do. That's what makes the six of us a good team. We all have different approaches."

Cat nodded, appreciating that Jeanie saw things that way. It was true—Cat used her sexuality and her preference for women to her advantage. She used what it took but never compromised her own morals or beliefs.

That night, at the party, Cat, Jeanie, and Christian made a number of connections. Christian watched in amusement as Cat made the rounds. She was able to get near just about every guy in the place. She'd walk up to the woman a guy was dancing with and begin dancing with her. She'd also get closer to the women that were near the men, talking to the women and discussing whatever. Since every guy at the party knew about Cat's apparent bisexuality, they encouraged their women to talk to her. Cat used that to her advantage—it kept her in on the action. Christian, of course, was able to talk to any and all of the women as well. Jeanie worked the men; she'd learned how to get away before it was necessary to get violent.

Christian kept his eye on both girls, rescuing them when necessary. Usually with a proprietary hand, or a dangerous look. Most of the guys had already sensed the undercurrent of danger in Christian. For all his good looks, his light blue eyes were shards of ice, and the nickel-plated gun he wore in a barely concealed shoulder holster said a bit as well. No guy was going to get into a gun fight over a woman— it wasn't worth the trouble. Besides, they'd seen the Viper Christian had driven up in; they knew the guy was a serious player. There was money to be made here.

Monday morning, Cat walked into the office looking like she hadn't slept at all. She hadn't. She and Kana had had a fight; she'd brought up Palani's name, and Kana hadn't responded well at all. It wasn't something she wanted to talk about, and it showed. Christian and Jeanie noticed Cat's mood immediately, exchanging a look. Rumor had it that Kana had been at the office all weekend. Now they wondered why.

"Everything okay?" Christian asked.

"Fine. Why?" Cat replied, way too quickly.

"Uh-huh," Christian said.

Cat looked back at him for a long moment, then blew her breath out as she saw that Jeanie was watching her too.

"Look, guys, I don't want to talk, okay? Can we just work?"

Jeanie and Christian exchanged another look, then nodded.

The three worked the rest of the day in relative peace. Donovan had stayed home, having been up half the night with nightmares again. Jeanie told Christian she was planning on talking to him about the whole thing that night.

"I'm tellin' ya," Christian said. "Shooting works…"

"Will you shut up!" Jeanie said, laughing all the same.

Cat had long since put her headphones on and was listening to music.

That night, Jeanie made dinner for herself and Donovan. He was looking worse and worse every time she saw him. She was beginning to worry about his health. It was time to talk to him about all of this.

After they ate, they sat on the couch, drinking wine. She leaned back against him, his arm around her shoulders.

"Donovan?" she said cautiously.

"Huh?" he said, his mind having been elsewhere.

She sat up, turning to face him.

"I think you need to see your parents," she said softly, looking directly into his eyes.

"What?" he asked, searching her face. She had to be kidding, right?

"Listen to me for a minute, okay?" she said, putting her hand on his arm. "I think this thing is eating you up inside now, babe. I think you need to reconcile it somehow."

"You think I should forgive him," Donovan said, his eyes narrowing.

"No," Jeanie said, holding up her hand. "I think you need to talk to them. I think you need to know why."

"Why?" he asked disbelievingly. "I need to know why the bastard beat me?"

"Yes," Jeanie said. "And you need to know why your mother didn't stop him, and why they left, and… just everything, Donovan."

He looked at her for a long moment, then shook his head. "I can't."

"You can, babe."

"I can't handle being in the same room with that man and not want to shoot him."

Jeanie nodded. "Okay, note to self—don't let Donovan talk to his parents while armed," she murmured, a grin starting on her lips.

Donovan looked back at her for a moment, then couldn't help but grin too. She always did that to him—made a joke when things were at their worst, or so it seemed.

"All I'm saying, babe, is talk to them," Jeanie said, reaching out to touch his cheek. "I don't want this to eat you up, okay? I love the man that you are, and something like this can take hold inside you and change you—I don't want that. I love you, Donovan. I don't want to ever lose you again, and not to something so insidious as buried anger and resentment."

Donovan's teal eyes searched hers. He could see that she really was worried. It was that worry that hit home. He knew she was right—he knew this could eat him up inside. He knew it already was doing just that. That it was why he wasn't sleeping. The nightmares were just solidifying his memories, making them worse and worse.

He reached out, touching her cheek, then leaned forward to kiss her lips softly.

When he pulled back he said, "Will you come with me?"

"Of course," she said, looking shocked that he'd even needed to ask.

He closed his eyes for a long moment, then opened them, nodding.

***

Joe was fast asleep when his phone rang. He reached for it tiredly, thinking he was going to ream out whoever was calling him at—he glanced at the clock—two in the morning!

"This better be good," he muttered. "Sinclair," he answered, his voice still a growl.

There was silence at the other end of the line, expectedly. Then Joe heard a distinct sniff, and he knew this wasn't work.

"Hello?" he said, softer now.

"Joe…" came Jordan's voice. She was crying.

"Jordan, what is it?" Joe asked, sitting up.

"Joe, I need you," she said, her tone bordering on hysterical.

"What happened, babe? Where are you?" Joe asked, endeavoring to stay calm.

"I need you, Joe, please…"

"Babe, I'll be there—just tell me where."

"Joe…" she said, still crying.

"Jordan, tell me where you are!" Joe said, sternly now. He could sense she was getting hysterical.

She was silent. Joe jumped out of bed, walking over to his desk and looking through the paperwork, trying to remember where she was at on the tour. He found the schedule he'd printed out, glancing at his watch.

"Vegas—Jordan, are you in Vegas?"

"Yes, Vegas. I need you," she said, sounding like she was losing it again.

"Are you at the hotel?" he asked, seeing that they were staying at the Hard Rock.

"No," she said tremulously. "I'm in the hospital, Vegas General."

"What?" Joe exclaimed before he could stop himself. "What happened, Jordan? Are you okay?"

"I'm not okay, Joe. I need you, please?"

"Okay, baby, okay," Joe said soothingly, even as he picked up his cell phone and dialed the number for the pilot he had hired on an on-call basis. "I'll be there as fast as I can get there, okay?"

"Majors," the pilot answered, sounding tired.

"It's Joe—I need to get to Vegas two hours ago."

"Meet me at the airport," Majors said, snapping to immediately.

"I'll be there."

Joe hung up his cell, then turned his attention back to Jordan.

"Baby, I'm heading to the airport. Can you hang in there for a couple of hours?"

Jordan was silent for a long moment. Finally she uttered a small "Yes."

"I'm comin', babe. I'll be there. Give me the number you're at."

"I don't know it," she said, sounding upset again.

"It's okay," Joe assured her. "I'll get it. You just stay there and wait for me, okay? I'll be there."

"Okay," she said, sounding relieved.

Joe was at the airport a half hour later. He'd called the hospital by then and talked to the doctor that had seen Jordan. She'd been attacked and nearly raped. Joe felt his stomach turn over. His first

165

thought was that it was Mark, her stepbrother.

His next call was to Vegas PD, asking what was being done in the case. Did they have a CSI over there yet?

"Yes, Captain," said Tom Jameson, the captain of vice for Vegas PD. "We've got someone on it already. Your girl isn't exactly cooperating, however."

"Shit," Joe said, grimacing. "I'll talk to her when I get there. She'll cooperate."

"We need to get a kit on her right away, Captain Sinclair."

"Okay, I'll work on it. Who do you have from your team on the case?"

"Benitez. She's at the hospital now."

"Can you patch me through to her cell?" Joe asked, even as he boarded the plane Jordan had bought him and waved to Majors, who was running pre-flight.

"You got it, Captain," Jameson said. "Incidentally, it's good to have fellow law enforcement on this. Makes things easier."

"I know what you mean," Joe said. "Thanks for your help on this, I really appreciate it."

"No problem. Transferring now."

Joe heard the line click, then a woman's voice answered. "Benitez."

"Good morning," Joe said smoothly. "This is Joe Sinclair, I'm a captain over here at San Diego PD. I believe you have my girl there."

"Your girl is Jordan Tate?"

"Yeah," Joe said, grinning. "Don't you read tabloids?"

Benitez chuckled. "No time, sir."

"Are you near the room they have her in?"

"Yes, sir. But she won't let me touch her."

"Do me a favor," Joe said. "Take the phone in to her and let me

166

talk to her. I'll make sure you can do your job."

"That would be very much appreciated, Captain."

A few moments later he was on the phone with Jordan.

"Baby, let her do her job. She needs to get evidence, okay?" Joe said softly.

"Can't you do it when you're here?" Jordan asked petulantly.

"No, baby. That's a CSI's job—it's important, okay? I need you to do this for me."

There was a long silence, and then she sighed softly. "Okay, if you say it's important…"

"It is, Jordie, trust me."

"Okay."

"Jord?"

"Yes?"

"I love you," Joe said softly. "We'll get through this, okay?"

"Okay," she said, her lips trembling.

"I'm on my way now. I should be there in an hour. Can you hold on till then, babe?"

"Yes," she said, sounding stronger now.

"That's my girl," Joe said, grinning.

Jordan handed the phone back to the CSI.

"We a go?" Benitez asked Joe.

"Yeah, we're a go. Just take it easy with her, okay? I know it's a pain in the ass, but she's really scared right now."

"Affirmative, Captain," Benitez said, even as her eyes softened at the tone in Joe's voice.

It was obvious to her that he cared about this woman a lot—hell, he was getting on a plane in the middle of the night to be by her side. Benitez couldn't help but want to help find the person that did this to her and make a good case against him.

An hour later, Joe strode into the hospital. Naturally, past an army of reporters who had conveniently heard about the incident already.

"Joe, is Jordan Tate okay?" one of them yelled.

"She will be," Joe told the man, continuing toward the doors.

"Do you know who did it?" asked another reporter.

"Whoever it was better be prepared to deal with me," Joe said, his tone all boyfriend at the moment, not cop.

Joe got to the doors then and walked inside, ignoring all the other questions coming at him. He spoke with a nurse, who told him he should wait for the doctor.

"Look, I don't have time for that right now," Joe said impatiently, wanting to get to Jordan as soon as possible. "Just tell me where she's at."

"But, sir—"

"Look," Joe said sharply. "It's late, I'm tired, and my lady is in this hospital somewhere scared to death. Tell me where the fuck she is, now."

The nurse jumped at the tone in his voice. Like many people in the country, she'd read all there was to read about the Sinclair and Jordan Tate romance. She was finding out how very intense Joe Sinclair was at that moment.

"Room 1022," she said.

"Thank you," Joe said, nodding curtly to her as he strode away.

"Is that her boyfriend?" asked one of the other nurses nearby.

"Oh yeah," said the first nurse, nodding as her eyes followed Joe down the hall.

Joe knocked lightly on the door to the private room Jordan was in. He didn't hear anything, so he opened the door cautiously and walked inside. Jordan lay curled up on the bed. She was wearing a skirt and blouse that were rumpled and torn in a few places.

Joe stepped close to the bed. Jordan's eyes were closed. Reaching out, he touched her cheek gently. She jumped, letting out a small scream as her eyes flew open.

"Babe, it's me," Joe said—unnecessarily, since she'd already realized that and was throwing herself into his arms.

He held her close as she whispered his name over and over again. He held her until she calmed down again, moving to sit on the bed so she could rest against him. When she was calmed, he pulled back to look down at her, brushing his thumb over her cheek, where there was a nasty bruise already.

"What happened, babe?" he asked gently.

She shook her head, burying it in his shirt. "Please just get me out of here, Joe."

"Has the doctor released you?"

"I don't care," Jordan said, shaking her head. She looked up at him then, tears in her gold eyes. "Please take me out of here."

"I will, babe," he said. "But I want to make sure you're okay first, okay?"

"I'm fine, Joe. I just want to get away from here," she said, gesturing to the hospital room.

Joe nodded, glancing around him and reaching for the nurses' call button. The nurse answered right away.

"Can you send the doctor down here as soon as possible, please?" Joe asked.

"Yes, sir," the woman replied crisply.

Joe wondered if it was the same nurse he'd chewed out earlier. When the doctor appeared no more than five minutes later, Joe was fairly sure he'd already been pegged as a pain in the ass.

"You wanted to see me?" the doctor said.

"Yes. She wants to go back to the hotel," Joe said, gesturing to Jordan, who was sitting with her face once again buried against his shirt.

The doctor looked at Jordan, then picked up her chart and read it over quickly.

"I'm waiting for one more test to come back," he began.

"Is it something you can contact us at the hotel about, once you hear?" Joe asked, feeling Jordan tense against him.

The last thing he wanted was for Jordan to cause a scene in the hospital. It would just be more fodder for the tabloids, and he knew she didn't want that, no matter how she was feeling at the moment. Joe was attempting damage control, as well as trying to comfort her. It was a new level in a relationship for him; he wrote it off as a minor drawback to dating a superstar.

The doctor looked thoughtful, then nodded, seeing too that Jordan was getting ready to rebel. Joe nodded toward the door, indicating to the doctor that he wanted to talk to him in private. The doctor nodded too.

"Babe," Joe said, pulling back to look down at Jordan. "I'll be right back, okay?"

She nodded, looking up at him. He could see her desperation to leave.

"Just hold tight, I'll be right back."

Getting up, he walked out the door with the doctor.

"Is there anything I need to know?" Joe asked.

"No." The doctor shook his head. "She had some minor contusions and cuts, but is for the most part fine physically. Emotionally may be another story."

Joe nodded. "I'll do my best to take care of that part."

"Mr…" The doctor paused.

"It's Joe."

"Joe, I think you should know, I got the distinct impression that Ms. Tate knows exactly who attacked her. She was terrified of anyone that came into the room, as if she knew this person would come after her again."

Joe narrowed his eyes, again thinking it was Mark O'Brien.

"Thanks, Doctor. I appreciate you letting me know, and for understanding her wanting to leave."

The doctor nodded. "If you need a back door, I can take you two through the emergency exit. It's pretty secluded."

"That would be great," Joe said, nodding.

Ten minutes later they were out of the building and in the car service sent by the hotel. The service whisked them into an underground lot and up a private elevator to Jordan's suite of rooms. Joe opened the door, leading her inside. She pulled back, looking around almost terrified.

"It's okay, babe," Joe assured her, his hand hovering near his holstered gun at his back all the same. "I'm with you, Jordan. Come on."

He pulled her gently through the door, his eyes scanning the room, his senses working overtime.

"Where's Jim at?" Joe asked, suddenly realizing he hadn't seen the bodyguard once. "In fact, how the hell did anyone get past him? I mean, that is his job, to protect you."

Jordan went still then. It took Joe a moment to realize she'd stopped dead in her tracks. He looked back at her. She stared at him. Suddenly, like a flash of lightning, it hit him.

"Oh, hell no," Joe said, shaking his head, his tone dropping to a deadly level. "He didn't…"

Jordan closed her eyes, nodding.

"He's dead. He's fucking dead," Joe growled. Then he saw the stricken look on Jordan's face. He pulled her into his arms, holding her close. "I'm sorry, baby. I'm so sorry,"

"He just wouldn't stop, Joe…" she said, shaking her head against his chest.

"Jesus. Where did BJ get this guy?"

Although he couldn't say much, he hadn't realized that Jim had obviously been dangerous. Joe gritted his teeth, fighting the urge to go and find the man and beat the living shit out of him. He'd been hired to protect Jordan, and he'd betrayed her trust by hurting her. That was beyond reprehensible, and Joe was going to see that he paid for it, dearly.

He walked Jordan into the bedroom and gave her one of the Valium tablets the doctor had prescribed. Then he helped her take off her clothes and get into the shower. He climbed in with her, gently washing her back, her shoulders, everything. He saw the various bruises on her body, and once again steeled himself against the urge to hunt down and kill Jim. Once done in the shower, Joe quickly dried off, putting on the robe the hotel supplied. He then wrapped Jordan in a huge bath sheet and carried her to the bedroom. Her eyes were already drooping from the Valium.

Laying her gently on the bed, he covered her up. Walking around the room, he made sure the door was secure, then called down to the manager of the hotel to tell him the codes to the room needed to be changed. The manager didn't argue, realizing whose room they were talking about. Joe went to the room bar then, and had a few shots of tequila to calm his nerves. He still couldn't believe her own bodyguard had attacked her. What was the guy thinking? That she wouldn't tell anyone? Was he nuts?

Joe realized suddenly that he hadn't called Midnight or Kyle. He picked up his cell phone.

Midnight turned over, groaning as the phone rang.

"I thought this part was over a long time ago," Rick muttered as Midnight reached for the phone.

"'Lo?" Midnight said into the phone.

"Night, it's me," Joe said. "Look, I'm in Vegas."

"Getting married again?" Midnight asked, grinning.

"No," Joe said. "Jordan's here. She was attacked tonight, by her bodyguard no less."

"Oh Jesus…" Midnight said, sitting up.

"I know," Joe said, nodding.

"Is she okay?"

"Yeah. But she's pretty freaked out."

"Understandably."

"I'm going to need to stay with her at least for a few days, until we can get someone else to take over the bodyguard work," Joe said. "Can you cover me?"

"Don't even worry about it, Joe. You just take care of Jordan. We'll be fine here."

"Thanks, Night," Joe said, thanking God again for such a supportive family.

"You just take care of her and you, and let us know how things are, okay?" Midnight said. "If you need anything, let me know."

"I will. Thanks."

"You sound beat. Have another shot, then go crawl back into bed with her, okay?"

Joe chuckled. She knew him well; he was still standing at the bar and had just poured himself another shot.

"Cheers," Joe said, holding up the drink.

"Be safe."

"Will do."

They hung up. Joe climbed into bed next to Jordan a few minutes later, pulling her into his arms gently and holding her close. His senses were on full alert, lest Jim try and come back.

CHAPTER 7

Jeanie dialed the number off the piece of paper Darrell had given her. She waited while the line connected. She was sitting in her gold Camaro, outside her and Donovan's house. She didn't want to call from the house, knowing Donovan was totally on edge about this meeting anyway.

"Hello?" a woman answered.

"Mrs. Curtis?"

"Yes, this is she."

"This is Jeanie, Donovan's wife," she said, her tone brisk and business-like. "Do you still want to see Donovan?"

There was hesitation at the other end of the line. "Yes, very much so."

"Fine. Be at 3640 Avant Drive at seven p.m. tonight."

"Okay," Donovan's mother said, sounding eager to agree to anything at that point.

"Then we'll see you tonight," Jeanie said, and hung up.

Donovan walked out of the house a minute later. Jeanie watched him as he came toward her car. He looked better today; he'd managed to sleep most of the night. Of course, she was sure that had a lot to do with the two bottles of wine they'd finished. Then again, that had been her plan.

Donovan got into the car, looking over at her.

"Tonight at seven."

He nodded, looking grave.

"Are you going to cook?" she asked.

"Why?"

"Because I want them to see what an incredible man you've become without their help," she replied succinctly.

Donovan grinned. She did have a way with words.

"I'll make your favorite."

"Ah, I knew I'd get something out of all this," she said, winking at him.

"Now I see your motives," he said narrowing his eyes at her.

Jeanie laughed, starting the Camaro and heading off toward work.

They had a raid that day, the culmination of a case Donovan had been working. When they hit the door, there was a lot of running. Cat, Donovan, and Christian went after three that ran through the house looking for a way out. Donovan had his guy cornered when the kid pulled a knife, bringing it up and out. Donovan blocked the knife with his right forearm, yelling as it sliced through his shirt and skin, and punched the kid in the face with his left hand. The kid was out instantly, and Donovan grabbed him, lying him down on the stomach and cuffing him.

Jeanie came running into the room, having heard Donovan yell.

"Oh shit," she said, seeing the blood on Donovan's arm.

Grabbing her radio off her waist, she yelled for a paramedic, moving to Donovan as she did.

"I'm fine, babe."

"Donovan, you've got a pretty good slice there."

He glanced down at his arm, noticing that she was right. It was a six-inch-long gash.

"Stitches," he said grimly.

"Yep," she said, nodding and grinning at the same time.

Three hours later, Donovan left the emergency room with a bandage on his forearm. Spider sent him home for the rest of the day. Jeanie finished up paperwork by four thirty and went home to make sure he was okay. He wasn't even home. She worried about him for the next half hour, until he walked in carrying bags of groceries.

"You're not supposed to be using that arm, Curtis," Jeanie said, giving him a dirty look.

"Then take one, Franco," he said, grinning.

He'd bought the food for the meal he was making that night. They put everything away. Donovan had rolled up the sleeves of his denim shirt, exposing the bandage that was on his arm. Jeanie noticed that it had seeped some blood.

"Babe, you need to change that dressing," she said, pointing to his arm.

He glanced down at the bandage and shrugged.

"I'm going to go take a quick shower anyway. I'll change it then." He leaned down, kissing her lips. "Want to join me?"

"If I do," she said, looking up into his eyes, "it won't be a quick shower."

He canted his head to the side. "Tell me again how that's bad…" he said, his teal-blue eyes twinkling.

"Mmm," she said, standing and wrapping her arms around his neck. "I'm all yours, Sergeant."

An hour and a half later, they were running to catch up, as usual. Both of them were grinning like bad kids. Donovan's hair was still damp, but he looked good—Jeanie had to hand him that. He'd shaved, and smelled great, as usual, wearing Tommy cologne. He wore beige Dockers with black boots, a dress belt, and a black Oxford.

177

It was a standard outfit for him. One he looked really good in, however.

He was standing at the counter, chopping vegetables, a towel thrown over his shoulder. His arm was once again bandaged, his sleeves rolled up as he worked. Next to him on the counter was his third glass of wine. Jeanie was sitting on the low island watching him.

She loved to watch him cook; he looked so good in the kitchen. He was the perfect combination of masculine, sexy, and talented. He did most of the cooking in their household, having been to a culinary school for all but two semesters before graduation. Donovan was always relaxed in his kitchen. All the same, she saw him tense when the doorbell rang.

"I'll get it," she said, standing and sliding her hand over his back soothingly.

Donovan nodded, a muscle in his jaw jumping as he clenched his teeth. She knew he was irritated that he was so nervous about seeing his parents again. She also knew he wanted desperately to simply hate them and write them off. But it was never that easy to do when things were unresolved.

Jeanie opened the front door and was surprised to only see a woman standing there. She looked at Donovan's mother, surprised by how small she was. She didn't know why she'd expected someone bigger—Randy was only 5'6"—but their mother was even smaller than that, only about 5'4".

"You must be Jeanie," Donovan's mother said, her eyes taking in every detail of the girl that was married to her son.

"Yes, I am," Jeanie said, opening the door wider to let her in.

"I'm Diane," Donovan's mother said, extending her hand.

Jeanie took the proffered hand, nodding. She led Diane down the hall toward the kitchen.

Diane's first impression of her son was that he'd grown into quite a handsome man. He was so tall! His sandy-brown hair still fell across his forehead, as it always had when he was younger. When he looked at her, however, she was so surprised—she'd forgotten how truly beautiful his eyes were, just like Randy's. They had Diane's mother's eyes.

Diane resisted the urge to go to Donovan and hug him, knowing that kind of gesture wouldn't be acceptable. She couldn't hide, however, her overwhelming admiration for the man her son had grown into.

"Donovan…" she said, shaking her head in amazement.

Donovan looked at his mother, remembering instantly everything about her. For some reason he remembered the times she'd taken his hand and placed it on her cheek. He'd never understood the gesture when he was little, but he'd so craved her attention he'd loved it. He looked at her hands. They were older now, but still the same.

He took a deep breath, expelling it slowly.

His mother's eyes took in the kitchen then, and the fact that he was obviously cooking.

"You cook?" she asked, amazed.

Donovan nodded. "I learned in a culinary academy," he said, his voice coming out hoarse.

"But you're a police officer now, aren't you?"

Donovan looked surprised that she knew that, but nodded.

Diane nodded. Donovan reached up with his right hand, rubbing the bridge of his nose, an indication that he was uncomfortable. His mother gasped at the sight of blood on the bandage he wore on his forearm.

"You're hurt?"

Donovan glanced down at his arm and nodded.

"He was cut on a raid today," Jeanie said. "We took him to the hospital and got it stitched up."

"We?" Diane asked, looking at her.

"Yeah, me and another member of our team," Jeanie said.

"You're a police officer too?"

"Yes," Jeanie said, smiling.

Diane nodded, looking surprised but not saying anything.

"Would you like a glass of wine?" Jeanie asked.

"Wine?" Diane glanced at the counter, where Donovan's glass was, and noticed that Jeanie had a glass there as well.

Once again she was surprised. Her son drank wine? Where had he gotten all this polish and class?

"It's a really good blend," Jeanie said, reaching for a crystal glass from the rack under the cabinets that hung over the low island.

She poured a small amount into the glass and handed it to Diane. Diane tasted it and was pleasantly surprised.

"This is wonderful," she said, smiling at Jeanie.

Jeanie grinned, pouring more into the glass.

"Donovan has a gift for picking the perfect wine with everything," she told his mother.

Diane looked at her son again, trying to reconcile the boy he'd been with this very sophisticated man standing in front of her.

"You've had some very good influences in your life," she said.

"My father notwithstanding," Donovan said evenly.

Diane hesitated for a moment, then nodded slowly, her look resigned. Part of her had held a shred of hope that Donovan wouldn't still hate his father, and her for that matter. She knew he had every right to hate both of them.

"And yes, I got lucky with role models after you left," Donovan said calmly. "Randy met and married a very good man, Joe. He helped me learn what being a man was about."

Diane nodded again. She'd read a great deal about Joe Sinclair, the man Randy had married. She'd also read things about her son—that was how she'd known about him being a police officer.

"Well, you have grown into a very handsome, very polished man," Diane said softly.

Donovan looked back at her for a long moment, not sure how to react to what she was saying. Part of him was thrilled that his mother seemed proud of what he'd become; another part of him wanted to snort and say, *Yeah, no thanks to you.* He finally nodded, slowly, his eyes averted from hers. Donovan turned back to the cutting board then, continuing to chop the vegetables for their meal.

Jeanie took that as a cue and invited Diane to sit down in the living room. Diane looked around her son's house in awe. Everything he owned seemed to only substantiate the idea that Donovan had become very refined. Diane knew that she wanted to meet Joe Sinclair at some point, if nothing else to thank him for rescuing the children she was foolish enough to abandon. She'd already learned that Joe Sinclair was responsible for Darrell having a successful construction business of his own, and for the center that Randy ran—even the house she ran the center out of. Joe Sinclair was definitely a savior of sorts, and Diane Curtis desperately wanted to thank him.

She and Jeanie made small talk. At one point, Diane caught sight of the ring that Jeanie wore, her engagement ring. Diane's breath caught in a sharp gasp.

"My God, that's beautiful," she said, reaching out to take Jeanie's left hand, holding it as she looked at the ring.

"Donovan has incredible taste," Jeanie said, smiling.

"I married you, didn't I?" Donovan chimed in from the kitchen.

Jeanie rolled her eyes. "I married you, remember?" she called back. "Get the story straight, Curtis."

Donovan walked out of the kitchen, wine glass in hand. "I asked first."

"Oh yeah, blah, blah, blah," Jeanie said, grinning as he walked around the couch and sat next to Jeanie on the love seat.

"And said the L-word first," he pointed out evenly.

"Oh, don't start!" she said, laughing.

"I'm just stating the facts, Sergeant," Donovan pointed out, a grin playing at his lips.

"Uh-huh," Jeanie said, narrowing her eyes at him.

"You know I'm right," he said, his teal-blue eyes sparkling as he looked at his wife.

Diane caught the look and felt her heart swell. Donovan was very much in love with his wife—that much was very evident. It made her feel so good. She'd always worried about Donovan, wondering what effect his father's abuse and her own negligence at stopping that abuse would have on him. Would it make him incapable of the love that Randy had obviously found?

Donovan caught the glazing of tears in his mother's eyes and wondered at it. It felt so strange, having her here. But he'd found that he didn't harbor near as much animosity toward her as he'd thought he would. And now he wanted to know some things.

"You came alone," Donovan said, his look searching.

Diane nodded. "I thought it might be better to talk to you first, before you see your father again."

"Why?" Donovan said, his eyes cooling a bit at the mention of his father.

Diane took a deep breath. "Because I was hoping to make you understand things a little better before you see him."

"Cloaking his sins again, Mother?" Donovan asked evenly.

182

Diane looked at him sharply, but then realized that was exactly what it appeared she was doing.

"Donovan, let me explain," she said beseechingly.

Donovan nodded, his expression a bit more closed now, but Diane rushed on anyway, hoping to explain before he shut down.

"Please understand, I'm not trying to make any excuses for what your father—or, for that matter, what *I* did when you were a child. There's no excuse for what happened to you," Diane said, feeling the lump in her throat rising. "If I could go back, Donovan, and change everything, I would. You don't have to believe me, but I have to tell you that I've regretted everything about your childhood for many, many years now."

The lump in her throat got the better of her then, and her tears flowed down her cheeks. She pressed on, knowing she had to say everything she'd wanted to say to him.

"I thought of how many times I went and hid from what your father was doing to you. I hated myself for so many years for that. But hating myself didn't fix anything for you, and I know that. And saying this now doesn't fix it either.

"When we left, Donovan, it was because we were scared Child Protective Services was about to take you and Randy away from us and put us in jail. At least your father, and he was scared, and ran. I didn't know any better, so I ran with him. It was a stupid, foolish thing to do, but something I can't change now, no matter how much I wish I could.

"It took years for our lives to get to a point where we really started looking at what we'd done by leaving you kids behind. That's when we started checking into how you were. That's when we found out about Joe Sinclair and his marriage to Randy. We were relieved that things were going well for her, and that you three were still to-gether. I found out from Social Services that Darrell begged to keep the two of you with him. That he told them he'd do anything it took to keep you two fed, clothed, and with a roof over your head. He was the man your father should have been."

Diane's voice halted as she smiled, thinking of Darrell.

"Your father had problems with his temper for years. He was constantly getting into fights. One night he went to a bar and got into a fight with a man there. Your father went to jail for assault. It was there that he was evaluated by a psychiatrist and diagnosed as manic depressive. He has vicious mood swings—that's why he would fly into such a rage with you, Donovan. He couldn't control it then, and believe me, he's spent a lot of years hating himself for what he did to you."

Again she paused, her throat constricting.

"He's the one that wanted to find you again, Donovan. He wanted to face you and tell you he was sorry. He even said that if you knocked him out, he wouldn't blame you a bit, that it would be the least he deserved."

Jeanie glanced at Donovan, having noticed how still he'd gone while Diane was talking. She was surprised to see tears in his eyes. She reached up, touching his cheek. Donovan smiled fondly, closing his eyes as a tear slid down his cheek. Then he looked at his mother.

"Why didn't you ever stop him?" he asked, his tone very affected and in no way accusing.

Diane shook her head. "I was a coward, Donovan. I was terrified to have him turn his wrath on me. I kept lying to myself, saying that it wasn't that bad, that he was just disciplining you. I was wrong. I have no excuse for not stopping him. You were my baby. I should have done something, anything…"

It was obvious she'd agonized over this for a while now. It was there in her eyes.

Donovan nodded slowly, accepting her answer.

Diane was shocked when she actually saw him flash the boyish grin she remembered from years before.

"And Dad wants to box, huh?" Donovan said wryly.

Diane laughed softly, feeling unbelievable relief and joy flood her veins. Her son was definitely an incredible young man. He had made so much out of his life and was happy, no matter what he'd been through as a child. It spoke volumes about what a strong character he had. Diane had no idea where he'd gotten this character from; she suspected he'd learned a lot from this Joe Sinclair.

"Donovan?" Diane queried later in the evening, while they were eating.

She'd already exclaimed repeatedly over Donovan's cooking abilities, saying he should be a top chef somewhere. His response was that he was the top chef—"in this house."

"Yeah?" he said, looking up at her, still shocked to be sitting across from his mother.

"Is there a chance I could ever meet Joe Sinclair?"

"Why?" Donovan asked, reaching for his glass of wine and taking a drink.

"I'd like to meet him," Diane said. "And to thank him."

"For?"

"For helping you become such a good man. For being so good to all three of you. For giving me grandchildren." She said the last smiling fondly, having met Cat and JT the day before.

"Randy had something to do with that too, Mom," Donovan said, grinning.

Diane stared back at Donovan openmouthed.

"What?" Donovan asked, not sure why she looked so shocked.

"You just called me Mom," she said softly.

Donovan looked back at her, his teal eyes gentling as he grinned. "You are my mother, remember?"

"Yes, but…" Diane said, shaking her head in wonder. "I never realized how good it would feel to hear you say it again."

Donovan chuckled, glancing at Jeanie, who was looking at him with pride shining in her eyes. He took her hand, putting it to his lips and kissing it softly.

"What was that for?" Jeanie asked.

"Because I love you," Donovan said, knowing that he'd never have reconciled with his mother if Jeanie hadn't pushed him to do it.

"Just remember that when it's time to do the dishes," Jeanie said, grinning as she winked at him.

The three of them laughed. It turned out to be a very nice evening, far from what Donovan had expected.

***

Dave was on surveillance with Cat that day. She noticed his unusually reserved manner as soon as they were in her Blazer. For a long while she didn't say anything, thinking that it really was none of her business. She had her own issues to mull over. She hadn't talked to Kana since the day she'd walked out of her house. It had been almost a week at that point. She wasn't sure what was happening, if they were just over, or what.

Once they were in place and waiting for their bad guy to make a move, they sat in the car, the silence stretching. Cat glanced over at Dave, noting that he looked perfectly at ease with the silence. She'd heard that about him, that his silence was something you'd have to get used to when you worked with him. Dave's phone rang at one point. He pulled it off his belt and answered it. Cat could only hear his side of the conversation.

"Dibbs," he answered, his face lit up with a smile. "Hey, honey," he said softly. He listened for a few moments, his face drawn with concern as he nodded. "I know, I need to do some checking, hon, and I will." He nodded a few times, then blew his breath out in a deep sigh. "Yeah, but if Liz is taking Nick down with her, we have a problem," he told his wife. They talked for a couple more minutes, then hung up.

Cat mentally filed the conversation away. She'd been hearing different things in the department about Midnight Chevalier-Debenshire's wild niece and the Assistant Chief's sixteen-year-old son. None of what she'd heard was good, and with the chief getting ready to run for Attorney General, things were bound to get very hairy real quick.

Dave looked over at Cat and was fairly sure he saw her mind working. To her credit, though, she simply looked back at him calmly. His lips twitched in amusement. He'd been lucky with her; she was a good narc. She had good instincts, a quick mind, and a different approach to the job that blended well with the rest of the team. He wondered idly what she'd been thinking but said nothing. They continued the surveillance in a more comfortable silence.

***

Joe sensed someone standing near the bed. Moving with the lightning reflexes that had kept him alive for years, he sat up, pulling out the gun he'd put under his pillow at the same time. Those same reflexes

187

recognized BJ Sparks instantly, and he immediately pointed the gun's muzzle at the ceiling even as Brenden's eyes widened in a cross between amusement and surprise.

"Heya, Joe," BJ said, his English accent clear, his grin sardonic.

"Gonna get yer ass shot one day, Beege," Joe said, shaking his head and grinning as he set the gun on the nightstand.

"Not with you on the job," BJ said, glancing down at Jordan, who lay fast asleep next to Joe.

Joe glanced down at her. She hadn't moved.

"She took meds," Joe told BJ.

BJ nodded. "Let's go talk," he said, indicating the door.

Joe got out of bed carefully, not wanting to risk waking Jordan.

He and Brenden settled in the living room, coffee in hand.

"So what happened?" Brenden asked.

"She was attacked," Joe said, looking contrite. "By her bodyguard."

"Fuckin' A," Brenden snarled. "I'll kill the bastard."

"I'm up to bat first, man," Joe said, his tone no less vengeful.

"Any idea where he ran off to?"

"No," Joe said, shaking his head. "Jordan didn't even tell me it was him till we got back here last night."

Brenden nodded. "I'll get someone on it right away."

"In the meantime, we need to get her better protection."

Brenden nodded, narrowing his eyes in thought. "John's got an assignment right now, or I'd use him."

"Is that Mackie?"

"Yeah."

Joe nodded. John Machiavelli was a man who'd been hired to protect the lead singer of a band called Fast Lane. The singer, Cassie Roads, had been attacked by her ex-boyfriend. Subsequent bad press

188

had turned a lot of people against Cassie, the victim. When Cassie had tried to take her own life, unable to handle the slanderous lies being spread about her anymore, it had been John who'd saved her. After that, John Machiavelli had become known as Cassie's knight in shining armor. The two had become a couple, getting married after John was shot trying to protect Cassie. It was a perfect Hollywood romance. John Machiavelli had taken on other bodyguard work, making more and more of a name for himself.

"So what are our other options?" Joe asked.

BJ was silent for a moment, then pinned Joe with a look. "Well, you could do it."

Joe's mouth dropped open. Then he started to shake his head. "Uh, no, I have a job already, thanks."

"Yeah, but man, she's not going to trust anyone right now, only you or me."

Joe narrowed his light blue eyes at BJ. "So you do it."

Brenden laughed. "I would, but I'm not licensed to kill like you are."

Joe blew his breath out in a sigh, shaking his head. "I would, man, but there's no way I can get away for that long. She's got, what, another two and a half months on this tour?"

"Yeah," Brenden confirmed. "You don't think the chief will let you off to do it?"

Joe dropped his head to the back of the couch, staring up at the ceiling. "Midnight'll let me do anything I need to do, Beege, but it'll put her in a bind."

Brenden nodded slowly. He could only imagine the balance Joe Sinclair had to try and keep between his job, his love life, and his friends, who were so close they were basically his family. Something always had to give somewhere.

189

Brenden left an hour later, after they'd discussed some other options. Brenden was determined to find Jim and beat the crap out of him for attacking Jordan. Joe was determined to help him do just that.

Joe walked into the bedroom and saw that Jordan was still sleeping soundly. Checking to make sure the room was secure, the extra lock in place on the front door, Joe went to take a shower. He was shaving and had just lifted the towel to his face to wipe it when he heard Jordan.

"Joe?" she queried, her voice worried.

"I'm here, babe," Joe said, walking to the bathroom doorway.

Jordan was sitting up on the bed, looking tired but still beautiful. Her hair fell around her shoulders like a dark curtain.

Joe walked over to the bed and sat down. He was wearing his jeans and hadn't put a shirt on yet.

"BJ's in town," he said. "He's working on finding Jim."

Jordan nodded, and crawled onto his lap. Joe wrapped his arms around her.

"How are you feeling, babe?" he asked.

"Sore," she said. "But okay, I guess."

Joe nodded. He was thanking God again and again for Jim having not succeeded in raping her. He knew how awful that would have been. Like Midnight, Jordan was very independent and didn't like to feel out of control. Joe knew from experience how Midnight reacted to being out of control, and it wasn't something he wanted to relive with Jordan.

"What happened?" he asked gently.

Jordan was quiet for a moment. Then she started talking, slowly at first but then rushing to get through it.

"When the show was over, I wanted to come back to the hotel.

Jim said I should enjoy a little bit of the Vegas nightlife. I told him that I was tired and wanted to go to the hotel. He kept telling me he could show me a good time. We were in the limo at that point, and I finally just let him have it. I told him that he needed to leave me the hell alone, and that I was the one calling the shots here. That he needed to back the hell off me before I had him fired. I guess that's what did it, because he grabbed me then, and told me that he'd take what he'd been wanting before that happened. I fought him and he hit me. The window between us and the driver was up—Jim had done it—so the driver had no idea what was going on. I managed to get to the button and push it long enough to break the soundproofing seal and screamed at the driver to stop. He stopped, and Jim jumped out and ran off. The driver got me to the hospital."

"God, babe," Joe said, shaking his head. "Had he been coming on to you?"

Jordan hesitated, then nodded. "I just figured he was harmless. He usually backed off when I told him no. But he wouldn't stop last night, no matter what I said."

Joe sighed. "Babe, next time you need to tell me if something like that is going on. Guys like that only respond to real threats."

"I just didn't want to make a big deal out of it," Jordan said, sighing.

"Jordan," Joe said, pulling back to look down at her, his fingertip under her chin. "When it comes to your safety, I want you to make a big deal out of anything that makes you uncomfortable."

She nodded slowly, moving to rest her head against him again.

"So what happens now?" she asked.

"Well," Joe said, "I think you need to cancel a couple of shows to—"

"No," Jordan said, shaking her head. "I'm not going to let that bastard ruin this tour for me."

"Jordan…" Joe said, already sensing the fight rising in her.

"No, Joe," she said, pulling back to look up at him. "I'm not letting him do that to me."

"Okay, okay," Joe said soothingly. "But we need to get you a new security guy, and I don't know how fast that can be accomplished."

"Can't you stay with me?"

"Yes, babe, I can for a few days, until I can get someone in here that I trust."

"I want you," she said succinctly.

"What?"

"I want you to be my bodyguard, Joe."

"Jordan…" he said, shaking his head slowly. "I can't—you know that."

"Why can't you?" she asked, her eyes welling with tears suddenly.

Joe sighed. "You know why."

Jordan pressed her lips together, not wanting to say what she was thinking, knowing it would only make him mad. She leaned against him, burying her face against his shirt again.

Joe held her, sensing her irritation with him and knowing it would only get worse. She was a bad combination of scared, desperate, and untrusting. It wasn't going to make it easy for him to find her a new bodyguard, one she'd accept. He hoped that somehow he could talk to John Machiavelli and convince him to protect her.

***

Elizabeth made her way into the local dealer's mansion. She spoke to one of the guys and told her what she was looking to get.

"Uh, yeah, just go on upstairs, shorty," the man with the gold teeth told her, rubbing his nose with his forefinger. "We'll be up to take care a' you in a bit," he added with a wink.

Elizabeth thought his phrasing was odd, but she nodded, figuring she'd do whatever she needed to in order to get the cocaine she was looking for. She made her way upstairs, entering the room the man had indicated. She wrinkled up her nose at the smell of alcohol and pot and glanced around. It was certainly shabbier than she'd expected, but she noted a nice balcony outside the French doors, so she wandered out there. She stood looking at the view of the pool where half-naked women gyrated to blaring rap music.

Suddenly the doors behind her slammed. Elizabeth jumped, turning around to look at the blonde woman standing there.

"Aren't you supposed to be somewhere else tonight?" Cat asked knowingly.

It took Elizabeth a long moment, and then recognition dawned.

"Oh my God…" she breathed, feeling her insides start to quake uncontrollably. "You work with… Oh my God…"

Cat nodded. "I'm not God, but I'm about to be your one salvation," she said succinctly.

Glancing behind her, Cat verified that no one had come into the room yet.

"Have you done any yet?" she asked.

"What?" Elizabeth asked, hoping to throw the woman off the scent

Cat gave her a narrowed look. "Just tell me if you've done any coke yet," she snapped.

Elizabeth was shocked, but shook her head.

"Good, then you're still able to attend your aunt's party."

"I—" Elizabeth began—she had no intention of going to that

party.

"Oh, like hell," Cat said, rolling her eyes and shaking her head. "You don't show up at that party and you're going to be buying more trouble than even you can handle."

Elizabeth decided it was better to shut up at that point. She knew she was already in deep trouble. This woman worked with Dave; she was a narcotics officer. And here she was in a drug house. She didn't know how much more trouble could she be in, but she didn't want to find out!

Twenty minutes later, they were in Cat's Blazer, driving toward Midnight and Rick's house. Elizabeth was shaking, she was so nervous. She had no idea what Cat would tell her aunt and uncle or how they were going to react. What was this woman's angle? Why had she interfered? Was she that big of a do-gooder that she somehow felt it was her duty? Or was it about her career? That was it! The woman hadn't been a member of Dave's team very long—maybe she was trying to get a promotion. Maybe she was trying to impress Midnight! That had to be it. Just as she turned to Cat to suggest that she could pay her to keep her mouth shut, Cat turned her head toward her. Her look was assessing; Elizabeth didn't understand it.

"I'm not going to tell them," Cat said as she tossed her cigarette out and rolled up the window.

"You're not?" Elizabeth asked, completely stunned.

"No," Cat said, shaking her head. "But I think you'd better think seriously about what you're doing."

"Why's that?" Elizabeth asked, already not liking the look Cat was giving her and starting to feel chastised once again. Were these people always going to try to run her life?

"Your family has a lot of juice in this city," Cat said. "And that can be used against you, and them."

Elizabeth was surprised by that statement. She understood what Cat meant by her family's power, but how could it be used against her?

"What do you mean?" she asked finally, her curiosity getting the better of her. "Used against me how?"

Cat shrugged. "Just that if they choose to, they can put you in rehab and keep you there until the desire to cause trouble is a distant memory."

"They wouldn't do that," Liz said, sounding high and mighty even though the thought made her quiver inside a bit.

"Maybe Mummy wouldn't, sweet cheeks, but you're talking about a Chief of Police now, and not one even I'd mess with."

"My aunt wouldn't do that!" Liz exclaimed, not nearly as sure as she sounded.

"Wanna bet on it?" Cat asked. "If she thinks it's in your best interests, I think you'd be surprised what she or your uncle might do."

Liz sat for a minute, contemplating that thought. Then she felt the need to ask the other question crowding into her mind. "What did you mean, it could be used against them?"

Cat gave her a quelling look. "You think those people back there are boy scouts, little girl? They figure out who you are, and they'll use you to get to them. Is that what you want?"

Liz swallowed convulsively. She hadn't really thought of it that way. But surely this woman was being dramatic.

"They wouldn't dare," she said, really hoping she was right.

Cat said nothing, only shrugging.

"But you're not going to tell them?" Liz asked, wanting to know before she walked into her aunt's party, the purpose of which was to announce that she was running for Attorney General.

"Nope," Cat said, shaking her head.

195

Liz breathed a sigh of relief. She kept silent the rest of the trip. At Rick and Midnight's house, Cat dropped her off.

"You're not coming in?" Liz asked, surprised, still thinking that Cat was just placating her to keep her from trying to run. There had to be some angle in this for her.

"Not my party," Cat said, smiling tightly.

Liz nodded mutely as Cat put the Blazer into gear and drove off. Liz spent the rest of the evening in a sense of unreality. She couldn't believe she'd come so close to getting caught and had managed to escape it.

***

Kevin slipped into bed behind Erin. She lay on her side, her back to him. She'd been asleep for hours; it was 2 a.m. Sliding his arm under her neck carefully, he pulled her back against him gently, leaning down to kiss her neck. She sighed in her sleep, then stirred, finally waking and turning her head to look up at him.

"Hi," she said quietly.

"Hi," he said, leaning down to kiss her.

When their lips parted, he glanced in front of her.

"I see you have a little visitor," he said, grinning.

Erin laughed softly, nodding.

"He said he couldn't sleep," she said, indicating Steven, who was lying snuggled up in front of her.

Kevin shook his head. "He just likes sleeping with Mommy," he said, winking. "Of course, I can't blame him," he added, grinning widely. "I like sleeping with you too."

Erin laughed again. "Let me take him back to bed."

"I'll get him," Kevin said, smiling as he got up.

He gently lifted the sleeping boy and carried him back to his own room. Tucking him into bed, Kevin looked down at Steven. He found that he cared as much for Erin's son as he cared for his own daughter.

Emily was his eight-year-old daughter, by Stacy. Stacy was a drama queen he'd been dating when he was in the police academy in Seattle. It had been with Stacy that his demons, as he called his addictions and problems, had run rampant. Stacy unleashed the fury that he normally held tightly in check. She had a way of pushing every button he had, and for that reason, he avoided her like the plague. It was difficult to do, considering she was the mother of his child. Unfortunately, she also had custody of his child.

Sighing, Kevin turned and left Steven's room. Going back into the bedroom, he sat down, taking off his boots, his shirt, and finally his jeans. Erin lay on the bed, watching him move around the room. Finally, he turned to her, getting into bed and pulling her close. Their lips met, and as usual he ignited her passion for him.

Erin had just gotten up the next morning to get ready for work when the phone rang.

She picked it up quickly, to keep from waking Kevin, although he stirred immediately.

"Hello?" Erin queried.

"Who's this?" asked a woman sharply.

"This is Erin," Erin replied, already fairly sure who she was talking to.

"Oh, the chick shacked up with Kevin," Stacy said sarcastically. "Is he there?"

"He's here, but he's asleep currently," Erin replied evenly.

"Well, wake him up, Erin."

Erin took a deep breath, wanting to tell the woman off for her attitude, wanting to say something about the fact that although Stacy didn't work, Kevin did, and needed sleep. She knew it wouldn't help to cuss Stacy out; the woman didn't listen anyway, and Erin also knew Stacy was likely to use any set-down Erin gave her against Kevin. It was bad enough that she withheld Emily from him regularly; Erin knew she couldn't further jeopardize his chances at seeing her.

"Please hold on for just a moment," Erin said in her best receptionist voice.

Kevin had rolled over by this time, so Erin sat down next to him, touching him on the shoulder.

"Hon," she said softly. "It's Stacy."

Kevin growled in his throat, abhorring conversations with his ex-girlfriend. Erin laughed softly and handed him the phone as he sat up. She went back to the bathroom, not wanting to eavesdrop on their conversation. Although she couldn't help but overhear anyway, at least his side of the conversation.

"What is it, Stacy?" Kevin asked without preamble. He listened for a moment, a scowl on his face. It deepened as he listened to her. "What the hell happens to the seven hundred bucks I send you every month?" he asked crossly. "Yeah, right, I'm sure, okay," he said, sounding far from convinced by her answer. He listened again for a bit, his brows drawing together in utter disbelief. "When?" he asked sharply. "That's tomorrow, Stacy," he said, glowering now. "You didn't know about this before now? Yeah, and I can say 'bullshit' in about ten languages," he said, narrowing his eyes.

Erin glanced over as he held the phone away from his ear. She could hear Stacy screaming at him. She walked back over to the bed, sitting down facing him. His eyes connected with hers as he shook his head slowly. When Stacy had quieted, he put the phone to his ear again.

"I'll be on the plane tonight," he said. "Have her ready."

He hung up without another word.

"What's up, babe?" Erin asked, knowing it must be bad if he had to travel to Seattle.

Kevin gave a short, sarcastic laugh, shaking his head in disbelief.

"She's managed to get herself into trouble again. She has a bench warrant out for her arrest, for passing bad checks."

"Nice," Erin said, knowing that Kevin busted his butt sending the woman seven to nine hundred dollars a month to help support Emily, much more than any court would have ever awarded Stacy.

"Yeah," Kevin said, irritated. "But apparently they finally caught up with her, and they're sticking her ass in jail tomorrow."

"Tomorrow?" Erin asked, stunned.

"Yeah."

"What about Emily?"

"Oh, I'm just supposed to come right up there and pick her up," Kevin said sardonically.

"Do we have to ever take her back?" Erin asked, her eyes gleaming evilly.

"Ninety days," Kevin said. "But her 'lawyer' is filing an appeal."

"Let's hope her lawyer is as inept as she is," Erin said, voicing her disregard for Stacy as a mother.

Kevin had told Erin plenty about Stacy's parental abilities. Stacy rarely cooked, she almost never cleaned, and she spent more time competing with her daughter for attention than anything else. Kevin often worried how well Emily was really taken care of. He'd always wished that Erin could be her mother. Now he was going to have the perfect chance to see what things would be like.

Erin was smiling. She was thrilled to have a chance to finally meet Kevin's daughter. She'd heard a lot about Emily from him, but he'd never dared take Erin with him on a visit to see his daughter, knowing that Stacy would blow a gasket. Stacy was extremely territorial, and she still considered Kevin her territory. Regardless of the fact that she'd left at a time in his life when he needed her the most, when he was recovering from the accident that had almost killed him. When he'd been diagnosed as an alcoholic, Stacy had taken Emily and left him. It had hurt him immeasurably.

"Oh my God," Erin said suddenly.

"What?" Kevin asked, already grinning.

"I can't go to work today," she said, her mind racing.

"Why not?" he asked, looking mystified.

"Hey, buddy. I'm about to have another baby—I have to prepare."

Kevin laughed, leaning forward and taking her in his arms and hugging her close. He knew she'd take it well that they were suddenly going to have a second child in their household for a while. She was just that way. Always willing to do what it took to make him happy. Always willing to go out of her way to help him through whatever he was going through.

Erin spent the day getting the extra bedroom ready for Emily. Kevin had left his credit card with her, instructing her to use it to buy whatever she felt the room needed. Erin vacillated at spending his money, but he insisted, stating that it was his daughter and he wanted her to have whatever Erin felt she needed in her room to make her comfortable.

Kevin spent his day trying to tie up as many loose ends as possible. When he got into the department, he went straight to Dave's office to see him. He stood in the doorway until the older man looked up.

"What's up, Mace?"

"I'm going to need some time off."

Dave nodded, motioning to the chairs in front of his desk.

Kevin sat down, stretching his legs out in front of him.

"So what's going on?" Dave asked.

"My ex called this morning," Kevin said. "She's being taken into custody in Seattle for writing hot checks."

Dave nodded, waiting for Kevin to continue.

"She needs me to take care of Emily for her while she's in jail," Kevin said, already feeling irritated again at the fact that Stacy could be so irresponsible, as well as giving him such short notice.

"When is she going in?"

"Tomorrow," Kevin said, his tone reflecting the fact that he knew it was a ridiculous situation.

"Nothing like fair warning, huh?" Dave said, grinning wryly.

"That's my ex for you," Kevin replied sourly.

"So how long do you need?"

"Well, I have to fly out tonight to get Emily. And then I'd like a week to make sure she's acclimated, make arrangements for day care and stuff like that."

Dave nodded. "You talked to Stevie about what you'll do on your case?"

"Yeah," Kevin confirmed. "We'll meet with them today, and drop the information that we're running back to Vegas to take care of some business."

Dave nodded. "Sounds good."

"So am I good to go?"

"Of course. You have to take care of your home and family," Dave said reasonably. "That's what we work for."

Kevin nodded, grinning. He appreciated a boss who understood that ideal. The people he'd worked for in the past weren't so under-standing, thinking that the job should always come first. Standing up, Kevin extended his hand to Dave.

"Thanks, man," he said sincerely. "I appreciate it."

"Have a safe trip," Dave said, smiling.

That afternoon, when Kevin got home to get ready for the trip to Se-attle, Erin showed him what she'd done in the extra bedroom. He was stunned. She'd turned the stark space into a warm, cozy room. She'd used things that had been in his garage, items that he'd put out there to be disposed of later. She'd had to go out and buy some things, like a comforter, sheets, and curtains. The theme she'd chosen was but-terflies, which was Emily's current passion. Erin had even managed to find a small desk for her at a used store. She'd brought it home and cleaned it up. It sat in the corner of the room with a seventeen-inch TV and DVD player on it. She'd also managed to find a few DVDs that she thought Emily might like, remembering that Kevin had told her Emily was into a lot of the Disney movies.

"And I'm sure Steven wouldn't mind sharing the ones that he has too," Erin said, smiling as she showed Kevin the little stash.

She also showed him the coloring books, activity books, pens, pencils, crayons, notebooks, and backpack she'd gotten for Emily.

"I also checked with Steven's school, and they said that we can enroll her there at least while she's here—that way she doesn't lose any of her schooling. I went ahead and got the paperwork, and filled out what I knew. Oh, and I checked with Sarah, and she said she'd be happy to pick Emily up from school when she picks up Steven, and watch them both until I get off work."

Kevin was blown away. She had accomplished so much, and

with so much thought as to what Emily would like. Even the back-pack and notebooks Erin had bought her had butterflies on them. He was speechless, finally taking her in his arms and kissing her deeply.

"Thank you," he whispered against her lips.

"You don't have to thank me, Kevin," she said, hugging him. "I'm so excited about her being here with us, I can hardly wait till you get back with her."

Kevin looked down at Erin for a long moment, staring deeply into her eyes. He was ever astounded at her ability to love. She didn't care who it was, what their situation was, or who they were. If she felt they deserved love, she gave it unconditionally. She'd never even met his daughter, and yet she was knocking herself out to make sure Emily was going to be happy with them, even if it was only for ninety days or less.

Kevin shook his head, unable to fathom how Erin did all that she did.

"What?" she asked, smiling at him, pleased that he seemed happy with what she'd done. She hadn't even told him yet how little she'd spent. She'd found almost everything either on sale or on clear-ance.

"You just amaze me sometimes," he said honestly.

"Is that bad?" she asked, grinning.

"No," he said, shaking his head. "It's wonderful."

Leaning down, he kissed her lips, pulling her closer. "You do so much for me," he said, moving his lips to her ear, kissing it. "I don't know how I ever lived without you."

Erin smiled, thrilled to hear him say that. "You did okay," she said shyly.

"No," he said, shaking his head and pulling back to look down at her. "I got by. I don't think I truly lived until I met you."

Erin hugged him, unable to think of the right thing to say but deeply happy that he felt that way. She knew that his life hadn't been filled with much love, and she was glad that she could make him feel so good now.

"What time does your plane leave?" she asked after a few long moments.

"At six," he said, glancing at his watch. He had three hours.

"Okay," she said, nodding. "I'll go pick Steven up and come home and make some dinner. I know you won't eat in Seattle."

Kevin grinned. She knew him well. She knew he'd avoid seeing his family, since there was always some kind of scene when he went there. So she knew he'd check into a hotel room, go over to pick Emily up in the morning, and then head back to San Diego.

"Why don't I go get Steven?" Kevin said. "That way you don't have to rush with dinner."

Erin thought about it, then nodded. "That would be great, if you have time."

"I have time. Besides, I want to talk to him a little bit about what's going on."

Erin smiled fondly. She loved that Kevin treated her son so well. Steven's real father had absolutely nothing to do with him. Kevin gave Steven attention, guidance, and affection, something the boy craved more than anything, especially from a male role model.

When Donovan had moved Erin and Steven into his house to protect them from Tyler, Erin's abusive ex-husband, Steven had been in heaven. He'd enjoyed having a man around to buddy around with. Unfortunately, Donovan, although very nice to Steven, had nothing in common with the child. Steven had enjoyed being around Donovan, but not near as much as he loved being with Kevin. Kevin thought nothing of getting down on the floor with Steven and playing with Matchbox cars, creating networks of roads or freeways for them to drive on. Steven ate up every second of the time Kevin spent with him, and Erin loved Kevin all the more for doing it.

A half hour later, Kevin drove back toward the house in his Durango.

"Steven," he said. "I wanted to talk to you."

Steven looked over at Kevin, worried. He was always worried that Kevin and his mother would break up, like Erin and Donovan had, and Kevin would leave them. It was something that he thought about a lot. Kevin noted the look on the boy's face, and wanted to reassure him quickly.

"It's about my daughter," he said. "Remember we told you that Emily is the same age as you?"

"Uh-huh," Steven said, nodding.

"And you know she lives with her mommy in Seattle, right?"

"Right."

"Well, her mommy has to go away for a little while, so Emily is going to come stay with us while she's gone."

Kevin paused, giving Steven a few moments to digest that information.

"She's gonna live with us?" Steven asked.

"For a little while," Kevin said. "Does that bother you?"

Steven said nothing for a moment, then shook his head. "Is she gonna stay in my room?"

"No," Kevin said, shaking his head. "Your mom got the extra room all ready for her today."

"Does she like cars?" Steven asked, addressing his chief interest.

"No, I don't think she likes cars," Kevin said, smiling. "But you can show her your cars, and maybe you can get her interested in them."

205

"Do I have to share my cars with her?" Steven asked suspiciously.

Kevin laughed, shaking his head. "I don't think so, little man. I think she's into butterflies, so I don't think you'll be losing too many cars to her."

Steven nodded, looking very serious. "She can be in my class at school."

"Would you help her in class if she needs it?"

"Yeah. I can show her math and everything, it's easy."

Kevin grinned. "Easy for you, maybe. I can't make heads or tails of it."

Steven grinned too. "I'm smart."

"Yes, you are," Kevin confirmed. "Smarter than any of the other kids in the school."

"Yeah." Steven nodded. "Well, except for Ginny, but she's a total geek anyway."

"Careful," Kevin said, winking at Steven. "The geeks usually turn out to be the prettiest girls in school at some point."

"Girls are gross," Steven said, making a face.

"Your mom's not gross," Kevin said, grinning.

"She's not a girl," Steven chided. "She's a woman."

"Right, but she was a girl once."

"Then she grewed out of it," Steven said logically.

"She grew out of it, not grewed," Kevin corrected gently, knowing that Erin wanted Steven to speak properly as often as possible.

"She grew out of it."

"Right," Kevin confirmed. "She did indeed grow out of being a geeky girl."

Steven nodded his agreement.

"So you're okay with Emily staying with us?" Kevin asked.

"Is she a geek?"

"No, she's not a geek, I promise," Kevin said, grinning.

"Good."

Kevin laughed, shaking his head. Kid logic was always inscrutable.

Later that evening, Steven and Erin drove Kevin to the airport. They walked him to the gate. Onlookers noticed the rather incongruous-looking threesome. Kevin was a dangerous-looking man, with his shoulder-length brown hair pulled back at the top, earrings in both ears. It wasn't so much his appearance that had people watching him, but his presence that they could feel. He had a wariness about him that kept him apart from most of the population. He liked it that way. They stayed away from him, he stayed away from them.

Then there was Erin, with her open, happy smile, beautiful blond hair, and blue eyes. She walked along next to Kevin, holding Steven's hand and looking totally happy. Beside her walked Steven, who, much like his mother, was a happy, smiling child. People tried to figure out where Kevin fit into that picture. Kevin knew that; he could see it on their faces. He grinned, knowing it just didn't look right. He didn't care.

When his flight was called for boarding, he turned to Erin, leaning down to kiss her quickly. Kevin was never one to be overly affectionate in public; Erin knew this. Kevin knelt down in front of Steven.

"I'll see you tomorrow, little man," he said seriously.

"I'll see you tomorrow, big man," Steven replied, his face serious as well.

It was their "cop" voice that they were using. It was a game they'd played since the first time Kevin had met Steven. Steven had asked him to produce his badge, and Kevin had done so, using his best cop voice.

"You're bringing Emily back, right?" Steven asked.

"Yep," Kevin said, nodding.

"Okay," Steven replied, nodding too.

Kevin stood up, looking down at Erin. "I'll call you when I know what flight I'm coming back on."

"Okay, be safe," she said, smiling up at him.

"Around Stacy?" Kevin queried doubtfully.

Erin laughed.

Kevin turned and got on the plane. Erin and Steven watched him take off.

CHAPTER 8

Donovan drove up to the hotel his mother and father were staying in. As he did, he saw his father standing outside, smoking. Seeing his father again triggered a number of memories all at once. Donovan parked the Mustang and got out. He found that he was actually about the same height as his father, who he'd always imagined to be so big.

John Curtis looked at his son, unable to believe that little Donovan had grown up so much. Diane had been right—he'd turned into a very handsome man. John found that he couldn't think of a thing to say to his son, however. It had been so long in coming, this meeting with Donovan. John had thought of a million things to say, but it was one thing to imagine how things would go and another to actually work up the nerve to say any of it.

Without any other ideas coming to mind, John walked up to Donovan's car, looking it over. He touched the polished black fender, smoothing his hand over it appreciatively. He looked over the dual exhaust.

"Ponyboy?" John asked, reading the license plate on the Mustang.

"My nickname," Donovan said.

John looked at him, waiting for the explanation. Donovan shrugged.

"It's from a movie called *The Outsiders*. There was a character in it named Ponyboy Curtis. That combined with the fact that I love

Mustangs—you know, with the pony on the front. The guys in high school started calling me it, and it just stuck."

John nodded, grinning. "It's different."

"Yeah," Donovan agreed. "You ready to go?"

John nodded, still looking a bit uncomfortable. Donovan unlocked the car and gestured for his father to get in on the passenger side. John got in, looking around the interior of the car. He noted it was immaculate, all leather. His son had excellent taste.

Donovan started the car and pulled out of the space, glancing over at his father as he drove out of the parking lot. John looked distinctly uncomfortable. Donovan wasn't sure how to make him feel more comfortable.

There was a long silence while Donovan drove, not even sure where they were headed. His father had called him the day before, asking if they could get together. Since the next day was Saturday, Donovan had agreed. They'd arranged a time to meet, and that was all.

"Your mother tells me you cook," John said after a few long minutes.

"Yeah," Donovan said, grinning. "I kind of followed a girl into the culinary academy."

John grinned, nodding wisely. "Girls will get you into the strangest things, sometimes."

Donovan laughed.

"Jay's extremely happy I did, though," he said.

"That's your wife, right?" John asked, still astounded that "little Donovan" had a wife.

"Yeah, Jeanie."

"She doesn't cook?"

"Well," Donovan said, grimacing, "the last time I let her cook, she just about destroyed one of my best saucepans, so I try to avoid letting her do that."

John laughed, shaking his head. "She is lucky to have you, then."

"I'll let her know you think so," Donovan said. "Speaking of which, I need to make a quick stop at the store—do you mind?"

"Not at all," John said, interested in seeing his son in all settings.

Donovan turned into the grocery store. Both men walked inside. John noticed many female heads turning to look at Donovan. He was further intrigued as he noticed what Donovan bought. Nothing he picked up was in either a box or a can. He picked up fresh fruit, vegetables, meat. He also grabbed flour, sugar, white and brown rice. Nothing he chose was processed. He was indeed serious about his cooking. John also noticed he spent a great deal of time picking out fresh herbs and seasonings.

John watched Donovan in silence, feeling a sense of unreality. Here he was with his thirty-two-year-old son, who he hadn't seen since he was eleven. Now they were shopping, and he was watching his son choose things he himself would never have known about. John was a macaroni and cheese, TV dinner, Spam kind of guy. He could see that Diane was right; Donovan simply oozed class now.

He also noticed that Donovan was an extremely polite man. Whenever he brushed past someone, he murmured, "Excuse me." When he addressed people, he did so politely, saying "Please," "Thank you," and "May I." He also articulated his requests in a way that showed he was not only educated but a complete gentleman.

Having been a construction worker's son, and further raised by his construction worker brother, Donovan being such a sophisticated man was a shock. Diane had told John that Donovan was nothing like the men in his family, that she was fairly sure it was the influence of Joe Sinclair.

John realized he owed Joe Sinclair a definite debt of gratitude. He and Diane had visited with Randy the day before, and found that their daughter had become a beautiful, intelligent, confident, and gentle woman. She was running a center that took in children, utilizing her bachelor's degree in child psychology to work with children displaced during police actions. Both Diane and he had been astounded at how shy, quiet Randy had blossomed into such a bright, vivacious woman. Once again, they were sure it had everything to do with Joe Sinclair. They were dismayed by the information that Randy and Joe had divorced the year before. Randy assured them that Joe was still her very best friend, and around all the time.

They'd also been enchanted by Randy and Joe's children, JT and Kat. Both kids were beautiful and very bright. They had seemed thrilled to find that they did indeed have grandparents. Apparently Joe's parents had been killed when he was twenty years old. So John and Diane were their only true grandparents. Randy had assured them that they would have an opportunity to meet Joe when he returned home. She explained that he was currently handling an emergency with his girlfriend. John and Diane had been surprised to hear her talk rather fondly of Joe, and not seem at all bothered by the fact that he had a girlfriend that he was "taking care of" at that point.

When they got out of the store, Donovan put the groceries in the car. As he went to put the cart in the cart return, he noticed an elderly man attempting to disengage a cart from the one in front of it. He was having a hard time. Donovan offered his assistance, freeing the cart for him. The older man thanked Donovan profusely, commenting on what a "nice young man" he was. John looked on with a proud grin.

Once in the car, John glanced over at Donovan. "Do you always do things like that?"

"Like what?"

"With the cart for that man."

Donovan shrugged, then grimaced. "Yeah, I guess I do. That's why I get called 'the boy scout' a lot by the team."

"The team?"

"Yeah, the team I work with at the department. Rogue Squadron is what we're called."

"And they call you a boy scout?"

"Yeah," Donovan said, grinning. He shrugged. "My cover is usually the clean-cut nice guy, the good boy playing at being bad."

"It seems to fit," John said. "But is that bad?"

"It's not the common definition for a narc," Donovan said, not sounding like he minded much.

"And that's bad?"

Donovan chuckled. "Well, it works for me. I just have to work with guys like Blue and Mace, who have totally different styles."

"What are their styles?" John asked, curious about the work that Donovan did.

"Well, Blue looks like he just stepped out of a movie, so he usually uses his looks to hook them and plays up the rich, successful dealer angle. And Mace looks like a very dangerous, hardcore dealer, with a major undercurrent of violence in him, so that's his angle."

John nodded. "Does your… cover," he began, trying to use the right word, "work as well as theirs does?"

"Yeah, it works," Donovan said. "They never expect me to be a narc—if anything, they think they're going to cheat me out of something. It never occurs to them that I might be busting them later."

John grinned, thinking it was pretty ingenious to use what you had naturally as a tool against people you were trying to arrest. If you weren't trying to pretend to be something you weren't, you'd be less likely to make a mistake. Donovan used what he had to do his job.

"Your team sounds very interesting," he said.

"Oh, that's just the guys," Donovan said, grinning.

"That's right. Your mother said your wife is a narcotics officer too."

"Yeah," Donovan confirmed. "So is Blue's wife."

"Really? You're all on the same team?"

"Yeah," Donovan said. "It just kind of worked out that way. Jeanie and I worked a case together, and we ended up needing Blue's help. He brought his then girlfriend Stevie in on it with him. The four of us worked well together, so Midnight made us a team. Mace joined us a few months later, and now we just got Cat."

"Okay, so what is your wife's cover?"

"Jeanie's got this very sexy but innocent look about her. Guys never think she's a narc—she's too beautiful—so she usually plays up the sweet, sexy but hands-off angle. Men fall all over themselves to please her."

"And the other two?"

"Well, Stevie is a very tough, very independent woman who's got a body that doesn't quit. She's sexy to the extreme and uses every ounce of it to get men to deal with her. Then there's Cat, who's brought a whole other angle to the work," Donovan said, hesitating, not sure if his father would be shocked when he heard about her.

"A whole other angle?" John asked, noting the way Donovan said it.

"Yeah," Donovan said, grinning. "She's bisexual, so she's able to play both the men and the women. She even laid a kiss on Jeanie last week, to make sure they were invited to a dealer's party, knowing that would get the guys' interest piqued enough to invite them."

John's eyes did indeed widen, and Donovan chuckled.

214

John cleared his throat pointedly, shaking his head. "It sounds like you definitely have an interesting group there."

"Oh yeah." Donovan nodded. "That's why we fit the name Rogue Squadron—we don't do anything like everyone else. We're kind of the ones that are out there on the edge."

John nodded. "Now, Midnight—that's the chief, isn't it?"

"Yeah."

"We read a lot about her," John said, then looked at his son more closely. "We also read that you were shot a few years back."

Donovan looked surprised for a moment, but then nodded. "I was shot twice, actually."

"We read that. But you recovered alright, right?"

"Yeah. My shoulder still gives me trouble every so often, and then I messed my back up on that same case a few months later."

"How?" John asked, always astounded at what a dangerous line of work Donovan had chosen.

"I was caught by an explosion and thrown through a plate-glass window."

"That was the explosion they thought killed the chief, right?"

Donovan looked over at his father for a long moment, then nodded slowly. "You two did read a lot, didn't you?"

John shrugged helplessly. "We did our best to find out how you kids were doing, without intruding on your lives."

Donovan grinned. "Making national headlines certainly helped that, didn't it?"

John chuckled, nodding. He was surprised at how easygoing Donovan was being. He'd expected things to be strained with his son, considering the past that they had. Diane had told John what an astounding man Donovan had become, and Donovan was proving that over and over again.

Donovan had been driving toward his and Jeanie's house as they talked. He pulled into their driveway as John looked over at him.

"Donovan," John said cautiously. "I wanted to talk to you, well, about—"

"Dad," Donovan said, putting his hand up in a halting gesture. "You don't have to say anything. Mom explained already."

"I know she did," John said. "But that doesn't relieve me of my need to tell you how sorry I am for what I did to you. I know that's not a lot of consolation," he went on, sighing in frustration. "But you need to know that I've hated myself for years for what I did. I was just too afraid to face you and tell you how sorry I was."

Donovan nodded, swallowing convulsively at the lump in his throat.

"Dad," he said, his voice coming out a bit hoarse because his throat was constricting with emotion at that point. "I think you need to know that I don't feel like you ruined my life. I think that in spite of what happened, I've turned out okay."

"You've turned out more than okay, Donovan," John assured him. "You've become a very admirable man. I know my genes had nothing to do with that. You should know that I know I owe a huge debt to Joe Sinclair for the way you and your brother and sister have turned out."

Donovan nodded, agreeing with his father on that. "Joe's a pretty great guy."

"So I understand."

They were both silent for a few moments. Donovan glanced out the front windshield, contemplating whether or not he should ask the question he wanted to. Finally he took a deep breath and plunged ahead.

"Can I ask you a question?"

John nodded.

"What did you hope to accomplish by coming back?" Donovan asked. "I mean, why now?"

John nodded slowly, having wondered when Donovan would ask that question.

"The truth is, Donovan, I've wanted to do this for a few years now. Ever since I got a handle on what caused me to be so violent. You know, in my day, people just had tempers—they weren't 'manic depressive' or 'psychotic' or any of that. There were no 'cures,' there were no answers. We just were the way we were.

"But once they told me that it wasn't something that I really could have controlled, other than to get out of the situation, I started feeling like I needed to at least explain it to you. I guess I really wanted to vindicate myself, you know, tell you it wasn't really my fault. But I know it was my fault. I know that at the time I was just so furious I couldn't control myself, but I think if I'd really given a damn, I would have tried harder. It was just so much easier in those days. Kids weren't abused, they were 'disciplined'—there was no line drawn that said when discipline turned into abuse. I kidded myself so many times, saying that I never crossed that line. But I did, I know I did, and for that I'm sorry."

John's eyes searched Donovan's, hoping that he was making some kind of sense. He and Diane had talked about it over and over again. She'd made him understand that no matter what they told themselves back then, it had still hurt Donovan immeasurably, and for that reason, John shouldn't expect Donovan to forgive him.

Donovan looked down at his hands for a moment, then up at his father.

"I learned way back," Donovan began, "that you can either be a victim or you can accept things and move on with your life. Joe was

217

key as an example of that. He took something that happened to him, a tragedy that had almost ruined his life, and used it to do something good. I don't know if it was the knowledge of what happened to him or if I just knew I couldn't live with playing the victim, but I decided to move on with my life and forget about what happened.

"Now, knowing why it happened, knowing that it wasn't something that you just chose to do to relieve your own stress, I can understand the situation better. Another thing I've learned is that it's very easy to assume how you'd be, or how you'd react if it were you. But the thing is, you never know how you'd be in a situation until you're in it. And you can't know how someone was feeling, or what they were thinking, or what was happening to them psychologically at the time of an incident. You can't be in their shoes, so it's pretty hard to make a judgment as to what you would have done in the same situation."

"What are you saying, Donovan?" John asked anxiously.

"I'm saying that I forgive you for what happened twenty years ago, Dad," Donovan said. "No matter what the reason, no matter what you did, it's over. I've gone on with my life. I'm happy, well adjusted, and I don't feel like it really had that much effect on my life."

John blinked a few times, unable to believe what he'd just heard. Donovan forgave him? It was far more than he'd even dared to hope for—he'd only been hoping that Donovan would at least allow him to explain. He'd never thought for a moment that Donovan would not only do that but actually absolve him of his sins.

"That surprises you," Donovan noted.

"Yes," John said honestly. "Your mother is right. You are one incredible young man."

Donovan grinned, incredibly pleased to hear his father say that. It was amazing what biology could do to you. He hadn't seen this man in twenty years, and yet his father's obvious pride in what his son had grown up to be made Donovan feel better than he could ever have thought it would.

"Come inside and meet Jeanie," he said, nodding toward the house.

"Gladly," John said, feeling the weight of years of guilt lift off his shoulders.

They went inside and found Jeanie sitting at the computer in their home office, typing away. When she heard them come in, she turned around with a huge smile, her eyes shining brightly. She could see by the smile on Donovan's face that things had gone well with his father. She was very happy for him.

"Jay, this is my dad. Dad, this is Jeanie."

Jeanie got up and walked over to them, extending her hand to John.

"It's very nice to meet you," she said, smiling.

"It's nice to meet you too," John said, taking her hand.

"I see where Donovan gets his height from," Jeanie said, grinning.

John laughed. "I think he's got an inch or two on me now. How tall are you, Donovan?"

"Six two."

"Yep. You're an inch taller than me," John said with a smile.

"And you always seemed so big to me before," Donovan said, his grin wide.

"You were the skinniest kid…" John said, trailing off as he shook his head.

"Thank God you fixed that," Jeanie said, poking Donovan in the ribs.

"Don't like skinny, huh?" Donovan asked.

"Nah, I like my man with a little meat on his bones," Jeanie said, winking up at him.

"Wow," John said, having noticed Jeanie's wedding ring when she poked Donovan. "That *is* a beautiful ring. Diane told me that your ring made hers look like it came out of a bubblegum machine."

Jeanie smiled brightly. "Donovan probably cleaned out his savings on this," she said, giving Donovan a narrowed look.

"Don't start that again," Donovan said. "It wasn't that much."

"Bull," Jeanie said, giving him a haughty look. "I know you."

"And?"

"And you never do anything halfway, Donovan Jacob Curtis, and I know you didn't on this, so just quit trying to BS to me."

Donovan grinned, refusing to reply. John watched the exchange, enjoying that they got along so well. Diane had told him that Donovan was very much in love with his wife. John could see that just by the way they looked at each other. There was no hesitation in their communication style—they said what came to mind. It was obvious that they were used to teasing each other a lot.

They unloaded the groceries from the car, and Donovan made the three of them lunch. John found out that Donovan was indeed a good cook. Even on short notice, he whipped up a smoked bacon and Gorgonzola salad, with mixed greens, beets, slivers of carrots, chunks of tomatoes, and sliced onions with a creamy vinaigrette dressing. He even had fresh French bread he'd just bought at the store, as well as the perfect wine to complement the meal. John was duly impressed, as Diane had been the week before. Donovan was indeed a very classy man.

***

Elizabeth drove up to her usual connection at the mansion in La Jolla. Getting out of the car, she looked around surreptitiously. She didn't notice the dark blue Blazer that had stopped farther up the street; she also didn't notice the fairly dangerous-looking young men watching her get out of her car.

She walked up to the door and was given entrance by Willy. He flashed a toothy grin at her. "You get the master suite tonight, baby girl," he said, making a sucking sound through his teeth as he ran a lecherous hand down her arm.

Elizabeth pulled away slightly, shuddering at the contact. Something in her head told her something was off, but she needed the drugs, and this wasn't the time to get antsy. She told herself to just go with it, and laughed off his looks and touch. She then made her way upstairs, assuming correctly where the master suite was by the opulent double doors at the end of the long hallway. Letting herself inside, she looked around. The room was as opulent as the doors, with a huge bed in the center draped with black velvet coverings and huge gold-covered eagles on top of the posts. Everywhere she looked was gold and mirrors. She looked at herself in a mirror, seeing how small she seemed compared to the huge room.

Before long the doors opened, and in walked four men. They all wore baggy jeans and tank tops or team jerseys with a number of chains around their necks and rings on their fingers. Elizabeth grew uneasy immediately and started to leave.

"Where you goin' shorty?" one man said, his gold teeth gleaming in the darkened room.

"Yeah, the party's just getting started," another man said, the tattoo over his eye, which read *THUG*, twitching as he blinked rapidly.

"I... I, um... I made a mistake..." she stammered, moving to leave again, but yet another man got in her way and stopped her, holding his hands up to stave her off.

"Whoa, whoa, hot little mama, you don't need to go nowhere," he said, reaching for her.

To Elizabeth's dismay, the man started moving forward to touch her. She backed up immediately. Before she knew it, another man was reaching out to touch her ass. She jumped at the contact and changed direction. Suddenly she was in a corner, and both men were looming over her.

"I don't think you understand," Elizabeth said, using her most reasonable tone.

"What's to get? You want what we got and we gonna give it to you," the larger of the men sneered.

Elizabeth thought about screaming, but then she remembered she was in a drug dealer's home, and who was going to help her? Certainly no one here. She felt sick suddenly, a cold tingle running down her spine. They were going to have sex with her—there was no doubt about that. The question was whether or not she'd fight them. But if she got the drugs…

Suddenly there was a commotion. Elizabeth couldn't see what was happening, but she heard various phrases like "What the fuck?" As the two men in front of her parted, she saw Catalina walking toward her, giving her a "shame on you" look she didn't understand.

"Honey, honey, honey," Cat chided. "I told you you can't be doing this right now." Cat glanced at the men, rolling her eyes. "Guys, trust me, you don't want to be tapping that ass," she said with a wink, reaching out to take Elizabeth's hand and pull her out of the corner.

"How the fuck do you know what we want?" said the taller of the two guys, reaching out to grab Elizabeth.

"Well," Cat said, chuckling snidely, "unless you want to get

222

yourself a nasty case of the clap, I don't think you do."

"The what?" the other man chimed in.

"Clap, honey, clap," Cat said, pulling Elizabeth to her again and putting her arm around her shoulders. "My girl got herself into a mess at a party we were at in Soho last month, and the doctor said she's not supposed to play for a while, but she just can't seem to help it."

Elizabeth said nothing, burying her face against Cat's shoulder. She was terrified, and praying that what Cat was saying would get her out of this.

"She's got somethin'?" the first guy said, sounding disgusted.

"Oh yeah," Cat said, her smile knowing. "But if you really think you want her…"

"No, no, fuck no," the second guy said, stepping back as if he could get whatever Elizabeth had by proximity.

Cat glanced down at Elizabeth, her grin still in place.

"Come on, baby girl, let me take you home. Did you at least make your score?" Cat asked solicitously.

Elizabeth shook her head.

Cat looked at both men. "I need to get her down to the man. She gets really annoying when she doesn't get her stuff, ya know?"

"Yeah, yeah, go," the first guy said, gesturing for them to leave.

Cat didn't waste time. She walked downstairs and marched Elizabeth right out the front door and to the Blazer. Elizabeth was shaking badly by this time. Cat put her in on the passenger side and got in on the driver's side.

"Did you take anything while you were there?" Cat asked.

Elizabeth shook her head, her eyes downcast. She was still dealing with what had almost happened. Cat nodded, then started the Blazer with a roar. She drove off, heading down the hill. Elizabeth

223

was silent for a long while, huddling against the passenger door.

"You're going to tell them, aren't you?" she finally asked, her voice tremulous.

Cat looked over at her, her eyes searching. "Is that what you want me to do?"

Elizabeth looked back at her for a long moment, and finally shook her head.

"Are you sure about that?" Cat asked.

"What do you mean?"

"I mean, you knew I had you nailed, yet you went back. Why?"

"I…" Elizabeth started, answers racing in her head, any number of smartass answers about how she always did what she wanted and no one told her what to do. But none of that was the truth, so she spoke the truth. "I can't stop," she said simply.

"Do you want to?"

Elizabeth debated her answer for a while. She knew she should want to stop, but part of her really loved the feeling of totally letting go of everything when she was high. She eventually shrugged by way of an answer.

"You don't know?" Cat asked evenly.

"I don't know," Elizabeth said, raising her chin a bit as her pride kicked in.

Cat nodded slowly, her look considering. "Do you have any idea what you were headed for tonight?"

"What do you mean?"

"Have you ever heard the term 'gang bang'?"

Elizabeth's eyes widened as she nodded.

"Well, you were going to be the entertainment tonight, sweetheart, the main course," Cat said pointedly.

Elizabeth swallowed, her look pensive. She knew Cat was right.

224

She'd known what was going to happen, but what scared her more was that part of her was willing as long as she got the drugs she wanted—what was one or two more men she'd had sex with? It didn't seem to matter anymore. None of them did.

Cat narrowed her eyes at the younger woman, knowing she wasn't getting through to her. "It wasn't just those two, little girl," she said. "It was half the men in that house."

Elizabeth's head came up, her look cynical now.

"Don't believe me?" Cat asked.

"No."

"Want me to take you back there, so they can all get their piece of you before they beat you to within an inch of your life, if not just kill you so you can't report them?"

Again Elizabeth's eyes widened, frightened. Even so, she was all bravado when she said, "They wouldn't have," shaking her head. She figured Cat was just trying to scare her.

Cat nodded, giving a short, sarcastic laugh. "Tell that to the Latina we found last week who'd been gang raped and left for dead. She was ripped from front to back. She almost bled to death because they'd raped her so many times. Interestingly enough, she was found on the beach just below that house. But hey, what do I know? I'll take you back there right now, and you can take your chances," she said, swinging the Blazer into a U-turn at the next light.

"No!" Elizabeth exclaimed, still not sure if she should believe Cat or not, but the mental picture she had just painted was enough to scare her.

Cat turned the vehicle around again.

Elizabeth thought about what could really have happened. She really hadn't thought beyond those two men, but maybe that was the problem—maybe she was more addicted than she realized.

"I can't quit," she told the other woman.

Cat looked over at her. Elizabeth wanted to put on a brave face, but she just couldn't do it at that moment.

"Do you only do coke?" Cat asked gently.

Elizabeth hesitated, not sure what all she should admit to, but decided to be honest and shook her head slowly.

"What else?" Cat asked, her tone still gentle.

"I've tried a lot of things, even meth," Elizabeth said, cowed.

Cat nodded, grimacing. "Do you really want to quit, Elizabeth?"

Elizabeth blinked a couple of times, her face drawn and serious. The addiction wanted her to say "Hell no," but she knew that she was headed down a dangerous path, so again she nodded.

"Well," Cat said, "there are a lot of good rehab centers here."

"No, I can't," Elizabeth said, shaking her head, instantly afraid.

"Why?"

"My family will kill me. Or at least disown me."

"I doubt that," Cat said. "I think they'd help you if they knew for sure you needed it. Trust me, babe, they already suspect you're using."

"They do?" Elizabeth asked, surprised. She thought she'd been careful.

"Oh yeah," Cat said. "Your brother-in-law is the best narc in the country—did you think you could fool him forever?"

Elizabeth was silent, realizing she had been foolish.

"Still," she said, "if I go into rehab now, what will that do to my aunt's campaign?"

Cat narrowed her eyes at the young woman. Elizabeth hadn't seemed to be worried about her aunt's campaign to become Attorney General when she was going to a drug house.

"What is it you think you want, Bet?" Cat asked.

Elizabeth noted the way Cat shortened her name, wondering at it. No one had ever called her that before. Then she realized there had been an edge to Cat's question. Narrowing her blue eyes, Elizabeth looked out the passenger window.

"I don't want anything," she said evenly. Her ego had kicked in again. She took deep breaths to avoid crying. She would not cry in front of this virtual stranger! She was not going to show weakness! She could feel the tears trying to clog her throat, and she clamped down on the feeling viciously, gritting her teeth.

Suddenly Cat turned off and headed toward the beach. Once there, she parked the Blazer and turned to Elizabeth.

"Tell me why you do drugs," she said simply.

Elizabeth didn't look at her for a long moment, staring out the passenger window instead. She needed to shore up her ego before handling that question. By the time she looked at Cat, the facade was very definitely in place once again.

"Because I like to party, that's why," Elizabeth said lightly.

Cat narrowed her eyes "Now try the truth."

"That is the truth," Elizabeth snapped.

"Are you hoping you'll get caught?"

"Why would I endeavor to hide my drug use if I was hoping to get caught?" Elizabeth asked condescendingly. She was using everything in her arsenal right now.

"You know what, little girl," Cat said, her eyes narrowing, her voice holding an edge of menace. "Don't even get bitchy with me. I'll drive your ass to your aunt's house and be done with you for good."

Elizabeth looked back at Cat for a long moment, surprised at her abrupt change in attitude. She'd actually reminded Elizabeth of Midnight for a moment. Elizabeth wasn't sure what to say at first. The last thing she wanted at this point was to face her aunt and uncle.

Turning, Elizabeth got out of the Blazer, her hands shaking. Cat did the same, grabbing her cigarettes and lighter. Moving to the front of the car, Cat leaned against the bumper, taking out a cigarette and lighting it.

It took Elizabeth a full ten minutes of debating, going over in her head what the repercussions could be. She knew rehab was going to be a nightmare; she'd heard about it from enough of her friends to know that. She wasn't sure how she was going to get out of this. With Midnight running for Attorney General, things were very focused on everyone in the family. That included her. She was terrified that her family would get thrown into the spotlight because of her, and that Midnight would lose the election because of her. It was just too much to fathom. Sighing, she walked over, moving to lean against the front bumper of the Blazer as well.

"Can I have one?" she asked, gesturing to Cat's cigarettes.

Cat shook one out of the pack and flicked open her lighter. They smoked in silence for another few minutes. Elizabeth was the first to speak.

"Would you help me if I wanted to quit?" she asked cautiously. She wasn't sure that she was even asking the right person, but Cat had been her savior so far.

Cat looked thoughtful for a moment, then nodded slowly. "It isn't going to be fun, you know."

Elizabeth nodded, looking reserved.

Cat was silent for a moment, her lips twitching. "We'll go to my place. I need you where I can watch you."

Elizabeth simply nodded, not wanting to argue with the one person that might be able to help her out of the situation she'd put herself in.

***

Joe waited backstage as Jordan took her final bow of the night. The crowd was cheering, screaming, and stomping. Jordan came running offstage, looking happy again. Joe was pleased that she was getting back into her routine. It showed that she was putting the incident with Jim behind her.

Joe hadn't gotten the opportunity to confront Jim, luckily for him. The bodyguard had disappeared. Jordan had asked Joe a couple of times to stay with her and be her bodyguard. He'd refused, telling her that BJ was looking for a replacement for Jim. Joe was doing any and all final screening on anyone that BJ found. If they passed muster, he let Jordan meet them. So far Joe had been through three candidates. Jordan had disliked each of them, for various reasons.

"Jordan," Joe had finally said after she'd trashed the third guy, "what do you want for my life?"

"I want you to protect me, Joe," she'd said tearfully. "I don't trust anyone but you."

Joe had shaken his head and walked away, going to the bar in the room and drinking a couple of shots. He didn't want to get into another argument with her about why he couldn't just quit his job and take care of her.

As he did every night, Joe escorted her back to her dressing room. Once the door closed behind them, she turned to him, putting her arms around his neck, kissing him deeply and pressing close. Joe gathered her into his arms, pulling her closer, his lips deepening the kiss. He knew she was on an adrenaline high, and it always made her horny.

When their lips parted for a moment, he looked down at her.

"Maybe I should find you a female bodyguard," he said, grinning. "I think it might be too dangerous, you having a man around after the concert."

She shook her head. "I only want you, Joe. You're the only one that turns me on now."

"Mmhmm," he said, grinning as he leaned down to kiss her again.

In the end, they made love on the couch in her dressing room. Joe had to admit, it was a new adventure with her every day. New cities, new places for her to drag him to and then become passionate. Two days before, they'd been in an exclusive but huge clothing store. She'd been trying on clothes, her main passion in life. At one point, she'd called Joe into the private dressing room, saying she wanted to show him the outfit she had on.

"Come out and show me," Joe had said.

"No, I can't. It's too sexy for that."

Joe had gotten up out of the chair he'd been sitting in to watch her model the mountain of clothes she'd taken into the dressing room. She opened the dressing room door and pulled him inside. She hadn't been wearing anything. They'd made love, laughing like bad kids breaking the rules. Joe was sure there'd be a story in the tabloids the next day. Fortunately, nothing had turned up.

That night they were in New Orleans, so Joe took her to dinner in a nice, quiet little French restaurant. After they'd eaten, they were lingering over drinks and having a quiet conversation when a man lurched over to the table. He made a grab for Jordan. She let out a startled scream even as Joe's hand whipped out, snatching the man's wrist before he could touch her. In the same movement, Joe stood from the table. He spun the man around, pressing him face first against the nearest wall, his wrist pulled up behind his back.

"That's not the way to approach a lady," Joe said evenly. "Did you need something?"

"She looks like she needs a good fucking," the man grunted, his voice slurred with alcohol.

"I take care of that just fine," Joe said conversationally. "Now," he went on, raising the man's wrist a fraction of an inch, making him hiss in pain, "if you don't want me to break your arm, you'll take yourself off somewhere else, quickly."

That being said, Joe released the man's wrist, moving to put himself between him and Jordan. The man predictably scampered away. Joe blew his breath out, shaking his head. There was no end to the nuts that roamed the streets. He was finding that out more and more, being around Jordan. She attracted them like bees to honey.

Turning, he looked down at her. She was pale, and shaking. He took her hand in his, pulling her gently from the table. As they moved through the restaurant, Joe saw that everyone was watching them. He pulled Jordan closer, his arm around her shoulders protectively. Pulling a hundred dollars from his pocket, he tossed it on the maître d's pedestal, surprising the man. Then Joe escorted Jordan out of the restaurant, his eyes watchful as he walked her over to the limo that awaited them.

Back at the hotel, he fixed her a drink, handing it to her as she sat down on the couch. She looked up at him, her gold eyes still showing the effects of the scare.

"You see why I need you?" she said tremulously.

"Jordan..." Joe began gently.

"No!" she exclaimed, standing and banging the drink down on the coffee table. "I don't want to hear it again, Joe, okay?" she said, moving toward the window and looking out. "I know," she continued, glancing back at him. "I know, okay? Just forget I said anything."

With that, she turned back toward the window, unable to hold back the tears anymore but not wanting him to see them. It irritated her that she was so afraid now. She didn't trust anyone anymore. She didn't even trust her own judgment anymore. In her heart she knew she was being unfair to Joe; she knew what his job meant to him, but she was so afraid now. With Joe there to protect her, she knew she wouldn't have to worry ever again, but she couldn't make him see that.

The problem was, she knew he'd left the department once before. And he'd done it to protect the ones he'd loved. He'd left when a ring of dirty cops had tried to kill Randy. He'd been afraid they'd come after his family next. He hadn't been willing to take that chance, so he'd left the department and moved the family back to England to his family's estate. Jordan knew this, and in her heart she felt that Joe was proving to her just how much she really meant to him, and that was sorely lacking compared to how much Randy had meant to him. And it hurt.

She was still facing the window when she heard the door to the room close. She turned around and saw that he'd left. The tears started in earnest then. Striding over to the bar, she poured a shot of Jack Daniels, drank it, and poured another. Finally she took the bottle and went to sit on the couch. When Joe didn't come back after an hour, she moved to the bedroom, taking the bottle with her. She was fairly drunk by that time, but she drank more, until she ended up throwing up in the bathroom. She fell asleep fully clothed in bed after that. Tears were still on her cheeks as she did.

Joe spent an hour walking along the streets of New Orleans. He walked until he felt calmer. Then he went to a bar and had a few drinks. He left an hour later, walking again. It irritated him that Jordan thought it was so easy for him to just give up what he'd done for most of his life. He didn't know why she couldn't see that he had responsibilities he had to take care of.

At two o'clock in the morning he sat at a sidewalk café drinking coffee. He picked up his cell phone and dialed Randy's number. She answered after three rings, sounding tired.

"Hello?"

"It's me," Joe said, grimacing as he glanced at his watch. He hadn't thought about the time. "Sorry I woke you."

"It's okay," Randy said, sitting up in bed and rubbing her eyes. "What's wrong?" she asked, knowing he wouldn't have called if there wasn't something wrong.

Joe sighed, shaking his head. "I don't know what to do here."

"About what, Joe?" Randy asked, moving to lean back against the headboard of the bed they'd shared for many years.

"Jordan wants me to take over being her bodyguard, and I just don't know how to convince her that I can't do that."

"Why can't you?"

"What?" he replied, shocked.

"Why can't you, Joe?"

"Uh, San Diego PD, captain, vice—ringing any bells, babe?"

Randy chuckled. "Yeah, I vaguely remember the job you've done for twenty years, Joe. But if she needs you there, what's to keep you from doing it for her?"

Joe hesitated. Why was Randy asking him this? Didn't she understand his responsibilities to the department after all these years?

"Joe?" Randy queried when he didn't say anything. "Let me ask you this," she said, changing tactics. "Do you honestly feel like the attempted rape was staged?"

"God, no," Joe said, shaking his head.

"Okay," Randy said. "And do you feel that it's possible this guy could try to attack her again?"

"Yeah, that's why I'm trying to find her a bodyguard," Joe said, sighing. "But she won't accept anyone else—she keeps finding fault with all of them."

"Maybe she's afraid to trust someone else she doesn't know. Look, let me ask you this, and be totally honest here. Do you love her?"

"Yes, I love her," Joe said sincerely.

"Then I don't see why this is a hard decision, honey."

"Randy, I'd have to leave the department, at least for a while. That'd leave Midnight in the lurch, and everyone else."

"Joe, if you'll recall, you left the department once before, when the people you loved were in danger. The department didn't fold because of it. Remember Devereaux and company?"

Joe's mouth dropped open at that statement. He couldn't believe he'd forgotten that. Jesus! He *had* left the department to protect his family; it had taken Midnight's "death" to bring him back.

"Fuck…" he breathed, realizing he'd been wrong.

"Uh-huh," Randy said, grinning. "If you love her, Joe, and she needs you, you need to be there for her. Unless that's it, and it's really that you don't want to be there for her…"

"That's not it!" Joe snapped, then winced. That was probably exactly how it looked to Jordan. "Goddamn it…"

"Not too far of a leap, was it, babe?" Randy said, smiling.

Joe blew his breath out, starting to grin. "I was being stubborn, huh?"

"Yep. And too set in your ways and attitude."

"I know."

"And probably a bit too judgmental about musicians and your perception of what you feel is their habit of being dramatic," Randy continued. "And—"

"I got it," Joe said, cutting her off.

Randy giggled. "Good."

"I'm an old man. What do you expect?"

"I expect you to go back to your girlfriend and apologize."

"And?"

"And tell her that you've now removed your head from your ass, and you'd be more than happy to take over watching out for the woman you love," Randy said, her smile in her voice.

Joe sighed. "I can't believe I wasn't thinking about that," he said, shaking his head.

"Well, it's a whole different kind of situation, Joe. You were dealing with dirty cops back then, people you considered a real threat. I don't think you really consider this creep that attacked Jordan as a threat, but he is, as long as he's out there."

"I know, I know," Joe said, nodding. "God, I can't believe I've been being so bloody stupid."

"If you're lucky," Randy said, grinning, "maybe she'll let you off with a piece of significant jewelry."

Joe laughed. "I don't think I'll get off that easy. Because if you were able to see that about me quitting the department before, so was she, and that's what's got her so twisted up."

"Probably," Randy said, remembering that Jordan felt like she was never going to measure up to Randy, since she'd known Joe for so long.

Joe sighed. "I think I'm becoming senile."

"I think you're very jaded when it comes to anyone outside of law enforcement."

"Not a good thing, considering who I'm dating."

"Nope," Randy confirmed.

"So I need to adjust my attitude."

"Yep," Randy agreed.

Joe blew his breath out in a disgusted sigh. "Thanks, babe. Thanks for helping me get my head screwed back on straight."

"Someone has to do it," Randy said, smiling.

"Yeah," Joe said. "And lucky you, huh?"

"Oh yeah," Randy said, laughing softly. "Go make nice, Joe."

"Ma'am, yes ma'am," he said, his tone crisp like a new cadet's.

Randy laughed, as did Joe.

They hung up a moment later. Joe stood up and stretched, wanting to hurry back to the hotel now. He knew he'd been narrow-minded, and he needed to do what he could to make it up to Jordan.

A half hour later, he walked into the hotel room, tossing the plastic room key down on the coffee table and leaning down to pick up the drink Jordan had left there. As he straightened, his sixth sense started to tingle.

Moving toward the bedroom area of the suite, he noted that the door was closed. He listened. He heard the slightest sound. Opening the door very quietly, Joe stepped inside. To his horror and instant fury, he saw Jim, his body covering Jordan's. She was obviously not fully awake, but it was very clear what Jim intended to do.

In two strides Joe was next to the bed. A moment later he hauled Jim off of her by two handfuls of his jacket. Joe literally threw Jim across the room, slamming him into the wall.

"Son of a fucking bitch!" Joe yelled, striding over to where Jim had slumped to the floor.

Hauling him up, Joe punched Jim in the mouth. Jordan was fully awake by this time, sitting up in bed, her scream adding to the commotion. Jim kicked Joe viciously, making him back off long enough for Jim to go on the defensive. Jim was a big man, and much younger

236

than Joe. But Joe had years of street fighting under his belt, and his complete and utter fury were to his advantage.

Jim took a swing at Joe, connecting with his jaw. Joe countered with a punch of his own, knocking Jim back. Jim realized quickly that he was outmatched, so he pulled out the knife he'd been carrying. He jammed it toward Joe, intent on shoving it into his chest. Joe brought his left arm up and out, knocking Jim's arm aside, and kicked him in the stomach, knocking him against the wall again. Joe didn't stop there, moving in to punch Jim twice, knocking him out with the second punch.

Joe stood over the other man's unconscious form, breathing heavily but watching to make sure Jim was indeed unconscious. Jordan jumped out of bed, moving to Joe. His outstretched arm kept her behind him. She grasped his arm, looking down at Jim. When he didn't move, Joe glanced down at Jordan.

"Call hotel security—tell them to get the police up here."

Jordan nodded and moved to the phone. Joe walked over to the closet where his bags were stored. Reaching into one, he pulled out his cuffs. He went back over to Jim, shoving him over on his back and cuffing him. He resisted the urge to kick the shit out of the man while he was at it.

"How did he know we were here?" Jordan asked a few minutes later as they sat on the bed.

"He had your schedule, babe, and he knew what hotel you were in," Joe said. "And he's probably been waiting for me to leave you alone so he could get to you." He said the last with his voice full of self-disgust.

"Joe," Jordan said, reaching up to touch the bruise already starting at his jaw. "You stopped him. That's what counts."

Joe shook his head, turning to her, searching her face.

"No, babe. I've been so fucking stupid," he said. "I'm sorry."

"Stupid how?" she asked, her eyes questioning.

"With not being willing to do this for you," he said, gesturing toward Jim's unconscious form. "It shouldn't even have been a question."

"What do you mean?" Jordan asked, her tone slightly different now.

"I mean," Joe said, reaching out to touch her face, smoothing his thumb over her cheek, "that when the woman I love needed me, I should have been willing to drop anything and everything to be there for her."

"You were, Joe—you came when I called you."

"Yeah, but then I was ready to turn you over to someone else for protection. And that's when I was wrong."

Jordan bit her lip, not sure what he was saying now and not daring to hope too much.

"What are you saying?" she asked, her eyes searching his.

"I'm saying if you still want me to protect you, you've got me."

Tears were in her eyes instantly, and she was hugging him tight a moment later.

She pulled back to look up at him. "Joe, are you sure?" she asked, wondering if he was just reacting to what had just happened with Jim.

"I'm sure. I had someone kick me in the ass an hour or so ago."

"Who?" Jordan asked, mystified.

"Randy."

"Huh?" Jordan said, totally lost.

"I called her, thinking she'd be on my side in this," he said, grinning. "As usual with the women in my life, she jumped all over me and told me I was basically being stupid."

Jordan bit her lip, trying not to laugh.

"Don't you dare," he said, narrowing his light blue eyes at her, grinning as he did. "She kindly reminded me that I'd left the department before for the people that I loved, so what was different this time."

"That was your family," Jordan said, trying to at least be fair.

"Well, you're the woman I love. And you're just as important to me, Jordan."

"I am?" she asked, actually awed.

"You didn't know that, did you?" Joe said, feeling like an even bigger heel now.

Jordan didn't answer, not wanting to add to the self-recrimination he was apparently already feeling.

"I…" she stammered. "I hoped that I meant a lot to you, Joe."

"You mean everything to me. I just haven't adjusted my thinking on rock stars yet."

"We're all pampered, over-paranoid attention junkies," she said, quoting back to him something he'd said to her a few times.

Joe grimaced, hating that she had it word perfect; he'd obviously said it a lot. He shook his head, looking down into her eyes.

"I'm sorry. That wasn't fair of me to say. I know better than to generalize, and yet I did it to you, and I shouldn't have."

She smiled at him, loving that he was able to admit when he'd been wrong. It was one of the many things she loved about him. She realized suddenly that he'd agreed to stay with her and protect her. It had her throwing herself into his arms again, kissing him deeply.

An hour later the police arrived. Jim didn't regain consciousness in that time, luckily for him. They took him away, and told Joe and Jordan to come down to the station the next day to make a statement. They spent the rest of the night making love. Joe reminded her over and over again that he loved her, showing her in every way he could.

Jordan fell asleep in his arms, as happy as humanly possible at that point in time. She knew no one could hurt her now. No one.

CHAPTER 9

Kevin's trip to Seattle hadn't gone well. Stacy's first priority was trying to talk him into staying and helping her beat the charges against her. When he refused, she screamed at him, telling him what a piece-of-shit father he was. He'd calmly reminded her that if it wasn't for the "child support" he sent her monthly, she'd probably be homeless, so she'd better remember that when she insulted his fatherhood.

Stacy next attempted to tell him that she did not want her daughter around "that bimbo" he was "fucking." Kevin told her that if she knew what was good for her, she'd better stop that train of thought, because he had no intention of putting up with it.

"What do you think you're going to do?" Stacy sneered.

Kevin narrowed his moss-green eyes at her. "Don't think anyone will care if I beat the shit out of you before you go to jail, Stacy," he said, his tone low and threatening.

Stacy was smart enough to back off then, knowing that Kevin usually didn't make idle threats. She also knew that as a former Seattle PD cop, other cops would probably look the other way if he did beat her. In truth, Kevin wouldn't risk getting himself into trouble by smacking her around, but the urge had been strong when she'd started talking trash about Erin. Stacy wasn't fit to even say Erin's name, let alone make any kind of judgments about her.

Emily, on the other hand, was thrilled to see her father, running to him and throwing her arms around him, hugging him so tight

Kevin could barely breathe. She was absolutely beside herself when Kevin explained that she was going to come stay with him in California for a few months.

"Can we go to the beach?" Emily asked, her little green eyes wide and excited.

"Of course," Kevin said, grinning. He noted that Stacy was positively glowering. He looked up at her. "Is her stuff packed?"

"I wasn't sure what to pack," Stacy said snidely. Kevin knew that meant Stacy hadn't bothered. If it wasn't going to garner her anything, why do it?

Kevin shook his head, knowing it was a waste of his time to try and argue with her. Instead he stood up and walked toward Emily's room. As usual, it was an appalling mess. Stacy didn't bother with housework. It took two hours to find enough clothing that actually fit Emily, let alone pack. In the end, Kevin just picked up everything that did fit and shoved it into a bag, noting that half of it wasn't even clean. He started to tell Emily to take any toys she wanted on the trip, then realized as he looked around that there weren't any. She was clutching a ratty teddy bear with one eye missing, so he assumed that it was her favorite.

Taking her hand, he walked out of the room, throwing Stacy a foul look. He wanted to get into it with her about the toys. Kevin had made a point of sending lots of things for Emily the year before, for Christmas, since he hadn't been able to make it back to Seattle. He wondered what had happened to the toys, but didn't want to get into a battle with Stacy with Emily looking on.

He left the small apartment that Stacy rented, his daughter's hand in his. He drove to the local toy store, taking Emily inside. He had her pick out a couple of things to take down to San Diego. He also bought her a LeapFrog pad, and three books to replace the one he'd sent her for Christmas, holding down his irritation when she didn't mention that she already had one. Kevin figured Stacy had probably pawned the toys to buy God knew what.

Kevin drove back to the airport then, getting them on the very next flight leaving for San Diego, not wanting to spend any more time in Seattle than necessary. The flight left in an hour, and he sat down with Emily at the gate. She played happily with the LeapFrog, beaming like it was indeed Christmas again.

Pulling out his cell phone, he called Erin. He told her when the flight would get in but not about everything else, not wanting Emily to hear him trash her mother.

"So how did things go with Stacy?" Erin asked gently.

"Not well," Kevin said, his eyes on Emily.

"Will you tell me about it when you get back?" Erin asked, knowing that he didn't want to talk about it in front of Emily.

"Oh yeah," he said, grinning, glad that Erin knew him well enough not to push at this point.

"Well, Steven and I will be there to meet your plane," Erin said, smiling.

"Good," he said, smiling too.

Five hours later, after a stop in San Francisco, Kevin and Emily walked off the airplane. Emily held on tightly to her father's hand, her eyes wide as she looked around.

Erin fell in love with Emily the minute she laid eyes on her. The child was absolutely precious. She was so tiny! Erin could see how tightly Emily was clutching Kevin's hand—she knew the child was overwhelmed, understandably.

Kevin walked over to them, looking down at Emily.

"Em, this is Erin. I told you about her—she's my girlfriend."

Emily looked up at Erin, then over at Steven, who stood sedately next to his mother.

Erin knelt down in front of Emily, then put her hand on Steven's shoulder. "This is Steven," Erin told the girl. "He's my son, and he's the same age as you are."

"Hi," Steven said, his face reflecting puzzlement that the little girl wasn't talking at all.

Emily bit her lip, not sure what to say to either of them.

"I understand," Erin said, smiling at her, "that you like butterflies. Is that true?"

Emily nodded slowly.

"Well, then I think this is probably for you," Erin said, handing her a brightly colored gift bag.

Emily looked up at Kevin. He nodded to her. "Go ahead, Em. It's okay."

She smiled brightly then reached into the bag, pulling out a purple-and-black stuffed butterfly.

"Oh…" Emily uttered, her voice tiny, her eyes shining brightly.

Erin couldn't help but feel moved by the joy on Emily's face. She glanced up at Kevin, and he smiled at her. He leaned over, kissing her softly on the lips.

"Thank you," he whispered softly.

The four of them left the gate then. Kevin had Emily's one bag and the few toys she now owned, so they left the terminal and walked to the parking garage. Kevin took them all to dinner at Boll Weevil, ordering a milkshake for Steven and Emily to share. Although Emily seemed to enjoy herself, Erin noticed that the child stayed very close to Kevin. It broke her heart to see how skittish Emily was, and it also made her wonder how Stacy really treated the child.

Later, when they got home, they showed Emily her room. She

stood staring at the bed that Erin had set up for her. She touched the bedspread with the colorful butterflies reverently.

"Emily," Kevin said, "Erin put this room together for you so you'd have a nice place to stay."

Emily turned, looking at Erin searchingly. It was like she was looking for Erin's motivations. Without a word, Emily walked over to Erin, putting her little head against her mid-section. Erin put her arms around the little girl, glancing at Kevin. He looked down at his daughter, his eyes pained. It bothered him that Emily seemed so uncommunicative. It also bothered him that Emily had apparently been neglected a lot. It hadn't escaped his notice that she was tiny, and that she seemed to weigh absolutely nothing.

Erin and he set about putting both kids to bed. Erin made a point of reading both of them a story. Emily sat and stared at her the whole time she read, as if trying to figure out what Erin was doing. It was pretty obvious Stacy never read to her daughter. Erin and Kevin tucked Steven in, then did the same with Emily. Again, Emily seemed surprised by Erin's attention. Kevin leaned down, kissing her on the cheek. Emily threw her arms around his neck. He hugged her to him.

"It's okay, baby," he said gently. "I'll be right down the hall if you need me, okay?"

Emily let go of his neck and sat back, nodding sedately, her eyes wide.

"Emily, do you want us to leave the hall light on for you?" Erin asked softly.

Emily looked at her, then at her father, in askance.

"Do you want that, Em?" Kevin asked.

She nodded.

"Okay, baby, we'll leave it on," Kevin assured her. "You lay down and try to get some sleep now, okay?"

245

Emily nodded, lying down. Kevin pulled the covers up over her again and made sure she had her bear. He noticed that she also had the butterfly clutched in her arms. He smiled, glancing at Erin. She smiled back at him, winking.

They left the room a few minutes later and went to their bedroom. A little while later, they lay on the bed, talking.

"I could just kick myself," he said stridently. "I should have checked on her more often."

"From here, Kevin?" Erin asked skeptically. "You had to believe that Stacy was taking care of her, babe."

"No, I didn't. I should have known," he said, shaking his head.

"Kevin, Stacy obviously did okay before," Erin pointed out. "She's just apparently done worse lately. I have to tell you, though, it breaks my heart to see how little she talks."

"I think she's just overwhelmed right now."

"What happened in Seattle?"

Kevin proceeded to tell her, including the part about her being the bimbo he was fucking.

"Oh, nice," Erin said, making a face. "Emily didn't hear that, did she?"

"No. I would have knocked Stacy's head off if she'd said something like that in front of my daughter."

Erin grimaced, thinking that Stacy probably said much worse when Kevin wasn't around.

Kevin sighed, shaking his head. "I guess all I can do is take the best care of her that I can right now. If Stacy's doing a lousy job, though, I'm going to find out, and if I have to I'll see about getting childcare services over to check on Em more often."

"That might get her taken away, though," Erin pointed out.

Kevin nodded. "I know—that's why I haven't done it before

now."

"Couldn't we see about keeping her here with us?"

"Stacy would fight tooth and nail."

"Why? It's apparent she doesn't really care about Emily. But then again, she'd lose a bargaining tool with you, wouldn't she?"

Kevin made a disgusted face, but nodded. "That and seven hundred dollars a month."

"Did she even say what she's doing with all that money?"

"Of course not."

Erin shook her head. "I'm sorry, Kev, but I have to say that I hate that woman, and I've never even met her."

"Trust me, you don't have to know her to hate her," Kevin said, rolling his eyes.

"Well, we've got Emily here with us now, so we'll see what we can do to make her the happiest girl around."

Kevin smiled, leaning down to kiss her softly. "Thank you, babe. For being so great about all this."

"You don't have to thank me, Kevin. I want to do this for her. You know I love kids, and your daughter is the most beautiful child I've laid eyes on since I had Steven. She looks a lot like you."

"Poor kid," Kevin said, grinning.

"Shut up!" Erin said, laughing. "I happen to think my man is gorgeous, thank you very much."

Kevin grinned, leaning in to kiss her again. They kissed for a while, then fell asleep.

In the middle of the night, Erin felt someone touch her cheek. She opened her eyes and found herself staring into Emily's.

"Are you okay, honey?" she asked softly.

Emily shook her head, her eyes wide.

"What's wrong?" Erin asked. "Are you afraid?"

Emily nodded slowly.

"Do you want to sleep in here for tonight?"

Emily looked surprised by the offer. She glanced at her father, who lay behind Erin, his arms wrapped around her. Then she looked at Erin again and nodded.

"Come on," Erin said, patting the bed next to her.

Emily climbed up on the bed and lay down. Erin placed her hand gently on Emily's stomach. Emily wrapped both her hands around Erin's, snuggling close to her. Erin felt tears sting the backs of her eyes. The child was too sweet for words. Erin and Emily fell asleep. An hour later, Steven crawled into bed behind Kevin. Kevin ended up on his back, with Steven sleeping against his side. Kevin had his arm under Erin's neck, and she had her arm cushioning Emily's head. Kevin had his other arm around Steven. When Erin woke the next morning, she couldn't help but laugh softly at the picture they presented, the four of them sleeping in the bed together. Kevin stirred, waking up and looking at the situation.

"I think we're going to need a bigger bed," he said, grinning.

"I think I'm going to love this," Erin said, grinning too.

"I think I love you," Kevin said, reaching up to touch her cheek.

Erin stared at him for a long moment, her lips parted in shock. "You do?"

"Honey, you had to know that."

Erin thought about it, then nodded slowly. "I guess I did, but you never said it, so…"

"You never said it," Kevin said, "but I felt it."

"I never said it because you didn't. Remember? I'm the one that made the mistake of falling for someone that loved someone else."

Kevin made a face. "That was Curtis, not me."

"I know," she said, touching his cheek. "But still, I was afraid to ruin things."

"Well, I'm ruining them then, but I love you."

She leaned down, kissing him softly on the lips, then pulling back to look down into his eyes.

"I love you too," she said, smiling.

"Damned good thing," he said, grinning.

She laughed softly. "Isn't it though?"

Things were just getting better and better.

***

Elizabeth slept heavily for a full day and a half. Whenever she woke for a few minutes, she felt like everything in her body was screaming at her to give it drugs. Her hands were shaking, her mouth was dry, she felt a horrible weight on her, a sadness that felt heavy and made her feel like she couldn't breathe sometimes. Part of her knew it was withdrawals, but another part of her told her that she was sick, and if she'd just get a hit of something, she'd feel so much better. It was a terrible feeling.

Cat was solicitous, checking on her often, asking how she was feeling when she did wake.

At one point she woke up and saw Cat sitting at the foot of the bed.

"How are you feeling?" Cat asked.

Elizabeth didn't answer right away, turning her thoughts inward, trying to decide how she felt. Finally she shrugged, looking sad. Cat nodded, knowing the feeling of hopelessness was setting in.

"Come on," she said, getting off the bed.

Elizabeth wondered what Cat was planning to do. The part of her that craved drugs and didn't trust anyone said this was somehow a trap. All the same, Elizabeth forced herself to get up and follow the other woman. Cat led her to the living room, telling her to sit down on the couch. Cat made her tea.

"Sugar?" she asked, holding up the cup.

"And milk, please," Elizabeth said softly.

Cat nodded, fixing the tea and taking it over to her. Cat sat down in the chair to the side of the couch, her look contemplative, but she said nothing. Elizabeth sipped the tea, glancing around at Cat's apartment. She hadn't noticed much before; it had been dark when they'd arrived. The apartment was sparsely furnished but still tastefully done. Not overwhelming, and certainly not as luxurious as her own apartment, but still nice.

Cat was watching her. Elizabeth wasn't sure what she was waiting for.

"So," Elizabeth said, breaking the silence, her tension high, "what happens now?"

Cat's lips curled in a sardonic grin. "Well, once you're through with the withdrawals, you go back to life."

"That's it?"

"Well, hopefully you go back with a better idea of why you do what you do."

"And what good will that do me?"

Cat shrugged. "I guess that depends on how honest you are."

"With you?" Elizabeth asked, feeling like she was being played.

"With yourself."

"Well, if this is all on me, then what do I need you for?"

Cat grinned. "Well, for one thing, talking to yourself usually gets you the answers you're looking for, not always the right ones. Also, it makes people think you're crazy if you talk to yourself and answer yourself too," she added with a wink.

Elizabeth laughed softly. She did like the way Cat talked to her; she didn't treat her like an idiot.

"So where do I start?" she asked.

"Wherever you want."

"You said why I do what I do," Elizabeth said. "What did you mean by that? The drugs?"

Cat nodded. "That and all the other things you do, the wild child stuff."

Elizabeth grimaced, shaking her head. "It's really dumb, you know," she said, her tone self-denigrating.

"What is?"

"Why I am like I am."

"Why is it dumb?"

Again Elizabeth grimaced. "Because it's so bloody cliché I make myself sick."

"Tell me," Cat said gently.

Elizabeth was quiet for a few minutes, sipping her tea. She was trying to gather her thoughts. Cat waited patiently. When Elizabeth started to talk, it just tumbled out, and she couldn't seem to stop herself.

"When I was five or so, it became very obvious that Susan was the favorite child in the family. Susan, perfect little Susan, who never put a bloody foot wrong. She was smart, she was cute, she was so mild-mannered and sweet. She never cried, she never yelled or made a fuss. Naturally everyone always asked me why I couldn't be like Susan." She made a disgusted face. "Who wanted to be like Susan? The mousy little thing, she was afraid of her own shadow.

"The problem was, if I didn't act like Susan they ignored me. So I did everything I could to be good like her. But I just couldn't do it. Eventually, however, I discovered the old trick of being loud. If I was

251

loud, and stood in the middle of a store and screamed, suddenly not only did my parents pay attention to me, but so did everyone else. Unfortunately, eventually they became immune to my screams.

"So I stepped up to breaking things. At first it was just dishes in the kitchen, or a glass. They came running, worried that I'd hurt myself. Suddenly I was the center of attention for a moment—they cared. Eventually, they stopped again. I guess they figured if I was bleeding all over their expensive Persian rugs, then they'd pay attention. So I moved up to Ming vases, Imari plates, Lladró statues, whatever it took." She shook her head, her lips curling in disgust. "They grew immune again and bought more insurance. Finally, I just started living for myself. I went out of my way to shock people, just to get something out of them. I no longer cared if my parents noticed or cared. They grew so used to everything I did, they merely shook their heads and walked away when I was in trouble." She took a deep breath, blowing it out sadly. "Have you ever read the story about the boy who cried wolf?"

Cat nodded, narrowing her eyes slightly.

"Well, I guess I did that once too often," Elizabeth said. "I guess I had them convinced that I just liked to make noise. Too well convinced," she said, pressing her lips together in consternation. It had really backfired on her.

"What happened?" Cat asked softly.

Elizabeth put her tea down on the coffee table, lying down on the couch, looking up at the ceiling. She felt the weight of what she was about to tell the other woman. She'd never told anyone else about it—well, not anyone that had ever believed her, anyway. Cat moved to sit on the floor next to Elizabeth's head. Reaching out, she touched Elizabeth's shoulder.

"What happened, Bet?" she asked again, her voice more gentle this time, the look in her eyes concerned.

Elizabeth saw it, and was surprised by it. Why did this woman care?

"Haven't you heard what a little drama queen I am?" she asked sharply, the knot in her stomach tightening. She was expecting Cat to nod and give up, but there was the tiniest part of her that wanted so desperately to reach out to another human being and finally receive understanding.

Cat didn't reply, her look direct.

"Didn't they tell you how I make things up to get attention? How I fuck anything that wears pants so I can get attention? How I make my entire family look bad, just to get back at them?" Elizabeth said, her voice full of self-loathing.

Cat's expression didn't change, and Elizabeth could see that she was waiting. "What happened, Bet?" Cat asked again, just as softly.

Elizabeth looked away from her, wiping irritably at the tears that had formed in her eyes instantly at Cat's tone. No one had ever talked to her like that, no one that hadn't wanted something from her. Maybe that was it.

"What do you want from me?" Elizabeth asked.

Elizabeth saw a flicker of amusement in Cat's eyes, then she shook her head slowly.

"You must want something," Elizabeth insisted.

"Everyone does, right?"

Elizabeth didn't answer. She stared back at Cat for a long moment, easily reading the sympathy in her blue eyes. She didn't trust it.

"Everyone wants something," Elizabeth said, her tone far too world-weary for her tender age.

"From you," Cat finished the statement.

253

"Right," Elizabeth said sharply. "So what is it you want, Catalina?"

Cat didn't answer, merely returning Elizabeth's steady gaze.

"Tell me what happened, Bet," Cat said then. Her tone told Elizabeth that she hadn't been dissuaded in the slightest from asking the question.

"Why?" Elizabeth asked, tears in her eyes again. She didn't bother hiding them this time. She was trembling inside both from the thought of telling her deepest secrets and the quiet desperation that was starting in her heart—it was so unexpected it was almost painful.

"Because I think you need to," Cat said, sounding sincere.

Elizabeth swallowed convulsively, trying to rid herself of the lump in her throat. Her eyes turned to the ceiling again as she began talking. She was trying to distance herself from what she was saying.

"When I was sixteen, my father worked for this high-prestige bank in London. He had a man that worked with him who came to the house a lot. He was around his mid-thirties, and decent looking. So as usual, I had to cause a stir. So when he came over the first time I flirted with him, much to my father's dismay. I was only really flirty that first time, but after that, when he came over he'd talk to me, say things like what a pretty girl I was, but always when my father wasn't in the room. At first I thought it was a game—how funny it was that he was flirting with me. If only my father knew!

"One day my parents were out at some thing for Susan's school. I was home alone. He came to the door. He said he had business to discuss with my father. I told him my father wasn't at home. He said he'd wait for him to return. I stupidly let him into the house and told him he could wait in the sitting room…"

Elizabeth's voice trailed off as she shook her head. The memories were flooding in, making her insides recoil at the pictures running through her mind.

"What happened, Bet?" Cat asked again, reaching out to take her hand. Elizabeth stared at Cat's hand holding hers. She felt the warmth of the other woman's hand and wanted desperately to tamp down on the now blooming feeling of hope. Maybe this time someone would actually hear her and believe her.

"He ended up raping me on the couch in the sitting room," Elizabeth said. "I was so stupid to even let him in the house. I was stupid to flirt with him,"

"He was scum for raping you," Cat practically snapped.

Elizabeth made a face, her look disparaging. "Oh, he didn't rape me, you see? I encouraged him—I was always playing with fire, you see, and he just took me up on my offer."

Cat's mouth dropped open, disbelief clear on her face.

"That's what he said, right?"

"No," Elizabeth said, her lips curling derisively. "That's what my father said when I told him what had happened."

"Holy shit," Cat said, aghast. "Did you tell your mother?"

"My father forbade me telling my mother. He said he would not allow me to spread slanderous lies about a colleague of his. He told me he knew that I'd been sleeping around, and that I was merely crying rape because I wanted attention as usual."

Cat shook her head, her look belying her disgust at what Elizabeth's father had done.

Elizabeth shrugged. "After that, I didn't bother to try and please them. If there was trouble I could get into, I did it. Why not be the slut my father thought I was? At least I'd have some fun doing it."

"When did the drugs start?" Cat asked carefully.

Elizabeth sighed. "About three years ago. I'd always smoked pot and drunk. Someone had cocaine at a party, so I tried it. I actually smoke it more than I snort."

Elizabeth moved to sit up, and Cat sat next to her on the couch. They were silent for a few minutes.

"You know what's really pathetic?" Elizabeth said wistfully.

"What?"

Elizabeth turned her head to look at her. "I really hate who I am now."

"So stop being what you hate."

"I don't know who to be anymore," Elizabeth said sadly. "I've become what I pretended to be for so long."

"Do you want to be different?"

Elizabeth nodded slowly. She honestly did, but had never really said it out loud before.

"Then you're already taking a step in the right direction, Bet," Cat said. "You've realized that you don't like what you're doing. You're making a conscious effort to do something different now, something right."

"But what if I can't do it?" Elizabeth asked, tears starting to well up in her throat again.

"You can," Cat assured her.

Elizabeth shook her head. "I don't know… I just…" she said, the tears coming in earnest now.

To Elizabeth's relief Cat didn't say anything else, simply taking her into her arms and letting her cry.

"Shhhh," Cat said. "It's okay, it'll be okay…"

Elizabeth lay against her and cried for a while, finally quieting as she grew tired again, drained from all the emotions she'd just gone through. To Elizabeth's surprise, Cat got up from the couch, taking her hand and leading her back to the bedroom, where she put her back into bed, covering her up. Cat then took up her spot at the foot of the bed again.

"Cat?" Elizabeth queried softly.

"Yeah?" Cat asked, looking over at her.

Elizabeth bit her lip, momentarily hesitant. "Will you stay in here with me?"

"Right here, Bet," Cat said, smiling gently.

Elizabeth nodded, feeling very grateful to this woman suddenly. Her last thought was that she should use her trust fund to buy this woman a house or something nice…

She was sitting in her parents' sitting room again, but her parents were there and they were watching him rape her. *Why aren't they doing anything? Why are they just sitting there?*

"You deserve this," her father was saying. "We've given you to him, since you wanted him so much."

She started to scream, she tried to claw at his eyes, but he didn't have eyes—he was just a faceless entity. She pushed at him, but he wouldn't get off her. "Help me!" she screamed at her parents. "Why won't you help me?"

"You want what we got and we gonna give it to you," the man sneered, but then it wasn't the banker anymore—it was one of the men who'd almost accosted her at the drug house, and there were more, many more men crowding around her now.

Where was Catalina? Had she left her too? She opened her mouth to scream again, but someone covered her mouth and they were pushing at her, grabbing her, hurting her. She bit down on the hand and then screamed as loudly as she could, yelling Catalina's name.

Suddenly Catalina was there. "Bet?" she shouted. "Wake up!"

Elizabeth woke with a startled cry, terrified. Cat was standing

257

next to the bed, her hand on her shoulder still.

"It's okay," Cat was saying soothingly. "It was a bad dream. It's okay."

Elizabeth felt herself shaking. She was still terrified—the dream had been so real. Cat put her arms around her, pulling her close and holding her, much like one would a child.

Elizabeth felt Cat's hand smooth her hair back as she said, "It's okay, Bet, it's okay. No one's going to hurt you. It's okay."

Elizabeth relaxed in Cat's arms, pressing her face to her shoulder, one hand grasping a handful of Cat's shirt at the waist. After a while, she started feeling sleepy again and began dozing off, but then she felt Cat starting to get up. Elizabeth immediately tightened her hand on the material of Cat's shirt, desperately needing the closeness of another human being at that moment.

"Stay, please?" she asked plaintively.

"Okay," Cat said, lying back down and putting her arms around her again.

In the end, they both slept that way. Elizabeth woke the next morning feeling much better. She moved her head, looking up at Cat, and realized she'd just met her best friend.

***

Stevie watched Kevin and Sergei talking. She knew Sergei didn't like to deal with women when it came to actual business. She was getting to the point where she wanted to slap the crap out of the man for being a stupid chauvinist, but instead she sat back and let Kevin do the talking.

It had been a long week. They'd been on Sergei's yacht for most of it. Stevie had determined that she definitely didn't like boats. She

258

hadn't actually gotten seasick, but the feeling of the water moving under her just didn't sit well with her. Leaning back on the bench seat on the deck, she let the breeze blow against her face. This would be nice if she were here with Christian, maybe. But not for work—she couldn't relax, couldn't let her guard down.

Sergei had gotten more insistent and more pushy about wanting her. He'd been coming on to her the entire time they were on the boat. Constantly trying to get her alone, putting his hands on her whenever he got half a chance. She knew it was part of the play here, but also that they'd better make the deal soon. Sergei wasn't going to be put off much longer.

Kevin glanced back at Stevie. He could see the twitch of her jaw as she clenched it, even if she looked perfectly at peace, with her rich auburn hair blowing in the breeze. He knew she was getting tired of being left out of the business dealings. Sergei only seemed to want her around to ogle, not to actually deal with. It went against Stevie's grain, and Kevin knew it.

The sun was just going down, and Sergei was telling him that the shipment was going to be in by the time they docked two days from now. Kevin wanted to find out exactly where the shipment was going to be; Sergei was vacillating on that information. Kevin knew that with some good vodka the Russian would start talking. It was a risk. Sergei was constantly trying to get Kevin to drink with him, and seemed suspicious that Kevin wouldn't do it. But Kevin also knew that things were getting to the point where they'd only have the guy on sale of narcotics, and without the evidence, it was going to be a hit or miss case. That wasn't good enough.

The small group—Kevin, Stevie, Sergei, and his two body-guards—went inside. Sergei predictably went to the bar. Kevin leaned down to Stevie.

"Have a drink with him—we need to loosen his tongue," he whispered.

Stevie nodded and went to the bar, her green eyes on Sergei's.

"What are we drinking?" she asked, her look bold.

"Vodka, what else?" Sergei said, a leering grin on his face.

Stevie shrugged. "Not my usual preference, but I can deal with that."

Sergei nodded enthusiastically, changing his game plan again. If he could get her drunk maybe he could get to her.

They drank for the next three hours. Kevin hung back, letting Stevie do the talking. She did exactly what Kevin had hoped for—getting Sergei bragging. When Sergei bragged, he said way more than was prudent. Especially when he was trying to impress Stevie.

"The warehouse," Sergei was saying. "It's not so big, but it has a room underneath, da?"

"A basement?" Stevie said, grinning. "Very ingenious, Sergei," she murmured approvingly, knowing Kevin was keeping track of every word.

"And it's no at the waterfront either," Sergei said, grinning with pride. "It's in town, in that… How you say? Gaslamp Quarter?"

"Cops'd never look there," Kevin put in, nodding his agreement that Sergei was indeed a brilliant dealer.

"Cops, bah!" Sergei spat with disgust. "The cops here, they are so stupid! In Russia, the KGB, they know everything, and they don't play silly games. They just come, shoot, and leave."

Stevie nodded, thinking, *Too bad we can't do that here.* "I've heard the KGB was pretty nasty."

"Nasty, vicious, hateful," Sergei said, narrowing his eyes. "But I am here now, and I make plenty of money off foolish Americans."

Stevie glanced back at Kevin. Did the idiot not get that he was insulting his clients to their faces? Probably not—he was pretty high. He'd snorted no less than ten lines of cocaine while drinking an entire bottle of vodka. Stevie had managed to make it look like she'd drunk more than she had. Fortunately, Sergei was stingy with his coke and didn't offer her any. She knew how to make it look like she was snorting, but it was always a fairly dangerous act she'd rather avoid.

The more drunk and high Sergei got, the more pushy he got. At one point, he leaned forward, putting his hand on Stevie's shoulder, sliding it downward and caressing her breast. Stevie pulled back, glancing at Kevin, who stood up immediately, warning Sergei with a look. Sergei glanced at Kevin, then nodded slowly. Stevie finally gave up trying to get information out of him. She wasn't in the mood to push too much, because if the guy slid his foot up her thigh one more time, she was going to reach down and break his ankle.

Getting up, she made a point of wavering on her feet, acting for all intents and purposes drunk.

"I'm gonna go to bed," she slurred.

Sergei stood up too, looking upset. Stevie didn't miss the hardon he had. Oh, she was so not staying around to deal with that! Kevin walked her to the cabin they were sharing.

"You okay?" he asked her as they got inside.

"Yeah," Stevie said, nodding. "He was playing footsie way too much for my tolerance," she added, her green eyes glittering.

"Ah." Kevin nodded. "Well, I'm going to go back and see what I can get out of him. We need to close this damned case."

"I know, I know," Stevie said, aggravated that she wasn't able to get the information out of Sergei.

"Hey," Kevin said, touching her on the chin. "You got the warehouse out of him. Let me see what I can do now."

Stevie nodded. "I'm tired. I think I'm going to just hang out here."

"No prob," Kevin said, nodding.

He headed back up to the dining room. Stevie lay down on the bed, mentally going over the week.

Sergei had taken to "checking" on them frequently while they were in their cabin together. The first time had been the first night on the yacht. Once they'd all retired for the night, Sergei had come wandering down the main passageway, fortunately being extremely loud in the process. He'd knocked lightly that first time, even as he started to open the door. Stevie had pressed against Kevin instantly, as if she'd been snuggling up to him. Kevin had glanced questioningly over his shoulder.

"What can we do for ya, Sergei ?" he asked evenly.

"Wanted to wish you *spokoynoy nochi*, a good night," Sergei said, eyeing Stevie hungrily.

"Yeah, cool," Kevin replied, nodding, not looking impressed.

The following night, when they heard him coming down the passageway Stevie threw her arms around Kevin, leaning up to kiss him deeply. Kevin hadn't been prepared, but covered it well by kissing her back. When Sergei opened the door without knocking, he got an eyeful. Kevin's hands were caressing her back, his lips devouring hers hungrily. Sergei stood staring, transfixed. Kevin and Stevie played it up, letting him get a good look before Kevin finally broke the kiss to stare at him pointedly.

"Good night, Sergei," Kevin said mildly, his face calm but his eyes narrowed slightly. He was metal under tension—even Sergei felt that.

Sergei finally nodded and walked out of the room. It hadn't stopped his nightly visits, so Kevin and Stevie had kept up the facade, even lying in bed one night with Kevin not wearing a shirt and Stevie wearing only a strapless bikini on top, to make it look like she was naked under the covers. They made it appear that they'd fallen asleep after having sex. Sergei stared at them for a full five minutes. Stevie felt Kevin's hand tensing and relaxing on her waist as he waited for him to finally leave. Kevin was always on his guard; he knew he was the only thing between Stevie and Sergei's desire for her.

Stevie lay on the bed, closing her eyes and wondering where Christian was at that moment. She found it quite amusing that she missed her husband like crazy. No man had ever excited her enough to make her miss him constantly. Christian did. Every moment she spent with him was exciting. It was downright disgusting. She grinned to herself, feeling so tired.

She must have fallen asleep, because the next thing she knew someone bumped into the bed, jostling it. She opened her eyes and saw Kevin.

"Okay?" she asked wryly.

He nodded, but she noticed right away something wasn't right. She sat up. He moved to sit on the bed, and she saw him waver ever so slightly.

"Mace?" she queried, looking him over.

"Need sleep," he muttered.

Holy fuck, he was drunk! Stevie heard the slight slur in his words. Shit, shit, shit! Was he crazy?

"You're drunk," she said, getting off the bed and walking around to look at him.

He looked at her, his face stony.

"Jesus fucking Christ, Mace! Are you nuts?" she raged.

He said nothing, only stared back at her, his eyes bloodshot.

"Fuck!" she exclaimed.

Moving toward the door, she shook her head. What had he been thinking? He couldn't drink—he knew that! Goddamn it! She slammed out of the cabin, heading down the passageway. She got up onto the deck, standing at the railing, letting the wind whip her long hair around her face. She stared out at the ocean, trying to get a handle on her anger.

Thinking about it, she knew there had to be an explanation. Kevin had been sober for over four years. She knew it would be the taste of alcohol that would have him drinking again. What had happened? She needed to find out. Until she did, she really didn't have a right to get pissed at him. She turned to go back to the cabin and found Sergei lounging against the rails, watching her.

Giving him a curt nod, she started back toward the cabin. His hand on her arm stopped her.

Kevin lay down on the bed, feeling the whole cabin spin. His mind kept replaying Stevie's voice in his head. "Fuck!" she'd yelled. "Jesus fucking Christ, Mace! Are you nuts?"

Yes, he was nuts. He'd made the mistake of trusting Sergei. They'd ambushed him, his bodyguards good-naturedly holding his head while Sergei poured the vodka down his throat. They were all laughing. None of them had any idea that Kevin had a drinking problem. Not that they'd have cared even if they had. After that, everything was a blur. Kevin had tried to leave the dining room a few times, but they'd stopped him. Sergei kept calling him back, handing him another drink, then another. Kevin couldn't stop, he couldn't say no. Damn it!

He lay back, trying to make the world slow down for a minute. God, he felt like shit. He closed his eyes and the world seemed to spin faster. He opened them, and he didn't feel much better. Jumping up off the bed, he ran into the bathroom and threw up. After ten minutes, he dragged himself off the floor and back to the bed. He felt marginally better. It occurred to him that he needed to go find Stevie and try to explain.

As if on cue, he heard Stevie's scream. He was off the bed, his gun in hand and throwing open the door. He made his way down the passageway, instantly realizing that Stevie was in Sergei's cabin. When he got there, Sergei's two bodyguards were in front of the door. Kevin put the gun in one man's face, his eyes flicking from one to the other.

"I'll fucking blow your head off if you don't get out of my way, now!" he growled viciously.

The man jumped, and moved out of the way.

"Open the door!" Kevin told the other man, gesturing with the gun.

The bodyguard did what he'd said. He shoved both of them inside in front of him. They were in some kind of outer room; the bedroom was to the right.

"Over there." He motioned with the gun, pulling out his cuffs and tossing them to the first bodyguard. "Put one on your wrist, loop it around that pipe, then put it on his wrist."

Kevin lifted the gun when they hesitated. The bodyguards hurriedly complied. Kevin moved to the bedroom, putting the gun at the small of his back. He opened the door and saw what he was afraid of. Sergei had Stevie on the bed. His body held her down, one massive hand holding both of her wrists even as she struggled. His other hand was between them, violating her, and he was just ready to plunge himself into her when Kevin grabbed him by two handfuls of shirt and literally threw him six feet across the room into the bulkhead. Sergei sank to the floor, out cold. Kevin moved to Stevie, who was busy grabbing the coverlet off the bed to cover herself. She had bruises already darkening on her face and her body.

"Jesus…" Kevin breathed, moving to her side.

He quickly found some cord and tied up Sergei, in case he came to. Then he turned to Stevie, picking her up in his arms. She wound her arms around his neck, burying her face against his shirt. He carried her back to their cabin, setting her gently on the bed.

"I'm going to get us out of here, Stevie," he assured her.

She nodded numbly, looking like she was in shock. Kevin made sure she was covered up and warm, then turned to their bags. He grabbed her set of cuffs and a second pair he always carried with him. He left the cabin and went to the wheel room; he knew Sergei's captain's room was behind it.

Kicking the door open, he walked in, his gun out and at the ready.

The captain jumped up out of bed wearing striped undershorts and nothing else.

"Get dressed right now," Kevin ordered. "Then get this fucking thing back to shore."

The captain nodded, not willing to get shot for anyone, least of all Sergei.

"You better be at the helm, getting us home, before I get back, or I'm going to learn how to drive a boat, real quick," Kevin said ominously. The captain nodded again.

Kevin went back to Sergei's cabin and cuffed both guards separately, then took them into Sergei's bedroom. He then cuffed an unconscious Sergei. He left them all there, taking a fireplace poker and ramming it in the door latching mechanism. Standing back, he kicked the poker with all his might, bending it enough on both ends that there was no way to get out from the inside. Then he headed back to the captain. The man was doing exactly what he'd been told. Kevin was satisfied that he was headed home.

He went back to the cabin, sitting down on the bed and looking down at Stevie. She was huddled under the blankets. Kevin blew his breath out slowly. This was not the time to lose it; he needed to get her home safely. He'd already fucked up badly, but now wasn't the time to mull that over. He picked up his cell phone, went into the bathroom, and made the calls he knew he had to make.

As the yacht docked, a team of seven officers swarmed on board. They took Sergei, his bodyguards, and the captain into custody. Kevin carried Stevie off the yacht. Dave met him at the end of the gangway, his eyes searching Kevin's. There was nothing to see; Kevin's face could have been set in stone. He followed Dave to his car, where he placed Stevie in the backseat.

"Get in," Dave told Kevin.

Kevin nodded, getting in on the passenger side.

The ride to the hospital was silent and thankfully quick. Dave got Stevie out of the car. She insisted on walking this time. Kevin hung back, but followed them into the emergency room.

An hour later, everyone was there. Everyone except Christian— they were calling him in from the field. He'd been told that Stevie had been nearly raped and hurt. By the time Christian hit the doors to the hospital, his blood was boiling and he had one question in his mind.

He strode right over to Kevin, who had stood when Christian walked in.

"Where the fuck were you!" Christian yelled, his punch coming right after that, knocking Kevin back a few paces.

Everyone moved to intervene instantly, even though Kevin made no move to fight back. Dave and Tiny pulled Christian back, and Donovan, Jeanie, and Cat got in front of Kevin. Dave walked Christian away, with Tiny right behind them. Cat turned to Kevin, reaching up to touch his jaw. Kevin jerked his head away, turning and striding down the hallway. Cat started after him, but Donovan stopped her.

"He's hurt," Cat said.

"I know," Donovan said. "But worse, he's been drinking."

Cat looked back at him as he pulled his cell phone off his belt.

"What are you doing?" she asked.

"Calling Erin," he said, glancing at Jeanie and nodding toward the hallway Kevin had walked down. Jeanie nodded, then went after him. Cat followed her.

"What's up?" she asked, clueless.

"Mace is a recovering alcoholic," Jeanie said. "If he was drinking, we have a problem."

They continued along the hallway, trying to locate Kevin, but he was gone.

"Shit," Jeanie said, pulling out her cell phone and calling Donovan. "He's gone," she reported.

"Fuck," Cat heard Donovan say.

"Should we have patrol watch for him?" Jeanie asked him.

"No, we need to handle this," Cat said, shaking her head.

Jeanie looked back at Cat for a minute, then nodded. "Donovan, Cat's right, we need to handle this. Kevin doesn't need this going anywhere, ya know? I'll go check the lot."

"Okay," Donovan said. "I'll head out and start looking around here."

"Got it."

The search was on for Kevin. The last thing they wanted was for him to self-destruct.

Down another hall, Dave had Christian leaning against a wall.

"Blue, she's fine—she'll be fine," he assured him. "We don't know what happened yet, but we do know that it was Mace that got them back to shore."

Christian took quick breaths, trying to calm down, but all he knew was that Kevin had been Stevie's protection and he'd failed her.

"I want to see my wife," he finally growled.

Dave stepped back, his head coming up. He knew Christian was still pissed, and he couldn't exactly blame him. There had to be more to all of this than there appeared to be. They needed to get the whole story.

Christian walked into Stevie's hospital room. She was sitting on the bed, her knees pulled up to her chest, her arms wrapped around her legs, her head down on her knees.

"Baby?" Christian said tentatively, feeling his heart lurch when her head snapped up. She had bruises on her face.

He walked over, searching her eyes. He touched the bruise on her cheek gently. That was when she lost her composure. The tears started, and Christian gathered her into his arms, holding her against him as she cried. When she finally quieted, he still held her, stroking her hair soothingly.

"Baby, I'm sorry," Christian said, so distraught she lifted her head to look up at him.

"I'm okay, Christian," she said softly. "I think I just need to put it past me."

"Jesus, babe…" Christian said, shaking his head.

"It could have been a lot worse," Stevie said. "If Mace hadn't gotten there when he did, Sergei would have raped me, and God knows what else. Mace stopped him."

Christian's lips twitched. He wasn't willing to be grateful to Kevin at this point.

"It shouldn't have happened at all," he said.

"It's my fault it did, Christian," Stevie said quietly. "It wasn't Mace's fault at all."

"How do you figure?" Christian asked, striving to hold on to his temper. He wasn't mad at her—he was mad at the situation. His wife had been violated, the woman he loved…

"I was there, remember?" Stevie said calmly. "I was the one that was stupid enough to leave the cabin. If I hadn't gotten pissed at him for drinking, I would have realized how dumb I was to do that."

"He was drinking?" Christian asked, his eyes narrowing dangerously.

"Wait, wait, wait," Stevie said, holding up a hand to stave off his anger. "They ambushed him—Sergei told me that. It's some stupid Russian custom, kind of like the whole tequila popper thing in TJ, you know? Kevin didn't plan to start drinking—they literally forced him into it."

Christian's lips tightened. He still wasn't willing to give in on the point.

"He was your protection."

"And he did protect me. When I screamed he was there a minute later. Christian, he launched Sergei across the room to get him away from me. That was a good six feet, and Sergei isn't a little guy—he's bigger than you. It wasn't Mace's fault," she repeated. Then she saw the look in Christian's eyes. "Oh God, you didn't do anything, did you?" she asked, just knowing from that look that he had. The guilty flash that crossed his face showed that she was right.

"Jesus, Christian! What did you do?"

"My wife was attacked and almost raped while he was supposed to be protecting her—what did you expect me to do?"

"Oh Lord…" Stevie said, shaking her head.

Christian looked wholly unrepentant.

Dave stuck his head in the room a few minutes later. "Blue, we need you."

Christian's head snapped around. "What's up?"

"Mace is gone. We need to find him, now."

Christian didn't move, but Stevie started to stand up.

"Where do you think you're going?" Dave asked her.

"I'm going to help find him," she said, looking up at Christian pointedly.

Christian said nothing, then after a long moment, in which his eyes narrowed at his wife, he nodded slowly, glancing back at Dave.

Rogue Squadron set off to find one of their own. They found out quickly that Kevin Elmasian knew how to disappear when he wanted to. Midnight put out a city-wide request for information on his vehicle. Rogue Squadron found out that Kevin had left the hospital, taking a cab back to the waterfront, where he'd picked up his Dodge Durango. Once in his vehicle, he may as well have been a ghost.

Erin was sick with worry, but she had to hold it together around the children. She told them Kevin was still on his case. Donovan's call had worried her; the subsequent calls had only deepened that worry. She knew Kevin had been forced to drink by the dealer he and Stevie were working, and that when Stevie had left the cabin in anger, she'd been attacked by that same dealer. It had been Kevin who had rescued her from actually being raped, but that hadn't been enough to keep Christian from decking him upon getting to the hospital. Kevin had disappeared after that. She was worried sick.

It was worse when, after two days, they still hadn't located him.

There had been reports from CHP of a Dodge Durango, Kevin's, doing 120 on the freeway. CHP had stopped him, and because he was a cop, he was asked to slow down. The reporting officer stated that Kevin had nodded, then left the scene doing at least eighty-five. There had been other reports of the Durango on the freeways; he had last been seen in the vicinity of Los Angeles.

***

Dave and Stevie were checking bars in Los Angeles, literally going bar to bar. Donovan and Jeanie were checking another area of the city, and Cat and Christian were down on Sunset. They were canvassing as much of the area as they could cover, and they'd been at it for two days.

"Yeah, he was here," the bartender at the Whiskey said, nodding.

"When?" Christian asked.

"Last night. Got into it with someone at the bar."

Christian looked at Cat. She grimaced.

"What happened?" Christian asked the man.

"Dunno. They took it outside."

"Would anyone else here know?"

The bartender favored her with a hungry look, then glanced around. "Yeah, you see that guy over there, by the stage?"

Cat glanced back. Seeing a heavyset man rolling cable next to the stage, she nodded.

"He was one of the guys that broke it up," the bartender said. "Talk to him."

"Thanks," Christian said, pushing off the bar and walking toward the stage.

Cat looked back at the bartender. "Give me a double shot of tequila, will ya?"

The bartender nodded, pouring the shot. Cat knocked it back, then pulled a ten out of her pocket and tossed it on the bar.

"Thanks," she said with a wink, then turned around to wait for Christian.

Christian came back to the bar a few minutes later, ordering a double shot of tequila as well. "Make it Herradura," he told the bartender.

"That's extra," the bartender said.

"No shit," Christian said, his light blue eyes impassive.

The bartender nodded, not liking Christian at all, cop or no cop.

After Christian drank the shot he threw a twenty on the bar and straightened up. "Let's go."

Cat followed him outside, waiting to hear what the man had said.

"He's fucked up, big time," Christian said gravely. "The guy said he thinks he might have gotten knifed in the fight too."

"Shit," Cat said, reaching for her cell phone. "So now we add hospitals to the search."

"Yup," Christian said, leading her back to the car as she called Dave.

"This isn't getting any better," Dave said, hanging up his cell.

"What?" Stevie asked, glancing over at him.

"Mace got into a fight at the Whiskey last night. He was apparently drunk off his ass, and the bouncer thinks he might have taken a knife to the gut."

"Fuck!" Stevie said, looking frantic. "We've got to find him, Dave."

"I know we do," Dave said. "And we need to find him fast."

"You can bet he hasn't had Adderall in at least two days."

"That's not going to help the situation at all."

They continued the search.

"Anything yet?" Kyle asked Midnight when he walked in the next morning.

"Nothing good," Midnight said, shaking her head. "He was at the Whiskey the night before last and apparently got into a fight. They think he might have been knifed."

"Shit," Kyle said, shaking his head.

Midnight sighed. She wasn't sure what she could do. She didn't want to put out an APB on Kevin until she had to. The last thing she wanted to do was run screaming to anyone, least of all the press. Kevin had a family and a reputation to protect, and an all-points bulletin would endanger that. But if it came down to his safety or the APB, she knew she'd have to do it, and pray that it wouldn't get out of the law enforcement community.

Midnight's phone rang. She snatched it off the cradle.

"Chevalier."

"It's me," Dave said.

"Tell me you have good news."

"I have news. It's not great," Dave said, resigned.

"What?" Midnight said, feeling a chill enter her blood.

"We got a hit on one of his credit cards and tracked him to a motel. But when we got there he was gone. There was blood on the bed."

"A lot?"

"Enough."

"Damn it," Midnight said, shaking her head. "Dave, I'm gonna have to do an APB. We've got to find him."

"I know," Dave said, blowing his breath out in a deep sigh. "Look, give me another twelve hours. If I don't have anything, we'll go with the APB."

Midnight was silent for a few moments, trying to weigh her decision. "If he's losing blood, Dave…"

"He knows first aid, Midnight. If he felt it was serious, he'd go to a hospital."

"Unless he just doesn't care at this point."

"We have to believe he wouldn't do that to Erin and the kids."

"He's done this much."

"I know," Dave said. "Twelve hours, Night. That's all I ask."

Midnight took a deep breath then blew it out slowly. "Okay, Dave, twelve. I'm going to send the rest of the Gang up on a plane in an hour. I'll have them call you when they touch down. Have a plan of attack for them. Just find him, please."

"I'll do my best."

***

Joe had just gotten himself and Jordan checked into their hotel in Sacramento when his cell phone rang.

"'Lo," he answered.

"Joe, it's me," Midnight said.

"Hey, Night, what's up?" he asked, grinning at Jordan as she led him to the elevator.

"I've got a man missing."

"Who?" Joe asked, stopping dead in his tracks.

"Mace."

"What happened?" Joe asked, glancing at Jordan, who was now

watching him with worry in her eyes.

"The case he and Stevie were working rolled on them. The guy got Kevin drunk and then attacked Stevie."

"What?" Joe exclaimed, heedless of the people around them who jumped. "Is Stevie okay?"

"Yeah, she's okay. She's up in LA with the rest of the Gang, looking for Mace."

"LA? What's he doing way up there?"

"That's where he ended up. And the newest wrinkle is that he got into some kind of fight and got hurt."

"Hurt how?" Joe asked, leaning back against the wall, staring unseeing up at the glass elevators that were moving up and down the tall building.

"Knife fight."

Joe blew his breath out. "Okay, so what do you want me to do?"

Midnight couldn't help but smile. Joe was always loyal, no matter where he was.

"Well, I was thinking, don't you know the watch commander for LAPD?"

"Yeah. Want me to call him?"

"Could you?" Midnight asked. "We need LAPD's help, but I don't want anything in writing—you know what I mean?"

"Ten four," Joe said. "I'll call him now."

"Thanks, Joe. I knew I could count on you," Midnight said, breathing a little bit easier.

"Always," Joe said, smiling. "I'll call you back after."

"Thanks."

They hung up a few moments later.

Joe led Jordan into the elevator, pushing the floor number for their room, and started dialing as he did.

276

"What's going on?" Jordan asked.

"Mace is MIA right now, and I need to see if I can help," Joe said as the call connected. "Yeah, Captain Yovonovich," he said. "Captain Sinclair, San Diego PD." He waited a few moments. "Hey, Cappy, this is Joe. Yeah, yeah, good—how's it going there? Good. Look, I got a guy that I need located. No, he's one of ours. He's one of my sergeants, his name's—Yeah, that's him, how do you know? Seriously? Okay, yeah, could you put me through? Thanks, man, I owe you."

They got to their floor with Joe still on the phone. Jordan started to step out of the elevator. Joe put his hand on her arm, still doing his job as her security even as he talked to someone on the phone. Jordan was constantly amazed by him.

"Yeah, this is Captain Sinclair, down in San Diego. I understand you dealt with Kevin Elmasian this morning?" He asked this even as his eyes swept the hallway, checking both directions, then led Jordan out of the elevator and down the hall. "Yes, what can you tell me about him? Did he look okay? Right, yeah, so he was edgy? No, no, he's a narc, but he had a case go bad and it threw him," Joe explained, opening the door to their room and once again checking it over before letting Jordan enter. "Okay, any ideas where he was headed?" he asked, heading over to the bar and pulling out the tequila bottle. Jordan took it from him and poured him a shot. He smiled at her gratefully, nodding as the other person talked. He knocked back the shot, holding the glass up to Jordan again. She poured him another. "Right, so you think he was headed north? Okay, that would put him Bakersfield way, or heading for Vegas if he went east? Okay, thanks." Joe knocked back the second shot.

He hung up and then dialed again.

When Midnight answered, he said, "He's headed either north—they guestimate he'd be around Bakersfield by now—or east toward

Vegas."

"Thanks, you're the best," Midnight said.

"Let me know if you need me."

"I will."

Midnight hung up, then called Dave to give him the information. The entire group fanned out. Time was running out. They needed to find Kevin fast.

CHAPTER 10

Kevin sat staring at the cards. Even drunk he could beat the house every time. *What are you doing?* part of his mind asked him. He shut the thought down. He didn't want to think. Shaking his head and reaching for his drink, he placed a bet and tossed down two cards. He was reaching for the cards when he sensed someone watching him. Reaching up to scratch his three-day growth of beard, he flicked his moss-green eyes to the side. Two uniforms, watching him. He bet again, then laid his cards out. He won yet again.

Glancing at the dealer, he saw the woman glancing nervously at the cops then back at him. She was cute, blonde with brown eyes. *Not as cute as Erin.* He slammed the door on that thought. He wasn't going to do this to himself, not again. Kevin inclined his head to the dealer, indicating that he wanted to play another hand.

She dealt him the cards, her eyes searching his face as if trying to figure out if he was a criminal. He looked like a dangerous man, with his long hair, pierced ears, and scruffy beard. There was an air about him that warned people off of him. His bright green eyes were calculating, with not a sliver of warmth in them. He looked cold and hard. Maybe he was a drug dealer or a hit man. Jenny had been dealing cards at The Mirage for six years; she knew dangerous when she saw it. All she knew was she was worried about what would happen when the cops approached.

There were two cops, Nevada PD. One was tall and thin, with

black hair and a mustache, and the other was shorter, a black man with a broad build. He looked like he lifted weights. The skinnier cop approached Kevin.

"Word is," the cop said, "you're a wanted man."

Kevin didn't look at the him, simply continued to play cards.

The cop leaned on the table, putting his face closer to Kevin. "We got a request to locate you."

Kevin's eyes flicked to him, his face impassive. "So you never located me," he said evenly.

"Nah," the cop said shaking his head. "We get a request to find you from the Chief of San Diego PD, we find you, man."

The cop put his hand on Kevin's arm. Kevin's eyes dropped to the hand, then narrowed as he looked up at the cop.

"If I were you, I'd remove that hand now."

"Sergeant," the cop said, trying to be amicable. "Don't make this tough, okay?"

Jenny raised an eyebrow. This long-haired guy was a cop? No way!

Kevin didn't answer, merely staring back at the cop with pure malice in his eyes. The cop wisely removed his hand. Kevin went back to playing cards, dismissing him with his silence.

"Look," the cop said, not willing to be dismissed so easily. "Don't make us take you out of here in cuffs."

Kevin gave the man a wintery smile. "Try it, see what happens," he said, his voice full of confidence.

The cop stared back at him, unable to believe this guy was really a cop. He'd been told Kevin Elmasian was a narc; he apparently didn't realize there was a time to drop the act. But Steve Sharkey wasn't ready to take this guy on. He walked back over to his partner.

"What did he say?" Sean Mich asked, his muscles flexing in the tight sleeves of his uniform.

"I don't think he's willing to go anywhere at this point," Steve said wryly.

"Fuck this shit," Sean said, and walked over to Kevin.

"Let's go," he said, putting his hand on Kevin's arm.

Faster than lightning, Kevin grabbed Sean's wrist and twisted it painfully. Before Sean could blink, he felt the muzzle of a gun pressed against his stomach. It was below the table, and they were so close together that no one could see the gun—no one except Steve, who grabbed his cell phone instantly. Kevin knew exactly how to work things.

"Keep your hands off me," Kevin grated. "I'm going to sit here and play cards, and you're going to fucking back off, you got that?"

"You're making a mistake," Sean said, his dark eyes staring into Kevin's.

"I'm the one with a gun pointed at your gut," Kevin replied. "Be smart, back off."

"They already know you're here."

"Who?"

"Your team—they know you're here."

Even as Sean said it, Steve connected to Dave, who was headed into the casino.

"Tell him to back off," Dave told the cop. "Mace might just fight his way out of here. Tell him to back off."

"You got it," Steve said, thinking these damn San Diego PD people did things all fucked up. But they had the okay of the Nevada PD Chief of Police, so they had no choice here.

"Sean!" he yelled over. "Back off."

Sean glanced back at Steve, thinking the guy was a fucking idiot. Steve gave him a look that reminded him they were under the direct orders of the police chief. Sean looked back at Kevin, who hadn't batted an eyelash. Sean put his free hand up in surrender. Kevin released his wrist instantly, and the gun vanished back into the holster under his right arm. Sean backed up, glancing at Jenny. The girl was actually grinning. Bitch!

Jenny glanced at Kevin again, still not sure about him but having enjoyed him getting the better of the Nevada PD cop who'd come on to her constantly. Once when he'd stopped her after leaving the casino, supposedly for rolling through a stop sign, he'd suggested that if she gave him a blow job he'd let her off with a warning. She'd taken the ticket. Kevin's moss-green eyes gazed back at her, dropping to the card shoe. She realized he was waiting for her to deal, as if nothing had happened.

Dave walked up to the cops at that point, tapping them and motioning them back with him. He told them about what had happened, then called in Tiny, Spider, and Kana, who took up positions to watch Kevin without getting too close to him. Rogue Squadron had a quick meeting behind a bank of slot machines.

"He's really on edge," Dave told them. "He cleared leather on a cop."

Christian rocked back on his heels, glancing at Stevie.

"If he's been drinking all day like they said, it's no wonder," Stevie said. "And he hasn't had Adderall either," she added, giving Christian a pointed look.

"Yeah, he's not really thinking right now," Jeanie said, shaking her head.

"He probably thinks he's screwed either way," Cat pointed out.

The rest of the group nodded.

"I think we should get Erin over here," Donovan said.

The group turned to look at him.

"She's probably the only weakness he has," Donovan explained. "If she approaches him, he's less likely to do anything crazy."

"Do it," Dave said.

Donovan was on the phone a moment later, telling Erin to get to the airport. Dave got on his cell at the same time, calling Joe. He got his go-ahead to use the plane Jordan had bought him; since Joe was with Jordan, the plane was in a hangar in San Diego.

"Tell her to go to Palomar Airport," Dave told Donovan, who nodded.

An hour and a half later, Erin was escorted into the casino. Dave met her at the front entrance.

"Where is he?" she asked, her face a mask of worry.

"I'll take you over to him," Dave said. "Erin, look, he's really on edge right now. He pulled a gun on a cop."

"Oh my God," Erin said, closing her eyes for a moment. "Dave, he hasn't had Adderall for three days. He's sitting in a casino full of noises that would put him on edge even when he's had his Adderall. If he's drinking too…"

"I know, Erin, don't worry," Dave said, touching her arm. "We just want him back safe, okay? Midnight's got everything else taken care of. But listen to me," he said, his look serious. "I want you to be careful when you approach him."

"Careful?"

"Yes, Erin. We don't know for sure how he's going to react to all of us being here. I don't want anything to happen, okay? So when you approach him, stay back. Don't get within his arms' reach."

Erin stared back at Dave, unable to believe this was happening. It wasn't Kevin they were talking about—this wasn't the man she knew and loved. All she knew was that she wanted him safe; she didn't care about her own safety. Finally she nodded, seeing that it was what Dave was waiting for. He walked her over to where the rest of the team stood, still concealed behind the slot machines.

"He's over there," Dave said, pointing to the tables thirty feet away.

Erin was shocked at the way Kevin looked. His face was covered with stubble. He was totally disheveled. Her heart ached at seeing how hardened he looked. All she could think of was how upset he must be. Dave warned her again to stay out of arms' reach, and she nodded automatically.

"We'll be covering you from here," Dave said. "Erin, you have to know that if he makes any move to hurt you, we'll have to take him down."

Erin's eyes widened, and she glanced at Donovan. He grimaced, nodding to her.

"No," she said, shaking her head. "I won't let you hurt him."

"Erin," Dave said, putting his hand on her shoulder. "You're a civilian. We're putting you at risk by sending you over there, but I don't want things to get out of hand. If he pulls his gun on another cop, I have a feeling we'll have a slaughter here, and I don't want that. These Nevada PD guys are pretty pissed that he got away with it once. Please, just do what I say, okay? We won't shoot to kill, but we'll have to stop him from hurting you or himself."

Erin shook her head, sickened by the thought. But she knew what Dave was saying was true. Kevin could have easily been shot when he pulled a gun on the first cop—drawing a gun on a police officer was usually suicide. It told Erin how dismal Kevin was really feeling. She knew she needed to help him, no matter what.

Walking out onto the floor, Erin watched him. He was playing cards like any normal patron, but Erin knew him better than that. She could see his jaw twitching, meaning he was clamping down on the thoughts racing through his head. He had an ashtray full of cigar butts next to his right arm, indicating he'd been chain smoking. He also had a drink in front of him.

Erin walked over to him.

"Not too close, Erin," Dave muttered under his breath as he and the rest of Rogue Squadron fanned out to cover her.

Heedless of Dave's warning, Erin walked right up to Kevin, standing next to the chair he sat in. She reached out, touching his cheek.

"Kevin?" she said softly, searching his profile worriedly.

There was a moment when he didn't move, didn't even breathe. *It couldn't be*, he told himself. He turned to look at her. There she was, her blue eyes searching his face, her hand touching his cheek. *My God!*

He blew his breath out in a rush, putting his hand out to her and pulling her to him, crushing her in a hug, his face buried in her hair. Erin responded by wrapping her arms around him, hugging him too.

"It's okay, babe," she whispered. "It's okay. I love you. I'll take care of you."

Kevin moaned against her hair, an expression of utter disbelief. He was near tears, his emotions running high. Glancing up, he saw the rest of Rogue Squadron walking over, with Tiny, Kana, Spider, and Rick coming up from the other side. He couldn't believe they were all there. Erin pulled back, looking up at him, then glanced over her shoulder.

"We've been lookin' for you," Christian said, grinning.

"You're damn slippery," Stevie said, standing in front of Christian.

Kevin's eyes fell on her, his look searching. Erin stepped back as

Stevie moved to hug Kevin.

"I'm so sorry," Kevin said, his voice distraught.

"It wasn't your fault, Mace," Stevie said. "And you rescued me from him."

"And got the two of you back home safe," Dave put in.

Kevin looked down at Stevie for a long moment, then glanced at Dave. Then his eyes went to Christian.

"Looks like you owe me a good right cross," Christian said, grinning and extending his hand to Kevin.

"Or a left," Donovan muttered.

The group laughed then, and all the tension drained away.

Jenny watched the whole scene with a sense of unreality. Tears had come to her eyes when she'd seen the way this cold, hard man turned to complete mush with the blonde girl. Then suddenly there were all these incredibly good-looking people standing around talking to him. They had to be cops, all of them, but they didn't look like any cops she'd ever seen. *Wow*, was all she could think.

By nine that night, three hours later, Kevin had been checked out at the hospital for his injury during the fight in LA. He'd been stuck with the knife, earning a deep puncture wound. The doctor gave him a round of antibiotics and told him to keep the area clean. Erin assured the doctor that they'd do just that. She was beyond relieved that his wound, although serious, wasn't something that wouldn't heal with care.

The entire team had decided to take the night off and stay in Vegas. The Mirage gave them a block of rooms, complements of the hotel. The manager was overwhelmingly happy that they'd managed to avoid a scene in the casino; he was also influenced by the Nevada Chief of Police.

Kevin was lying on the bed in the hotel room, still feeling a sense of unreality. He couldn't believe his entire team, as well as the other members of the Gang, had actually been searching for him for three days. He'd had no idea that they'd be that worried about him. He had, in fact, convinced himself that they were more than likely glad to be rid of him and all his problems. Kevin wasn't used to loyalty among his teammates, nor the tenacity of his boss or the Chief of Police. Why did they care? It was a mystery, where these people got their loyalty. It hadn't occurred to him that they actually cared about him. It had started to sink in over the last three hours, as Erin told him what all they'd gone through to find him.

Hitting the bottle again had also, in his mind, assured him of losing Erin. There was no way she'd put up with this serious lapse, beside the fact that he'd caused Stevie to get hurt. It was just beyond his abilities to grasp that Erin loved him unconditionally. No one had ever done that; there were always conditions, limits, and boundaries. He felt like he'd busted through all of them, shattered them. He never went halfway on anything. Yet here she was, flying to Vegas to help rescue him from himself.

Erin walked into the room, her eyes going to him lying on the bed, and smiled warmly. She went over to the bed, setting down the food she'd brought him. Kevin sat up, reaching out to touch her cheek, his eyes searching her face.

"Please don't ever scare me to death like that again, Kevin," she said softly.

"I wasn't trying to, babe."

"I know," she said. "Why did you take off?" she asked, her tone non-accusing.

Kevin shrugged, leaning back against the headboard. "I just figured I'd screwed up so bad that there was no coming back. By the time we got Stevie to the hospital, I was already convinced I'd fucked up, but when Blue nailed me, that confirmed it in my head."

Erin grimaced as she reached out to touch the bruise that was still dark on his jaw where Christian had hit him.

"I just had to get away, Erin," Kevin said. "I was sure I was out of a job, and with the drinking, I didn't think you'd want to deal with me either."

"Kevin," she said sternly. "You're always reminding me that you're nothing like Donovan or Tyler. Please remember that I'm not Stacy or your mother." She touched his lips, looking into his eyes. "I love you, no matter what happens, no matter what you do."

He took a deep breath, blowing it out slowly as he nodded. She was right. He had assumed she'd be like Stacy, who'd taken off on him when he'd been diagnosed as an alcoholic. Stacy hadn't been willing to go through all that with him; he hadn't been worth it to her.

"Now, eat," Erin said, handing him the box.

She'd bought him Chinese food, one of his favorites. She knew him so well. He started to eat. There was a knock at the door a few minutes later.

"I'll get it," Erin said, giving him a narrow look. "You keep eating."

Kevin grinned. She was a mother, girlfriend, and lover all wrapped up in one beautiful little blond package. And he loved her more than anything in the world.

Erin opened the door to find Midnight and Kyle standing there.

"Midnight," she said, surprised.

"Hi, Erin," Midnight said, smiling and reaching out to hug her. "How's he doing?"

"He's okay," Erin said softly.

Midnight moved into the room as Kyle hugged Erin. Kevin had

stood up, looking apprehensive. This was the chief and Assistant Chief. Were they here to fire him? Or were they here to arrest him?

Midnight walked over, her look searching. She could see he was nervous. Then she realized he had no idea what her intentions were. To his utter shock, she hugged him.

"It's good to see you're okay," she said.

Kevin had no idea how to respond. He nodded, glancing at Kyle, who had also come over. Kyle extended his hand to Kevin, nodding in agreement with Midnight's statement.

"You got checked out?" Midnight asked, glancing at Erin, who nodded.

"Yeah," Kevin confirmed. "Chief, I—"

"It's Midnight, Mace," she interrupted. "This is family business, not police business, okay?"

Kevin nodded. "I just wanted to tell you that I'm sorry for all the trouble..." he said, trailing off as he shook his head.

He'd cost her so many man hours—ten officers out searching for him. Not to mention how many favors she'd probably had to call in to keep him from getting his ass shot or arrested. It was unfathomable what a huge pain in the ass he'd just been.

"Mace." Midnight touched his arm. "Relax. Trust me, you have no idea how much grief the rest of my crew has caused me over the years," she said with a grin.

"Worse than this?"

"Oh yeah," Midnight said. "Had to send my best narc after Stevie, had to send people after Joe countless times, even had to rescue your girl from her creep of an ex once," she said, winking at Erin. "That's what family does, Mace, and you're part of this family, whether you recognize it or not."

Kevin stared back at her, unable to believe what she was saying.

She really did consider him part of her family. Lots of departments claimed that law enforcement was "a family," but when it came right down to it, greed, jealousy, and foul play always became key. But not with Midnight, not with her department. It suddenly occurred to him why people were so loyal to Midnight Chevalier. She gave her people 110% of herself, and they gave it back to her equally. She earned their loyalty, and she'd just earned his for as long as he lived.

Unable to put his thoughts into words, he inclined his head to her, lowering his eyes.

"Thank you," he said sincerely, his voice full of the heartfelt appreciation he had for her and for what she'd done for him.

Midnight and Kyle stayed for a few minutes, then left, telling him to get some rest.

"We'll all meet for breakfast downstairs, then maybe we can relieve this place of some of its cash," Midnight said on the way out, winking at him and Erin.

Kevin chuckled, nodding. Erin laughed, her arm through his, holding his hand tight.

After he'd finished eating, he set aside the white box and took Erin into his arms, kissing her deeply.

"I'm sorry for everything I just put you through," he said. "I love you."

She kissed him again, stroking his cheek. Pulling back, she looked into his eyes. "I will always be here for you, Kevin. Don't ever doubt that again, okay?"

"Okay," he said, his eyes shining. He leaned in to kiss her again, caressing her back, pulling her closer.

He took his time and made love to her, reminding her that she was the woman he loved. It often amazed her how gentle and sweet he could really be with her. She loved him more for the side of him that he showed no one else. It made her feel so special there were no words to really describe it.

Afterward, as they lay catching their breath, he leaned up on his elbow, looking down at her.

"Erin," he said, gazing down into her eyes.

"Hmm?" she purred, her face serene.

"I don't ever want to lose you."

"You won't," she assured him.

"Marry me," he said, his lips an inch from hers.

"What?" she asked, unable to believe she'd just heard him correctly.

He pulled back to look down at her. "Marry me, Erin. I need you more than anything in the world."

Tears were in her eyes instantly, and she was nodding, so happy she could barely contain it. He smiled brilliantly, kissing her deeply.

"Can we do it here?" he asked, not wanting to wait.

"In Vegas?" she said, still smiling brightly.

"Yeah, I don't want to wait. I want you to be mine, now."

"Can we at least wait until tomorrow?" she asked, giggling like a giddy schoolgirl.

He sighed. "If you insist," he said, grinning.

The next morning, at breakfast, Erin shocked everyone by telling them that she and Kevin were getting married. Kevin sat back, watching everyone's faces. He was surprised that they all looked extremely pleased at the prospect. Even Joe and Jordan had shown up at the hotel early that morning. Joe had wanted to make sure for himself that Kevin—"one of my people," as he put it—was okay.

After breakfast, the women commandeered Erin to go shopping for a dress to get married in. The men took Kevin out to celebrate and find him something suitable to wear. Kevin and Erin had decided to get married that evening at 6 p.m.

Joe, Rick, Spider, Tiny, Dave, Christian, Kyle, and Donovan first took Kevin over to New York, New York, where they all went into Hamilton's to the cigar bar and had a few drinks—except for Kevin, who stuck to Coke—and cigars all round. Then one of the guys had the idea of heading over to the huge amusement park. Oddly enough, their idea of a bachelor party consisted of daring each other to get onto the bigger rides. Kevin couldn't help but enjoy himself. It was like being with a bunch of high school buddies. They ate hot dogs, cotton candy, peanuts, popcorn, and ran through every kind of soda they had, plus a few combinations that became dares in and of themselves. By three o'clock, Joe said they had to get over to finding Kevin something to wear. Kevin said he needed a jewelry store.

Joe nodded wisely, taking him down to a place that sold quality jewelry. Kevin bought Erin an engagement/wedding ring combination. He'd been ecstatic to find an antique reproduction set that literally screamed Erin. He knew she'd love it. The guys then ushered him to a store to get him into at least a suit. He was cajoled, harassed, and downright threatened that he had to look good to marry Erin. He took it all in good humor, beginning to sincerely feel like part of the family.

Erin was taken to the best salon in town, where she got pampered beyond belief. Midnight and Jordan banded together to make sure she had the best day of her life. Jeanie, Stevie, Kana, and Cat participated fully in helping out. Jeanie and Stevie picked out nail colors for Erin's toes and fingers while Kana and Cat perused books for hairstyles.

"Are you going to have a veil?" Cat asked Erin, who was getting a facial at that point.

"I don't think we should go that formal, do you, guys?" Erin asked, glancing over at Midnight, who was sitting across from her.

"It's your day, Erin," Midnight said, shrugging. "Do you want a veil?"

"I didn't have one last time," Erin said, grinning.

"Well, that's good enough reason to have one this time," Kana said.

"Sounds like a good idea to me," Jordan put in.

"I second that," Jeanie said.

"Me three," Stevie said, laughing.

In the end, they took Erin over to a bridal shop and let her try on anything she wanted. The dress that was very much her was a vision of white lace, with cap sleeves off the shoulder.

"Absolutely perfect," Midnight pronounced.

"Definitely," Jordan agreed.

"Oh yes," Cat said, smiling. "What do you think, babe?" she asked Kana.

Kana canted her head to the side, her look measuring. "It's definitely you, Erin."

"Is that bad?" Erin asked, grinning.

"Not at all," Kana said with a wink. "I just like them a little less innocent."

Cat elbowed her as everyone laughed.

"You should get that one, Erin," Jeanie said.

Erin bit her lip, then picked up the price tag. As her eyes widened, Midnight stood up and took the tag from her.

"Don't worry yourself about this, young lady," she said.

"But—"

Midnight held up her hand. "No buts, just go find a veil."

Erin stood staring at Midnight openmouthed. Midnight quirked a grin. "Call it a wedding present."

Cat, Jeanie, and Stevie hustled Erin over to pick out a veil.

The veil ended up being a simple ring of flowers with ribbons trailing down the back.

Midnight paid for everything at the bridal shop, including the shoes, stockings, and undergarments the girls picked out for Erin.

"We're all gonna look like shit," Kana said with a grin. "But you"—she touched Erin on the nose—"are going to look beautiful, babygirl."

Erin smiled brilliantly, her eyes shining with tears.

"God, don't do that," Cat said, grabbing her arm and walking her out of the store. "Kana can't handle women crying, especially not cute little blondes," she said, winking back at Kana, who laughed.

Erin laughed softly.

They took her back to the beauty salon to get her hair and makeup done. Jordan grabbed Jeanie and Stevie and said she needed to "go on a mission." The three of them left the salon promising to be back in an hour.

An hour later they returned and presented Erin with a small box. Erin looked at the three suspiciously, then opened the box. She was stunned. Nestled inside the velvet was a pearl pendant, accented with two gold flowers with diamonds at their center, on a chain that was a beautiful delicate figaro design. There were earrings and a bracelet to match.

"Every woman has to have a wedding set," Jordan said, winking at Erin.

"These are so beautiful," Erin said, overwhelmed at how generous they were all being. Her eyes welled up with tears.

"Hey, none of that," Kana said, grinning.

Erin laughed, trying desperately not to cry.

"At least I haven't started her makeup yet," the stylist said.

The women laughed.

They took Erin back to a restaurant once her hair and makeup were done. They made her sit down and eat a salad and some bread, knowing that she wouldn't stop to eat later. Then the women decided they'd better get something together to wear. Erin insisted on accompanying them, saying she'd go crazy with nothing to do.

The group made it back to the hotel at 4:00 p.m. At 4:30, Joe's plane touched down in Las Vegas, carrying Tammy, Rhiannon, Jess, Susan, Randy, JT, Kat, Steven, and Emily. Susan escorted Steven and Emily to Erin's room, surprising her beyond belief.

When Erin opened the door, seeing Steven and Emily standing there with Susan, it was almost impossible not to cry. It had occurred to her during the course of the day that Steven and Emily would miss her and Kevin's wedding, but there was really no way to change that now. Susan had been taking care of Steven and Emily while Erin was in Vegas.

"Mommy!" Steven cried, throwing himself into her arms happily.

Emily clapped her hands, smiling brightly. She had changed significantly in the two weeks she'd been with Erin and Kevin. Once she was assured that she would never be yelled at for talking, asking for things, or wanting something, she became a different child. Nothing like the little mouse she'd been when she arrived.

Erin glanced at Susan. "Do they know?"

"Not to my knowledge," Susan said, smiling.

Erin took both children by the hand, leading them into the hotel room and sitting them down on the bed.

"You look pretty, Mommy," Steven said, reaching out to touch a curled tendril of hair almost reverently.

"Thank you, Steven," she said, smiling at her son. He was always her biggest fan.

She looked at Emily. "I have to ask your permission for something."

"What?" Emily asked, her green eyes wide.

"Well," Erin said, kneeling down and taking Emily's hands in hers, "I'd like to know if it's okay if I marry your daddy."

Emily's eyes opened wide as saucers, even as Steven's mouth dropped open, his eyes dancing with excitement. He looked at Emily, waiting for her answer.

"That would mean that my mom would be your mom too," Steven prompted when Emily didn't answer.

Emily looked at Erin for confirmation.

"Well, stepmom," Erin said, smiling.

Emily let out a small gasp and threw her arms around Erin, hugging her and nodding vehemently. Everyone in the room smiled. Susan handed Erin a garment bag and a small overnight bag.

"The children's clothes for the wedding," she explained.

Erin unzipped the bag and saw formal clothes for the kids inside. She looked askance at Susan.

"From Dave and me," Susan supplied, smiling.

"Thank you!" Erin said, hugging her.

It was unreal, how generous her friends were.

"Hey, this is your last wedding," Midnight explained with a shrug. "We have to do it right."

Erin smiled, liking that everyone seemed to feel that this marriage to Kevin was perfect for her. There had been a lot of surprise about her involvement with Kevin originally. They were so different, no one had thought it would work. But it did, much like Susan and Dave's marriage worked. Erin and Susan had become closer because of that fact. They were both with men who were very complicated, intense, and worked a job that entailed them being someone they weren't on a constant basis.

At 6:00 p.m., Kevin stood at the makeshift altar in the wedding chapel. Steven in his little suit and Emily in her white lace dress walked down the aisle first, surprising him. He hadn't known they'd been flown in. He glanced at Dave, who nodded toward Joe. Kevin shook his head in amazement, winking at Emily and extending his hand to Steven as they walked up. Everyone grinned as Steven took Kevin's hand, shaking it very seriously.

Donovan and Christian had been elected to given Erin away. Kevin had asked Dave to be his best man, and Erin had Jeanie and Stevie as her bridesmaids. Erin had indeed gasped at the ring Kevin had presented to her. It was a beautifully engraved antique reproduction ring in platinum, with a half-carat marquise-cut diamond in the center and a circle of small diamonds for the wedding band.

"I didn't get you one," she whispered, feeling bad.

"Couldn't wear it anyway, babe," he said, kissing her cheek.

"Oh yeah, that whole undercover thing," she said, grinning.

He chuckled. "Uh-huh."

In less than twenty minutes it was over, and Kevin and Erin were married. Kevin was given permission to kiss his bride. He stepped forward, his hand cupping her face, his eyes staring down into hers.

"You look so beautiful," he said, then leaned down and kissed her softly, deepening the kiss a moment later—and a moment after that, the cat calls and hoots started.

Erin and Kevin laughed, turning to everyone as they started

clapping.

They had the reception at the Hard Rock Café, deciding it was right about their style. The kids were happy. JT and Kat were about the same age as Steven and Emily. It was a fun night.

Back at the hotel, Susan took charge of the kids. Dave had made a point of upgrading to a suite so they would be able to play together.

"Might as well get used to this, huh?" he told Susan with a grin.

"Well, we won't have four at a time, regularly," Susan said, smiling.

"Thank God," Dave said, wincing as the kids laughed uproariously at something on TV.

Most of the rest of the Gang hit the casino. Kevin and Erin went up to their room.

"I can't believe this is really happening," Erin said, shaking her head.

"What is?" he asked, glancing down at her.

They'd been given a penthouse suite as a gift from Donovan and Jeanie.

"This," she said, putting her hand on his, her engagement ring glittering in the recessed lighting.

Kevin smiled. "I honestly can't believe it either. But I'm glad it is."

Erin bit her lip, staring up at him. "I love you so much, Kevin," she said softly.

"You proved that to me, Erin. By sticking by me."

She nodded, knowing that too many people in his life had let him down when he really needed them.

"I was really thrilled to have the kids here for the wedding."

"Yeah, I understand Joe was responsible for that," Kevin said, shaking his head again in amazement. "These people are unbelievable in their generosity."

"I know. Midnight paid for my all my wedding wardrobe, and Jordan bought me the jewelry. The other girls paid for the salon and everything. They were just great."

Kevin smiled. "You have a pretty nice extended family, Erin."

"They're your family too. Remember what Midnight told you."

He nodded, looking out the picture window at the lights of Vegas spread out before them.

"I'm going to go and change," she said with a secret smile.

He narrowed his eyes at her, grinning all the same.

"I'll wait right here," he said, his eyes twinkling.

Ten minutes later he was speechless. She was a vision in white silk and lace.

"My God, you're beautiful," he said, awestruck.

Erin smiled, walking over to him and wrapping her arms around his neck.

"I love you," she said, pulling his head down to kiss him.

They kissed for a long time, standing in front of the picture window. Finally, he swept her up off her feet, carrying her to the bedroom and lying her on the bed, kissing her again. Erin loved that he did things that were so romantic. She was a major romantic herself, and had always wanted a man that would be that way with her. She knew Kevin probably never had been with anyone else, but he was with her, and she loved him more for that.

They made love for hours, taking their time and enjoying each other thoroughly. Afterward they lay together talking.

"Kevin?" she said, propping herself up on her elbow, her finger tracing patterns on his chest.

"Yeah?" he asked, sounding very sated and comfortable.

"I just realized something."

"What?"

"We're married."

Kevin chuckled. "Yeah, babe, that's what that whole 'I do' thing was about this evening."

"I know that, you brat," she said, making a face at him. "But the thing is," she went on, placing her hand flat on his chest and looking at him seriously, "if you're a married man, you have a much better chance at getting custody of your daughter."

Kevin stared back at her for a long moment. He hadn't even thought of it, but she was absolutely right. Then he grimaced. "My latest escapade might fuck that up, though."

Erin chewed at the inside of her cheek, thinking about that. "I don't think there were any official reports made."

"How could there not have been?"

Erin looked back at him. "Midnight protects her family."

He stared back at her, surprised. "But she talked to the Chief of Police for Nevada PD."

Erin shrugged. "She asked for his help. That doesn't mean there was a report."

Kevin thought about that, wondering if it was indeed possible that a report hadn't been filed. Other than the insane act of pulling a weapon on a fellow cop, he hadn't really broken any laws. Was it possible?

"We need to find out before we even try anything," Kevin said. "I don't want to put Emily through that if they're just going to nail me on this."

"We'll check," Erin said.

"We'll need a good lawyer. That's not going to be cheap."

"We'll figure it out, Kevin," Erin said, determined. "I don't want her going back to Stacy."

He looked back at her for a long moment. It warmed his heart so much that she loved his daughter this much. That she was willing to do whatever it took to make sure Emily was taken care of. It was more than he could have ever hoped for.

"I love you," he said, putting his thoughts into words.

Erin smiled down at him. "I love you too, Kevin, and I want us to be a family."

Kevin grinned. "Going to fix me yet, aren't you?"

"At least," she said, grinning back at him.

Jordan, Joe, Midnight, and Rick hung out at the high-stakes tables. Midnight and Jordan watched the boys play.

"Joe looks content," Midnight observed.

Jordan glanced over at her. "You think so?"

"Yeah. He looks more relaxed than he has in years."

Jordan looked over at Joe, happy to hear that. She worried all the time that she was hurting him by asking him to be her security. If Midnight thought he was more relaxed now, then maybe it wasn't such a bad thing. In truth, Joe worked his ass off constantly at the department, but there was always more. With Jordan, he got plenty of time to relax and enjoy himself.

"So I hear you're going to be California's next Attorney General," Jordan said, smiling.

"Yeah, well, we'll see," Midnight said, her tone unconcerned.

"You will certainly be a good contender."

Midnight laughed. "Yeah, but I don't play politics very well."

"No," Jordan said. "But maybe that's what the people need to see for a change. Someone who doesn't play the games."

Midnight shrugged. "It's not like I'll lose much if I don't win.

I'm still the Chief of San Diego PD—no one has asked me to resign."

"I doubt they will," Jordan said. "Joe said they're probably shitting bricks, praying to God you don't win."

Midnight laughed.

Cat, Kana, Christian, Stevie, Jeanie, and Donovan were hanging out at the blackjack table, Kana and the boys playing, the other girls watching. Cat grabbed a waitress, ordering another drink for herself and Kana.

"You guys want anything?" she asked, her hand on the waitress's arm.

"Beer," Donovan said.

"Me too," Jeanie said. "Rolling Rock."

"Tequila," Christian said.

"Southern Comfort and Coke," Stevie put in.

The waitress took down everyone's orders and walked away. Cat watched her go.

"Quit it," Kana said with a grin.

Cat laughed, shaking her head.

When the waitress came back Cat paid for everyone's drinks, having ordered them from the bar, rather than the "free" drinks that were always watered down.

Dressed all in black, Cat was attracting attention left and right. One man walked over, seeing that she wasn't standing with a guy and noting the wedding rings on the two guys and two of the other women with the group.

"How about you and I go get a drink somewhere," he said, smiling down at Cat.

He was nice looking, dark hair, dark eyes, tall, nicely built. Cat noted the tan line of a wedding band on his left finger. So the wife was at home, was she? Or was she upstairs, asleep in the hotel? Cat hated guys that lied about their marital status by taking their wedding ring off. It was downright disrespectful.

"Sorry," she said. "I'm with someone."

The guy's eyebrows furrowed. He'd thought he'd guessed right about her being single.

"So where's your man at?" he asked, thinking, *What the hell, if I can cheat, so can she.*

"I don't have a man," Cat replied, enjoying this game. It always gave her a laugh to fuck with guys like this.

"You just said you're with someone," the guy said, trying to figure this chick out.

Kana had turned her head, listening in on the conversation. She knew Cat thoroughly enjoyed shocking people.

"I am," Cat replied, staring up at him.

"Uh…"

"She's with me, idiot," Kana said, her tone low. "So back off."

The guy looked shocked, then stared at Cat, who smiled sweetly in confirmation.

"Go away now," Kana said, not looking back, her eyes still on her cards.

"Look, bitch," the guy said, feeling his ego being bruised.

Kana stood up, turning to face the man. She was as tall as he was, and slightly broader. The man's eyes widened. They widened further when Kana brushed the sides of her jacket back, revealing a nasty-looking gun at her hip and a badge clipped to her belt. He glanced at Christian and Donovan, hoping to get some support from the men in the group. They were both turned to face him, and as he watched they held up badges. He looked to Jeanie and Stevie. Jeanie grinned, her badge at her waist as well. Stevie nodded, holding her badge up too.

He finally looked back down at Cat. She lifted her shirt, expos-ing a fair amount of tanned and toned stomach as well as… *Fuck!* A badge. He beat a hasty retreat.

Kana started grinning first, then Christian started laughing, and Donovan joined him. Before long all of them were laughing.

"Did you see the look on his face?" Cat said, shaking her head.

"I think you scared him right out of cheating for good, babe," Kana said, winking at her.

"Ah, you noticed that too, huh?"

Kana nodded.

"Noticed what?" Jeanie asked.

"He's married," Donovan said. "He took his wedding ring off."

"The tan line was obvious," Stevie said.

"Yup," Christian agreed.

***

Nick stared in shock at Elizabeth.

"What did you do?"

"Had my hair colored," Elizabeth said, rolling her eyes at him.

"Why red?"

Elizabeth shrugged. "It looked like a good color," she said, grin-ning.

She'd been itching to make a change; she was tired of looking the same. She could see she'd surprised Nick. He was staring at her as if she'd lost her mind.

"Oh, lighten up, Nick," she said, making a face at him. "It's my hair. I can do what I want with it."

Nick nodded, thinking she really must be bored. Finally he

walked away, going out onto the balcony of her apartment and sitting down. Elizabeth watched him go, wondering what was happening with him. Since getting herself straightened out, she'd found that she was becoming more empathetic with people who had been nice to her all along.

The fact was, Nick was thinking a lot about his life lately. He'd really started to miss Mikeyla. He'd gone out with a few girls, and while yes, they'd had sex, he'd found they weren't as smart or funny as Mikeyla was. Now, missing her was center stage. He wanted to see her, to talk to her. Unfortunately, he still wanted to make love to her too. He knew that wouldn't help.

Elizabeth walked out onto the terrace, looking down at him. She moved to straddle his lap, her head canted to the side.

"What's wrong, Nick?"

He looked back at her for a moment, then blew his breath out, shaking his head.

"Come on," she cajoled. "You can tell me. My hair's not that bad," she said, laughing softly.

Nick grinned, shaking his head. "It's not your hair, Liz."

"So what is it?"

He sighed, leaning back in the chair, his blue eyes scanning the horizon. "I miss Keyl."

Elizabeth nodded. "Have you talked to her at all?"

"Nope. Not since Joe's birthday party."

"So go talk to her."

"If it was that easy…" Nick said, trailing off as he shook his head.

"It is, Nicholas," she said, giving him a "you should know that" look. "You go over to my aunt's house, you knock on the bloody door, you ask to see Keyl, and then you talk to her. How much easier can it get?"

"And if she won't see me?"

"You keep going back until she will."

"That simple, huh?" he said doubtfully.

"Bloody hell," Elizabeth said, reaching over to the table for her cigarettes and lighting up. "You men always complicate things needlessly. Don't you understand that we want someone who's willing to pursue us?"

"I broke up with her, Liz, remember?"

"So?" Elizabeth said, blowing out a stream of smoke. "You can un-break up with her just as fast—you just have to have the balls to face her."

Nick narrowed his eyes at her. "I have the balls to face her. I just happen to know what everyone still thinks happened between us."

"So?" Elizabeth countered yet again. "You can tell her differently, Nicholas. If Mikeyla Marie Debenshire doesn't want to believe you, she can just stay alone."

"And you think she'll just believe me?" Nick said angrily.

"I think if she really wants to believe you, she will. You're in love with her. If she's stupid enough to throw that away, then she doesn't deserve you."

Nick looked back at her for a moment, then shook his head, laughing. Elizabeth Endicott did not know the meaning of candy-coating. But she was right. He was still in love with Mikeyla. Maybe he should try to see her. He'd made no effort since she'd verbally slammed the door on him that night at Joe's party.

An hour later he found himself in front of Rick and Midnight's front door. He knew Rick and Midnight were in Las Vegas with his father, so he figured he was safe trying to see Mikeyla. He knocked and waited, trying to figure out exactly what he was going to say. Marie,

Ricardo's nanny, answered.

"Hi, Marie," Nick said, smiling at her.

"Hello, Nick," Marie said, her English accent sweet.

"Keyl here?"

"In her room," Marie said, nodding and opening the door wider so he could enter.

"Thanks."

Nick walked down the hall toward Mikeyla's bedroom. Her door was open a crack. He peeked in, not wanting to surprise her too much. What he saw surprised him instead. She was lying on her bed, wearing a scant black spaghetti-strap camisole shirt and black panties that cut high on her hips. Her eyes were closed.

Nick thought he'd die. He had not been wrong about her body. It was incredible. Her shirt was cut off, so it exposed her stomach, flat and tanned. She was definitely gorgeous. He knew he couldn't try to talk to her at that moment—his mind was far too distracted.

Get it together, Masterson.

Taking a deep breath, he concentrated on relaxing. When he felt calmer, he turned and knocked lightly on the door. He heard her stir.

"Come in," she called a few moments later.

Nick pushed open the door, noting her surprised look.

"Nick," she said, moving to sit up, belatedly glancing down at what she was wearing. It was no less than her bikini, and he'd seen her in that. "What are you doing here?"

He shrugged, moving to stand by the bed.

"Just wanted to come by and see how you are," he said conversationally.

"How I am?" she asked, her eyes narrowing suspiciously.

Nick canted his head to the side, telling her without saying it that she was being too defensive. She looked back at him for a long moment, then blew her breath out with a sigh, shaking her head.

"I'm fine, Nick. How are you?" she asked, her tone more even.

He sat down on the bed, grinning at her.

"I'm okay," he said, glancing at the clock. "Since when do you go to bed at eight o'clock?"

She made a face at him. "I was tired," she said simply.

He nodded, looking unconvinced.

"Fuck you, Nick," she said, giving him a dirty look.

"You wouldn't—that was the problem," he countered with a boyish grin.

She looked back at him for a long moment, then couldn't help but laugh, slapping him on the arm in the process. Laughing, he grabbed her arm, tugging her toward him. She turned her back to him, ending up against his chest, his arms wrapped around her and one hand still holding her wrist. She had to admit, even if only to herself, that it felt good to be this close to him again. They sat that way for a while, her in his arms, her head against his shoulder, his cheek pressed against the side of her head comfortably.

"You're never going to guess who called me," she said, picking at the links of his watch aimlessly.

"Who?"

"Remember Xavier Zunin?" she asked, glancing up at him.

"Yeah…" he said, narrowing his eyes. He knew he wasn't going to like this.

"Well, he called, and apparently he's heard that you and I broke up…"

"And he wanted to hook up with you," Nick said, gritting his teeth.

"Yeah."

"Who else called you?" he asked, wanting to know exactly how much new competition he had.

"A few other guys," she said vaguely.

"Who, Keyl?" he asked evenly.

She shrugged, picking more determinedly at his watch. Nick noticed the action, and knew he really wasn't going to like this.

"Who?" he asked again, putting his lips right next to her ear.

She shivered at the feel of him so close to her again. It felt so familiar, so safe, so comfortable…

"Jessie, Scott, Larry Gorkie, and…" She paused, knowing he was going to be mad about the last name. "Tommy Landry."

"What?" Nick exclaimed.

Tommy Landry was his best friend. Or had been up until that moment.

"Motherfucker…" Nick breathed, thinking seriously about beating the crap out of the guy. "I'll kill him."

Mikeyla couldn't squelch the quick smile that touched her lips. Wiping it off her face, she glanced up at him.

"You did break up with me, Nick."

He looked down at her, his expression telling her that he knew that.

"Keyl, you have to know that they're after the same thing I wanted from you."

She turned her head away from him, narrowing her eyes. Yes, she did know that. It irritated her no end that these guys thought it would be so easy to get her into bed.

"Do they think I'm easy, Nick?" she asked, her voice holding a hint of accusation. "Do they think I slept with you?"

His finger on her chin tipped her head up to look at him. "No, Keyl, I never said that we hooked up like that, okay? I think you know me better than that. It's not my style to lie like that. Tommy knows better than anyone that we never had sex—he had to deal with my hits on the football field when I didn't get any."

Mikeyla grinned. "Well, you obviously didn't knock any sense into him."

"He'd never be able to handle your father," Nick said knowingly.

Tommy Landry was far from the clean-cut guy that Nick was. Tommy had tattoos, piercings, wild, spiked hair, and a fairly nasty pot habit.

"My father wouldn't let him within a hundred feet of me," Mikeyla said.

Nick laughed, nodding. "Try miles, babe."

Mikeyla laughed.

He hugged her, giving her a gentle squeeze. "I miss you so much, Keyl," he said softly.

She turned around in his arms, looking up at him.

"I miss you too, Nick," she said honestly, despite knowing she shouldn't tell him that.

His lips were on hers before she could even take a breath. Her head told her she should stop him from kissing her. But Nick was such a good kisser, and she really had missed him. Giving in and kissing him back, she put her arms around his neck as he gathered her closer. His lips moved over hers expertly, his hands caressing her back, wrapping around her.

Mikeyla was surprised by her body's reaction to Nick's kiss, but she still wasn't sure. She was shaking by the time he pulled back to look down at her.

"This is what makes me crazy," he said, his voice a husky whisper.

"What?" she asked, looking up at him wide-eyed.

"I know you want me, Keyl. I just don't understand why you

won't…"

She looked back at him. "How do you know?"

He looked at her like she was losing her mind. "I can tell, Keyl, by the way you react to me."

"How I react? Like what?"

"Like how you're breathing heavy right now, and when you do that little moan—it makes me crazy."

"Well, this is all new to me."

"We could take it slow…" Nick said, his tone hopeful.

Mikeyla looked considering, then nodded slowly. "As long as you'll stop if I say so."

"My father made sure I know that no means no, Keyl," Nick said seriously.

"Slow would be good, but…" she said, looking nervous, "I heard it hurts."

Nick grimaced. "Yeah, I guess it does hurt girls the first time, but that doesn't mean it has to hurt the whole time."

"Have you ever been with a virgin?"

He nodded. "A couple of times."

"Jesus, how many girls have you been with?" she asked, jealous in spite of herself.

He grinned, liking that she was jealous. "I didn't keep count."

She scowled, but then got back to her point. "Did it hurt them when you did it?"

He looked thoughtful for a minute, then nodded. "Yeah, the one girl tensed up for a few minutes, but once she relaxed again things went okay."

"The one?" Mikeyla said wryly. "And the other one?" she asked, her lips curling derisively.

Nick looked back at her, thinking, *I'm nuts for telling her any of this!* "She wanted to lose her virginity, so she pushed it, so she didn't even stop when it hurt, apparently."

Mikeyla chewed at her bottom lip. "So it hurts at first, but it doesn't the whole time?"

"I guess," Nick said. "I've never been on your end, Keyl," he added, grinning.

"Yeah, yeah, I know," she said, rolling her eyes.

"Is it the fact that it hurts that's kept you from doing it?" he asked. "'Cause it's going to hurt with anyone you do it with, Keyl."

"I know," she said, nodding.

He took a deep breath, blowing it out slowly. "Guys like Xavier won't take their time. They'll be doing it for the conquest."

She dropped her head to his shoulder. "I know," she said again. "And they haven't invested a year into this relationship like you have either."

"They aren't in love with you, either," he said, surprising even himself.

Mikeyla looked up at him, her eyes wide. "You are?"

Nick pressed his lips together. He hadn't meant to say that, but it was true. Finally he nodded. "I didn't really realize it until you weren't mine anymore. I know, I'm stupid, but it's true."

"Well, you are stupid," she said, narrowing her eyes at him. "Because if you'd said that a long time ago, we never would have had to break up."

"Huh?"

"If you'd told me that you were in love with me, I would have slept with you, Nick. You never did, so I figured I was just going to be another notch for you, and I'm too good for that."

He grinned. She sounded a lot like her mother. Midnight knew exactly what she was worth, and she'd obviously taught her daughter well.

"Well, I am," he said, leaning down to kiss her softly.

She snuggled against him, feeling really good suddenly. He loved her—why hadn't he just said that before? It had taken leaving her to make him realize it? Men were so stupid sometimes!

In the end, they sat up talking. He outlined how many different ways he was going to kill his best friend for trying to score with her while his back was turned. He had her laughing so hard at one point she was in tears. Mikeyla fell asleep with her head on his chest, her fingers entwined with his. Nick lay there next to her, holding her, feeling like he'd just gotten insanely lucky, having recaptured her heart. He fell asleep thinking along those lines.

The next morning, Nick woke to the feeling of her lips on his neck. He groaned softly, turning over onto his side to face her, pulling her closer to him. He kissed her softly.

"Good morning," she said, grinning up at him.

"Hiya," he said, his grin evil. "Well, we finally slept together."

Mikeyla laughed, nodding. "Everyone's going to talk now."

"Oh yeah," he said, rolling his eyes.

"Nick?"

"Yeah?"

"Did you sleep with Elizabeth?"

He sighed. "Will you believe me if I tell you that no, I didn't?"

"Is that true?"

"Yes, it's true. I wouldn't lie about it, Mikeyla. I won't say I didn't sleep with a couple of girls while we were broken up, but I will tell you that they were not you, and it made me really realize how much you meant to me."

She nodded, pleased by what he was saying. She'd never been

convinced he'd slept with Elizabeth, if for no other reason than being fairly certain that Elizabeth was too worried about not only her father and mother but Dave too, if he'd thought that she'd slept with an underage boy.

She smiled brilliantly. Test given and passed with flying colors. She'd known that he'd slept with a couple of girls at school—they'd been rude enough to tell her. The fact that he'd been honest with her was what mattered the most. She moved to kiss his lips, her hands sliding through his hair. Nick groaned again, pulling her close to him and deepening the kiss. His hands slid over her body, caressing her. As they kissed, things became more heated, and it became obvious to both of them that this was going to be their first time together.

Nick took his time, being so gentle with her it brought tears to Mikeyla's eyes. In the end, it didn't hurt near as much as she'd expected, and it was certainly worth the wait when she had her first orgasm.

When the waves stopped washing over her, she relaxed against him, breathing raggedly. He caressed her back tiredly, his chest heaving as he tried to catch his breath as well.

"I've been avoiding that?" she finally said breathlessly.

Nick laughed. "Yeah."

"Well, damnit," she said, grinning. "No one told me it felt that good."

"I don't know that it does with everyone, Keyl," he said seriously. "I have to say, it felt a hell of a lot better with you than it has in a long, long time."

"Oh yeah?" she asked, inordinately pleased with that thought.

"Yeah," he said, kissing her forehead, then brushing his lips back and forth over her skin. "I love you, Keyl."

"I love you too, Nick."

It was an amazing morning. Thank God her parents hadn't come home yet. They called a little while later, telling her they wouldn't be home that night either, since Kevin and Erin were getting married. Mikeyla did her best to hide her happiness that they'd be gone for another day. That meant she could spend more time with Nick, and maybe get him to make love to her again.

CHAPTER 11

Midnight had her first debate with one of the other candidates. It was being broadcast, and she was doing everything she could not to get nervous about it. And failing miserably.

"Hey," Rick said from the doorway to her office. "Lunch?"

Midnight grinned, nodding. He always showed up when she needed stress relief.

He took her to lunch. They had a couple of glasses of wine and talked. By the time he took her back to her office, he'd helped her take the edge off her nervousness. She kissed him deeply in the elevator, telling him she loved him for everything he dealt with for her.

"You're worth it," he said with a wink. "Most of the time."

"Hey!" she said, slapping him on the arm and laughing.

He laughed too, pulling her to him and kissing her again. They were still kissing when the elevator opened on his floor. There were a number of cheers and cat calls. They laughed, looking a bit embarrassed. The Debenshire love affair was legendary in the department, so catching the couple kissing in the elevator was a shock to no one.

Later that evening, Midnight was still grinning about their indiscretion. She waved away the over-excited assistant trying to get her ready. She had no intention of looking like some made-up Barbie doll on TV. Glancing across, she saw what was considered to be her biggest competition.

Art Longelo was currently the Assistant Attorney General. He was fifty-five years old, tanned and decent looking in a smarmy kind of way. With dark hair slicked back and dark eyes that tended to look right through people, Art had been singularly indistinguishable as an Assistant AG. Up until six months ago, when suddenly the slick Democrat had started shaking hands and kissing babies right along behind his boss. The act screamed political move.

Yet he was the strongest candidate the Democratic party had to offer. They were selling his Harvard law degree and his eight years' "experience" as Assistant Attorney General. Privately, Midnight's irreverent attitude was *Always a bridesmaid, never a bride.* However, she never expressed her attitude to the press, to the surprise of everyone that knew her.

The slander of Midnight and her career had started almost immediately upon her announcement to run. The first thing they'd delved into was, of course, her past. They brought out the fact that she'd been a gang leader. When asked about that, Midnight had shrugged and said, "My record speaks for itself." It became a litany that she used every time she was questioned about some new piece of garbage Longelo's people dredged up.

At one point, they'd tried to slam her because of where her campaign funds had come from, citing her husband's rich family and saying she was trying to buy the election. Midnight one-upped them by publishing the list of names who had contributed to her campaign. It read like a who's who of the rock and law enforcement world:

Richard Joshua, Mikeyla Marie, and Ricardo Martinez-Debenshire: $1,500,000

Joseph Michael Sinclair IV: $1,000,000

Jordan Tate: $1,000,000

Brenden James Sparks & Allexxiss Ramsey-Sparks: $1,000,000

Jerith and Nicolette Michaels: $1,000,000

Billy Montague & Skyler Kristiani: $1,000,000

Robert and Annabelle Debenshire: $500,000

Deborah Endicott: $500,000

Elizabeth Endicott: $200,000

Governor John Davies: $10,000

Randissi Curtis-Sinclair: $10,000

Division of Law Enforcement Director Phil Griffin: $2,000

Assistant Chief Kyle Masterson & Rhiannon Templeton-Masterson: $2,000

Lieutenant Spider Nguyen & Tammy Nguyen: $1,000

Lieutenant Kana Sorbinno: $1,000

Sergeants Nathanial & Jessica Ako: $1,000

Sergeant David E. Dibbins & Susan Endicott-Dibbins: $1,000

Sergeants Donovan and Jeanie Curtis: $1,000

Sergeants Christian and Stevie Collins: $1,000

Sergeant Kevin Elmasian and Erin Elmasian: $1,000

Sergeant Catalina Roché: $1,000

It totaled $7,732,000, but anyone reading the list who knew Midnight Chevalier at all knew that only her friends, family, husband, and children had contributed to her campaign. She hadn't asked the everyday citizen to give her anything up front. When the press outlined this information in a follow-up story, indicating who each person was, Midnight was asked for a statement. Her comment on this practice was simple. "The people shouldn't have to pay for their Attorney General." Her simple comment had sent people to their mailboxes in throngs. Letters of support and checks and cash were regularly dropped at the department. Officers on the beat were handed checks made out to "Chevalier for Attorney General." Midnight couldn't believe it.

She was quickly seen as the people's candidate, although she absolutely refused to use the phrase, not wanting to become a politician in the ugliest sense of the word. She also refused to engage in the mud-slinging that was happening all too frequently in the political world. Every time Longelo's people came up with something new, Midnight simply shook her head and pointed to her record. She responded to any direct questions about things that had actually occurred. She knew some of the garbage would come up during the debate—it was inevitable.

The stage was set. Midnight took her position behind the podium. Closing her eyes for a moment, she reached for Rick in her mind. She knew he was standing ten feet away, behind a camera, watching her. She could feel him there, and drew strength from him.

The debate began.

"Chief Chevalier, if elected, what would you say are your most immediate goals as Attorney General?" the moderator asked.

Midnight waited a few moments, gathering her thoughts. "I'd have to say that most important to me is the reduction of domestic violence. I also feel that it is highly important for the state to take a more aggressive role in lending assistance, training, and resources to local law enforcement."

The moderator nodded, then turned to Longelo. "Mr. Longelo?"

"It's been the practice of the Attorney General's office to initiate assistance only after assistance has been requested. Also, we don't feel that domestic violence is the issue it once was. My platform is one of educating people to be more understanding and empathetic with society's less than successful members. People need to understand that it takes an entire community to raise a child, and when that chain is broken the mitigating circumstances behind a child's behavior are to blame, not the child."

"You're saying the child isn't responsible for their own actions?" Midnight asked.

"I'm merely saying that society creates the climate in which the child lives, and until society is better able to teach these children, it is the responsibility of the state to do so."

"You're saying their parents aren't responsible for doing that?" Midnight said, forgetting quickly that this was a moderated debate and opting for the free-form debate she preferred.

"Ms. Chevalier—" Longelo began.

"It's Chief Chevalier or Mrs. Debenshire, Assistant Attorney General Longelo. Pick," Midnight said, her automatic reply when a man tried to put her in her place by calling her "Ms. Chevalier."

"I'm sorry?" Longelo said, not used to dealing with a woman as quick-witted as Midnight.

"Indeed," Midnight couldn't help but utter. "But back to the issue at hand," she said, as a ripple of laughter went through the audience. "It has long been a democratic platform that a child—or an adult, for that matter—is not responsible for themselves, but rather society is responsible for the formation of each person's actions. Frankly, I don't see how we can teach our children that actions have consequences when our own government is consistently telling them that they aren't responsible for what happens to them."

"Are you saying, Chief Chevalier," Longelo said, trying desperately to catch up, "that a child that comes from a broken home where they were abused has no remnants of that upbringing that lends itself to his future actions?"

"Certainly," Midnight said. "But I don't feel that is a justifiable defense in the case of that child becoming violent. If society teaches children that regardless of your reasons your actions are your own, a child would be less likely to commit violent crimes. Instead, the climate today is simply commit the crime, then come up with reasons for your actions, whether it be a broken home, abuse, neglect, or that little Jimmy down the street broke your GI Joe when you were five. Either way, the child grows up taking no responsibility for his or her actions. It's a dangerous stage to set."

Longelo rocked back on his heels, unable to come up with an appropriate response.

The moderator, having realized that this debate wasn't going quite normally, forwent the questions he was going to ask and turned it over to the audience.

A woman stood up.

"Is it true, Chief Chevalier, that you had a very rocky childhood?" she asked, having been thinking about what she'd read about Midnight being a gang member.

"Yes, I did," Midnight said. "My parents, while staying married, also ceased to act as parents to myself and my younger brother. I lived in a rough neighborhood where you either joined a gang or were beaten up by one. The consequence of my actions was that my younger brother was killed in a gang fight," she said, her eyes glistening slightly with tears that she forced back.

Rick stepped out from behind the camera, heedless of the crowd. His eyes were locked on Midnight. Midnight shook her head slightly, her way of telling him that she was okay. The cameras picked it up, and many more people fell in love with the Debenshire romance. There was a murmur throughout the crowd in reaction to Midnight's statement—that was not something that had been reported by the press.

Another woman stood up, addressing a question to Midnight.

"Chief Chevalier, you said you want to reduce domestic violence. What would you do to achieve that?"

Midnight looked back at the woman for a long moment. "My first goal would be to strengthen current laws on domestic violence. I'd also like to see a bigger campaign on domestic violence awareness. Too many people still believe that being abused is something to be ashamed of, rather than something that requires action. I would want to work directly with local law enforcement to target repeat offenders and their current situations to attempt to curb further occurrences."

There was a ripple of approval through the crowd. People were nodding. Rick looked out over the audience, grinning. He wasn't sure why Longelo had even bothered to attend. In the end, the crowd only wanted to ask Midnight questions. Midnight fielded every one of them with intelligence, information, and her usual quick wit.

The last question pertained to her campaign fund.

"People who I'm close to, and who believe in me, donated the money to help me run," she said, glancing at Rick.

"Aren't you rich, Chief Chevalier?" Longelo asked, his jealousy over the idea evident.

"No," Midnight said, shaking her head. "My husband's family has money, and he has a trust fund, but I'm not personally rich."

"Your own husband donated a million and a half to your campaign, Chief Chevalier. That makes you rich."

"No, that makes him not only rich but also blindly in love with his wife and her latest campaign to rid the world of injustice and overrated politicians."

Laughter once again went up from the audience. Midnight kept a straight face.

It was a good night.

"God, I was too flippant!" Midnight said, sinking into the passenger seat of Rick's Mustang.

"You were not," Rick said. "Unless Dumbass asked a loaded question—then yes, you were flippant, because you knew he was just being an asshole."

Midnight's lips twitched. "It isn't how I want to present myself."

"But it's you, love," he said, reaching over to touch her cheek. "The woman that pulls no punches and always sticks to her guns."

Midnight sighed, shaking her head. "I don't think that impresses people."

She was wrong. When the ratings came out for the debate, she had won by a landslide. People who were interviewed about it said it was fantastic to see a woman so knowledgeable about the law and law enforcement, but at the same time aware of the real problems in the state. They found her sense of humor extremely refreshing. One woman was quoted as saying, "She'll bring a personality back to the state, one it's been lacking for years!"

Naturally, there were the men who commented that she was one hot-looking woman, and that they wouldn't mind having her arrest them. Rick merely raised his eyebrow at that, shaking his head.

"They've obviously never seen you run a suspect down and cuff them," he said with a grin.

Midnight laughed. Things were getting interesting, that was for sure, but she knew that sometimes life had unintended consequences.

You can find more information about the author and series here:

www.sherrylhancock.com

www.facebook.com/SherrylDHancock

www.vulpine-press.com/midknight-blue-series

Also by Sherryl D. Hancock:

The *WeHo* series follows a group of women from Los Angeles as they navigate the ups and downs of love, life, work, and everything in between.

www.vulpine-press.com/we-ho

The *Wild Irish Silence* series. Escape into the world of BJ Sparks and discover how he went from the small-town boy to the world-famous rock star.

www.vulpine-press.com/wild-irish-silence-series